THE
TEMPORARY
AGENT

ALSO BY DANIEL JUDSON

The Gin Palace Trilogy

The Poisoned Rose
The Bone Orchard
The Gin Palace

The Southampton Trilogy

The Darkest Place
The Water's Edge
Voyeur

Stand-Alone Titles

The Violet Hour
The Betrayer
Avenged

THE
TEMPORARY
AGENT

DANIEL JUDSON

THOMAS & MERCER

Text copyright © 2016 by Daniel Judson

Published by Thomas & Mercer, Seattle

www.apub.com

Amazon, the Amazon logo, and Thomas & Mercer are trademarks of Amazon. com, Inc., or its affiliates.

ISBN-13: 9781503934993

ISBN-10: 1503934993

Cover design by Rex Bonomelli
Cover photo by Rex Bonomelli

Printed in the United States of America

for Wendy

PART ONE

PART ONE

One

Cahill was no stranger to suffering, his own or that of others.

But the night he lost Erica was without a doubt the longest of his life.

Oblivious to his own gunshot wound, he drove his Jeep as fast as he dared along the dark back road, heading for the abandoned service station a few miles north of New Haven.

Erica was in the passenger seat, barely conscious, her white fisherman's sweater soaked with blood.

The service station was his fallback position—his Alamo—and he had stocked it several months ago with emergency supplies, among which was a trauma kit.

He had received training in field medicine, would do what he had been taught to do—apply a compression bandage to the entry wound to at least slow the bleeding, then inject Erica with twenty milligrams of morphine, followed by another injection of three grams of ampicillin. He would cover her with an emergency blanket to keep her from going into shock, then retrieve a clean cell phone from his stored gear and use it to send a distress call via coded text message to the only person he could now trust.

After that, all he would be able to do is stay with her and keep her stable as he waited for expert help to arrive.

Such help was only an hour away and would leave immediately upon receiving the SOS. Cahill was certain of that.

But he knew enough about dying to know that the moment Erica's lungs began to fill with blood, each gasp she took would only serve to bring her closer to her last.

He was still driving, the service station less than a mile away, when he looked at her and saw the telltale pinkish foam gathering in the corners of her mouth.

The simple autonomic function of her lungs filling themselves with air was likely causing the expanded hollow-point bullet lodged near her heart to shift, damaging even more vital tissue with its jagged edges as it did.

The very act of staying alive was killing her.

Death was something Cahill had seen before, more times than he cared to remember.

Was something he had once faced himself, his torso shredded by grenade fragments.

No stranger at all to suffering, he was nonetheless unable to bear hers.

He told her to look at him and she did, with fading eyes.

Even if he could have taken her to the nearest hospital, five miles in the other direction, it was obvious to him that she wouldn't survive the drive.

He began to tell her to hang on, to stay with him, that everything was going to be okay. But her eyes were already glassy, her face pale and absent of expression.

Inside his heart, a rage was building.

Aimed not at the men who had come after them but at himself.

He should not have been so foolish as to fall in love with her.

He should have simply walked away that night they'd first talked.

And he never should have allowed himself to believe that it wouldn't come to this.

He had of course taken precautions, more so than usual once she had entered his life. But his enemies knew as well as he that the human heart, located just left of center mass, was the best target.

And they had struck at his without mercy.

Leaving Cahill now with only one thing he could do.

Beg the woman he loved for her forgiveness.

Two

Six hours earlier, they had been together in a motel just off the Merritt Parkway.

In the four months they'd known each other, every one of their encounters had occurred in such a place, during the transition from afternoon to evening.

Naked together, the rented room growing steadily darker until full night surrounded them.

A sanctuary from their respective lives, if only for a few hours.

Cahill had arrived at the motel first, paying for the room with cash and handing over one of his fake driver's licenses when the desk clerk asked for identification.

He had then circled the exterior of the motel once, casually, but carefully taking note of each of the cars parked in the narrow lot.

He had no doubt that he would easily spot the vehicle of some local private investigator waiting for them there.

He was also confident that he would have shaken any car that might have picked up his trail and attempted to follow him there.

He never took a direct route anywhere, made a point of circling blocks at random, often several times, and of entering and then exiting parking garages, always watching his rearview mirror as he made his careful maneuvers, his trained eye ready to take note of anything that appeared even remotely suspicious.

These habits were even more carefully observed whenever he drove beyond the city limits to one of the several out-of-the-way motels he had scouted and deemed suitable for their needs.

Once Cahill had entered the room, he adjusted the thermostat—Erica preferred it warm so they would both work up a sweat—and then stood beside the window, watching for her.

After she arrived and parked, Erica waited behind the wheel of her BMW until he sent her a text indicating he was certain she had not been followed, either.

When it was clear, she exited her vehicle. Cahill eyed the lot for any sudden movements as she headed for the room.

They had been seen together in public only twice, first meeting at a crowded private fund-raiser at Yale. Black tie, Cahill in a fitted tuxedo, Erica in a black cocktail dress.

His eyes had been drawn to her all night.

She had glanced at him only occasionally, but each time, she had met and confidently held his stare.

Their second public meeting had been at a luncheon several days later, in a hotel restaurant downtown.

A local journalist, Erica had been writing a PR piece on the charity Cahill had recently founded, so the meeting with the religious and community leaders who comprised the charity's board had the appearance of being purely business.

Though Cahill avoided making the papers whenever possible, he had attended the luncheon simply to look at her again.

It was afterward, though, when Cahill had quietly pulled Erica aside and told her that he would like to see her again that she had replied, "I would like that, too. But my marriage is ending, and things are a bit . . . rough, so we would need to be discreet."

Even if her situation hadn't required it, Cahill would have practiced all possible discretion.

He lived these days like a ghost.

Not an eccentricity or a game—though he would admit he did enjoy the act of evasion.

It was a necessity that had simply become a part of who he was.

So Cahill had no reason to expect that anyone would be waiting for them when it came time to dress again shortly after eleven o'clock.

Cahill rose and crossed the dark room to where their clothing lay scattered.

He heard Erica roll onto her back as he searched for his jeans.

"I shouldn't fall asleep like that," she said.

Cahill found his jeans and pulled them on. "You were tired, Erica."

"It's dangerous. Coming home at midnight is pushing it as it is. What if we didn't wake up? What if one night we slept through till morning?"

"It's okay," Cahill said. "I'll set the alarm on my phone from now on. An easy fix, right?"

Erica switched on the bedside light but remained in the bed. She watched him pick up his shirt.

He was fit, had the hardest body she had ever known, but she was staring at his torso for a different reason.

It was mapped with dozens of scars, some of which were jagged fragment wounds, while others were the flat, dulled patches indicative of high-temperature burns.

Others still were the fine, raised lines—some almost perfectly straight, others sharply curved—that had been left by the many surgeons who had worked to sew him back together five years ago.

The sight of his long-healed wounds saddened her and filled her mind with questions she knew not to ask.

She pushed the sorrow from her thoughts and ignored her reporter's nature.

"So I heard from my attorney today," she said. "We've got our court date finally. It's still a few months away, but at least the end is in sight."

"That's good news."

"You and I will probably still have to be careful for a while, even after the divorce goes through."

"Whatever you need," Cahill said. "Whatever it takes to see you."

He pulled his shirt on, then sat on the desk chair and reached for his leather boots.

Clipped inside the left boot was a neoprene holster containing a Kimber Ultra Raptor II compact 1911.

Three-inch barrel, short for a .45, so a weapon best suited for close-quarter combat, though Cahill could shoot tight enough groupings with it at fifty feet.

Fully loaded, cocked and locked, its grip rested just above the top of the boot.

A pair of spare seven-round magazines was in a small mag pouch secured inside his right boot.

As was the case with Cahill's wounds, the sight of his firearm always brought to Erica's mind a number of questions, but she let those go, too.

There was a strange kind of comfort in this for her—in not needing to know the details of a man's past to know who that man was.

He'd been a marine, once—an elite marine, she knew that much.

Now he was a philanthropist—and an effective one at that.

She'd never known so little yet felt so close.

Or so safe.

She watched as Cahill pulled on his boots.

"So, are you going to stay in bed all night?" Cahill teased.

She smiled. "I just might."

"The room's paid for."

"But you're leaving."

"Not if you aren't."

Now she teased him. "You know that the night we finally get to sleep all the way through to morning is the night you'll lose interest in me."

"Doubt that."

"Yeah, who am I kidding, I'll probably be the one to lose interest first. Like all women, I'm all about the chase, you know? The thrill of the conquest."

Cahill looked at her for a moment.

She was tall—as tall as he was—and had piercing blue eyes and long blonde hair.

"Strong Nordic stock." Cahill frequently teased her about this, though in reality he admired her athletic build and the natural strength she possessed.

Her response was to tease him right back with "Stoic Yankee Protestant."

This never failed to make him smile.

"Checkout isn't till noon," he said.

She thought about that, then laughed and began to shake her head.

"What?" Cahill said.

"It's just so sad that spending a few hours a week in a cheap motel is the best part of my life right now. I mean, who could have seen that coming? When little girls imagine their futures, they don't ever imagine this."

"We can stop. Until you're completely in the clear, I mean."

"Like I could stop." She waited, then said, "You know, this is where you're supposed to say you couldn't stop, either."

"It wouldn't be easy."

"I think maybe you can do better than that."

"I'd go insane and die without you."

"That's better." She smiled. "Was that so tough?"

"No." He thought for a moment. "Our time will come, Erica. Because we want it to. In the meantime, we need to endure. Trust me, I know what it's like to have to keep up appearances or lose everything. If it seems to you like I'm holding back, it's because I don't want you to feel any more pressure than you already do. We both have commitments, though, and we both need to be smart about how we conclude them. Right?"

Erica nodded.

"If we could take off tonight," Cahill said, "go somewhere and start over, I'd do it in a heartbeat."

"That's all I can think about sometimes."

"Yeah, me, too."

"C'mere," she said.

He stepped to the bed and sat on the edge of the mattress.

She reached up and touched his face.

"I love you," she said.

"I love you, too, Erica."

He leaned down and kissed her.

"We staying or going?" he asked.

"Going."

"So it's rise and shine, then."

"Yes, Sarge."

It was Cahill's turn to watch her dress—slacks and a camisole, soft wool fisherman's sweater over that, black shoes.

He was already thinking ahead to their next few hours together.

Then they stood in the center of the room, embraced, and kissed for a long moment before finally parting.

Cahill exited first, making a quick visual scan of the parking lot as he walked toward his Jeep.

The only vehicle present that hadn't been there when he arrived was a beat-to-shit Ford Crown Vic with New York State markers.

Not an unusual thing to see outside a motel just a few quick turns off the Merritt Parkway.

Erica knew not to park near Cahill's vehicle, so her BMW sedan was at the far side of the lot. At least two dozen cars, a mix of newer and older models, stood between her Beemer and Cahill's Jeep.

The Ford was three spots past Erica's vehicle, close to the very end of the rectangular lot.

Cahill reached his Jeep and stared at the Ford for a moment before deciding he wanted a closer look.

Something told him to do that, and he never ignored his instincts.

Knowing that Erica was watching him from the motel room window, he shook his head once, indicating that she was to hold her position.

He started walking, had passed the first car, then the second, was just passing the third—the front seat of the vehicle in question about to come into view—when he saw something he didn't like.

The right bumper of the Ford jostled, sinking down slightly, then rising up.

Right away the left bumper did the same.

This could only mean one thing: the passenger had quickly gotten out of the vehicle, followed immediately by the driver.

From behind, Cahill heard the sound of straining tires.

He glanced quickly over his shoulder, just as a Ford Econoline cargo van moving at a high rate of speed made the turn into the motel parking lot.

The rear end of the van swung wide, but the driver compensated, correcting the vehicle's path.

12 *Daniel Judson*

The badly tuned engine gunned, and the van hurtled across the lot.

Aimed straight at the door of the motel room Cahill had just exited.

From the corner of his eye, he detected something else he did not like.

The motel door was open.

And Erica was standing in it.

In a calm voice, Cahill called, "Get back inside, Erica. Lock the door and get down."

To his dismay, she hesitated. Cahill had seen even trained men freeze when faced with sudden violence, but there wasn't time for that now, so he called to her again, this time more firmly.

"Lock the door and get down."

Erica snapped out of her trance yet still refused to move. He could tell that she was considering making a run toward him.

"Lock the door, Erica. Now."

She did as ordered, flinging the door closed with two hands, but not before looking at him.

The last thing he saw was the look of fear on her face.

There was, though, no time for that, either.

In a well-practiced move, Cahill dropped down to one knee.

In his peripheral vision he saw the two men who had exited the Ford just seconds before clearing the back of the vehicle.

A quick glance told him that the passenger was armed with a cut-down, pump-action shotgun.

The man was raising the weapon, holding it single-handed by its pistol grip—and leveling it in Cahill's direction.

With his right knee on the pavement and his other knee raised, Cahill pulled up his left pant leg, exposing the top of his leather boot.

A second later, the compact 1911 was in his right hand, his thumb switching the safety lever down.

A second after that, he was rising to a shooter's crouch and completing a 360-degree grip of the firearm with his left hand.

Shoulders relaxed, he extended the weapon forward till the sights were directly between his right eye and his first target.

The front sight was in focus, the target forty feet away a blur, just as it should be.

Cahill waited till the sight alignment was perfect, then exhaled gently and went to work.

Three

A controlled pair—two rapid-fire shots into his target's center mass—dropped the man armed with the shotgun and forced the driver to take cover behind the Ford's left rear fender.

The man had panicked and scrambled clumsily, and Cahill knew that meant his adversary had no real training or firefight experience.

But even panicked and clumsy men were dangerous, so Cahill immediately fired two more rounds into the Ford's right rear fender to keep the driver's head down.

He then quickly turned his attention to the cargo van.

An ammunition count was running in his head—the Kimber had been loaded with a round in the chamber and a seven-round mag in the grip.

Eight rounds total, and he had just fired four.

He was already thinking of when to best access the backup mags holstered in his right boot.

The van skidded to a stop, its nose just feet from the motel room door. Parked almost parallel to the one-story building, the van blocked Cahill's view.

More important, it gave the van's passenger a clear shot at Cahill.

The man's window was down and he thrust out one arm.

In his hand was the last thing Cahill expected to see.

An Uzi submachine gun.

The passenger pointed the weapon at Cahill, or rather in Cahill's general direction. This was another indication that these men were not professionals—anyone who had been properly trained would know not to hold an Uzi with one hand while his arm was fully extended.

The first round would likely miss, and the kick produced by the rounds that followed would throw the weapon upward and far off target.

Cahill ducked and dove between two cars as the shooter opened fire, scattering nine-millimeter rounds everywhere.

The rear window to his right shattered, followed by the windshield, and after that there was the repeating dull thump of car metal and plastic absorbing dozens of rounds.

Cahill had fired an Uzi before—there wasn't a firearm he hadn't handled at least once—and there was something dramatically different about this weapon.

Instead of a continuous metallic drumming sound—the sound of a rate of fire averaging around five or six hundred rounds per minute—the sound coming from the muzzle of this weapon was more like fabric being ripped, indicating a much higher rate of fire.

There was no time to process this, however; Cahill had to displace, had to do it now.

He fast-crawled on his elbows and knees till he reached the front end of the vehicle to his right, then drew both knees to his abdomen and crouched there.

The van's passenger laid off the trigger, and in the sudden silence Cahill heard voices yelling in a language he did not immediately recognize.

He heard, too, the side door of the van slide open, followed by scuffling feet.

Many scuffling feet.

This was followed almost immediately by the sound of something heavy banging on the reinforced-metal lock of a motel room door.

The unmistakable clanging of a handheld battering ram at work.

Still ducked in front of the car, Cahill held the 1911 out to the side and sent two rounds of suppressing fire in the direction of the van's passenger door, then immediately raised his head just enough to look over the hood and through the shattered windshield and back window, quickly surveying the scene.

As he did this, he pulled up his right pant leg with his left hand and grabbed the two single-stack mags from their neoprene holster.

Before he could do anything more, though, the man armed with the Uzi opened up again with another poorly aimed barrage.

Cahill put his head down and waited the man out.

The instant the man laid off the trigger of the automatic weapon—more than likely to re-aim—Cahill rose without hesitation to a standing position, firing the 1911 despite only holding it with one hand.

There was no time to drop the mags and acquire a double-handed grip, which meant the short-barreled weapon would kick substantially up and to the left, preventing him from getting off an immediate follow-up shot.

But he didn't need it.

The single round was a dead-on head shot, and the man instantly sagged into a lifeless heap in his seat, dropping the Uzi to the pavement.

Cahill's magazine was now empty, but a round remained in the chamber, so he ducked again for cover, sliding one of the mags upside down into his shirt pocket as he released the empty mag from the pistol.

He then performed a "wet" reload—slapping a loaded magazine into a firearm while a round was chambered.

This would save him from having to fire that last shot, pause to drop the empty mag and insert a loaded one, release the 1911's locked-open slide to chamber a round, and only then apply his left hand to the grip and begin the process of reacquiring his target.

Every second was precious, especially now that the clanging had ceased, which meant that the motel room door had been breached.

The driver of the van was still behind the wheel, his head turned so that the back of his skull was all Cahill could see. The man was shouting orders at the three-man team rushing through the open motel room door.

In a language that sounded Slavic.

Out of time now, Cahill rose again and began his advance.

He intended to close the distance between himself and the van in a matter of seconds, but in his haste he forgot about the Ford and its driver.

The shots that rang out weren't the controlled pairings of a pro, but the wild firing of a man repeatedly pulling a trigger as fast as he possibly could.

The driver of the Ford had regrouped and was positioned behind the rear end of his vehicle.

Cahill had moved too far from his cover position to return to it, so he continued toward the van, putting his faith in the fact that the man shooting at him was not aiming.

He focused his attention instead on what was directly ahead.

Raising his 1911, Cahill didn't bother aligning the front sight with the man behind the wheel; only feet away, the man was well within the "point and shoot" range.

Feet away and getting closer.

The man turned, and by the look on his face, Cahill knew he'd only just now realized that his passenger had been shot dead.

His second realization was that Cahill was closing on the passenger door.

The driver began to reach frantically for something in his waistband—a weapon, Cahill was certain.

Before he could do anything more than that, Cahill was at the door.

And put two hollow-points into the man's forehead.

Six rounds left before another reload.

Yanking open the passenger door, knowing it would shield him to a degree from the wild shots coming at him from the Ford, Cahill grabbed the passenger by the collar of his jacket and pulled him out, then climbed into the van.

Moving over the passenger seat, he drew the firearm from the dead driver's waistband and cut between the two front seats, into the cargo van's back compartment.

Tucking the backup firearm—a Glock 17—into the back of his jeans, Cahill moved to the side hatch through which, mere feet away, was the motel room door.

As silently and quickly as he could, Cahill exited the van.

The room was dark—Erica had done the smart thing and killed the lights after closing and locking the door.

And by the banging coming from inside the room, Cahill knew she had locked herself in the bathroom, too.

That door was not reinforced, yet it still took a total of three blows from the heavy battering ram to send it off its hinges.

Cahill counted each one as he approached.

The light from the bathroom now illuminated three men bottlenecked in the bathroom doorway—one still held the battering ram, another had an Uzi drawn, and the third wrestled with the fallen door that stood between them and their objective.

Erica screamed, and Cahill felt his blood go cold.

Entering the room, he fired at the armed man first—a controlled pair to the back of his head.

The man with the battering ram was next. Cahill dropped him with a second pair before he could even let go of the heavy object.

The third man had time to reach for his pistol and begin drawing it—but that was as far as he got.

With Erica somewhere behind the last man, Cahill hadn't wanted to risk missing, so he decided to forego the instant kill of a head shot and put two rounds into the man's heart instead.

Six shots, six hits, all targets down.

The slide locked open on the empty mag. Cahill depressed the release, letting that mag fall to the floor, and inserted his last one. Spinning to face the motel room door, he released the slide, sending it forward and racking a round into the chamber.

The driver of the Ford, armed now with his fallen comrade's cut-down shotgun, was already in the doorway.

He was yelling something, and though Cahill couldn't understand the words, he recognized a desperate battle cry when he heard one.

Some men can only act bravely when angry.

It was a race now to see who could raise his weapon first.

Cahill won, putting two through the man's open mouth, severing the spinal cord just below the cerebellum, and causing all motor function to instantly cease.

The man, suddenly silent, dropped and landed in a heap in the doorway.

Cahill's ears were ringing severely when he called to Erica, "Are you hurt?"

He heard no answer, so he called her name again.

She finally replied with, "I'm okay."

"Stay where you are."

Cahill rushed to the motel room door, 1911 raised. He checked the dead man blocking the door, then made a quick visual survey of the lot—or, with the van in the way, what he could see of it.

Sensing nothing—no sounds, no hint of motion—he hurried back through the room to the bathroom.

Erica was crouched down in the only open space—the tub.

Cahill pulled the door aside, stepped to her, and held out his left hand.

"C'mon," he said calmly, "we're out of here."

She reached up and grasped his hand. Pulling her up and guiding her over the broken door, he positioned her behind him.

"Stay with me," he instructed.

He started toward the door, making sure she didn't stray out of line or fall behind.

"You're going to need to step over a body in a second," he said. "Don't look down, okay?"

Erica did as she was told.

Pausing to make one more quick check of the scene, Cahill led her out into the open.

Once they were around the cargo van, it was a straight line to his Jeep—a dozen steps, max.

He shifted position, placing Erica at his right side so his body was between her and the battleground to their left, his right arm crossed over his left so he could keep the 1911 pointed in the direction of the Ford, just in case.

They moved in this way toward his Jeep, the two of them bent slightly at the waist.

Once they reached his vehicle, Cahill leaned Erica against it and placed himself in front of her to shield her as he pulled his keys from his pocket and unlocked the passenger door.

His attention was fixed to his left—not on the entrance to the lot on the right.

And this, he determined later, was what allowed the leader of the hit team to approach them unseen.

The man only needed to take a few steps before he was in range.

And once he was, he raised his weapon and opened fire.

Four

The abandoned service station was located on a two-lane back road in a town called Amity.

Cahill had discovered it after he had arrived in New Haven, during his standard recon of the area. It had been purchased by a developer just prior to the crash of the housing market back in '08. Shortly after the deal had closed, the developer died, leaving all his assets to his much-younger second wife. His will was currently being contested by his adult children from the previous marriage, which left his holdings—this dilapidated building among them—in limbo.

To confirm that it would suit his needs, Cahill had affixed motion-activated game cameras to trees along the edge of the property, one camera facing the front entrance, the other facing the rear. Weekly checks of each camera's removable memory chip had told him that no one had visited the property for a full month.

Only then did he cut the back door's padlock, replacing it with an identical one to which he had the key, and hide a stash of emergency supplies under a rotted floorboard.

Just as he had been trained to do.

He had also buried a more complete cache of supplies in the undeveloped land out back.

And the shovel he had used for that purpose was now the means with which he would bury the body of the woman he loved.

His injury was bad, made the work slow going; he had to stop several times to reattach his makeshift dressing.

But within a half hour he had dug out a grave that was four feet deep, after which he carried her body, wrapped in a bloodied blanket, from the car.

Kneeling down, he carefully lowered her into the cold November ground.

Nearly every move he made gave rise to a pain that caused him to grunt.

But that pain was nothing compared to the burning in his heart.

At first he couldn't bring himself to cover her with dirt, but he reminded himself that this was only temporary. He had no intention of leaving her family without answers for any longer than was necessary.

If all went well, he'd determine in a matter of days who had ordered the hit.

And why.

But he could only accomplish this if he remained free.

Whatever happened to him after that, he did not care.

Whatever price he'd have to pay to achieve his goal—to make those who were responsible suffer—he would willingly pay it.

Once he had finally buried her body he bowed his head and folded his stained hands, offering her last rites—or as close to them as he could get.

It had been a long time since he'd had any thoughts of God.

Now Cahill implored him to take Erica's soul. And to guide him and give him the strength he would need.

It was only then that he had what it took to leave her.

Pushing forward was all he had now.

Minutes later, he'd dug out the sealed PVC tube that contained his gear and carried it to his vehicle.

Retrieving the two camouflaged game cameras from their respective trees, he tossed them into his vehicle as well.

He then swept the dirt with the tip of his shovel, smoothing the surface of the grave and covering it with debris before clearing away his boot prints as he backtracked from the scene.

It was a less-than-thorough cleanup and in no way removed all traces of his presence—but he only needed to buy a few days.

Back in his Jeep, he unsealed the PVC tube and removed its contents: various weapons, survival gear, necessary electronics, a field first-aid kit—all packed neatly inside a Ranger backpack.

He unzipped the pack and grabbed the first-aid kit.

As he peeled off his makeshift dressing, his wound started bleeding again, but he applied a sterile battle compress fast, binding it to the surrounding skin with surgical tape, and soon enough the bleeding stopped.

The kit also contained a box of oral cephalexin and a vial of ampicillin, along with several packaged syringes.

As he would have done for Erica, he injected himself with three grams of the ampicillin and put the cephalexin in his shirt pocket for later.

His eyes then went to the kit's sixteen-ounce container of oral morphine, but he decided against that.

An hour's drive was ahead of him still, and he needed to stay awake.

No doubt the pain—physical and otherwise—would fuel him.

PART TWO

Five

Tom received the first call on his cell phone at ten o'clock on a Friday morning.

But he was at his job and unable to answer—Specialty Fabrication Inc.'s policy prohibited any employee from engaging in cell phone use while working.

It was just one of the many rules that were strictly enforced by the foreman who seemed to be always watching from a glass-enclosed office high above the crowded machine-shop floor.

Tom had programmed his phone to generate a specific vibration whenever Stella called or texted, but what he'd felt in his pocket wasn't that. The notification for all other incoming calls or texts was a set of five rapid vibrations, followed by a set of five more.

Five-and-five was the pattern that had suddenly buzzed in the pocket of his jeans.

Even if cell phone use hadn't been prohibited, or his foreman wasn't likely to be watching, Tom wouldn't have dug out his phone to see who was calling, because that would have been unsafe.

He had come too far and sacrificed too much to do something as foolish as losing a body part to the prewar-era press brake machine he operated nine hours a day, five days a week—for fifteen dollars an hour and no benefits.

Tom was in the dingy break room located just off the work floor when he finally checked his phone.

The call he had missed had come from a number he did not recognize. And no voice mail message had been left.

A wrong number, then, he decided.

Placing the phone facedown on the table, he proceeded to eat his lunch. Stella always texted during his noon break, and sure enough, a few moments later, his phone buzzed on the tabletop with a familiar pattern.

Two quick vibrations, a pause, two quick vibrations, another pause, two quick vibrations.

Stell-a . . . Stell-a . . . Stell-a.

It was a staccato pattern that he was unlikely to ever miss, especially as he worked the hydraulic press, which sent its own steady vibrations, like currents of electricity, through the concrete floor and up his legs.

The other members of the day shift spoke Portuguese and Tom did not, so he sat through lunch alone. Even if he could understand their language, or they better spoke his, he still would have kept to himself, simply because he wasn't much of a talker.

Reticence was more of a habit than an indication of his nature.

But there was another reason why he chose to sit alone.

Stella's lunchtime texts had recently begun to include the occasional selfie.

Picking up his phone, Tom saw at the top of the display screen the small preview of a text message.

It contained a minuscule photograph—not so small, however, that his eye couldn't immediately detect a significant degree of bare skin within its frame.

He calmly entered his four-digit passcode with his thumb to open the message.

And there was Stella, facing her ornately framed bedroom mirror, her cell phone held off to the side to capture her full reflection.

She was wearing a white Oxford shirt, a string of knotted pearls, and nothing else.

The shirt was unbuttoned and open.

The long string of pearls was her ever-present trademark.

A brief message accompanied the selfie:

Come straight home tonight.

The command was a joke they shared. Tom always went straight home.

Where else would he go?

Where else would he want to be after a long shift of stamping and folding metal?

He sent a reply:

Yes, ma'am.

This was another of their jokes, one that Stella enjoyed because it emphasized the differences in their ages.

She was forty-five, Tom thirty-three.

This difference was something Stella called attention to often, but Tom seldom thought of or even cared about it.

He'd seen the world, more or less, by the time he was twenty-four.

He'd seen men die—comrades and enemies alike.

He'd seen family members die, too, this when he was just a boy—too early, by far, to have learned firsthand what certain men were capable of. And while he more often than not kept the details of his past to himself, Stella knew enough about him to know about that.

Of course, he understood why she would enjoy calling attention to the fact that her live-in boyfriend was a younger man.

As grounded as Stella was, she was not above vanity.

Her reply read:

That's a good boy.

Tom smiled.

They exchanged a few more texts—the errands she needed to run today, that maybe they could splurge tonight and get takeout.

Today was her only day off, and the last day of Tom's work week.

A precious alignment of free hours, and the energy that came with it, that they knew better than to squander.

Tom signed off, too, then paused to take another look at the photo he had received.

Stella wore her dark, curly hair cropped to the exact length of her oval face. Twirled strands often fell in front of her eyes, which she would pull back and tuck behind her ears with long fingers, only for those strands to fall free again, often seconds later.

For some reason, Tom loved that gesture—the futility of it and that it was something she did so often that she didn't notice doing it anymore.

Prior to taking the selfie, Stella had shaken her head, tousling her hair so her face was partially obscured.

Tom could still see, though, her dark-brown eyes looking boldly at the camera.

Locking with his.

He could see, too, her delicate features—Anglo nose, high cheekbones, sharp jawline.

He'd never had beauty in his life before—beauty that slept when he slept, woke when he woke.

Living beauty, breathing beauty.

He couldn't imagine life without that now.

Not that he'd have to.

Tom took one last look at the photo before deleting it along with their text conversation. He then deleted from his call history the incoming call he had missed.

He kept his phone as clean as possible. And he only ever needed to glance at a number—any number, no matter how long—to commit it to memory.

Returning his phone to his pocket, Tom went back to his lunch.

The image of Stella would linger in his mind as he worked this afternoon, which was, of course, why she had sent it.

Tom had washed up in the men's room and was about to punch in and head back out to the shop floor for the second half of his shift when his phone buzzed again.

Five rapid vibrations erupted in the bottom of his jeans pocket, followed by another five.

Stopping to check the phone, Tom saw on the display the same unfamiliar number that he had seen just an hour before.

He waited for the call to go to his voice mail, then watched the phone's display for notification that he had received a voice message.

Ten seconds passed. Fifteen seconds. Twenty seconds.

Nothing.

So either a long message was being left or the caller had hung up and left none at all.

It was a minute past one o'clock now. Tom had missed punching in exactly on the hour, one of their petty foreman's many requirements, but that didn't concern him. Tom was the best machinist in the shop, could do this work in the dark.

What was the man going to do? Fire him?

What Tom was concerned about was the fact that it was unusual to receive a call from anyone but Stella.

Actually, Stella rarely called, preferring to communicate by text.

But in the six months he and Stella had been together, Tom's phone had been virtually dormant.

And while he was still using the same phone he'd purchased upon his discharge from the navy five years ago, he could count on one hand the people with whom he had exchanged numbers.

The incoming number did not belong to any of those select few.

In this day and age, no phone number could remain private forever. Tom understood that eventually his own would fall into the hands of some telemarketer and from there spread to countless others, at which point his only connection to the outside world—a limited connection, by his own choosing—would likely begin to ring frequently with numbers he did not recognize.

Today seemed to be that day.

Nearly another minute had gone by—no voice mail.

This wasn't a distress call, then, one that could not be ignored.

The protocol in place had established that any attempt at contact by his former commanding officer would come from a specific number.

That number and no other, so Tom would know to answer.

Since this wasn't that number, he was in the clear.

Returning the phone to his pocket, Tom pushed through the thick fire doors and walked out onto a noisy shop floor crowded with heavy machinery that raged like giant beasts.

The afternoon shift had begun without him.

He glanced up at the glass-enclosed office. Seeing that Tom was looking at him, the foreman raised his left arm and pointed at his wristwatch.

Or he started to, because before the man could complete the gesture, Tom shifted his line of sight and, looking straight ahead, ignored him.

Six

The sun was already behind the surrounding high hills when Tom exited the machine shop just after five and started across the poorly lit parking lot, covered from head to boots with a fine, metallic dust that turned his dark hair and full beard prematurely gray.

And made him look more than a little like a ghost.

Inside his truck, he texted Stella to let her know that he was on his way, then started the motor and turned on the heater. Before he could even shift into gear, Stella responded.

Meet you in the shower.

Canaan Village, in Connecticut's isolated northwest corner, was barely a stopover on Route 7 as it wound through the foothills of the Berkshire Mountains. All of three blocks long, with a single traffic light. Unchanged, more or less, since the end of the Second World War.

The last of the truly small towns.

No street cameras, a small police force, and an insular population—these were just some of the reasons why Tom had chosen to end his years of roaming here.

Steering his truck into the narrow alley that led to the small parking lot behind Stella's building, Tom pulled into his space, climbed out of his truck, and locked the door. He moved back through the alley on foot and stepped out onto the open sidewalk.

Main Street was busy—well, busy for Canaan. It was a Friday, though, and despite the colder-than-usual November evening, a number of townspeople were out.

The only restaurant in town had already begun to fill up. The second-run movie theater, its grand marquee framed with blinking yellow lights, was, like the town itself, something out of another era.

By eleven at the latest, however, the town would be all but closed up, the only foot traffic beneath their windows being a handful of moviegoers leaving the last showing of the night.

After that the town would come to a complete stop, silence and stillness settling in till morning.

Unlocking the street door, Tom entered the narrow stairwell and began to climb the steep steps toward the only door above.

Before he was halfway up, his phone vibrated once again. Five vibrations, then five more.

Drawing his phone from his pocket, Tom saw on the display the same unfamiliar number that had called twice already.

He stood there for a moment, staring at it.

Stella had no doubt heard the street door open and close and was waiting for him to climb the stairs and enter their apartment.

She was likely wondering why it was taking him longer than usual to do so.

Still, Tom lingered.

If he answered and the caller was a telemarketer, then he could forget the whole thing. It would be the same if someone had simply misdialed.

But if it wasn't either of those?

If it was the call he had sworn he would answer?

The call that could potentially turn his quiet life upside down.

Yet, if this were that call, the fact that it was coming from a number unrecognizable to Tom meant that it was contrary to protocol.

Of course, that number could have been abandoned for a variety of reasons. But there was a protocol for that, too.

If I change phones, Carrington had instructed, *I will text you a confirmation code from my new number.*

Tom had received no such text.

He had, in fact, heard nothing at all from Carrington since the night he'd passed on the lucrative contract Carrington had offered him.

Walked away from more money than he could easily spend and began his years of drifting.

Drifting that eventually led him to Stella.

No, this isn't that call, Tom decided. *It can't be.*

And more important, he didn't want it to be.

Those days were behind him.

In terms of years as well as miles traveled.

He powered down his phone, pocketed it, and resumed climbing the steep stairs.

Reaching the door at the top, he thought only of the woman waiting for him beyond it.

And the hot shower they would take, and the few hours they would have together before sleep took their exhausted bodies.

Seven

They'd met six months ago.

Tom had been drifting from place to place for five years but was looking, maybe, for somewhere to stop.

Stella was the only waitress at a converted railcar diner he'd gone to for lunch by chance.

A woman, from what he'd overheard as he ate, who seemed poised between a life that had ended and one that had yet to begin.

So they had that in common.

Every day for a week, while Tom reconnoitered Canaan Village and the surrounding towns, determining whether there were employment opportunities and looking for a cheap place to rent, he ate breakfast and lunch at that diner, and each time picked up just a little more information about the woman he couldn't stop looking at.

He'd learned that Stella had never married and was fiercely independent. Though currently single, she had a loyal following: business owners and tradesmen and law enforcement officers—both local cops and state troopers from the Troop B barracks just north of town.

These men filled the diner to capacity and beyond every morning and every noontime, asking Stella how she was doing, sympathizing with her, offering advice, making jokes, complimenting her.

More than half of those men, Tom noted, wore wedding bands.

Tom couldn't help but think of the suitors in *The Odyssey*—the unruly men jockeying for the hand of Odysseus's queen as Odysseus was enduring his twenty-year journey back from Troy.

A number of these men—the more prominent business owners—had in the past encouraged Stella to run for a seat on the board of selectmen or even for state office.

Everyone in town, it seemed, knew Stella.

More important, everyone knew that she was smart.

Tom eventually learned that Stella had once owned what the locals referred to as an "empire"—a long list of properties, most located in Canaan.

Her first acquisition had been a failing women's clothing shop, which began turning a profit within three months of her taking over.

She'd been all of eighteen at the time, using as a down payment on the business loan the money she had earned working nights during high school.

From there she just kept moving, taking bigger risks, but always gambling on herself.

She had a knack for being in the right place at the right time. By her midtwenties she had earned her real estate license and immediately focused on commercial properties.

While her intelligence and ambition were widely acknowledged, it was the fact that she had regularly invested in her community—buying up several retail properties and, as landlord, offering incentives for startup businesses to come in and create jobs—that had earned her the admiration of her neighbors.

And their interest in her running for office.

You could make a real difference, they'd said.

It helped, too, that she was the daughter of a beloved state trooper captain and his obstetrician wife. Lifelong Canaan residents, long dead now.

One helped start your life, and the other protected it.

With her business savvy and deep roots in town, how could she lose?

And how could their small town not benefit?

By the time she was thirty, Stella had purchased and turned around dozens of troubled properties in town. She owned one of the historic homes in the heart of Canaan, leased a new Mercedes sports coupe every other year, collected luxury watches, vacationed—when she took time off—in northern France.

She had even acquired the only two auto dealerships in town.

Her empire was spreading.

But then the recession hit.

The dealerships—the last of her acquisitions—were the first of her assets to be lost.

And as the recession refused to ease up, everything that she had worked so hard for began to slip through her fingers.

A domino effect, each loss causing the next loss, which in turn caused the loss after that, and so on.

Now, at forty-five, bankrupt, she was facing the daunting task of just keeping her head above water in a still-suffering economy.

And did so by working the same job she'd held back in high school.

It was a job she was lucky to have, yes, she would be the first to admit that. But Tom knew that while this would be a less-than-satisfying arc for any person, it was even more so for someone like Stella Quirk.

The only property she'd held on to was located on Main Street—yet another investment once, as much for herself as for the town, with a mortgage that was currently upside down, and so dramatically that none of her creditors had taken it.

A modest storefront with a small apartment above.

The storefront was vacant, like too many other storefronts in town, and Stella had moved into the apartment above two years ago, when her home had been quickly—so quickly—lost to foreclosure.

A month after they started dating, Stella asked Tom to move in with her.

She'd never done anything like that before, she'd told him, had always been cautious with men.

It was her nature, but there was also the fact that everyone in town watched her so closely, and that a person—a *woman*—in her position had to be careful.

Should she one day actually run for office—and there were days back then when she had seriously considered doing that— her past relationships with men would, at best, become common knowledge, and, at worst, be held against her.

There were, she'd confessed, aspects of her sexuality— appetites that she could not ignore, or at least ignore for long— that she did not want in the spotlight.

By then, Tom had already been spending several nights a week at her place, the others in a cheap motel on the edge of town.

Cheap or not, paying for the motel room was just a waste of money, Stella had said.

Live with me, Tom. I don't give a fuck anymore what anyone thinks. I don't care if everyone knows.

It was obvious to Tom in the days after he moved in that Stella's having a live-in boyfriend—and one so much younger than she— was the talk of the town.

He could see the resentment in the faces of her "suitors" whenever he passed them on the street.

He could see in their unsmiling faces their dislike for the grim-looking stranger who had come out of nowhere and gotten himself invited into Stella's bedroom.

Such attention was not something Tom had wanted or needed, but what was left of Stella's world had a gravity that he didn't understand, but also didn't doubt. He was pulled toward it, and into her.

And maybe, between the two of them, a new life would be possible.

He often wondered what would have happened had he not stopped for lunch that day six months ago.

He almost hadn't, at that moment wasn't particularly hungry, but how often does one see an actual railcar diner anymore?

And the town he had been passing through—Canaan—seemed to Tom like the kind of place in which a man like him might be able to come safely to a stop for a time.

Eight

The steam drifting with them as they moved from the shower to her bedroom smelled of green apples and lavender.

Tom knew no cleaner smell than that.

Scrubbed and naked, they stood in the middle of the dark room and embraced, Tom behind Stella, his arms around her waist, Stella with her arms reaching back, her hands on his lower back.

They were halfway between her bed, still unmade from this morning, and the tall window that looked out over the small back parking lot.

Tom occasionally saw her in that window when he returned from work.

Sometimes she would be dressed in black lace underwear, and sometimes she was undressed save for her string of pearls.

And other times, she would place both hands on the windowsill and brace herself as Tom took her from behind, the combination of their muted reflection in the glass and Stella's potential exposure sending waves of heat running through her.

Tom was six feet, weighed 210. Stella had been with many men, a few physically bigger than he, but never one as powerful. She'd made a point of telling Tom this.

She'd also made a point of telling him that she had discovered long ago that she needed to be possessed—taken. So she had always sought out men she thought might play that role well, men who would control her behind closed doors and therefore allow her to privately surrender the respectability that was expected of her.

Pulling him against her, she whispered, "First time fast, second time slow, okay?"

Tom's response was to kiss the back of her neck. She felt his beard brush her soft skin and the warmth of his breath.

She felt, too, his own need building.

"I don't want you to hold back, Tom. I need you not to be able to."

Locking his arms around her waist, Tom lifted her and carried her to the bed. She felt as if she weighed close to nothing, and the sense of being so small and vulnerable thrilled her deeply.

He moved quickly, decisively—she could do nothing to stop him.

The next thing she knew, her feet were on the floor again and she was bent over the edge of the mattress, Tom pressing her down into it with one hand, the other reaching between her legs, spreading them.

"Fuck me," she said. "Like all the men in town want to. Fuck me like they all wish they could."

Tom had never once been taken aback by this, even the first time such wild words had flown out of her. If anything, he rewarded her for revealing her darkness to him. Stella had fallen even harder for him because of this, felt suddenly safe in a way she had never before known.

No recrimination or embarrassment with Tom, no need to even explain or discuss afterward.

Their shared secret, one that, for her, bonded them.

Later, things went more slowly. On her back, his mouth on her, she experienced a full release. Her second orgasm was always significantly better than her first, which was why she preferred to get the first out of the way as quickly as possible.

The second one always washed away so much clutter as it broke inside her.

And each one that followed washed away even more.

How could losing everything be so bad if losing everything brought me this?

It was a thought that made some sense out of the senseless.

A belief that made bearable what she had for so long been unable to bear.

Finally, when Tom was on top, she watched his face as he rocked steadily above her. She was spent, all of her overwhelming and urgent desires burned off, so it was about him now, his pleasure, giving him the time he needed to build to his second climax.

She'd never known this, either.

She knew the signs, knew when he was close, and when she felt him about to let go, she pulled him down to feel the full weight of him pressing upon her, then whispered into his ears things that were for him, that sent him over the top.

As he came, she clutched at him, wrapping her arms around him, riding out with him the fierce storm moving through his body till he finally was still again.

⌣

"When the food arrives, should I answer the door like this?" Stella said.

Tom watched from the bed as she placed her cell phone back on her dresser and stepped in front of the ornately framed mirror mounted on the wall beside it.

She faced the mirror, her skin slick with sweat, most of it hers, some of it his.

"If you want to," Tom said.

"Is that a dare?"

"If you want it to be."

"You know I love dares."

"Then it's a dare."

She smiled. "That might be pushing it."

Tom smiled back and said nothing, watching Stella watch his reflection in the mirror.

Her eyes scanned the many scars on his muscular torso. Some were star-shaped and jagged, others near-perfect straight lines that ran for several inches.

Often as they lay together, Stella would absently trace the tips of her fingers over his long-healed wounds, moving from one to the next.

She had asked once how he'd gotten those wounds, but Tom had merely smiled and said, "You should have seen the other guy."

A joke meant to deflect the issue. She had never asked again.

"Did they say how long till the food gets here?" Tom said.

"The usual fifteen minutes."

"Enough time for us to shower again."

"Actually, I want to tell you something."

"Okay."

She gulped down some water, sat on the edge of the bed, and faced him.

"So, I had a meeting today." She paused, as if uncertain where to begin. "Ben says it's time for him to sell the diner. And he asked if I would be interested in buying it."

"Are you?"

"I don't know. I probably couldn't get a loan, but even if I could, a diner is a lot of work."

"You do pretty much everything already. Ben barely comes in for more than an hour in the afternoon, right?"

Stella shrugged. "To be honest, I kind of like not being that . . . thing I used to be. There are advantages to being a failure."

"No one thinks of you as a failure, Stella."

"We can argue about that later. I mean, I can't wait tables six days a week for the rest of my life, that's for sure. And this might be a chance for me to start to rebuild things, maybe even get back some of what I lost. It might even be my only chance." She paused again. "I have to tell you, though, I'm starting to really like this lack of responsibility. I just do my job and go home. My personal life is my personal life; my nights are mine."

Tom understood what she meant by this, what it meant to be truly free of any and all responsibilities.

He'd spent years drifting, caring about nothing, having to worry about nothing.

Eating, sleeping, working, reading.

A man on his own, all the choices his.

That kind of life was always a safe bet.

"Does Ben need an answer right away?" Tom said.

"Not right away, but soon. I don't have any money saved, so I wouldn't even be able to come up with a down payment. The only reason I was able to bring the mortgage on this place current was because of the rent you pay me."

"How much does he want for the business?"

"We didn't get that far."

"Maybe you should find out."

"Why? Are you secretly rich?"

Tom shook his head.

"Damn it," Stella joked.

"It would be better to know than not know, right?"

"My credit is shot, Tom. Beyond shot."

"Mine's not."

"To be honest, I don't think you have the kind of credit a bank is looking for. I mean, considering the way you've been moving around. It's not like it used to be, when banks were begging people to borrow money."

"Maybe I know someone who wouldn't mind cosigning. As an investment."

"I appreciate that, I really do. But I don't even want to think about it now. I shouldn't have brought it up. Not till I had thought more about it, anyway."

"No harm in thinking out loud."

She smiled. "Sure there is." She took a breath, let it out, and said, "So work was okay for you today?"

"The day went fast enough," he said. "Your errands went well?"

"Yeah, except I ran into pretty much every one of my regulars everywhere I stopped."

"Ah, the suitors," Tom said.

"Jealous?"

"Only when you want me to be."

"Oh, I always want you jealous."

She leaned forward and kissed him.

"You're right, we should shower quick," she said. "Food will be here soon."

———

They were dressed—Stella in her silk robe, Tom in clean jeans and a T-shirt—when they heard the knock on the street door below.

"I'll get it," Tom said.

"Let me give you some money."

"I've got it tonight."

Before she could protest, Tom had unlocked the apartment door and was heading down the steep stairs.

Opening the street door, he saw the usual delivery kid, the one Stella always joked about greeting naked.

The kid had recently started eating at the diner several mornings a week, sitting at the counter, nursing a cup of coffee and picking at a muffin, quietly watching Stella.

Just another one of her suitors, as far as Tom was concerned.

He paid the kid, tipping him well despite the fact that doing so almost cleaned out the cash he carried, then headed back up the stairs and entered the apartment.

He found Stella standing in the hallway between the living room and the bedroom with an expression on her face that Tom did not immediately understand.

Or like.

He was about to ask her what was wrong when he realized that she was holding her cell phone to her ear.

She nodded. Then she said, "Hang on."

Holding out the phone with one hand, she covered the mic with her thumb and said, "It's for you." She paused, then: "She said it was an emergency."

Tom closed the door, handed Stella the bag of takeout with one hand, and took her cell phone with the other.

He had never given Stella's number to anyone.

And of the few people from his past who might one day reach out to him, none were female.

So it was baffling enough that a woman was calling, but what really concerned him was that someone looking for him had called Stella's phone.

Of course, Stella and he weren't exactly a secret.

And the frequency of their communication by cell phone—not to mention the nature of the texts they sent each other—was a clear indication of their living situation.

And though his phone was shut down, the last time it had been active, it was occupying the same GPS coordinates that her phone currently occupied.

So Tom had a pretty good idea what to expect as he placed the phone to his ear and said, "Hello."

Nine

"Tomas Sexton?"

Tom did not recognize the female voice, and this bothered him immediately. But he kept his mind clear and his body calm.

Fear had long since been conditioned out of him.

"Who is this?" Tom said.

"Tomas Sexton?" the female repeated. *Tah-mis*, she said, instead of *Toe-maas*. Everyone called him Tom, just plain Tom, but those who knew him well knew the correct pronunciation of his first name.

"Who is this?" Tom repeated.

"I'm told you won't need to write this down."

She began to rattle off a series of numbers.

The first, a single digit, was followed by several double-digit numbers.

She spoke evenly, pausing for only a second between each number. Her voice was a soft and soothing alto.

"Do you need that repeated?" she asked.

Tom said he didn't.

There was a moment of silence. Tom listened for any telltale background noise but heard none. He had already determined that she had no noticeable accent and that there were no tones in her voice that would indicate excitement or stress.

Finally, she spoke again. "I look forward to meeting you, Tom. I've heard a lot about you."

Before Tom could say anything else, the call abruptly ended.

A quick look at the phone's display confirmed what he already knew. The number was the same one he had seen on his own phone three times that day.

Lowering Stella's cell, Tom hesitated.

"What's going on?" Stella said.

He replied with the only thing he could say. "I'm not sure."

He handed her phone back to her and headed down the hallway to the bedroom.

"You should get dressed," he said.

"What's wrong? Who was that?"

"Get dressed, okay?"

Stella followed him into the bedroom. "Tom?"

"Get dressed, Stella. Please."

He reached under Stella's dresser and pulled out a black canvas shoulder bag. Moving to the bed, he opened and upended the bag, dumping its contents onto the tangled sheets.

Stella dropped her robe and grabbed a pair of jeans. She watched him as she pulled them on.

The bag contained two bottles of spring water, several protein bars, a Leatherman multitool, a mini-flashlight, a Moleskine notebook, metal draftsman's pen, and two smartphones and chargers.

Tom grabbed the phones and powered them up. Stella had pulled on a T-shirt and was about to put on a dark sweater when Tom handed her one of the phones.

"The only number programmed into this is the number to this phone." He held up the one he'd kept. "And vice versa, okay?"

"Okay."

"We're leaving our phones here, using only these for now. And we should shut our phones down, too."

Stella clearly balked at the idea of being separated from her phone. But then she focused on the more important point in Tom's statement.

We're leaving our phones here.

"Where are we going, Tom?"

"Out for a minute. You'll need shoes."

Stella looked around the floor for her boots. Spotting them, she hurried to where they were and began pulling them on.

"Out where?" she said.

Tom ignored the question. He quickly shoved the items on the bed back into the shoulder bag, then moved to his nightstand, opened the top drawer, and removed his Kindle.

It contained the thousands of books he had read in the past five years.

It was also his only secure means of deciphering the code he had just received.

On his way back to the bed, he grabbed a hooded sweatshirt from the closet.

Powering up the tablet, he placed it into the bag, secured the flap, then pulled on the sweatshirt and shouldered the bag.

"Please tell me what's going on, Tom. Who is that woman?"

"Not someone I've ever met. I didn't recognize her voice."

"Why did she call you on my phone?"

"We'll know more in a few minutes, Stella."

"Are we in danger?"

"If we were, I think we'd know it already."

He saw the look of confusion on her face.

"We'll only be gone for a few minutes," he assured her. "I just need to keep you in sight until I know exactly what's what. Okay?"

She nodded stiffly.

They left her building together, holding hands as they walked steadily toward the entrance to an alleyway five paces from the street door.

The early movie had ended, so moviegoers were leaving the theater. Others were waiting for the next showing. This meant that there were more people than usual on the sidewalk.

Tom studied the face of every person who approached.

In the back parking lot, he led Stella to his truck.

"You'll drive," he said. "Okay?"

She nodded. He let go of her hand and gave her his keys.

"Where are we going?"

"The McDonald's on Route Forty-Four." Before she could ask why, Tom said, "They have free Wi-Fi."

They parked in the back of the lot, within the long shadow of the restaurant.

Tom studied the parking lot for a moment, making certain they hadn't been followed.

He could feel Stella watching him.

Satisfied that they were in the clear, Tom removed the tablet from the shoulder bag, located the Wi-Fi signal, and logged on. He tapped the "Home" icon on the display. Within seconds, the Amazon.com homepage had opened up. Without signing into his account, Tom typed a title into the search box and was brought to a new page. The Kindle edition of Thomas Paine's *Crisis*.

He scrolled down the page till he found a review entitled: "These Are the Times That Try Men's Souls."

"There's a notebook and pen in the bag," Tom said. "Could you get them for me?"

Stella quickly found the notebook and pen, pulled them out.

Tom took the notebook, tore out a page, and handed it to her.

He looked at her, then said, "I'm going to point to some words and you're going to write them down, okay?"

Stella nodded.

The review was lengthy, its many paragraphs comprised of dozens of sentences. Tom began scanning, stopping first at the ninth word in the first sentence, underneath which he placed the tip of his index finger.

Man

From there he skimmed again, counting as he went and stopping this time on the word *fallen.*

He continued to skim the review, word by word, line by line, pointing to key words as he found them.

Meet

Black

Revolution

Four

Six words in total.

Man Fallen Meet Black Revolution Four

The instant Tom had read the last word of that directive, he exited the page and shut down his tablet.

"What's it mean?"

"It's a distress call. Someone I used to know is in trouble."

It took Stella a moment to respond.

Minutes ago they had been about to eat dinner.

Minutes before that they had been together in her bed.

"What kind of trouble?"

"I don't know."

"Who is the call from?"

"That's the problem."

"What does that mean?"

"There isn't a lot of time, Stella, but I'll tell you what I can, okay? And then I have to go."

"Where?"

"New York City."

"For how long?"

"It's seven now, so I should reach the city by ten thirty, if not sooner. If I can get on the road again by eleven thirty, I'll be back here before you leave for work in the morning."

"Why don't I come with you?"

"It would be better if you stayed behind."

"Why?"

"Please, let's get back home. I'll explain on the way."

Ten

Tom would have preferred that Stella wait for him in the roadside motel just south of Canaan, the place where he had stayed several nights a week prior to moving in with her, but she refused.

She'd be fine at home, she assured him. The police station was a minute away, plus she had the phone number of every cop and half the state troopers in her cell.

Any one of them would come running—to save her if necessary, comfort her if she were scared, or keep her company should she get lonely.

"Maybe I'll just invite them all over for a party while you're gone," she teased.

The joke, whispered into Tom's ear, was her way of letting him know that she was okay.

Okay with what he had told her, and what he had to do.

Before leaving, however, Tom secured the apartment, as much for his peace of mind as hers.

He dug a wind chime out of a kitchen drawer that had hung outside her bedroom window during the summer months, then grabbed a hammer and nail and suspended the chime above the downstairs door.

Opening the door even an inch would rattle the chimes, and that sound echoed up the stairwell and could be heard even in the back bedroom.

Tom then grabbed an empty can from the recycling bin, half filled it with coins from the jar of change on Stella's dresser, and instructed her to balance the can on the old brass knob of the apartment's front door after he was gone.

The knob was so wobbly that someone just gripping it from the other side would be enough to cause the can to fall to the floor and all the change to spill out.

His final security measure was taking the triangle-shaped block of pine Stella used to wedge the bedroom door open on windy nights and flipping it around to show her how it could also be used to wedge the door closed from inside the bedroom.

All of these precautions would, should the worst happen, buy her enough time to get to the chrome-plated Smith and Wesson .357 Magnum in her nightstand drawer.

Her father's service revolver from his days as a state trooper.

A weapon that, years ago, the man had taught his only daughter to use effectively.

It was ten minutes past seven o'clock when Tom left. Stella watched him from the bedroom window as he unlocked the metal toolbox bolted to his truck's bed and removed yet another shoulder bag, also identical to the one he had kept hidden under her dresser.

In it were various survival necessities for two, as well as $1,000 in twenties.

Kept there for this very reason.

At the truck's door, Tom paused to look up at the bedroom window and the woman standing in it.

She was not posed provocatively this time, but all Tom could think about was getting back to her—to the life they'd made in six short months, even to the long hours they both worked so they could spend their nights together.

A simple existence, but that was all he wanted.

She waved to him. He nodded, then got behind the wheel.

Heading south on Route 7, New York City a good three-plus hours away, Tom had plenty of time to prepare mentally for whatever awaited him.

Consider all the options—the ways in, the ways out.

All that needed to go right, all the things that could go wrong.

And those things that could go very wrong.

Eleven

Tom was on I-84 eastbound, about to cross the border into New York State, when he pulled his truck to the shoulder and stopped.

The last time he'd been in the city, he had gone there to meet with the same man he was expecting to see tonight.

Hoping to see. Counting on seeing.

This was five years ago, when Tom had decided not to sign on as a private military contractor with Carrington's fledgling security firm.

There was reason now, though, for Tom to doubt that Carrington would be the one to meet him tonight, since the first of the several protocols that had been broken was the very protocol put in place to confirm the identity of the sender of any message Tom might receive.

The call should have come from Carrington himself, no one else.

That was protocol number one: voice-to-voice communication.

Texts, even those coming from a known phone, could be sent by anyone.

Also, texts could be ignored by the receiver.

Therefore, protocol number one was critical because it would leave no doubt that the message had come from Carrington, and Carrington would know that Tom had received it.

There were only two reasons why Carrington would reach out in this manner.

Someday I may need your help, the man had said. *Or someone we know will need ours.*

At the time, Tom had wanted to know why Carrington had come up with such an elaborate system.

You're an asset to me, Tom. The more secret an asset is, the better, so I prefer not to draw attention to you, should I need you.

Carrington had paused, then said, *And frankly, it would benefit us both greatly if my enemies never saw you coming.*

Parked now on the side of the dark highway, Tom considered all the reasons why this did not feel right.

The voice he had heard tonight was not Carrington's.

The call had not come from Carrington's number.

And perhaps more important, Tom's first name had been mispronounced.

Though not in and of itself a broken protocol, it was at the very least an indication that the caller was not a friend.

Still, all the other established protocols had been observed.

The code in the review of Thomas Paine's *Crisis. Black* instead of *zero dark,* the standard military designation for midnight. *Man fallen* instead of *man down*—another of Carrington's variations that meant someone had been injured and was assumed to be currently in distress. And *revolution four* was the correct term for one of the five locations in and around New York City that Carrington had selected, all of them Revolutionary War landmarks.

Maybe Carrington was the fallen man, and someone who knew the code—if Tom knew it, then likely others did as well—was reaching out for help.

Someone who knew not to leave a voice mail. Someone determined or desperate enough to keep calling till Tom finally answered.

And who then adapted when Tom did not.

But of the people who might also be aware of Carrington's system of encrypted communication, Tom could not imagine that one of them was female.

The Seabee Engineer Reconnaissance Team that Carrington had commanded, and in which Tom had served, had been an all-male team.

And the combat marines their team supported at Forward Operating Base Nolay in Afghanistan's Sangin Valley had all been male as well.

Then again, Carrington had been in the private sector for a number of years and would have made all kinds of associations by now.

Female or not, Tom thought, *the question isn't simply who the caller is, but how she got Stella's number. And how she knew to call it when I had shut my phone down.*

Tom needed answers—all kinds of answers. And he would find those only by continuing forward.

Shifting into drive and steering back onto the interstate, he resumed his course toward New York City.

Eight blocks from his destination, Tom parked his truck and began to walk.

It was a Friday night, chilly but not cold, so Manhattan's Lower East Side was busy.

Bars and restaurants full, a steady stream of people on the sidewalks, cars passing on the narrow streets.

Tom reached the corner of Rivington and Forsyth Streets and immediately spotted two black SUVs parked nose-to-tail halfway down Rivington.

He then looked toward a small restaurant called the Gentleman Farmer.

During the Revolutionary War, several of General Washington's spies had regularly used it as a meeting place.

And the street it was on—Rivington—had been named after a publisher whose loyalist newspaper was in reality a means of dispensing crucial information about the British to Washington and his officers.

Normally, Tom enjoyed historical places, made a point of always pausing reverently in their presence to sense their aura. To remember the important events these places had witnessed, honor the generations of men and women that had moved through them over the course of hundreds of years.

But there wasn't time for that tonight.

After a careful survey of the area, he crossed Rivington and headed for the front door.

Through the storefront window he could see a man seated alone at a small corner table, his eyes fixed on the tumbler of whiskey before him.

A man at that moment lost in thought.

To Tom's relief, that man was James Carrington.

Twelve

Tom's sense of relief quickly gave way to concern.

Carrington was here to meet him, yes—that was good. But that did not explain why the man himself hadn't made the call that brought Tom here.

Tom entered the restaurant but paused just inside the door to scan the dozen or so tables.

PMCs—private military contractors—were generally easy enough to spot, but none of the diners here fit that bill.

When Tom looked back at Carrington, the man had already stood up and was downing what remained of his drink.

Carrington peeled off two twenties from a wad of bills and placed them on the table. He was returning the wad to his pocket and smiling as he headed toward Tom.

Clearly in a hurry.

Things were in motion now that Tom was here.

Carrington extended his hand.

"It's good to see you again, Tom."

"It's good to see you, too, sir."

Carrington's grip was firm, his handshake enthusiastic. He was fewer than fifteen years older than Tom, and yet he was the closest thing to a father Tom had known for a long time.

He was wearing dark-blue jeans, a shirt and tie, dress shoes, and a wide-collared leather coat.

Though Tom had seen Carrington in civilian clothes before, it always struck him as odd. He almost didn't even recognize the man.

"You don't have to call me 'sir' anymore, Tom." He looked Tom over quickly, then said, "You look good. Older. I mean that in a good way."

Before Tom could respond, Carrington told him there wasn't a lot of time and that they needed to move.

He led Tom out and onto the sidewalk, where they faced Rivington.

"Honestly, Tom, I didn't think you were going to show up."

"Thought about not," Tom said.

"The breach in protocol was unavoidable. I'll explain when I can. But you're here now, and that's what matters."

"Why am I here?"

Carrington casually reached up and brushed his ear twice with the tip of his index finger.

Tom understood the gesture.

A warning that someone could be listening.

"Some people need to talk to you," Carrington said. "I work with them from time to time. I trust them, and so can you."

"Who are they?"

"She's NSA. He's private sector."

This at least confirmed for Tom how the mysterious female had known to call Stella's phone.

"I won't be able to go with you," Carrington said. "I'm sorry about that."

"Where am I going?"

"Not far. This won't take long, Tom. Just pay attention, ask any questions you need to ask. And feel free to say no. Do you understand?"

Tom nodded.

The two black SUVs pulled to a stop in front of them, and the back passenger-side door of the first vehicle swung open.

Carrington faced Tom. "You remember what John Locke wrote in his *Second Treatise on Government*, right?"

A baffling question. But Tom knew the answer, so he nodded.

"Tell me," Carrington said.

"He wrote that the first law of nature is self-defense."

There was a touch of fatherly pride to Carrington's smile. "And thank God the founding fathers read him, right?"

This comment did nothing to clear up Tom's confusion.

Carrington looked at Tom squarely and said, "You understand what I'm saying, right?"

He didn't, but he trusted that at some point he would understand, so he nodded again.

Carrington said, "Good."

From inside the SUV, a male voice said, "Let's get moving."

Tom ignored that and waited for further instructions from his former commanding officer.

"It's so good to see you, Tom," Carrington said. "And civilian life clearly agrees with you. I wasn't sure it would, but I'm glad to know I was wrong."

He extended his hand again.

Tom took it, but this time there was something in Carrington's palm.

A small flip phone.

Out-of-date, practically ancient.

As they released hands, Tom palmed the phone, then discreetly pocketed it.

"Remember," Carrington said, "feel free to say no. There's no shame in looking out for oneself."

Carrington stepped back, and Tom turned and got into the waiting SUV.

Through the heavily tinted window, Tom watched a man join Carrington on the sidewalk—shaved head and scarred face, dressed in a black nylon jacket, khaki pants, and black tactical boots.

The very gear that made private military contractors—at least certain types of PMCs—easy to spot.

The scarred-face man said something to Carrington, who nodded and spoke.

The way the man quickly turned away told Tom that Carrington had given him some kind of order.

Maybe even an urgent one.

Tom watched the two men—Carrington standing still, the scarred-face man walking away—till they were gone from his sight.

——— ———

In the front seats of the SUV were two men in dark suits. Both had short, neatly trimmed hair and earpieces affixed in their right ears.

The man in the back seat beside Tom was dressed in jeans, a black field jacket, and tan workman boots.

He was also wired with an earpiece.

This man stared at Tom, his right forearm resting across his lap and his right hand just inside his open jacket, poised to grasp the weapon holstered there.

Glancing over his shoulder, Tom saw that the second SUV was following them closely.

Tom looked back at the man beside him, who was staring at him in a way that was both stoic and aggressive.

One of the reasons he had turned down Carrington's job offer was so he wouldn't have to deal with such men.

Men who mistook violence for adventure.

Men who were just a little too eager to use their deadly skills.

And who no doubt practiced long and hard to radiate an air of danger.

Not all PMCs were like that, of course. Most were quiet professionals. Some were retired special forces, others combat veterans who had served multiple tours of duty. Smart men, capable men, modest. Men who simply wanted to do the job and get paid and make it safely back home to their families.

And though only a fraction of those Tom would encounter were likely to be like the man now sitting next to him, a fraction was more than Tom cared to experience.

As much as he disliked the fact that he was now sitting beside the very kind of man he wanted to avoid—the very man he never wanted to become—Tom couldn't help but be amused by the effort this man was making to intimidate.

He decided to pass the time by looking out the window to his right.

The two SUVs were heading north on the FDR, following the western edge of the East River.

Ten minutes later, they pulled into a parking garage on Seventy-Second Street.

The driver steered the SUV to higher and higher levels, the nose of the tail car always just inches away.

Each level contained fewer and fewer vehicles, and in a far corner of the sixth level—the emptiest so far—waited a shiny black limo.

The SUV pulled up alongside it and stopped.

The driver pressed a switch that unlocked Tom's door.

The man beside Tom said, "Get out."

Tom did. A man in a suit held open the limo's rear passenger door.

Walking over to the limo, Tom looked inside at the two occupants.

A female in her midthirties, tops. Dressed in a dark business suit—jacket, silk blouse, dark nylons, sensible-but-still-stylish shoes. Fine brown hair pulled back into a tight bun. Smile confident but warm.

She sat facing the back of the vehicle.

The other occupant faced the front. Older, late forties. He was dressed in a business suit as well, but his was perfectly tailored, showing off his powerful athlete's frame. His hair was full but well trimmed, his face clean shaven, his skin tanned and taut.

Everything about him said affluence.

"Thank you for meeting us, Tom," the woman said. "My name is Alexa Savelle." Her voice, a soothing alto, had no accent of any kind.

There was no doubting that this was the woman who had called Stella's cell.

Savelle introduced the man as Sam Raveis.

Raveis simply stared at Tom. The only expression that Tom could detect on the man's face was a slight look of curiosity.

Savelle patted the empty seat to her left. On her lap lay a tablet in a black leather case.

"Please, Tom, sit with us," she said. "We need to talk to you. And there isn't a lot of time."

Thirteen

The limo door closed with a solid *whoomph*, and immediately the wind coming off the river that had been echoing steadily through the open garage was silenced.

The driver remained beside the door, his back to it, his arms at his sides and his hands hanging loose.

Tom recognized his mannerisms as those of a well-trained bodyguard.

The interior of the limo was rich with the combined smell of new leather and perfume.

Another woman's scent only made Tom think of Stella waiting for him back at her apartment.

His obligation to Carrington was all that kept him here.

Alexa Savelle spoke first. "Did Carrington tell you why you're here?"

"No."

"Would you mind telling me what he did tell you?"

"That you were NSA." Tom nodded toward the man in the expensive suit. "And that he was private sector."

"Did he tell you anything else?" Savelle asked.

Tom wondered if they were the ones Carrington had indicated could be listening and whether this was a test of Tom's honesty.

"He told me that he works for you from time to time. And that I can trust you."

Savelle smiled. "I'm hoping you will, Tom."

Up to this point, the man introduced as Raveis had been silently but actively watching Tom—studying him, sizing him up. Finally, he spoke.

"Jim Carrington is a good man," Raveis said. "Reliable, which goes a long way with me. He drinks too much now and then, but not so much that it interferes with business. At least it hasn't yet. I understand he offered you a job a few years back but you turned him down. I'm curious. Why?"

"I wanted to be on my own for a while."

"You were in the navy for eight years, correct?" Raveis said.

"Yes."

"You requested the Seabees when you enlisted. Construction Battalion. Why was that?"

"I wanted to learn a skill." He paused, then said, "I didn't want to be one of those guys who gets out of the military and can't find a job."

"Killing the enemy is a skill, no? You seem to be proficient at that."

Tom chose to ignore that comment.

"Your records indicate that you started out as a builder. A carpenter. So what did you want to do? Build houses?"

Tom shrugged. "Sure."

"Yet you currently work as a press brake operator. Stamping metal in a machine shop for barely more than minimum wage."

"Not a lot of houses being built these days."

Raveis watched him for a moment more. "Better times are bound to come, right?"

"If this is a job offer—"

"It's not a job offer, Tom. As much as I'd value a man like you working for me, I have no intention of wasting my time or yours."

"Then why am I here?"

Raveis looked at Savelle, who opened the tablet on her lap. She tapped the screen several times with her index finger, then began to swipe left to right, scrolling through documents.

"You did a year at Yale before enlisting in the navy." She looked up from her tablet. "We're assuming that means you know your way around New Haven, to some degree or another."

"Yeah."

"You were in the top tenth percentile of your class, but your father's sudden death the summer after your freshman year left you with no money for school and no family to help you out. So you turned to the military, like young people in a jam often do."

"It's interesting how a single event can completely alter one's life, don't you think?" Raveis said.

It seemed to Tom that both Raveis and Savelle were watching for his reaction.

He offered none.

"After completing basic training," Savelle continued, "you attended 'A' School, after which you were assigned to NMCB. It was during the subsequent Expeditionary Combat Skills training that you caught the attention of your then-commanding officer, who introduced you to Jim Carrington. On Carrington's recommendation, you began to receive nearly all the specialized training the navy has to offer, after which you were assigned to the Seabee Engineer Reconnaissance Team under Carrington's command. You served both in Iraq and Afghanistan as a support unit for the marines, often accompanying Force Reconnaissance units to forward operating bases, which as a Seabee you constructed and maintained but also defended."

"It's your work with the Recon Marines that interests us," Raveis said.

Savelle picked up the thread. "On the night of April 11, 2009, a Recon squad was returning to base after a long-range patrol when they were ambushed by heavily armed insurgents. Disobeying the direct orders of a superior officer, who was later court-martialed, you led a successful rescue mission."

"Not your first such mission," Raveis said. "But as it turned out, your last. Do you mind telling us what happened?"

Tom nodded toward the tablet. "It's all there, isn't it?"

"It is," Raveis said. "A grenade attack. You were defending the rear as your team and the Recon squad were executing a fighting retreat. According to the after-action report, you would have likely been killed if not for a certain Recon staff sergeant who placed himself between you and the grenade. In fact, the fragments that did hit you had traveled through his body first, greatly reducing their velocity and lethality."

"It was a bad night for a lot of people," Tom said.

"But a lucky night for you," Raveis noted. "Not only did you get to live to fight another day, you were later awarded the Silver Star for your actions." He nodded toward Savelle. "Alexa here only has a Bronze Star."

Tom glanced at Savelle's hand then and saw that she was wearing only one ring.

A bulky, gold school ring.

He focused on it more closely and recognized it as a West Point ring.

"After only two months of rehabilitation, you were back with your unit." Savelle stopped reading, then said to Tom, "Only a certain kind of man would go back, especially when he didn't have to. Apparently, Carrington wanted to transfer you stateside. He even put in the paperwork. But you talked him out of it, which he says is just one of the reasons why he thinks so highly of you."

Savelle resumed scrolling through documents, skimming and reading. "Three months after your return, your enlistment was up. For the first time in eight years, which at that point was close to your entire adult life, you were a civilian."

"Around that same time," Raveis said, "Carrington retired from the navy and joined the public sector, starting his own private security firm. Lots of money to be made in that line of work, even in a troubled economy. More so if you're the right kind of person, which, it turns out, Carrington is. So he starts building his business, making a name for himself, and meanwhile you relax for a few months, travel around a little, then decide, somewhat suddenly, to pass on Carrington's offer. To me that's odd enough, but then you do something even odder, Tom. You become a drifter, pretty much living out of your truck for five years. From what we can tell, all you did was move from place to place and job to job and read books on your Kindle."

Raveis paused, looked squarely at Tom, and said, "I can see why you finally settled down. She's a very attractive woman. In great shape for someone her age." He smiled, his taut and tanned face showing few creases. "And the pearls are a nice touch."

Tom felt a wave of rage, yet he just calmly reached for the door handle. Before he could do more than grasp it, though, Savelle placed her palm on his forearm, stopping him.

Her touch was gentle.

"I'm sorry, Tom. Raveis is an asshole by nature, but he's being an even bigger asshole now because we need to determine your state of mind, and we need to do so as quickly as possible. We have to know if you're prone to violent outbursts, like men who have been injured in combat can be. Because if you are suffering any kind of posttraumatic stress, we can't use you. It's as simple as that. We need to know we can count on you one hundred percent. And frankly, the way you've been living your life the past five years doesn't exactly fill us with confidence."

"You probably shouldn't count on me, then," Tom said.

Raveis said, "You're willing to just walk out without knowing what it is we need you to do?"

"I'll live with it."

"Can you live with letting a man die?"

Tom didn't move.

"How about letting the man who saved your life die? The man who almost *died* saving *your* life. Who by all accounts *should* have died saving your life. Could you live with that?"

"Charlie Cahill is in trouble," Savelle said.

Her palm was still resting on Tom's forearm, and she was looking at the side of his face.

"What kind of trouble?"

"He has disappeared," Savelle said.

Tom looked at Raveis, then back at Savelle. Her eyes, he noticed, were dark brown—like Stella's.

"What would you need me to do?"

Savelle reached across Tom and tapped his window twice. The driver opened the rear passenger door.

The sound of the wind echoing through the parking structure returned.

"There's a lot to cover," Savelle said. "I'll bring you up to speed as we take you back to your truck."

Tom studied Raveis one more time.

"I appreciate you not jumping out of your seat and twisting my head off," the man said. "No hard feelings, I hope."

Tom didn't see the point in replying. He was about to exit the limo when Raveis spoke.

"It's important to know who you're dealing with, no? What they're capable of. And the means at their disposal. Wouldn't you agree?"

"I do," Tom said.

He turned and got out. Savelle followed him.

A black sedan was waiting for them.

A moment later, the two of them sat shoulder-to-shoulder in the vehicle's back seat.

Its driver was a woman no older than Tom.

She glanced at him in the rearview mirror.

The sedan followed the two SUVs and the limo as the caravan wound its way down to the street level.

Once clear of the structure, the three lead vehicles headed across town on Seventy-Second.

The black sedan peeled off and made several turns till it was back on the FDR, where it sped south in the left lane.

Fourteen

"Have you and Cahill been in contact since his discharge?"

"No."

"How well did you know each other?"

"Not very well. He and his Recon Marines were tight-knit, didn't really hang out with outsiders. I was just a Seabee, so I was an outsider."

"Did you two have any interactions before the night he saved your life?"

"I think we exchanged books once or twice, but that was it. I was aware of him. It was a small base, and he was kind of a star to his men."

"What do you mean?"

"He was . . . exceptional. Everyone knew it. His men looked up to him, and he took care of them."

"Do you know what he's been up to these past four years?"

"No."

Savelle swiped the tablet several times, then held it so Tom could see the screen.

Displayed on it was a newspaper article. The headline read:

EX-MARINE OPENS FREE YOUTH GYM

Below the headline was a photograph of Cahill standing amid several teens, male and female, all of whom were dressed in boxing gear.

Behind them was a fully equipped boxing gym—rows of hanging heavy bags, wall-mounted speed bags, and a regulation-size boxing ring.

"Cahill made the papers often," Savelle said. "At least he did at first. He opened a number of these gyms, each one in a city with high dropout rates and out-of-control gang violence. Open to all, boys and girls. And absolutely free. The only catch was all schoolwork had to be completed before training for the day could begin. To that end, Cahill staffed each gym with volunteer tutors. Within six months of the first one opening, the dropout rate in that district fell to nearly zero and the graduation rates rose to one hundred percent. He changed lives, Tom. He gave at-risk youth a place to go and learn discipline and respect. Detroit was the first gym, New Haven the most recent. There have been five in total."

Savelle swiped through several more articles. Tom watched them go by, saw in one article a photo of Cahill standing with a priest on his left and a man in a business suit on his right.

The headline above that photo read:

YOUTH CLUB RECEIVES CORPORATE SPONSORSHIP

"I'll send these to your Kindle," Savelle said. "Along with everything else we have on Cahill. His education, service, and medical records, as well as every after-action report he wrote. I need you to look through all the material tonight and get back to me first thing in the morning."

"What am I supposed to be looking for?"

"We consider it very likely that someone from Cahill's past has taken him in. It would be someone who isn't too far away. And who had some kind of medical training. Maybe a classmate of his who went on to become a doctor or nurse, maybe someone he worked with during his rehabilitation at Walter Reed. Or even a medic from his unit."

"Why would Cahill need someone with medical training?"

"He was wounded last night."

"How?"

"I've included the police reports." Savelle paused. "But the short answer is that he was shot. We've been through everything with a fine-tooth comb, but you knew Cahill. Maybe not as well as I had hoped, but you knew the men he served with and wrote about in his after-action reports, so maybe you'll catch something we missed. A name, a connection—something, anything that may give us an idea where he is."

"The NSA isn't law enforcement. Why is Cahill's disappearance a concern of yours?"

"There are some questions I won't be able to answer, Tom. I'm sorry."

"Then maybe you can tell me why this is a concern of Raveis's."

"Let's just say he has a personal interest in what happens to Cahill."

"I'm going to need more than that," Tom said.

Savelle looked at him, then nodded and said, "I'm not surprised you didn't know. Apparently, most people didn't."

"Know what?"

"That Cahill comes from money. Big money. Old family money. And the rich and powerful take care of their own."

"Raveis works for his family."

"Again, Tom, I can only tell you so much."

Tom took a moment to consider that, then said, "Why drag me down here if all you need is for me to read over some reports? Reports you're going to e-mail to me."

"The way you lived these past five years sent up some red flags. An intelligent man choosing to live some Jack-Kerouac-*On-the-Road*-thing could just as easily be another homeless vet struggling to cope with what he'd seen and done. And the fact that you're working a job that is, well, beneath you—that concerned us, too. We needed to meet you in person so we could determine whether or not you were up to this."

"Up to what?"

"We're all in agreement that when and if we do locate Cahill, you should be the one to approach him."

"Why?"

"People who have almost died together in combat share a bond that can never be broken. Trust me, I know."

Tom glanced down at her only ring.

He wondered if beneath her silk blouse she had scars similar to his own.

"Cahill is likely to react better to you showing up than anyone else we could send. Considering his current state of mind, anyone else would be at risk of being shot dead on sight."

"What do you mean by 'his current state of mind'?"

"Cahill wasn't alone last night. He was with a woman. Two witnesses saw the shooting from their rooms. According to them, she was shot, too."

"Shot by whom?"

"Seven men came after them initially. A hit team. The police reports identify them as Chechen. Cahill killed every one of them. Before he and the woman could get away, though, an eighth man appeared. He wounded Cahill and shot the woman in the chest."

A bright light suddenly filled the interior of the sedan.

Headlights, approaching rapidly from behind.

The driver flipped on the indicator and steered the sedan into the right lane.

A white box truck passed in the left lane, traveling at a high rate of speed. That, combined with the November wind coming off the East River, caused their vehicle to waver as the truck pulled ahead.

Swerving into the left lane, it sped onward.

"Where's he going in such a hurry?" the driver said.

Tom saw that she was wearing the same earpiece setup as Raveis's men.

He turned his attention back to Savelle. "Why would a Chechen hit team be after Cahill?"

"That's one of the things we'd like to know."

Tom thought about that for a moment, then said, "Chest wounds aren't necessarily fatal. The woman could still be alive."

Savelle shook her head. "Two spent shell casings were found at the scene. Their locations suggest they came from the firearm used to shoot both Cahill and his girlfriend. The rounds were Remington Golden Sabers. Nine millimeter, 135 grain hollow points, plus-P load, to be exact. It's difficult to imagine she could have survived the devastation caused by such a round, especially at such close range." She took a breath, then said, "I've read your service record, Tom. You've seen chest wounds. They're a fucking paradox, aren't they? There's only so much you can do when you're out in the field, and yet it can still take time for your man to die."

Tom thought of the fragility—the startling fragility—of the human body.

He'd seen flesh torn and burned, faces and torsos mutilated, limbs severed, missing hands and feet that were never again found.

Men in agony, lost to fear, the course of their lives in a single instant forever altered.

It had taken him years to even consider being with a woman again.

Years before he knew he could lie naked in the dark and touch soft flesh for pleasure without seeing in his mind the things he'd witnessed and wished he could forget.

To imagine Stella's body torn in any way was unbearable.

"Will you help us?" Savelle said. "Help us find your friend before he does something that can't be undone."

Tom almost felt compelled to point out once more that he and Cahill weren't friends.

Not back then—and not now.

Instead he said, "What is it you're afraid he'll do?"

"Take his revenge. And throw what's left of his life away. Wouldn't you?"

Tom used his silence to let Savelle know that he needed more than that. It didn't take her long to understand.

"There was an incident a few years ago," she said. "With his family. This much is public information. In fact, I've included the relevant newspaper articles and court records."

"What kind of incident?"

"You'll understand once you've read everything. You'll see why this is so urgent. Maybe you can help us, maybe you can't, but right now Raveis is determined to do whatever it takes to find Cahill. If it helps, consider this a search-and-rescue mission. And a chance for you to maybe repay your debt."

"What makes you think I feel indebted?"

"I saw it in your face the instant I said his name. And anyway, who wouldn't be?"

Tom glanced at the driver watching him in the rearview mirror, then looked back at Savelle.

"I'll need a few things from you in return first," he said.

"Okay."

"All the data that was collected from Stella's cell phone—I want it erased. Mine, too. All of it deleted, every scrap. Can you do that?"

"I'll take care of it," Savelle said.

"And Stella is to be kept out of this from now on."

"Of course."

"I have your word."

"You have my word."

Tom knew he had no choice but to trust her.

The only ring she wore helped him with that.

"How will I get in touch with you?" he said.

She showed him a small business card on which were written ten digits—an area code and phone number.

The handwriting was precise and confident.

"This is to a clean cell I'll have on me at all times. Call me and I'll meet anywhere you want."

Tom glanced at the business card. "Okay."

Savelle smiled. "That memory of yours must come in handy." She returned the card to her jacket pocket and tapped her tablet's screen several times. "I've sent the documents to you. They're encrypted. To open them, use the last four digits of the phone number I just showed you."

The sedan decelerated then.

Tom looked through the windshield and saw that they were about to exit the FDR.

Savelle was watching him. "When I reentered civilian life, I encountered a lack of loyalty from others that I found . . . unnerving. And, frankly, disorienting. I see now why Carrington speaks so highly of you. And why he has kept you in his back pocket all these years."

The vehicle made a sharp turn onto Houston Street and came to a stop at a red light.

The intersection ahead was empty—no traffic visible in any direction.

Tom was now just blocks from his pickup.

He would be home in less than three hours.

Just like he'd promised.

"There's one more thing," Savelle said. "You're off the books, of course, but I can't guarantee your involvement in this won't come to the attention of whoever sent the hit team after Cahill. Just to be safe, you might want to make sure your girlfriend is somewhere no one can find her. You might even want to take care of that now rather than later. One innocent woman is already dead. None of us wants another."

Tom stared at Savelle for a moment, then said, "Thanks."

He reached into his pocket for his smartphone as the traffic light turned green and the sedan proceeded into the empty intersection.

The phone was in his hand and he was about to make the call to Stella when the vehicle's interior once again filled with a bright light.

Overwhelmingly bright and growing ever-brighter.

Headlights, and high up. Identical to the truck's that had passed them on the FDR moments before.

But coming from the left this time.

Casting shadows that shifted and swelled inside the sedan as their source grew closer and closer.

On an intercept course and closing awfully fast.

Fifteen

The sound of a gunning engine was the last thing Tom heard for a time.

He didn't hear the crash of the high-speed impact. Metal colliding and collapsing, dense automotive plastic splitting, tempered glass shattering.

He felt the impact, though—felt the sudden change in the sedan's direction and the G forces that sudden change had instantly generated.

He felt, too, Alexa Savelle grab his left hand as her side of the sedan lifted and the sudden shift in direction quickly morphed into the early stages of a rollover.

Once the vehicle was fully committed to the roll, the violence was remarkable.

Tom was flung against the passenger door, striking the window with the side of his head.

Savelle slammed into him, her right shoulder driving into his torso.

Tom reflexively tried to grab her with his right arm, but that meant releasing his phone. The moment he did, it was lost in the turmoil.

As quickly as he had been flung to the door, Tom was suddenly upside down. He hung weightless for a microsecond before being claimed again by gravity and landing headfirst on the sedan's ceiling.

He must have blacked out briefly, because the next thing he knew the sedan was completely still.

He was breathing hard, so hard that he should have heard it, maybe even heard nothing *but* it.

All he could hear was dead silence.

The sedan's interior was still filled with wide beams of bright light that illuminated churned clouds of dust and smoke.

The windows of every door had broken, the bits of scattered glass sparkling like diamonds.

Tom was still stunned, reeling from the crash and roll, when he detected a faint ringing in his ears.

Distant at first, but it grew steadily louder and louder. He almost brought his hands to his ears in a vain attempt to stop the rising sound.

But before he could, the ringing ended and he was at last hearing clearly.

What he heard first was the rushing November wind and the hissing of steam escaping the sedan's cracked radiator.

And then he heard something else.

A vehicle coming to an abrupt stop and several of its doors opening and closing.

Several pairs of heavy feet scrambling.

Running in the sedan's direction.

Tom's initial thought was the wild hope that they were running to help.

It was when he heard men yelling in a language he could not recognize, but feared was Chechen, that he realized they weren't rushing to lend assistance.

The exact opposite, in fact.

Raising his arm to shield his eyes from the blinding bright light, Tom could see that the driver was still buckled in and suspended upside down, her arms hanging limp beside a head that was motionless.

Looking to his right, he saw that Savelle was limp and motionless as well.

Motionless except for the rising and falling of her chest as she breathed in and out.

Tom heard the men moving along both sides of the overturned sedan, a single voice shouting commands.

It would require significant concentration for him to even begin extricating himself from his twisted position on the roof. He and Savelle were entwined in such a way that he could not immediately figure out how to separate himself from her.

As he struggled to get free and right himself, he suddenly heard the sound of liquid being spilled.

Lots of it. Some of it was splashing onto the pavement outside the shattered windows, but the majority of it landed on the underside of the two tons of steel above him.

Tom scanned the boots of the men now surrounding the sedan.

A pair, at least, was outside each door.

He focused finally on the boots nearest to him and saw that the pavement around them was shimmering.

It was when he smelled the pungent odor of gasoline that he understood what was about to occur.

His heart surged, pumping adrenalized blood into his limbs.

Sixteen

Tom scrambled, ignoring the sudden pain shooting through his torso as he pulled himself free of Savelle.

Getting onto his hands and knees, he ignored, too, the carpet of broken glass cutting into him.

He reached out for Savelle's shoulder, shook her, but she did not react.

The only weapon he possessed was his Leatherman tool, but that was useless to him.

He remembered, though, the earpiece he'd seen their driver wearing.

Identical to those worn by Raveis's men.

Raveis's *armed* men.

Might she, too, be armed?

Lunging through the narrow space between the two front seats and turning onto his side, Tom reached around the driver.

Her full bodyweight pressing against the seat belt made it difficult for him to open her jacket. Finally he slipped his hand inside, hoping to find a firearm in a waistband holster on her right side.

Finding nothing here, he searched for a shoulder rig along her ribs.

Not finding that, he reached around to her left side and located at last a leather holster secured to her belt.

His heart rose, only to sink again: the holster was empty.

The weapon had to have either been flung out during the rollover, or fallen from the holster when the driver came to rest upside down.

But Tom was on his side and would have to roll onto his stomach to make a visual search of the ceiling.

The fact that the pairs of boots surrounding the sedan had started to flee one by one told him that he wouldn't have the time for that.

It wasn't long before the single pair of boots standing outside the rear passenger door—Tom's door—was all that remained.

A gasoline container landed beside those boots, and by the sound it made Tom knew it was empty.

The boots paused before taking a step backward.

This was followed by the unmistakable click of the lid of a Zippo lighter being flipped open.

And that was followed by the sharp snap of the thumbwheel rolling briskly over the flint.

Once, then again, and then a third time.

Silence came right after that, during which Tom expected the lit Zippo lighter to be tossed onto the fuel-drenched vehicle.

Out of desperation, he began to scan the ceiling directly below the upside-down driver.

And there he saw it.

Her firearm.

A SIG Sauer p232.

Not far from which lay his smartphone.

He wanted both, of course, but knew he had to go for the weapon first.

He reached for it, but it was just beyond his grasp.

Rolling onto his stomach, he elbow-crawled over broken glass, turning onto his side again and pulling himself between the two front seats.

He felt his skin slicing as he scrambled to get closer to the weapon.

He strained his arm as far as it would go, felt his rear deltoid overextend, and then he finally had the muzzle between his index and middle fingers, which was enough for him to spin the weapon around and bring the butt close enough for him to grab with four clawing fingers.

There was no time to retrieve his smartphone.

And there would be no point in him possessing the thing if he were dead.

Wiggling his way out from between the front seats, he returned to the backseat compartment while establishing a solid one-handed grip on the firearm and pulling back the hammer with his thumb.

He was doing the only thing he could—what his basest instincts and years of training were telling him to do.

What hope, though, did he really have?

If he shot out, wouldn't the men surrounding the sedan shoot back?

If they killed or even just wounded him, then Savelle and her driver would be left to burn.

But Tom had to do something, had to act.

He was extending his arm, about to open fire on the only target outside his window.

A single pair of boots.

Before he could extend his arm fully, though, he heard a sudden burst of small-arms fire.

Not close, but not far away, either.

Several more bursts followed.

Turning his head toward the noise, Tom looked through the driver's-side window and saw a black SUV a half block away.

Its two front doors wide open.

Tom saw, too, two men approaching with weapons raised.

One of them took quick aim with his pistol and fired three rapid shots.

The sound of a sharp grunt coming from behind Tom caused him to look back at where the man with the lit Zippo had been standing.

Tom did so just in time to see the man drop into view.

Shot in the head, he landed hard on his side.

And then Tom saw the still-burning lighter tight within the man's grip.

His lifeless body sagged as his lungs emptied for the last time.

All Tom could do was watch as the man's hand fell to the pavement.

The shimmering gasoline that coated the ground around him ignited with a blinding flash of orange light.

The dead body was engulfed in flames that quickly burned blue.

And instantly spread.

The area surrounding the vehicle was consumed, as was the vehicle's undercarriage.

And, Tom knew, its exposed gas tank.

The heat hit him like the blast from a furnace, and the oxygen inside the sedan was instantly sucked out.

Seventeen

He had seconds, if that.

Tom discarded the pistol and withdrew his Leatherman tool, swinging its four-inch serrated blade open with his thumb.

Reaching between the front seats, he grabbed the seat belt holding the driver and sawed through the dense fabric.

Two strokes were all that were needed.

The driver fell free and, still unconscious, slumped onto the glass-covered ceiling.

Tom heard a voice outside the sedan, yelling, but in English this time.

He yelled back, "Driver's door! Driver's door!"

But doing this voided Tom's lungs, and inhaling only filled them with the gathering smoke.

Holding the steering wheel with his right hand for leverage and bracing his back against the side of the passenger seat, Tom pushed the driver with his left hand across the ceiling and toward the window.

As he did, he saw something being laid over the flames directly outside.

A jacket.

A black nylon jacket.

It did not smother the flames but covered them enough to provide a clear extraction path for the driver.

A pair of hands in tactical gloves appeared in the window, seizing the driver by the collar of her jacket and pulling her through and out.

By the time she was clear, the nylon jacket was in flames, but Tom didn't care about that.

He slid once more into the backseat, turned onto his right side, and shoved Savelle with both hands toward the rear window—the only exit not currently blocked by flames.

The smoke that seconds ago had been gathering was now filling the cramped space, stinging Tom's eyes and burning his throat and lungs.

The rear window of tempered safety glass was shattered but still in place, so Tom rolled onto his back and began to stomp at it with the heels of his boots.

It was then that Savelle regained consciousness.

To Tom's surprise, she quickly assessed the situation and began stomping at the rear window with him.

They were out of sync at first, but then in unison.

Their third collective stomp heaved the opaque sheet from its frame, and almost immediately the still-intact window was pulled clear.

Seconds later someone appeared there, lying on his side on the pavement so he could fit into the narrow space between the street and the overturned sedan's trunk.

Through tearing eyes, Tom recognized the face of the man who had met Carrington on the sidewalk outside the Gentleman Farmer.

Scarred face, shaved head.

Reaching inside with one outstretched arm, the scarred-face man grabbed Savelle's ankle and dragged her through the window.

Alone in the car now, Tom thought only of one thing.

The smartphone in the front compartment.

If things go wrong, I will text you from this number and this number only, he had said to Stella prior to leaving the apartment.

She had looked at him with concern and asked, *What are you afraid might happen, Tom?*

He hadn't replied, simply wrote down in his notebook the four-digit code Stella was to look for and showed it to her.

1111—easy enough for him to type quickly with one hand, should time not be on his side.

And meaningless to anyone who might intercept it.

Tom now needed her to execute the emergency protocol she had promised to follow, no matter what.

The scarred-face man appeared in the rear window again, reaching through it for Tom.

"Give me your hand!" the man yelled.

But Tom ignored him—ignored the heat and the fumes and the smoke, too—and dove once again into the front compartment, feeling around blindly, this time for his only direct connection to Stella.

He felt only broken glass.

He'd pushed his luck too far, had taken in too much smoke.

He was choking, his lungs aching for oxygen, his eyes rolling back behind their tightened lids when his fingertips brushed the phone.

He closed his fist around the device just as he felt a pair of hands clutch both of his ankles and begin to pull him backward over the broken glass.

One swift, violent motion that reminded him of the start of a carnival ride, and Tom was out.

Flat on his back on the pavement, looking up through eyes blurred from tears at the starless November night sky.

Eighteen

"We have to move!" the scarred-face man said. *"Now!"*

Tom was gagging and coughing, could barely see, but he knew the reason for the man's urgency.

The relatively thin metal shell of the sedan's fuel tank was burning, heating the gasoline within.

He rubbed his eyes, clearing his vision enough to see that the scarred-face man was standing protectively between Tom and the bodies of the Chechens, his firearm held in a two-handed grip, extended forward but muzzle tilted so it was aimed at the street.

A quick count of the fallen told Tom there were four.

The scarred-face man's partner was already on his way to the cover of the SUV with Savelle.

Tom looked and spotted the unconscious driver lying on the pavement. Rising, he staggered to her, knelt, and scooped her with his arms, then rose again and headed toward the SUV.

Reaching it and moving behind it, Tom lowered her to a seated position, gently leaning her against the back bumper.

Touching her shoulder with his left hand to keep her upright, he saw that his palm and fingers were torn and bloodied.

He was clutching his smartphone with his right, and the palm was just as torn up.

He looked at Savelle, leaning against the back bumper as well. Her face was smeared with smoke stains.

She nodded once, and Tom nodded back.

Sirens could be heard in the distance, approaching fast from at least two directions.

The scarred-face man said, "You shouldn't be here when the cops arrive."

He was standing beside Tom, holstering his weapon.

Now that the man wasn't wearing his jacket, Tom could see that he had a thick but hard build. He was older, maybe in his mid-fifties, maybe even early sixties. He spoke with a heavy Cockney accent.

"Can you make it, Seabee? Or do you need help?"

The scarred-face man was smiling.

His teeth were so perfect, they had to be false.

Before Tom could reply, the overturned sedan's fuel tank burst under the pressure generated by the buildup of expanding gases.

The fuel that sprayed from it ignited in midair and fell back to the street like burning rain, instantly doubling the size of the inferno.

All eyes turned to the blaze—except for Savelle's.

She watched as Tom turned and started walking away.

Touching the display of his smartphone with his thumb several times as he went.

He was pocketing his phone when he turned a corner and was gone.

Tom's injuries became evident as he made his way to his pickup.

The side of his head was cut, and though it was a simple flesh wound, capillaries were bleeders, so beneath the layer of smoke covering the right side of his face was dried blood.

His left forearm was burned in several places, the skin dark pink and blistered and aching sharply.

And the mysterious pain Tom had felt when he'd first pulled himself free of Savelle revealed itself to be banged-up ribs on his right side.

Not broken, but definitely bruised.

All that plus the cuts to his palms and elbow and knees.

And the burning in his throat and lungs.

He'd suffered graver injuries, of course, and had moved on foot through more treacherous places than this, so he chose to be grateful that he wasn't worse off.

He was grateful, too, that he was alive and on his way back to Stella.

What he needed was for her to text him, as he had instructed her, and let him know that she had reached her secured location.

This was all that mattered right now.

It wasn't till he was more than halfway up the Saw Mill River Parkway that he felt the phone finally vibrate.

The message was what he had instructed her to send.

What he most wanted to read.

SAFE

He was just under two hours away, so he replied with:

2 hrs.

Now that Stella was safe and he had informed her that he was on his way, the gravity of his situation began to sink in.

The horror he had just escaped. Horror that reminded him of a chaotic firefight in a barren landscape that had always struck Tom as having been carved out by the clawed hands of Satan.

Ambushed by insurgents during a late-night sandstorm, Cahill's squad had been pinned down by heavy fire.

The arrival of Tom and his men allowed the Recon Marines, some wounded, to begin a fighting retreat to the waiting armored Humvees.

Tom and Cahill took position and began laying down suppressing fire—Cahill with a M249 SAW, Tom with his M4 carbine.

Ammo was running low as more insurgents began to come up from the south.

But as Tom and Cahill were readying to displace and catch up with their men, a grenade came out of the night and landed in the sand.

A Soviet-era F1, ten feet from Tom's position.

He could recall—would never forget—Cahill falling onto his side, facing Tom, his back to the grenade.

A human barrier between Tom and the device.

The last thing Tom remembered before the blast was being eye-to-eye with Cahill for a second, maybe two, maybe less.

A long time, whichever it was.

When Tom was a mile from his destination, he texted Stella one last time, informing her that he was a few minutes away.

Turning into the parking lot of the roadside motel, he saw her car parked outside the room farthest from the manager's office.

He also saw the vehicle parked next to hers.

An unmarked state trooper's cruiser, a solitary figure seated behind the wheel.

As Tom steered his truck into a parking spot, he got a look at the driver.

His name was Conrad, and he was one of Stella's more loyal regulars at the diner. He had known Stella all her life, had gone through the public school system with her and worked for her father during the final years of the man's career.

Conrad had also, Tom knew, expressed without reservation his feelings about Stella letting into her life a man who hadn't held a steady job for five years.

A man who looked like trouble.

Conrad and Tom stared at each other as Tom shifted into park and killed the motor.

Stella appeared in the doorway of her room, dressed as she had been when Tom left her—black sweater, jeans, boots, and pearls.

She was smiling as Tom approached, but her expression darkened when she got a good look at him.

Battered and torn and burned, walking toward her.

She hurried to him, hugged him once, and led him inside. Conrad's off-duty vehicle pulled away.

Nineteen

Tom was seated on the edge of the bed, his torso bound with surgical tape to keep his ribs from moving, the burns on his forearm
treated and covered.

His face washed clean of smoke and blood, the superficial
wound on his scalp sealed with a liquid bandage.

His beard and hair badly singed, making him look even more
ragged than usual.

Stella packed up the leather doctor's bag that had belonged to
her mother. She placed it on the bureau top, then sat beside Tom.

"So that first time I saw you with your shirt off and asked you
about your scars and you said, 'You should have seen the other
guy,' you weren't just making that macho joke guys make, were
you? You were talking about Cahill. He was the other guy."

Tom nodded. "Yeah."

"You didn't want to tell me the truth back then, I get that. My
father had wounds from Korea he never liked to talk about. I think
it was more about his scars reminding him of the men he'd seen get
killed than any pain he himself had suffered. But that is kind of a
big thing to keep from the person you love, you know."

"I know. I'm sorry. I'd just like to keep the past in the past if
I can."

"Who wouldn't? But one way or another it always seems to come back around, doesn't it?"

Tom nodded.

Stella studied him for a moment, then said, "Before you left tonight, I asked you what you were afraid might happen. You didn't answer then, but I need to know now if this is what you were thinking might go down?"

"Not this, no."

"But you knew something could happen."

"Carrington's in a dangerous business," Tom said. "One I want nothing to do with."

"Dangerous in what way?"

"A man can cross a line and not even know it."

"What does that mean?"

"You can start as a private military contractor but end up something else."

"You mean a mercenary?"

"No, worse."

"What's worse?"

"I was in Iraq for my first deployment. What a lot of people don't know is that while there were one hundred thousand service members in Iraq, there were also seventy thousand PMCs contracted by our government through private firms like Blackwater. The terms of their contracts essentially made them above the law. And whenever someone is above the law, it's usually a short road to his first atrocity."

"You weren't afraid you'd cross that line yourself, were you?"

"No. I was afraid of what I'd do if the guy standing next to me crossed that line." Tom paused. "It's important to me that I never think of myself as above the law. Or associate with men who do."

"Why?"

"My mother and sister were killed by men who thought they were above the law. And my father got killed when he decided to take the law into his own hands and hunt them down."

"Jesus."

"Yeah."

"So Cahill is doing what your father tried to do."

Tom nodded.

"And Carrington employs mercenaries. That was the job he offered you. The job you turned down."

"He could be legit. A lot of private security firms are. Maybe I didn't want to find out."

"But you still went to meet him."

"I had to."

Stella thought about that. "You said Cahill is a Recon Marine. What is that? I've never heard of them before."

"Most people haven't. The army has Delta Force; the navy has the SEALs. The marines have Force Reconnaissance."

"And you were Seabee recon, right?"

"Not the same thing. Recon Marines are tier one, the elite of the elite. They know their shit. If Cahill doesn't want to be found, I doubt anyone is going to be able to find him."

"So what are you going to do?"

"What they've asked me to do. Look through his files, see if anything stands out. But you're what matters now, Stella."

"Don't use me as an excuse."

"To stop me, someone was willing to let two women burn to death."

"Are we sure it was you they were trying to stop?"

Tom realized he hadn't considered that.

There were, after all, three people in the sedan. One was an NSA analyst associated with a man who, as far as Tom was concerned, was as shadowy as they come.

A man, for whatever reason, determined to find Cahill.

Had the men who attacked the sedan believed that Raveis was in the vehicle?

That he had slipped out of the conspicuous limo with Tom and Savelle?

But these sudden speculations only served to make the situation seem that much more dangerous.

And more likely to spin out of control.

And spread far beyond New York City.

Spread as far north as the quiet town of Canaan, then sweep through it like a violent storm.

"I appreciate your concerns," Stella said. "But I'm pretty much surrounded every day by cops and state troopers. I have my carry permit, and Ben has no problem with me keeping my .357 under the counter in my purse. You don't have to worry about me."

"Easier said."

"I already called Ben and told him I won't be in today and probably not tomorrow. You need some sleep, and I'm wide awake. So why don't I look through the documents? You said they were looking for anyone Cahill might have known who had some medical training. I can do that. And remember, my father was a state trooper. I've read my share of police reports. I can maybe help you make sense of those."

"This is my responsibility, Stella."

"You're not on your own anymore, Tom." She smiled and said, "I'm sorry, but I'm older than you, so you have to do what I tell you."

He smiled, too. "That's convenient for you."

Stella stood and walked to the desk.

On it was an oversize purse.

From it she removed Tom's Kindle.

"You said the documents were encrypted. What's the code?"

Tom hesitated, his mind cluttered with dangers he could foresee and dangers he could barely imagine.

But Stella was right. He was tired, and the sooner he gave Savelle and Raveis what they wanted, the better.

He recited the four digits.

"I'll take care of this. You're going to need your strength, so rest up. Doctor's orders."

When he didn't move, Stella returned to the bed and helped him lie down.

It took all he had to hide the pain doing so caused.

"I'll be right here," she said. "I'm not going anywhere, okay?"

Tom looked at the bedside table and saw her father's chrome-plated .357 Magnum.

Within easy reach.

Next to it were Tom's two cell phones—his emergency smartphone and the flip phone Carrington had slipped him.

He was certain his former CO had given him that phone so they could contact each other directly—without the use of codes—should the need arise.

What was likely intended as a comfort was instead the exact opposite.

The life he had built, once he was finally ready to build one, was what he wanted.

All that he wanted.

This tiny device—out-of-date, limited in terms of power and options as cell phones went these days—represented a direct line to the very life Tom had refused.

And the world he would have preferred to avoid, occupied by the kind of men he wanted never to become.

Twenty

Tom drifted in and out of a shallow sleep.

At one point he dreamed of the grenade landing in the sand.

That moment—those fast seconds—when his life was about to end and everything both sped up and froze all at once.

He hadn't dreamed of that in a long time.

Waking and lying still on the motel bed, that night was all Tom could think about for a while.

He remembered Cahill and himself, shredded and burned and bleeding, being transported by helicopter across the desert to the aid station.

He couldn't really remember the pain, but he remembered feeling an acute loneliness.

Or more accurately, homesickness.

Thanks to the morphine in his blood, it became close to all he could feel.

He'd of course heard the stories of wounded and dying men of all ages crying out for their mothers.

The same terrible stories had emerged from every war.

He had thought of his own mother, too, and maybe he would have cried out for her if she hadn't already been dead for years, along with the other members of his family.

No home, then, for which to long.

No family to think of beyond the men beside whom he had trained and served for eight years.

So Tom had ignored the ache in his heart and had given in to the sensation of all the world's edges being dulled as the opiates flooded his brain.

At some point he had overheard the two medics tending to Cahill.

Maybe he'd heard them, or maybe he had only dreamed it at some later point and now recalled it as a memory.

Either way, one medic had yelled to the other over the noise of the rotors, "Yeah, this guy's never going to be the same again."

And the other had simply nodded in agreement.

What was it Savelle had said about what she called Cahill's "current state of mind"?

Something about an incident with his family a few years back . . .

Something, for her, that called into question his emotional state.

And made a violent course of action likely, if not inevitable.

It was, Tom thought now, an odd thing to know so little about the person to whom he owed so much.

But the state of Cahill's mind aside, the man was likely involved in something serious. Something that attracted men willing to murder to achieve their goals.

And now, so was Tom.

He lay still for a while longer, letting his mind wander where it needed to go.

Memories arising and falling, thoughts emerging that caused yet more memories to arise.

It had been a long time since he'd reflected upon his own life in this scattered way.

It was first light when Tom decided that he'd had all the rest he was going to get and looked for Stella.

She was seated in the room's only chair.

Tom's notebook was on her lap.

The two pages visible to him were filled with handwritten notes.

Sitting up, Tom suppressed a loud grunt.

Stella, lost in her reading, hadn't heard him move.

He moved to the edge of the bed and said to her, "How's it going?"

She looked up at him, almost startled, and asked if he was okay.

He told her that he was and asked if she had found anything.

She nodded and said, "Actually, yeah, I have. Lots."

Twenty-One

They sat side by side at the foot of the bed, Stella with Tom's notebook on her lap.

"Cahill is an interesting guy," she said.

"How so?"

"He grew up privileged. Park Avenue, prep schools, estate out on Long Island, chauffeurs, the whole thing. He graduated from Dartmouth first in his class, so he pretty much could have had any job he wanted. Not that he needed to work, because his trust fund was released to him the day he was handed his college diploma. Ten million dollars. Can you imagine that?"

"No," Tom said.

"And that was just the trust fund set up by his late grandfather. His family has vast real estate holdings. Hotels; apartment buildings; banks in New York, Chicago, London, Paris—you name the city, his family owns something there. Their overall wealth is estimated to be over a billion." She paused. "Which kind of makes you wonder why he joined the marines. I mean, of all the things he could have done. For that matter, he could have gone in as an officer. He was offered that but refused it."

"You got all this from the documents Savelle sent?"

"I haven't even had the chance to read everything yet. They really must be desperate, because it looks like she sent you every record a person can leave behind." Stella paused. "It's actually pretty scary."

"What is?"

"The amount of information they managed to collect. A person's entire life, right there. But what I find curious is how fast they got all this. You met with them at, what, eleven? At that point, Cahill hadn't even been missing for twenty-four hours. Doesn't that seem pretty fast? I mean, say these records weren't legally obtained—say some NSA hacker stole them for Savelle. Each one came from a different source. A lot of different sources—private institutions, hospitals, courts, banks. That's a lot of information to gather in such a short period of time."

"You think they'd already been collecting Cahill's records?"

"They had to have been. And for a while."

Tom thought about that, then asked if she'd come across anything about an incident with Cahill's family.

She had.

"There were dozens of newspaper articles about it. They were dated about four years ago. Apparently, there was a very public legal battle over Cahill's trust fund that ended with Cahill being both disinherited and disowned."

"What was the fight over?"

"Whether he was fit to manage his own affairs. The battle got pretty nasty, according to the articles. Suits and countersuits were filed, the psychiatrist from one side contradicted the psychiatrist from the other. Eventually, the lawsuits were dropped and Cahill walked away with his trust fund intact. But it's clear that he was cast out of his family. Wills were changed, and according to one article, so were the locks to all the private properties the family shared. Another article reported that the family had begun to employ bodyguards after that." She paused. "It's like they were afraid of him. Of what he might do."

"In what way was he supposed to be unfit?"

"His family alleged violent outbursts, self-destructive behavior, mood swings, painkiller addiction." Stella shrugged. "Classic posttraumatic stress."

Tom said nothing.

"I noticed something else, too, in his school records."

"What?"

"Cahill was a troubled youth. Rebellious, out of control. Wild, even. He was thrown out of several prep schools before he turned fourteen. But then everything suddenly turned around for him and he became a model student."

Tom considered the transformation from troubled youth to Dartmouth graduate to marine grunt to squad leader.

He had never seen a better noncom leader than Cahill.

Nor had he seen anyone as poised under fire.

But what would it take to bring such a man full circle?

Trigger whatever it was that had caused him to be troubled in the first place?

And unleash in him an anger and madness that could not be controlled?

Tom had seen exactly that in his own father.

"Where's his family now?"

"His parents are in Europe and his sister's in Colorado. So even if Cahill weren't estranged from his family, he still couldn't go to them for immediate help. I mean, I can't imagine he'd try flying with a fresh gunshot wound."

Tom saw her point.

"Anything in the police records that might help find him?"

"They're just rudimentary, but that's to be expected at this point. There are supposedly a number of witnesses—other guests at the motel and the night manager—but their statements weren't included."

"Is that unusual?"

"No. The detectives simply wouldn't have had the time to process the statements they took. You know, actually sit down and open their notebooks and type their notes into a computer."

"Savelle seemed to know what the witnesses had said."

"Maybe she talked to one of the detectives. I know law enforcement will cooperate with government agencies. More so now than back when my father was alive."

"So what *do* the reports include?"

"Basic crime scene documentation. Locations of the deceased, direction in which their bodies lay, placement of spent shell casings, inventory of personal belongings, inventory of the weapons recovered, that kind of thing. Cahill had checked in under a fake name using a fake ID, but his prints were found in a number of locations, which I'm guessing is how they confirmed he was in fact the room's occupant."

All military personnel were fingerprinted upon induction, the prints stored in a national database that was easily accessible to a wide range of authorities.

Tom asked what weapons had been recovered.

"Various handguns, a cut-down shotgun, and an Uzi. Where they were found suggests they all belonged to the hit team."

"They came prepared, didn't they?"

Stella nodded. "There was also a bloodied pocket knife found." She checked her notes. "The manufacture is Cold Steel, the model the Recon One. Cahill's prints were also on that, but none of the deceased had knife wounds."

"Savelle said something about an eighth man being the shooter."

"The police have sent out a blood sample for DNA analysis. Maybe the guy's in the system."

"Have they been able to determine ownership of the weapons?"

"Not yet. Firearms aren't registered like vehicles are. There's no state or national database the police can type a serial number into and instantly get a name and street address. The detectives will have to contact the ATF, who contacts the firearm manufacturer, who directs them to the wholesaler, who directs them to the seller the weapon in question was shipped to, and then the seller manually looks up the buyer's 4473 form. That takes time, especially when there are multiple weapons from different manufacturers to track down. Takes even more time if the original buyer ended up selling the firearm privately or trading it in. And that's assuming any of those weapons were legally purchased, which is unlikely. Statistically speaking, properly obtained firearms are rarely used to commit crimes. And, of course, Uzis are illegal in this state, so there'd be no paper trail to follow."

"Anything about the firearms that stands out?"

"A number of the spent shell casings were .45 caliber, but no .45 was found. And there were no prints on the casings."

Tom knew that while the military-issue sidearm was the Beretta M9A1 chambered in nine-millimeter, Cahill and his fellow Recon Marines had opted for the .45-caliber Colt 1911.

It was likely that Cahill would choose the same powerful firearm in his civilian life.

What was unlikely was that he would leave it behind if he could help it.

"Anything else?"

"The attackers arrived in two vehicles, both of which had been stolen. So were the tags on them." Stella flipped through her notes again. "Oh yeah, the deceased had tattoos. A skull on their torsos, rising suns on the backs of both hands, and rings of skulls chained together around the fingers."

"Every one of them had those?"

"Yes. According to the detective's report, that identifies them as members of the Obshchina. The Chechen Mafia."

"What the hell is Cahill into . . ." Tom said softly.

He was more thinking aloud than asking.

So it surprised him when Stella said she had some ideas about that.

Twenty-Two

"Cahill has founded a bunch of charities," she said.

Tom nodded. "Boxing gyms for underprivileged youth."

"Right. The first one was in Detroit. The next was in Oakland, then Chicago, then Camden, New Jersey, and then finally the one here in New Haven. I got the idea to look this up because I know New Haven is ranked as the fifth most violent city in the country. There are a lot of lists like that online, actually, but more than a few list the same five cities in their top ten."

"Violent how?"

"Gang violence. That doesn't necessarily mean street gangs, though. It can also mean affiliates of foreign cartels. Russian, Mexican, Serbian, Chechen. That means trafficking in drugs and stolen vehicles and firearms on an international level. Worse than all that, though, it means human trafficking, too. The flesh trade. Sex slaves. Runaways, mainly, but also women brought here from overseas under false pretenses, only to be bought and sold."

"It's difficult to imagine someone like him being involved with that."

"Maybe he's not part of it. Maybe he was trying to fight it."

"How?"

Stella repeated what Savelle had told Tom last night. Wherever Cahill opened a gym, dropout rates fell and graduation rates rose.

"Gangs have territories, and they prey on those who live within them. That's how they make their money. The last thing any criminal would want is a stabilizing influence to be introduced into his feeding ground. From what I've read, Cahill was clearly a stabilizing influence wherever he went."

"How do you know this?" Tom said. "About gangs, I mean."

"My father was concerned that the gang activity in Hartford and New Haven would one day make its way here. He tended to want to teach me everything he knew. Even when I was little, he would do that. Even when my mother thought it wasn't appropriate. It was our thing, though, you know? He was never shy about his desire for me to go into law enforcement. He had his heart set on his daughter joining the FBI. But when I grew up, it wasn't what I wanted to do."

Tom began to understand a little better now why so many of her friends were state troopers.

Or rather, why so many state troopers were drawn to her.

What man didn't want a true equal?

"Were there any attacks on Cahill in any of the previous cities?"

"No, but it looks like he never stayed in any of those very long. He'd set up the gym, start it with his own money, get it staffed with local boxing instructors and tutors, and once it was self-sufficient, he'd move on. A few months, tops. He's smart, too, because he not only involved the community's religious and civil leaders, he also landed corporate sponsorships and integrated each gym with local law enforcement athletic leagues. Kids not only had somewhere to go after school, they were often working out next to cops, building relationships that would have never existed otherwise. The guy made a difference, Tom. He dramatically improved lives and communities."

"Not really the actions of someone unfit to manage his own affairs."

"I thought the same thing. And he opened his first gym just six months after the lawsuit was dropped. Would someone really snap back that quickly?"

"Doubtful."

Stella was quiet for a moment. "You know, there's a big difference between street gangs and foreign cartels. Street gangs are dependent on the youth of their neighborhoods to increase memberships. Or even just to replenish it when current members are sent to prison or killed. Dry up the flow of new members and a gang weakens and falls apart. But that's not the case when a gang isn't homegrown. They import their members from overseas. You can't dry up a supply of new members by making positive changes to the community."

"Is there a Chechen gang presence in New Haven?"

"That's the thing. I went to the National Gang Center website, and none of the linked articles said anything about foreign gangs, just the usual street gang activity."

"Yet a Chechen hit team was sent after Cahill. And Savelle and I were attacked by Chechens."

Stella nodded. "So maybe this has nothing to do with Cahill's charities."

Tom thought about that. "You said he stayed longer in New Haven than he had in any of the other cities."

"Yes. He arrived six months ago. Like I said, he left every other city after just a few months. Once one place was up and running, he'd move on to the next."

"Any idea why he stuck around?"

"I'm guessing it's the same reason you stuck around Canaan. He saw a woman he couldn't live without."

Tom smiled. "Is there anything about her in there?"

"Not much. Just her name. Erica DiSalvo."

"How did the cops identify her? I mean, her body hasn't been found, right? Were her prints in the system, too?"

"No. The only car in the motel parking lot that didn't belong to a guest or employee was registered to Robert DiSalvo. That's her husband. She went missing the same night Cahill did."

"She's married?"

"Yeah, I did a quick search on her name and her husband's name. She's a local journalist and he's a bigwig in commercial real estate and construction."

"A jealous husband?"

"They were divorcing. But maybe, yeah. I mean, men do crazy shit, right? Maybe she wanted out but he didn't. The guy could afford to hire a team, that's for sure. And being in construction means he probably knows someone who knows a person who knows a guy."

Tom took a breath, let it out.

"None of this tells us where Cahill went, though, does it?"

"No. But I started wondering about something."

"What?"

"Why boxing gyms? Why would Cahill go around setting them up? So I went back and looked at his prep school records, and sure enough, at the age of fourteen, which is apparently when things turned around for him, he joined a boxing team. He boxed all through school and at Dartmouth, too. So it makes sense that he'd pick that as the means of turning other troubled kids around, right? I mean, if that's what turned him around, he'd want to pass that experience along." She paused. "But again, those aren't really the actions of a person whose own family would be afraid of him, right?"

Tom agreed, then asked what prep school Cahill had attended.

"That's where it gets good. He went to Taft. That's right here in this state, in a town called Watertown. You said Savelle believes Cahill would have gone to someone close by. Watertown is less than an hour's drive from the motel where he was attacked. That's pretty close."

"Who there would he have gone to for help, though?"

"If his old boxing coach is the man who turned him around, then maybe they've stayed in touch over the years. A mentor is a pretty powerful figure in a person's life. So I tried to find out who the boxing coach was when Cahill was a student there. Maybe the man had some kind of medical training. Or maybe he would know someone who did. Most prep schools have on-call doctors who live on or close to the campus."

"What did you find?"

"Nothing. My resources are pretty limited, though. I went to Taft's website and did a Google search with all the keywords I could think of. I bet your NSA friend could help out with that, though."

Tom looked at Stella but said nothing.

Stella said, "What's wrong?"

"I'm impressed, don't get me wrong. But you figured all this out in a few hours and with limited resources. Savelle had to have had these records for a while, right? So how did she or some NSA analyst not find this already?"

Stella shrugged. "Possessing records and combing through them are two different things. I mean, we hear that on the news all the time, don't we? Some bomber on a watch list slips through the cracks because no one was actually watching him. Maybe Savelle is scrambling to cover her ass."

Tom nodded but remained silent.

Stella's eyes narrowed. "What are you thinking right now?"

"I'm thinking that everything almost adds up but doesn't. You know what I mean? It feels like I'm being asked to build something quickly with guesses or estimates instead of actual measurements. And I don't like that."

"These people went to a lot of trouble to get you all this information, only to leave you feeling like you haven't been given the whole story."

"Exactly. So either the information itself is incomplete and therefore faulty, or things are being intentionally left out."

"Neither sounds good."

"Nope."

Stella looked at Tom closely. "So what are you going to do?"

"The only one I know I can trust is Carrington. But there are some things with him that don't add up, either. Those lapses in protocol, his involvement with a man like Raveis. I'll be honest. My gut tells me that you and I should run. Just go north and keep moving till our trail disappears." He stopped short.

"But?" Stella said.

"Whatever he's into, whatever he has become, I owe Cahill my life. That's a debt I can't ignore. And what if Carrington is in trouble? We didn't really get to talk before I was sent to meet Savelle and Raveis. I can't turn my back on him, either."

"Then don't. Can you contact him? Use the review he used to contact you to send him a coded message back?"

Before Tom could answer, one of the two phones on the bedside table began to vibrate.

It was the flip phone Carrington had slipped to him outside the Gentleman Farmer.

Tom looked at Stella, then back down at the phone.

Finally taking it and flipping it open, he pressed "Talk."

There was no reason for him to bother checking the caller ID.

Carrington began reciting double-digit numbers. After completing them, he asked if Tom needed them repeated.

"No," Tom said.

Carrington ended the call.

Twenty-Three

Stella retrieved Tom's Kindle from the desk.

"I'll pull up the review."

Tom said, "No, not yet."

"What's wrong?"

"Carrington told me that we'd never use the same review twice."

"But how are you supposed to know what the new one is? And anyway, he hasn't really followed all of the protocols so far. I mean, you said that's one of the things about him that doesn't add up."

Tom thought for a moment.

"It could be an emergency," Stella said. "Should we at least go to the review you used before and give it a try? If we come up with gibberish, at least we'll know he's working from a new one."

"Hang on a sec," Tom said.

"What?"

He recalled what Carrington had said as they stood on the sidewalk outside the Gentleman Farmer.

You remember what John Locke wrote in his Second Treatise on Government?

He recalled, too, the answer he had given.

Less than a minute later, Tom had found the e-book in the Kindle store and was scrolling through the recent reviews.

He didn't have to go far before he found what he was looking for in the title of a review posted just the day before:

"The First Law of Nature Is Self-Defense."

Using the list of numbers, Tom parsed the message quickly.

"What's it say?" Stella said.

"He wants me to meet him this afternoon."

"Where?"

"That's the thing. He didn't use any of the predetermined locations."

"What did he say?"

"He highlighted three words for the location: *Washington's*, *spy*, and *rest*."

"What does that mean?"

"A man named Benjamin Tallmadge was Washington's spymaster during the Revolution. All Carrington's other locations were Revolutionary War landmarks in and around New York, so this fits."

"So you have to figure out some place in New York that has a connection to Tallmadge."

"I don't think it's in New York."

"Why?"

"Tallmadge settled here in Connecticut after the war. In Litchfield. He died there."

It took Stella only a moment.

"His grave," she said.

Tom nodded.

"Litchfield is just twenty minutes south," Stella said.

A quick Google search showed Tom not only photographs of Tallmadge's headstone but the address of the cemetery where it was located as well.

"At least I won't have to go far this time," he said.

"I'm coming with you," Stella announced.

"No, I need you to stay here. Just in case."

"In case of what?"

"In case of anything. Please, Stella. Humor me here. I need you to stay out of sight, okay? I need you to do that for me."

She was displeased but didn't press the matter.

"I'm thinking that we should move to a different motel," Tom said. "In theory, anyone monitoring Carrington's phone could determine our location now. Since we don't know what's going on, I'm taking every precaution." Tom looked at her. "I'm sorry, Stella. Just a few hours ago some madmen tried to burn me and two other people alive. I have to know that you're safe."

"I get it, Tom. I do. But you'll have to do me a favor."

"What?"

She nodded toward the .357 on the nightstand. "Take that with you."

"I can't."

"Why not?"

"First of all, I don't have a carry permit."

"Likely neither will the men who might try to kill you."

"Second, that was your father's service revolver, right?"

"Yeah."

"And I'm assuming that when he gave it to you, he transferred it to your name."

"Yes."

"So if I were caught with that, or had to use it, or lost it, you could end up in jail for having given it to me." Tom shook his head. "Anyway, I'm not about to leave you unarmed. I don't care how many of your trooper buddies are waiting outside the door."

Stella waited a moment, then said, "So what time are you supposed to meet Carrington?"

"Two."

"Good. That gives me time."

"Time for what?"

"To call Conrad," Stella said. "I want him to grab something for me."

"I'm thinking we should leave him out of this."

"I trust him, Tom. Like you trust Carrington. Anyway, you can agree it would be better for him to go back to our place and get what I need than for us to."

It still took him a moment to give in. "Yeah. But it would be better if you used the landline."

Stella nodded. "He should be on duty by now, so I'll call his cell."

Tom asked Stella to have Conrad meet them at the motel so she could relay in person what she needed and where they were going. Then Conrad could catch up with them later at a location that only the three of them would know about. They couldn't be too careful at this point.

A total of ten minutes had passed when a state trooper's four-door sedan pulled into the parking lot.

Tom dropped the key at the manager's office while Stella and Conrad spoke—Conrad still behind the wheel, Stella standing with her arms folded across her stomach by the driver's door.

Conrad looked at her in that stoic way of his, then glanced through the windshield at Tom as he was leaving the office and walking toward his pickup.

Looking back at Stella, Conrad nodded and said something Tom couldn't hear. She reached in through the open window and touched his shoulder in thanks, then stepped back as the four-door reversed, turned around, and exited the lot.

Tom asked if everything was okay.

Stella told him everything was fine.

Though he sensed something was off, he didn't press the matter.

"Before we leave, we should turn off all of our electronics."

Stella nodded. "Okay."

Minutes later, Tom was leading the way in his pickup, Stella following in her vehicle.

He watched the rearview mirror as much as he watched the road ahead.

Five miles south, there was another roadside motel.

Tom got a room, paying for it with cash.

Then he unlocked his pickup's bed-mounted toolbox, removed a duffel bag, and led Stella toward their room.

"What's in the bag?" she asked.

Twenty-Four

They had checked in at eight o'clock, and less than an hour later Tom was ready to go.

His dark hair and full beard, both singed badly in the fire, had been buzzed down to the length of a few days' stubble by Stella.

She had used the electric clippers that Tom carried in the duffel, along with, among other things, a change of clothes, which he was now wearing.

Crisp jeans, dark sweater, nicer work boots, and a fleece-lined windbreaker with a fold-down collar.

He looked like a workman cleaned up for a date.

Or if not a workman, then maybe—thanks to the buzz cut—an off-duty state trooper.

Either way, he didn't look like the man who had drifted into Canaan six months ago.

More important, he didn't look like the man who had met with Raveis and Savelle less than twelve hours ago.

Not exactly, anyway, and any change in his appearance could only benefit him going forward.

After he'd been cleaned up, Tom and Stella had lain facing each other on the strange bed, Tom in his new clothes, Stella stroking his face carefully, to avoid his wounds.

Neither had said a word.

Closing her eyes, Stella had pulled Tom's face to hers and kissed him.

She continued kissing him even when they heard a car door open and close and heavy footsteps begin to approach.

Stella didn't stop till Conrad's knocking brought the private moment to an end.

The trooper was holding a small wooden box.

He entered and handed it to Stella.

Remaining by the door, he looked at Tom and said without smiling, "Nice haircut."

"I asked Conrad to get this for me," she said. "I had forgotten all about it till a little while ago. It was in a foot locker that belonged to my father. Some of his things are stored in my basement."

She handed Tom the box, and he knew by its weight what it contained.

Tom opened it and peeled away the oilcloth in which it was wrapped. He looked at the government-issue .45-caliber Colt 1911.

"My father brought it home from Korea," Stella said. "It was the sidearm he carried through the Chosin Reservoir. It's not registered in my name, or anyone's name, for that matter, so there's no way it could be traced back to me."

Conrad removed an envelope from his shirt pocket and handed it to Stella. She passed it to Tom.

Inside the envelope was a slip of white paper—an official-looking form, complete with the seal of the State of Connecticut, signed and dated by a state trooper named Edward Sirkin.

Printed across the top in bold letters:

TEMPORARY PERMIT TO CARRY PISTOLS AND REVOLVERS

"Apparently, when you and I first started dating, Conrad and his buddies ran a background check on you to make sure I wasn't getting involved with someone who was trouble. A background check is required for a carry permit, so that was already out of the way. And because you were in the navy, your fingerprints are in the system. And your expertise with firearms means they waived the requirement of an NRA safety course certificate. So the permit is actually legit . . . just processed a lot faster than normal."

Tom wasn't sure what to say.

"You'll need to come to the barracks at some point to get your photo taken and trade that in for a permanent permit," Conrad said. "But you're good with that for now, statewide. It won't do you any good in New York, of course. Or Massachusetts or New Jersey."

Conrad handed Stella a small paper bag next, which she also passed to Tom.

Inside were three magazines—the seven-round mag the weapon had been issued with, and two eight-round Chip McCormick Power Mags.

"The mags are loaded with the best personal defense round out there," Conrad said. "UltraDefense by a company called Liberty Ammunition. Plus-p load, made of nickel-plated copper, not lead, so the round is less than half the weight, which means it leaves the muzzle at nineteen hundred feet per second instead of the usual eight hundred feet per second. As you know, that's fast for a forty-five. And it fragments upon impact, doesn't mushroom like your standard hollow point, so you've got five razor-sharp pieces scattering in a star pattern through your target at over twice the speed of sound. The shock wave created by the foot-pound energy alone is enough to damage internal organs. Hit a man with this and he's going down." Conrad paused, then said, "You know what constitutes self-defense in this state, right?"

Tom did. And he had no intention of spending even a night in jail, never mind serving a prison term.

Yet he also had no intention of letting himself get killed.

So, then, a fine line to walk from here on out if I'm going to make it back to Stella.

Conrad had one more item for Tom.

A pair of tactical gloves.

They were made of vented ballistic nylon, with thickly padded palms and knuckles reinforced with a dense, hard polymer.

The gloves alone, Tom thought, were effective weapons.

"There are no prints or DNA on the Colt," Conrad said. "And none on any of the mags or the rounds in them. You might want to keep it that way, in case you need to ditch the weapon."

Tom understood the significance of a state trooper, sworn to uphold the law, offering such advice.

Tom also understood that this—that everything Conrad had done and said—was a favor to Stella.

"I field stripped and oiled it," Conrad said. "It's in great shape for not having been fired in sixty years."

Folding the oilcloth back over the Colt, Tom closed the box and set it and the paper bag on the bed.

"Thanks," he said to Conrad.

The trooper nodded, lingering for a moment, then left.

Stella watched him get into his four-door and drive away.

"He's off duty at six," she said. "He'll be back then. If you're not, that is."

"Doesn't his wife or girlfriend mind?"

"He's single."

"I'm grateful that he's so . . . devoted to you, but I'm curious why."

"My father hired him a few years before his retirement, kind of took him under his wing. My mother, too. Maybe they saw him as the son they never had. A lot of the time, when I'd go over to have dinner with them, he'd be there. I think there was the hope, despite the age difference, that I'd date him. I love him like a brother, but I've never been attracted to him."

"It's pretty obvious that he's in love with you."

Tom remembered the day he had stopped at the diner for lunch and first saw Stella.

And the men—the steady stream of men—who filled the tiny restaurant just to interact with her.

Every man in town, it had seemed to Tom.

Or at the very least, every law enforcement officer.

And now here they were, relying on those men for their lives.

He was about to apologize to Stella for getting her involved in this, but before he could speak, she said, "You're coming back to me, Tom. Okay? Do whatever it takes to make sure of that."

Tom told her that he would.

He had a little over an hour before he had to leave to meet Carrington.

He and Stella spent that time lying on their sides on the bed.

Facing each other in a long embrace that reminded Tom of everything he had to lose.

Tom traveled south on Route 63, coming out of the high hills and passing through stone-bordered farmland that had changed little since first being settled nearly four hundred years ago.

Above him clouds the color of battleships crowded the November skies.

He was a mile north of Litchfield when he pulled to the side of a two-lane country road and shifted into park.

With his tactical gloves on, he removed the eight-round magazine he had loaded into the Colt before leaving the motel, then lowered the safety lever and turned the weapon sideways.

Holding the slide with an overhand grip, he racked it, ejecting the chambered round into his left palm.

The weapon was now unloaded, its slide locked back and the breech open.

He placed the Colt inside the console between his two front seats and locked the lid.

The three magazines went into his glove compartment, which he also locked.

The loose round went into his shirt pocket.

Removing the gloves, Tom placed them into the pockets of his jacket.

Despite having a carry permit, Tom saw no reason to be armed at this point.

It was Carrington he was meeting, after all.

Continuing on, Tom entered the Village of Litchfield a minute later.

A quaint old town, its hilltop Main Street lined with Colonial-era homes.

A long, sloping village green displayed monuments to every war since the Revolution.

Along the green's south side were brick storefronts that housed fashionable clothing boutiques, antiques shops, and pubs.

The historic cemetery was on East Street, just past the village.

Two black SUVs were parked inside its entrance.

The scarred-face man—the man who had met Carrington outside the Gentleman Farmer the night before, then less than an hour later had helped save Tom's life as well as the lives of Savelle and her driver—was standing next to the lead vehicle.

Tom parked not far from the SUVs and walked over to the man, who gestured for him to raise his arms.

Tom did, and the man patted down his torso.

Tom observed the man's face as he checked Tom thoroughly, more likely searching for listening devices than weapons. Neither said a word.

But Tom couldn't ignore the fact he was face-to-face with someone to whom he owed his life.

Someone that Carrington had put on his tail last night as a precaution.

Pausing on the pockets of Tom's jacket, the man removed one of the tactical gloves, looked at it briefly, then returned it to its pocket and completed his search.

"He's waiting for you over there," he said, pointing to the northeast.

Tom passed headstones that had been worn by centuries of exposure, some to the point where the engravings were unreadable, until Carrington came into view.

Standing by a gravesite, his head bent.

A few rows away stood the scarred-face man's partner, watching Tom as he approached.

When he was finally beside Carrington, Tom saw that it wasn't a gravestone Carrington was looking at but an aboveground granite crypt.

The engraving on it was worn, too, but still clear:

Hon. Benjamin Tallmadge
Born Feb. 25 1754
Died March 7 1835

Carrington glanced at Tom, smiled, and said, "That's the Tom I remember."

Tom didn't understand at first, then realized Carrington was referring to his buzzed-down hair and beard.

Looking back at the crypt, Carrington said, "I'm glad you're here. There are things I need to tell to you now. And a few small confessions I need to make. But first things first. Do you have the cell phone I gave you?"

Twenty-Five

Tom removed the flip phone from his pocket and told Carrington that it was powered down.

Carrington said, "Good." He took the phone from Tom and proceeded to remove its battery.

"I hope you'll forgive the violation of your privacy, but I needed to hear what Raveis and Savelle said to you. This phone is equipped with a hot mic, which means it's also a live transmitter that remains active even if the device is shut down. The only way to disable it is to remove the battery."

He slipped the now-inert phone into one pocket of his jacket and the battery into another.

"I tried to let you know that I'd be listening with that little gesture of mine," Carrington said, "but that was as specific as I could get with Raveis's men observing us." He paused, then said, "And five years ago, we thought there was no privacy left. You should see the ways they have these days to eavesdrop and track."

"Why did you need to hear my conversation with Raveis and Savelle?"

"We'll get to that. Another thing I should confess is that I recorded your conversation with them as well. In case they tried later on to deny ever having talked to you."

Tom was about to ask why Raveis and Savelle would want to do that, but then he remembered that the flip phone had sat on the nightstand from the moment he arrived at the motel to the moment he had picked it up and left.

"You heard Stella and me talking," he said.

Carrington nodded. "I'm sorry about that, too. Truly, Tom. It was an invasion of your privacy, yes, but I needed to know what was in the documents Savelle e-mailed you."

Tom had never considered Carrington to be an ends-justify-the-means kind of man.

In the nearly eight years he had spent under Carrington's command, he had never once seen his commander act in that manner.

It had always been the exact opposite, in fact.

Tom couldn't ignore this, but he chose not to dwell on it now. There were matters more urgent, more pressing questions he needed answered.

"Why did you need to know what was in the documents Savelle e-mailed me?"

"We'll get to that, too." He looked at Tom closely, glancing at the cut on his scalp, then down at his hands. "You don't seem too worse for the wear. But you always were as tough as nails."

"That wouldn't have mattered if your men hadn't showed up." Tom paused. "How are Savelle and the driver? I never got her name."

"Her name is Durand. She sustained a concussion but should be out of the hospital by now. Savelle is resting at home."

"Where does she live?"

"Manhattan. Why?"

Tom shrugged, then said, "Your men were carrying firearms in New York City. They shot and killed four men. How are they not on Rikers Island right now?"

"They're fully licensed and bonded bodyguards with permits to carry within the five boroughs. And even in a tyrannical city like

New York, defending oneself and others from imminent harm is still legal."

Tom asked what the names of his men were.

"The one with the shaved head and scars is Hammerton. He's former SAS. He has worked for me from the start. This one over here is Simpson. He was Secret Service, back before it was moved from Treasury to Homeland Security and fell to shit."

Tom studied Simpson.

Tall, lanky, dressed in jeans and a leather coat that reminded Tom of what submariners had worn during the Second World War.

Black leather lace-up boots with thick soles, mirrored aviator sunglasses.

Midthirties, tops, which made Tom wonder why he was no longer working for the government.

Tom looked back at Carrington.

"They were using that phone to track Savelle and me."

"Yes."

"You told me that you trusted her. And Raveis. So why have your men follow us?"

"What was it you said to your girlfriend, Tom? That I was in a dangerous business. The more accurate statement would be that I'm in business with dangerous people. You trust blindly, and you won't last very long. I learned quickly to take any and all precautions."

Before Tom could ask if breaching protocol in their initial contact was his way of taking precautions, Carrington looked down at Tallmadge's crypt and said, "This man has been a hero of mine since I was a kid. My father would tell me bedtime stories about him. On my birthdays he gave me books about the Culper Spy Ring and Washington. That began my lifelong fascination with the Revolution. And with codes.

"It's amazing," Carrington continued, "how close Washington came to losing to the British. I mean, the man lost more battles than he won. Defeat after defeat, for years. What turned things around was that he embraced espionage. And Tallmadge here was his spymaster. Very few people have ever heard of this man, and yet I believe we never would have won our freedom without him and the men and women under him."

Tom looked at his former skipper closely and saw that the man looked tired.

"I was hoping to keep you from getting involved in this, Tom. That's why I broke so many protocols—so you wouldn't show. I know you passed on this kind of work for a reason. But I should have known you would have answered even the sketchiest of distress calls from me."

"Why did you contact me at all, then?"

"It wasn't my idea."

It took Tom a moment to understand what that meant.

His conclusion wasn't a pleasing one.

"Savelle came to you and asked for me," he said.

Carrington nodded. "You specifically, yes. On Raveis's behalf. She wanted me to contact you and set up a meeting."

"How did they even know about me?"

"She obviously knows the details of Cahill's life. And yours. I wondered about that, too, and the only answer I can come up with is that Savelle wasn't lying when she said you should be the one to bring Cahill in. Because of what you and he went through."

The math was simple enough: How many others owed Cahill an equivalent debt?

And Tom had a history of leading rescue missions.

"Anyway, like I said, I tried to keep you out of this. Something in my gut told me there was more going on."

"Like what?"

Carrington shrugged. "With a man like Raveis, it could be anything."

"Who is he, anyway? What does he do?"

"Like me, he recruits and provides security personnel to corporations. Bodyguards here in the states and PMCs for our government overseas. But I'm small time compared to him. Hell, I'd kill to have a tenth of his business. In reality, though, Raveis is a power broker. He has connections in every government agency: CIA, DOD, FBI, DHS, ATF. The alphabet soup of law enforcement and intelligence organizations. You name it and he has someone on the inside. When politicians or CEOs or the ultrawealthy need something done, something sensitive or even illegal, he's the person they call. Or rather, they call their lawyer, who contacts someone who meets with him."

Tom remembered what Savelle had said about Raveis's interest in Cahill being personal.

"Raveis is working for Cahill's family," Tom said.

Carrington shook his head. "No. They turned their backs on him a long time ago. Whatever his reasons may be, Raveis is serious about finding Cahill. I'd bet good money you aren't the only person he has searching for him, though I'm thinking right now that you may have the best chance of finding him."

"What do you mean?"

"Your Stella may be on to something, Tom." Carrington smiled. "She's a smart one. Where'd you find her?"

Tom ignored the question. "What do you mean, she may be on to something? The boxing coach?"

"Yes. And she's right about something else, too. There's collecting data and there's processing it. Savelle is Raveis's informant in the NSA. I can tell you that much for certain. But this is in no way a sanctioned NSA operation. You need to understand that, Tom. This is all Raveis. And since Savelle's affiliation with him is off the books, she can only do so much for him before putting herself at risk of being exposed. She can steal files, sure—that's easy—but she can't exactly assign a dozen analysts to process and interpret them for her."

"You said Raveis has other people searching. Have any of them found what Stella found?"

"I have no way of knowing," Carrington said. "But the bigger an operation, the more opportunity for leaks. And outright betrayal. Which might explain how a Chechen hit team knew where you and Savelle were last night. What it doesn't explain is why they tried to kill you. And in the most brutal way possible. I mean, if they wanted you dead, why not just shoot you both when you were trapped and get out of there? Why risk setting a car on fire, then sticking around to make sure its occupants don't escape? Why was it so important that you both burn alive?"

"A message," Tom said.

"But a message for who? Cahill? Raveis? Or whoever—or whatever—connects them?"

"What do you mean by 'whatever'?"

"Corporation. Institution. Government. With Raveis, it could be anything—or anyone." Carrington paused. "Everyone works for someone. Even a man like Raveis."

Tom took a moment to consider the possibility of crossing paths with men even more powerful than Raveis.

It was a less-than-comforting thought.

"I'm thinking you should call Stella and tell her to focus on the boxing coach," Carrington said. "Keep looking, keep digging. I'll be honest with you, Tom. Her finding this lead the way she did could be just what it looks like. The right piece of information in front of the right person. I mean, that's how they found bin Laden, right? A handful of people saw what the agencies were missing. But we're both smart enough to know that while it could be that, it could also be something else. Someone could have wanted you to find that information. You and you alone."

"Why?"

"That's what we need to know. Think about it. Savelle asked me to contact you on Raveis's behalf. For a noble reason, too. So you could help her save the man who had saved your life. Raveis is someone you don't say no to, not if you don't want to be crushed, but there was no way I was going to just give you to them. So I told her how to contact you, skipping a few important protocols, thinking that would keep you away. I didn't even correct her when she mispronounced your name, thinking that alone might keep you from answering. My point is, I was the friendly face that brought you out into the open. You could easily be the friendly face that brings Cahill out in the open. For whatever reason."

Tom paused a moment before saying, "So what now?"

Twenty-Six

Carrington removed a folded piece of paper from the pocket of his jacket and handed it to Tom.

"What's next is up to you. I was contacted by Savelle this morning, told to give you this address and send you there."

Tom didn't unfold the paper.

"Why didn't she contact me with this herself?" Tom said. "And why get you directly involved like this?"

"Those were my first thoughts, too. Raveis employs a chain of command. Actually, it's more like a chain of evidence, to keep him removed from any and all activities."

"So this is from Raveis."

"Via Savelle, yes." Carrington paused. "Raveis needs his buffer and Savelle understands better than anyone that no form of electronic communication is completely safe, so a good old-fashioned courier was their only option. Sending me keeps it in the family, if you will. And saves her from having to risk meeting with you in public again."

Tom unfolded the paper and read the address.

"What is this place?"

"After his legal troubles with his family ended, Cahill apparently disappeared for six months. I mean, he completely fell off the radar. One morning he left New York City by bus and didn't make another blip till he showed up in Detroit six months later. You've been living a quiet life since your discharge, Tom, but you still left a trail. Your cell phone use, as limited as it was, and the books you downloaded to your Kindle—those two things alone can tell anyone with resources where you were at any given time. And a pattern of movement can easily be drawn from that information. Add to that the fact that you withdrew money from ATMs and drove your pickup through tollbooths—in full view of security cameras in both instances. So you know that disappearing completely is no easy thing. Cahill didn't just wander off into the wilderness for six months, Tom. He went deep and stayed deep."

Tom thought of his own long recovery and gradual reentry into the world.

Rebuilding himself piece by piece, hour by hour, day by day—not just the tissue that had been torn and sewn back together, but his mind and soul.

His spirit, his very being.

And the injuries he had sustained were nothing compared to Cahill's.

Tom looked once more at the paper.

"So what does Cahill's disappearance have to do with this address?"

"He left a trail in every city he has lived in since Detroit, including New Haven. But about a month ago, that trail abruptly ended. He moved out of the apartment he'd been renting—in one of the poorest parts of the city, by the way. He abandoned the vehicle he'd been leasing in a parking garage, his spot paid up for a full year. The witnesses at the motel said he drove off in a Jeep Wrangler, but no such vehicle is registered to him and no Jeep was stolen from any of the motel's guests or employees. It's likely he paid for it with cash and used a false ID to register it. Something is up, Tom. Something happened that made him suddenly go dark. Or maybe something is about to happen. Then two nights ago someone somehow tracked him to that motel. You know the rest."

"When did you learn all this?"

"A few hours ago."

"Savelle told you."

"Yes." He paused. "She seems a little more forthcoming suddenly."

"Meaning?"

"It's just a hunch, but if Raveis is the reason she was almost killed last night, then maybe she's having second thoughts about whatever it is he's involved in. And has her involved in." He paused again. "If you ask me, she sounded scared. Very scared."

"So this is the address of the apartment Cahill moved out of?" Tom said.

"No. One of Raveis's teams went through that, found nothing. It was like Cahill had scoured the place before he left. As for where he went from there, where he's been living for the past month, no one seems to know. He did, however, establish a safe house. A secret place he could go to if he needed, where he could keep emergency supplies, lay low for a time in, or bug out from. This is the address of that place."

"Savelle told you this?"

"Yes."

"If it's a secret, how does she know about it?"

"I didn't ask. And she didn't offer."

Tom took a minute. "Why would Cahill need a safe house?" he said finally.

"That's the million-dollar question, isn't it, Tom? I mean, who does that, right? And where did he learn the skills needed to go dark? Completely dark. That's not something Recon Marines specialize in. We're talking tradecraft. And where did he go that first time he went dark? Where was he for those six months?"

"You think Cahill is some kind of operative."

"Historically speaking, a charity makes the perfect cover for any number of clandestine activities. And Cahill is a recruiter's dream. Ivy League education, former Recon Marine, independently wealthy. But whose operative? That's what I'd like to know. Government? If so, ours or someone else's? And of course, as we both know, corporations have their own security forces. Their own private armies. What a lot of people don't know is that they have their own special activities divisions, too. Their own mini-intelligence agencies, their own black ops squads. That could explain why Raveis is so interested in finding Cahill."

"He works for Raveis."

"Maybe. Or maybe he works for one of Raveis's rivals. It's possible he knows something about Raveis that Raveis doesn't want known."

"In which case I'm the friendly face that draws him into the open."

Carrington nodded. "And leads his enemy right to him."

Tom processed all of this, then looked at the address again: 190 Front Street, New Haven.

"Do you know the area?" Carrington asked.

Tom nodded. "Yeah. It's by the Quinnipiac River on the western edge of the city. The neighborhood is a mix of old industrial buildings and prewar cottages with some newer condos crammed in. I remember that it had more than its share of derelict buildings, which I'm guessing would make for a good safe house, right?"

Carrington smiled. "How did a freshman from Yale make his way to a neighborhood like that?"

"I was in love with an art major. She and some other students rented studio space in an old factory there."

"Easier times," Carrington said.

Tom nodded.

Carrington smiled, then said, "I looked up the address on Google Earth and it appears to be an old machine shop or something. A two-story brick front with a one-and-a-half-story loading dock and bay door behind it. It's right on the edge of the river. The windows are painted over and the parking area is covered with grass, so it's likely Cahill chose the place because it wasn't currently in use."

"Any kind of security system?"

"I was told there are no active utilities. No phone or electricity means no alarm."

"And Savelle wants me to head down there now," Tom said.

Carrington shook his head. "Like I said, our next move is up to you. If you go, I'm not sending you alone. Simpson and Hammerton will drive you and go in with you. They'll be with you all the way."

Tom glanced at the man standing a good fifty feet away. The leather coat, heavy-duty boots, and mirrored aviator glasses were overkill, there was no doubt about that.

In general, Tom only trusted men who didn't call attention to themselves.

But if Carrington trusted him, then so would he.

Looking back at Carrington, Tom said, "I'd need to get something from my truck first."

"The Colt Stella gave you."

Tom had almost forgotten about the invasion of his and Stella's privacy.

The information, private and otherwise, that Carrington now possessed.

And the change in Carrington's character that small betrayal denoted.

"Yeah, the Colt," Tom answered.

"Simpson has a sidearm for you. You probably know this already, but every Colt issued during Korea and Vietnam was purchased by the government prior to 1945. I'd rather if it comes down to it that your life didn't depend on a relic from seventy years ago." Carrington took a breath, let it out, then said, "This shouldn't take long. Just get in, have a look around, then get out and report back to me. Standard recon."

"What is it I'm looking for?"

"According to Savelle, you're looking for any indication that Cahill went there after he was attacked. If he did, then maybe you can find something that tells us where he went from there."

"Okay," Tom said. "But what am I really looking for?"

"There are some things no one seems to want to talk about, Tom. One is the possibility that Cahill's wound was worse than anyone thinks. The other is that there has been no sign of the woman he was with. You might walk into that place and find two corpses. Or worse, one corpse and one armed and mentally unstable special operator."

"In which case, I'd at least have a shot at bringing him out," Tom said. "In theory, anyway."

"It's a bad situation, I know. You've faced worse, though. My gut tells me that Cahill is long gone and this will turn out to be a big waste of time. But the more it looks to Raveis like we're on board— the more we do things his way—the better, don't you agree?"

Tom nodded. "I do, yeah."

Carrington paused. "It was smart of you to stay out of this business, Tom. When I first started, all I could see were the differences between me and a man like Raveis. But then you find yourself doing things you never thought you'd do. Caring less about things that used to matter because no one else seems to care. And that's the moment you start to see all those precious differences slip away."

"So get out," Tom said. "Walk away."

"It's too late for that. I made my deal with the devil. But it's not too late for you."

"What are you saying?"

"You need to help Cahill. You owe him, I get that. I'll do what I can to help you, and if in the process Raveis shows his hand in a way that helps me, then so be it."

"Helps you how?"

"The less you know the better."

Tom said nothing at first.

What was there for him to say?

Carrington was right; the less Tom knew, the better off he'd be.

"How should I contact you after I've searched the place?"

"I won't be far away. Hammerton will bring you to me after. Face-to-face communications between us from now on only, okay? But if something happens and you get separated from my men, for whatever reason, send me a text with the year Tallmadge here died and I'll reply with a safe location where we can meet."

"Okay. I probably shouldn't leave my truck here, though."

"There's a commuter lot by the entrance to the highway. You can park it there. And I'm assuming you and Stella have clean cell phones."

"Yes."

"How clean?"

"So far we've only used them to text each other a few times."

"When?"

"Last night. The phones weren't activated till a few hours before that."

"They should still be good, then. Don't use that phone to contact me, though. No matter what happens, okay? It will keep that phone clean, which will help keep Stella safe."

Tom nodded. "Thanks."

"Call her now," Carrington said. "Tell her to find out what she can about the boxing coach. I'll look into it, too. When you're done, meet you by the vehicles."

Tom nodded, but Carrington stayed where he was.

"If Cahill is black ops, Tom, then he's a dangerous man. And if Raveis has other men looking for him, then they're just as dangerous. You don't use sheep to hunt a wolf. Keep your eyes open, okay?

Trust your gut. If you see something you don't like, just get the hell out of there. Cahill may not be the man you remember. Wounds can change a person. Physical and otherwise." Carrington paused. "Don't forget that before he turned traitor, Benedict Arnold was a hero of the Revolution. He betrayed everyone he knew—everyone he had fought beside, everything he had fought for—not for money or ideals but out of pride. Injuries and insults eventually became too much for him to bear." Carrington shrugged. "Maybe Cahill resents what serving his country has cost him. Maybe he feels forgotten or neglected. It happens, right?"

Tom knew that it did.

Though his own stay in the hospital was relatively brief, he'd seen men who were broken in every way possible.

"Make your call, Tom." He looked up at the darkening sky. "I think it's going to rain any minute now, so you'd better hurry."

As Carrington began walking away, he waved for Simpson to follow him.

Tom wondered if this offer of privacy was Carrington's way of making up for having eavesdropped on Stella and him.

The bodyguard followed Carrington toward where the vehicles were parked.

Alone at the gravesite, Tom called Stella. He relayed to her what Carrington had said about the boxing coach.

"You won't believe this, but I just found him," she said.

"What do you mean?"

"I just got off the phone with Taft. I told them my son had been a student there and I was looking for his old boxing coach. They transferred me to the athletic director, and he told me everything I needed to know."

"What did you find out?"

"The boxing coach was Richard Mercer. He was *also* the school's resident physician."

"You said his name *was* Richard Mercer. Are you telling me he's dead?"

"He passed away four years ago."

"Shit."

"I know. He would have been our guy; he fit the bill perfectly. Medical training, trusted friend, located an hour from where Cahill was shot. And he had been a doctor with the marines in Vietnam, so that might explain why Cahill joined up after he graduated college. I really thought we'd found him."

Tom fell silent for a moment.

"You still there?" Stella said.

"Yeah."

"What should I do now?"

"I don't know. Did you eat?"

"Not yet."

"Order something in. I won't be long. And don't worry about me, okay?"

"Ditto. Let me know when you're on your way back, if you can."

"I will."

Another moment of silence, and then Stella said, "I love you, Tom."

"I love you, too."

They ended the call and Tom began walking toward the cemetery's entrance.

As it came into his view, he saw that one of the SUVs had already gone.

Simpson and Hammerton were standing next to the one that remained.

At the commuter lot, his tactical gloves on, Tom locked the three loaded magazines in the console between the two front seats and transferred the empty Colt to the heavy-duty toolbox secured to the bed of his pickup.

Then he locked up the truck, pocketed his keys, and met Carrington's men by the SUV.

Simpson handed Tom a Beretta 92F—the civilian version of the M9A1 he had carried when he was part of Carrington's Seabee recon team.

It was a weapon Tom had put tens of thousands of rounds through during the course of his eight years as a Seabee.

Tom half racked the slide to confirm a round was in the chamber, then removed and checked the magazine.

He noted that it was a ten-round mag, not the fifteen-round mag that was standard issue for that firearm.

"Connecticut law only allows ten-rounders now," Simpson explained.

He offered Tom a spare mag.

Tom reinserted the first mag into the grip, then took and pocketed the spare one.

Hammerton had watched Tom the entire time, as if to assess Tom's familiarity with the firearm.

By the man's reaction, it was clear that he had passed the test.

"Ready, Seabee?" the Brit said.

Tom nodded.

He had no holster, so he tucked the weapon inside the waistband of his jeans at the appendix position.

All three men climbed into the SUV.

Simpson steered onto Route 8, heading south.

Tom was in the passenger seat, Hammerton behind the driver.

His eyes never left Tom.

Twenty-Seven

Tom had not been truthful with Savelle about one thing.

He had seen Cahill following his discharge from the navy.

Or at least he had tried to. He had traveled to the VA hospital in New York where Cahill was receiving treatments for his injuries.

Tom had arrived just as Cahill was coming out of one of his many surgeries.

Unconscious in his hospital bed, connected to monitors and IV bags, his torso covered with bandages.

Tom knew a man who had a long road ahead when he saw one.

He'd waited for as long as he could, but Cahill had remained unconscious.

Tom eventually left without saying what he had gone there to say.

He went back a few days later but was told that Cahill had been transferred to a private hospital.

Tom wanted to know which hospital, but the nurse said she couldn't give out that information even if she had it.

It wasn't long after that that Tom had met with Carrington and informed him that he was no longer interested in contract work.

He'd seen enough of what conflict wrought and wanted to know a life without it.

For five years, he had.

Or close enough to it.

And for the last six months, he had known something more.

Something so simple it was elegant.

Now he had burns on his arms, deep cuts on his palms, and ribs that ached sharply whenever he breathed deeply.

And Stella was hiding in a roadside motel.

Missing out on her most profitable day at work, alone and waiting on Tom, no doubt worrying about him despite her assurances otherwise.

Maybe Carrington was right about Tom's debt.

If Cahill wasn't the same man who had saved him five years ago, then Tom was free and clear, right?

If he had crossed the line Tom had refused to cross and sold his hard-earned skills to the highest bidder, then he'd willingly gone to a place Tom could not follow.

A place from which Tom could not rescue him.

A place darker than dark.

It began to rain.

A heavy November downpour that significantly reduced visibility and drummed on the roof of the SUV so loudly that nearly all other sounds were drowned out.

None of the three men inside the vehicle spoke.

If Tom hadn't been given their credentials by Carrington, he would have known by their silence that these men were experienced—in one capacity or another.

He had observed the same pre-mission reverence in Cahill's Recon Marines.

And he had gotten lost in it a number of times himself as well.

Given himself to it, willed himself to disappear within it for as long as he could manage.

After twenty minutes on Route 8, Simpson picked up I-84 east, then I-691 after that for fifteen minutes before finally turning onto I-91 south.

Another twenty minutes and the SUV was rolling down the Front Street exit.

"ETA five minutes," Simpson said.

He switched on the CD player.

Jimi Hendrix's cover of "All Along the Watchtower" blasted through the half dozen or so top-of-the-line speakers positioned throughout the vehicle's interior.

Tom glanced back at Hammerton, who was looking out his window.

The man smiled slightly, then looked at Tom and shook his head. Something about Hammerton's amusement told Tom that these two men had not been partners for long.

As the SUV turned onto Front Street, Tom felt the first hit of adrenaline enter his bloodstream. That familiar metallic taste in his mouth.

Despite the sharp ache it would cause, he drew in a deep breath and repeated the mantra he had picked up a long time ago:

The way out is through.

The way out is through.

The way out is through . . .

PART THREE

Twenty-Eight

Front Street was just as Tom remembered it.

A riverside neighborhood that was a mixture of industrial buildings and quaint cottages and rows of modern condos, all crowded together on a narrow street.

Not the most private place for a safe house, Tom thought, but not a high-traffic area, either.

And 190 Front Street was as Carrington had described it.

Both Hammerton and Tom took a good look at it as Simpson switched off the CD player and steered the SUV slowly past.

A brick workshop, windows painted over, the front a two-story structure, the rear a slightly less than two-story loading dock area that sat flush on the river's rocky edge.

The parking lot was overgrown with now-dead grass, some of which was easily knee-high.

Simpson drove past the Grand Avenue Bridge and found a place to park a block away.

He turned off the motor and lights, then opened his jacket and removed his SIG p229 from his cross-draw holster. He half racked the slide to check that a round was chambered.

Tom knew that a p229 chambered in a .357 was the weapon of choice of the Secret Service, affirming what Carrington had told him about the man.

"You chambered a round when you holstered your weapon this morning, correct?" Hammerton said.

Simpson looked in the rearview mirror and nodded.

"So you shouldn't need to check it again, correct? Rechecking tells me you're nervous, and I don't like working with nervous."

"I know you're the badass here, Hammerton, but maybe you should just go fuck yourself."

"Guys," Tom said, "let's just do what we came here to do, all right?"

Simpson continued casting an angry look Hammerton's way via the rearview mirror.

Smiling but not looking at the mirror, Hammerton addressed his team. "Leave cell phones behind, gentlemen."

Simpson asked why, to which Hammerton replied, "Because I say so."

Tom understood the need for them to temporarily surrender their phones. Anything in their possession, should something happen, could potentially provide intelligence to the enemy. While Tom's smartphone was his only direct connection to Stella, it was also, in the wrong hands, a threat to Stella's safety.

He removed his phone from his jacket pocket and handed it back to Hammerton. Simpson removed his, too, but was clearly reluctant to hand it over.

"What, do you have dirty pictures of your wife on that?" Hammerton said. "Trust me, she sends me the same ones she sends you."

Simpson's neck flushed an angry red. He handed his phone to Hammerton, who placed all three phones into a small combination lockbox.

After closing and locking the box, he slid it under his seat.

"I'll take point," Hammerton said. "Simpson, you're middle. Seabee, you cover the rear."

Despite the heavy rain that awaited him, Tom couldn't get out of that vehicle fast enough.

As they did, Simpson took off his leather overcoat and swapped it for a heavy canvas field jacket.

The man swung it on, and Tom noted what looked to be the end of a black metal rod sticking out of the top of an inside pocket.

The rod, easily two feet long, was no doubt a breaching tool.

They backtracked on foot to the old shop, Hammerton leading them not to the front door but to the loading dock area around back.

Beside the garage-style door was an entrance.

A steel door seated in an iron frame set within a brick wall.

Simpson stepped past Hammerton, moved to the door, and removed the tool from his jacket.

Within seconds, he had prized open the steel door.

Hammerton, his SIG p226 drawn, entered the dark shop.

Simpson returned the breaching tool to his pocket, then withdrew his firearm and followed Hammerton in.

Tom made a quick survey of the street behind them before entering and closing the heavy, broken door as quietly as he could.

It was pitch-black inside till Hammerton removed a flashlight from his pocket and clicked it on.

But that did very little against the tomblike darkness.

Adding Simpson's flashlight to the mix didn't help much.

No one made a sound as both men slowly swung their lights around the room.

Tom saw in the narrow, sweeping beams glimpses of heavy machinery that were familiar to him.

The space, in fact, was crammed with everything from hydraulic presses the size of trucks to small table saws.

And there were still other machines hidden under heavy canvas covers.

Hammerton stepped forward, Simpson behind him.

Tom followed Simpson, listening as they moved around the maze of machinery for the sound of any activity coming from the entrance behind them.

"This is just a workshop," Simpson whispered.

"It's dormant," Tom said. "Has been for a while."

Both men looked back at Tom.

Hammerton said, "How can you tell?"

"The smell. These machines haven't been used for a long time. And anyway, they're too close to each other. There's not enough room to work."

Hammerton glanced at Simpson, who shrugged.

To the left was the entrance to the two-story part of the building. It looked like a living space—a small galley kitchen and, beyond that, what appeared to be a room with couches and chairs.

Tom noted, however, that the furniture seemed crammed together as well. Not so much carefully arranged as maybe hastily stored.

Hammerton led them into the kitchen area, stopped there to try the light switch mounted on the wall just inside the door.

Nothing.

He then moved through the kitchen to the living room doorway.

Everywhere he shined his flashlight, his SIG was aimed.

Something to his right caught his attention.

He moved deeper into the room, Simpson reaching the doorway seconds later.

He, too, looked to his right, paused briefly, then stepped into the room.

Tom passed through the doorway and saw what had captivated both men.

Stacks of wooden crates.

Dozens of crates, maybe close to a hundred, lining two walls of the room.

Three crates were on the floor, separate from the stacks, their lids removed and packing straw strewn nearby.

Hammerton led Simpson and Tom to the opened crates, shined his light into one.

In a nest of straw, wrapped in clear plastic, were several AA-12 automatic shotguns.

The next crate contained Barrett 82A1 .50-caliber sniper rifles.

The third, Uzi submachine guns.

Simpson picked up an Uzi and tore open its wrapper to get a better look.

"It's the new model," he said. "The Uzi-PRO, introduced about five years ago."

Tom could see that this version was a mix of metal and polymer, unlike the versions he'd seen before, which were composed almost entirely of stamped metal.

"Improved ergonomics for better accuracy, significantly increased rate of fire, and more compact," Simpson said. "And the cocking handle is now side-mounted to accommodate a Picatinny rail along the top of the receiver." He paused. "That nasty little thing is even nastier now."

Tom recalled the list of weapons that had been recovered from the motel parking lot.

He recalled, too, that the assumption had been that the Uzi recovered there belonged to Cahill's attackers, not Cahill himself.

So if this was Cahill's safe house, then why did it contain a crate of weapons identical to one of the weapons recovered at that scene?

More than that, why did this place contain a cache of military-grade weaponry at all?

"Do me a favor," Tom said to Hammerton, "shine your light on the serial number for a second."

In the light, Tom looked at the combination of two letters and four digits stamped into the rear left side of the receiver, then said, "Thanks."

Simpson seemed confused by this, but the way Hammerton was looking at Tom indicated that the Brit knew what Tom had done, and why.

"Your friend seems to have quite the arsenal," Hammerton said. "Kind of odd, don't you think? That he stores all this in a building with no active security system?"

Tom didn't respond. Odd, indeed. And on top of that, he saw nothing to indicate that a wounded man had brought a dying woman here.

Simpson returned the Uzi to its crate, then turned and made a visual sweep of the room.

He announced, "Stairs," and started crossing the room toward them.

"Hold up," Hammerton ordered.

Tom gestured for Hammerton to shine his flashlight on the stacked crates.

When Hammerton did, Tom saw a label on one crate that sent a chill down his spine.

M67 Grenades

"What the hell?" Hammerton said.

He moved his light to the next stack of crates.

M112 Demolition Block

"C-4," the Brit said. "Jesus."

Simpson was at the bottom of the stairs and shining his light upward.

Hammerton turned from the crate and said again, "Hold up."

Ignoring him, Simpson started up the stairs.

Hammerton moved quickly. Reaching the stairs and looking up, he repeated his order, but the sound of footsteps climbing meant that Simpson was continuing to ignore him.

Then Hammerton started up.

When Tom reached the bottom of the stairs, he saw in the single beam of moving light an open doorway at the top.

Tom withdrew the Beretta from his waistband, thumbed the safety up to the "Off" position, and gripped the weapon with two hands as he followed Hammerton to the top.

The open doorway led to a narrow hallway at the end of which was another open door.

Hammerton's beam reached into the room beyond, but there was no sign of Simpson within.

Nor was there any sign of his flashlight.

Just an empty room, the view into which was limited by the narrow door frame.

Hammerton waited for a moment, whispered Simpson's name several times, got only silence back.

Finally he proceeded forward, Tom close behind him.

Reaching the doorway, Hammerton moved to angle himself so he could cover more of the room with his flashlight.

As he did, there came the sound of sudden movement from within.

Nothing loud, simply a brief rustling of fabric rubbing against fabric that indicated motion of some kind.

A person swinging his arm, perhaps.

Followed almost immediately by something metallic landing on the floor.

Rolling forward, then coming to a stop.

Hammerton's reflexes were fast; he had his flashlight aimed at the item as it came to a stop right before them.

Both men saw the device clearly.

An M84 stun grenade, well within the five-foot range necessary for its blast to utterly disable a person.

But registering what it was was all they had time to do.

The flash-bang went off, blinding them with a few million candela of white light and deafening them with 180 decibels of sudden noise.

Their senses overwhelmed and their balance compromised by the wave of compressed air that tore through them, both men instantly dropped.

Tom felt hands grabbing at him, then dragging him farther into the darkened room.

The hands dropped him on the wood floor and then the Beretta was stripped from his grip.

Twenty-Nine

Tom's vision returned well before his ability to hear.

Or rather, before he could hear anything more than a ringing that sickened him.

Deeply nauseated, he was glad he hadn't eaten in a while.

Looking over, he saw Simpson on his knees with his hands joined together on the top of his head, fingers linked.

Next to Simpson lay Hammerton, also just regaining consciousness.

Beside Simpson stood a man in tactical gear—black pants, black shirt, black boots, and a Blackwater vest.

A pair of night-vision goggles hung around his neck, foam ear protectors still in his ears.

A Glock, held in a gloved hand, was pressed against Simpson's temple.

His other hand gripped Simpson's collar.

Tom scanned the room and saw two other men, both similarly dressed and equipped.

A moment passed, and then Tom realized there was a fourth man in the room.

He wore civilian clothing—dark wool pants and sweater, shoes, and a raincoat.

Expensive materials, tailored.

In his midfifties, Tom estimated. Graying hair, low hairline, thick eyebrows.

He was looking at Tom and smiling.

Tom understood two things right away.

This man was the leader.

And he had been standing there waiting for Tom to regain all his faculties.

What Tom didn't understand was the man's smile.

It was the smile of an old friend.

Fond, reassuring, almost cheerful.

Behind the leader and his flanking thugs loomed two flood lamps on aluminum tripods.

Both lamps were on, their bare bulbs aimed at Tom, their stark light forcing him to squint.

Despite his disorientation, Tom could remember Carrington telling him there were no active utilities in this building.

The leader spoke several times, doing so with the same warm smile, but Tom still could only hear ringing.

Finally, the man spoke to the two thugs standing behind him. They advanced on Tom, roughly lifting him to his knees and expertly binding his hands together behind his back with plasticuffs.

They did the same with Hammerton, then Simpson.

Tom and Carrington's two men were now in a row.

An executioner's row.

The leader spoke to Tom several more times.

Eventually, the ringing in Tom's ears diminished enough for the man's words to seep through.

So did the man's accent, which was Slavic.

Maybe Ukrainian.

Or Croatian or Czech or Serbian.

Or Chechen.

Tom knew, though, that there were more important things to focus on right now than where exactly in Europe or Asia this man had been born.

"Can you hear me now?" the Slav said. "Can you hear me now? Hello? Can you hear me now?"

Tom nodded.

"Good," the Slav said. "Welcome back to reality, though it is likely you will be wishing for unconsciousness again before we're done."

This was also said with a smile, one that was at once friendly and taunting.

Before Tom could reply, Hammerton spoke.

"Our employer knows our location."

The Slav took a step to his right and bent at the waist so he was face-to-face with Hammerton.

Tom noticed a considerable limp in the Slav's right leg.

He detected, too, a grimace on the Slav's face, which told Tom the cause of the man's limp was probably recent.

"Ah, yes, your trusted employer. Tell me, dear soldier, how do you think we knew to be here waiting for you?"

It took Hammerton a moment to respond.

"Bullshit," he said.

"Betrayal is a difficult thing to comprehend, no?" the Slav said. "And an even more difficult thing to bear, once the truth finally sinks in."

The Slav moved back to Tom. "I've been instructed to tell you before we begin that he is sorry it had to go down this way. But business is business."

Tom said nothing.

"I am right now going to give you a choice, Tomas. I can call you that, no? Tomas? Such an old-world name, no?" The Slav smiled again, then continued. "I'm told the freedom to choose is important to you, and that giving you a choice in this matter might make things go more quickly. The old way of doing things—my preferred way of doing things—takes time. Hours, sometimes days. Certain men can endure quite a bit of pain, both physical and psychological. I am told that you are likely one of these men. I am also told that we do not have a lot of time to waste. Our window is closing, so it's now or never."

He raised his left hand and snapped his fingers.

One of the two men behind him stepped forward and handed him a smartphone. Tom's Beretta was tucked into the waistband of the man's black pants. He wore a utility belt to which were attached mag holders, a knife sheath, and a carbon-fiber holster containing a black tactical flashlight.

The Slav said, "It seems your woman is very clever. Very clever indeed."

Holding the phone with one hand, he pressed the display with his thumb.

After a brief delay, an audio recording began to play, Stella's voice coming from the micro speakers.

"It's me," she said. "I was wondering if you could check something out for me."

Her voice continued.

"I need to know if a man named Dr. Richard Mercer had any children. And if he did, where they're living now." A pause. "No, I'm fine. He should be back before four, but if he isn't, I'll let you know." Another pause. "Okay, but find out what you can and call me back, please. Thanks, Joe."

The Slav thumbed the phone's display and ended the recording.

"That was made shortly after you left the motel. And this was made just fifteen minutes after that."

He pressed the display again.

A cell phone was ringing, then Stella answered.

"You found something?" She paused. "Wait, let me write this down." There was excitement in her voice. "Okay, go ahead." A pen scratching paper could be heard. "And her name?" More scratching. "Does she have any medical background or anything like that?" Another pause. "You're kidding me. And you said her husband is a vet? Oh, a *veterinarian*. Wow. Thanks for this, Joe. I owe you big-time." She listened for a moment, then said, amused, "Okay, I owe you anything except that."

The Slav ended the recording. "I'm sure you have many questions right now. Like how were you tracked to that motel? Take a moment to think about it. How long had your truck been out of your sight while you were in New York, being hand-fed all the information you would need to not only find your friend but to make you want to find him? To feel obliged to find him? About an hour, correct? Plenty of time for a tracking device to be attached to your vehicle."

It was imperative that Tom remain calm, he knew that.

"He is a traitor, you know. Your friend. Cahill. The kill order came from the highest levels of your own government. When the plan failed, a new one was developed, quickly. But Jim Carrington is known for thinking on his feet. That plan, Tomas, is you. It relied solely on you finding the traitor and killing him. The first part of your objective has now been achieved, thanks to your woman, so all that remains now is the final part."

Emotion on the battlefield—any emotion, every emotion—was a hindrance.

But inside Tom, rage was mixing with adrenaline.

A volatile mix that could lead to a mistake he could not afford to make.

"And why would I want to kill him?" he said.

It took all he had to keep his voice even.

The Slav smiled. "Ah, yes. The man who saved your life. Why would you kill him, indeed? The simple answer is because in this matter, I am afraid, you will have no choice. It must be you. Everything now depends on it being you. And so it will be you."

"I'm not killing anyone," Tom said.

His tone was not as calm as he would have liked.

"Defiance is the first reaction, yes," the Slav said. "But you will comply. And you needn't bother yourself with the why, Tomas. It's best for men like us to leave the big picture to those who are paid to think on that scale. I know that you understand what I mean by this. We are men who know our limits, what we are good at, and what we are not good at. So do yourself a favor—do your country a favor—and obtain the address from your woman, then go to that place and put two bullets into your friend's brain. That's all that is being asked of you. To kill for your country one more time. Tonight."

Tom shook his head.

"Predictable," the Slav said. "But not the end of the road. The beginning of it, in fact."

The Slav thumbed the display of his smartphone again.

But this time he brought it to his ear. "Stand by," he said, then lowered the phone and snapped his finger.

The man directly behind him stepped forward with a netbook.

"We are pressed for time," the Slav said, "so there is no point in me threatening to kill your colleagues here. No point in making you face the difficult choice of either killing the man who saved your life five years ago or watching the men who saved your life last night die right next to you. Instead, we will, as they say, cut to the chase."

He nodded to the man holding the netbook, who turned the device so Tom and the men kneeling beside him could see the screen.

On it was a live video feed.

The camera panned from left to right, showing two men in civilian clothing, ski masks, and gloves.

Both men were armed with pistols.

One held up a roll of duct tape as the camera panned past him. Tom recognized the room in which they stood as a motel room.

Identical to the room where Stella was waiting for his return.

He also recognized eavesdropping and recording equipment in the background.

As well as black parachute cord, a blindfold, and a ball gag.

"You are about to go on a mission via live video feed," the Slav said. "Rest assured, my men are professionals, so they will not harm her any more than they need to. Abduction, of course, is a rough business. Should she, say, fight back, they will do what they must to subdue her. However, they are more than capable of committing unspeakable acts. Barbaric acts. So if and when I give the order to begin hurting her . . . well, I will leave the rest to your imagination. A smart man like you will have no problem piecing such an ugly scenario together. And anyway, from what I've been told, she might not mind it. You two like it rough, no? She says things to you about all the other men in town."

Tom attempted to rise from his knees, but the man who had handed the Slav the smartphone was at Tom's side fast.

Pressing the muzzle of his Glock against the top of Tom's head, he pushed down on Tom's shoulder with his free hand.

Tom's eye went to the Beretta in the man's waistband.

Just inches from Tom's face.

"You are thinking of options right now," the Slav said. "Your brain is frantically calculating. I can see it in your eyes. Maybe if you force us to kill you, no harm will come to her. After all, what would be the point, right? Or if you somehow kill us right now, then maybe my men standing by will not act. Or if you kill us after they storm her room, this will buy you time to call the authorities and have her rescued. These are all false hopes, Tomas. If my men get no further word from me within three minutes, they proceed with their mission. And, once their mission is completed, should they report to me but hear nothing back, then starting tonight your Stella spends the rest of her life in a room with no windows, the toy of the worst men this world has to offer. Kept alive until we no longer need her. Until she is so broken that no one will pay for her."

He paused to let those words linger, then said, "There is only one way to save her."

It was a moment before Tom could speak.

"Call off your men," he said. "Leave her out of this, and I will do whatever you want."

The Slav shook his head, drew a breath, and let it out. "Appeasement. Another miscalculation. You know as well as I do that in order for you to fully commit to your mission—for you to truly want to succeed, *need* to succeed—we must have her in our possession. And at our disposal. This is the only way. Again, Tomas, whether or not any harm comes to her is your choice. I must stress that. I must make that perfectly clear. You *can* save her. You can *choose* to save her. Simply kill a traitor. You both will be free to walk away. And those who matter will know that you have served your country once again."

"Don't believe him, mate," Hammerton shouted. "She's fucked and you're dead, no matter what you do. Trust me."

The Slav said, "Ignore your colleague. He is not thinking about you, or her. He is concerned only with his own neck."

"A lot of my mates are going to be hunting your ass, motherfucker," Hammerton said. "Ex-SAS, with all the time in the world. You're the one who should be concerned. You won't be safe anywhere."

The Slav raised his hand and casually, almost dismissively, gestured toward Hammerton.

It was as if he had dispatched an attack dog.

The man with the netbook stepped forward and stomp-kicked Hammerton in the chest, sending him sailing backward into the brick wall, hard.

Tom had never seen a kick so powerful.

Hammerton sunk to the floor, rolled onto his side, and lay still, gasping.

But that was what he had wanted. From the corner of his eye, Tom saw Hammerton reach for something at the small of his back.

Something hidden in his belt.

Lying in that position, his hands cuffed behind him, meant that the Slav and his men were blind to his actions.

Tom felt his heart rise just slightly and looked quickly forward.

The Slav said, "Shall we get this over with, Tomas?"

"Don't do this," Tom said.

The Slav looked at him. "Your objection has been noted," he said.

Tom used the time left to stare at the Slav, committing everything about the man to his memory.

Every line in his face, the shape and color of his eyes, the teeth he flashed with that well-practiced smile of his.

"You will want to brace yourself," the Slav said. "Whichever way this goes, I am certain it will not be easy for you to watch."

He raised his smartphone and said, "Proceed."

Thirty

Tom stared at the netbook screen.

The video camera was a micro unit, which the cameraman attached to a pair of glasses that he put on as he followed the other two men to their motel room door.

When they opened it, the sound of the late-afternoon rain was all that could be heard through the netbook's speakers.

The men exited and quietly made their way along the front of the motel to the next room.

Stella's room.

At her door, the cameraman knelt and began to work.

A tension tool—a small piece of flattened metal with a ninety-degree bend at its end—appeared in his left hand, a stainless-steel lock pick gun in his right.

He inserted the bent end of the tension tool into to the deadbolt, then slid the pick gun's smooth metal blade alongside it and began to rapidly pull the trigger.

Each trigger pull made a sharp clicking sound, but it took only a half-dozen pulls before the bolt was unlocked and the tension tool spun freely.

The cameraman then did the same with the doorknob lock, though it took considerably more clicks before the knob turned freely.

He backed away and pocketed his tools as one of his associates stepped to the door and gripped the handle.

Turning it, he opened the door just a crack.

As he did, a loud sound came from inside the room.

The jingle of metal coins being scattered on the floor.

Tom knew then that Stella had rigged the doorknob just as he had rigged their apartment door before leaving for the city: with a container of some kind filled with loose change and balanced on the knob.

The armed men, caught off guard by the abrupt sound, shoved their way into the room, tromping on the fallen coins as they fanned out with their weapons drawn.

As the cameraman swept the room, everything looked like a blur at first.

Tom felt two conflicting desperations—to see her and not to see her.

The view on the netbook's screen slowed and came into focus.

The room appeared empty.

Behind the cameraman, someone closed the motel room door, muting the sound of the heavy rain.

It was then that another sound could be heard.

Running water, coming from behind the closed bathroom door.

The shower, judging by the volume of water flowing.

Any hope that Stella had heard the racket made by her improvised alarm was gone from Tom's mind now.

What replaced it was the knowledge that she was as vulnerable as a person could get.

Naked and wet—but more than that, deaf and blind to the approaching threat.

The cameraman settled his line of sight finally on the closed bathroom door.

He gestured to his associates and began to move forward.

One of the two men cut in front of him and stood outside the door. He waited for the other two to take their breaching positions.

The cameraman to the right and the other man directly behind.

The point man looked into the camera, then faced the door and reached for the knob.

He tested it. Found it unlocked.

He nodded toward the camera before facing the door one more time, then turned the knob completely and eased the door open slightly, allowing the first churning wisps of steam to escape.

The door was ajar by maybe an inch when the first shot was fired.

From inside the bathroom.

The door exploded at dead center, splinters flying from a hole the size of a nickel.

Another gunshot followed the first, a second hole appearing just below the first one.

A perfect keyhole pattern.

Both bullets hit the point man in the chest.

He was dead before he knew what happened.

The second man, his Glock drawn, fired wildly into the steam-filled room.

Panic shots, a left-to-right spray of bullets aimed straight ahead.

He was halfway through his clip of eighteen rounds when another shot came from the bathroom.

The camera caught the bright-orange flash of a .357 Magnum discharging a round.

This time, there was no wooden door to shoot through, nothing at all to diminish even slightly the speed or energy of the powerful round.

The second man folded and fell as if he'd been struck in the chest with a sledgehammer.

Only the cameraman remained now.

As he moved backward in quick retreat, his weapon drawn, he kept looking into the bathroom.

The amount of steam Tom saw told him that Stella had run hot water only.

So she wasn't in the shower.

She had run it to provide cover.

And as a decoy.

It wasn't until much of the steam that had collected in the tiny bathroom had been drawn out to the colder motel room that the cameraman finally glimpsed her.

The live video feed showed Stella, fully dressed and on her back on the tile floor, the soles of her feet planted firm and her knees raised and slightly spread.

Her head was up and the .357 was at a forty-five-degree angle to the floor.

Held there by two steady hands.

Right arm bent slightly with the elbow outward, left arm bent more deeply, elbow pointed down to the floor.

A perfect Weaver-style grip.

But the cameraman saw her too late.

Before he could lower his weapon and take aim, Stella fired the .357 once, then again.

The last view the camera showed was of the ceiling as its operator reeled backward. A blur of motion and background noise that ended when the video feed on the netbook's screen turned to static.

Silence fell as the Slav stared, dumbfounded, at the display.

Even his men were frozen, distracted.

The Glock at the right side of Tom's head had drifted slightly off target.

In his peripheral vision to the left, he saw that Hammerton was cutting through his plasticuffs with a blade he had retrieved from a hidden sheath located at the small of his back.

Little more than the tip of a double-edged blade connected to a metal handle designed to fit between the index and middle fingers of a clenched fist.

Thin, too—but more than enough for the task.

It only took a second, maybe two, tops—forever, it felt to Tom—but then the plastic tie was finally severed and Hammerton's hands were free.

In his right hand was the stubby but gleaming blade, held ready in a fist the size of a grapefruit.

Instantly, Hammerton scrambled to his feet.

And Tom, still bound, his heart pounding adrenaline into his bloodstream, rose up fast from his knees.

Thirty-One

Hammerton moved like an enraged bull.

He went first for the man holding the Glock to Simpson's head.

Grabbing the weapon with his left hand and controlling it expertly as he guided it off target, he slashed at the man's throat with the blade in his right.

A horizontal motion, lightning fast.

Nothing short of a killing stroke.

Riding the momentum of his swing, Hammerton spun slightly, stripping the Glock from the man's grip just as the man, raising both hands to his open throat, began to drop.

Tom knew they had entered a world—a confined world, a surreal world—in which violence of action was all that mattered.

Moments from now—seconds from now—the fastest and the strongest and the most savagely vicious would be the winners.

And the losers would be dead.

The rules were simple enough.

Once Tom was on his feet, he charged the man next to him, whose firearm had also drifted off its target.

Bending at the knees and turning to the left slightly, he drove his right shoulder squarely into the man's solar plexus.

Running as fast as he could, he drove the off-balance man into the nearby brick wall with all his force and weight, then straightened up fast, cocked his head to the right, and slammed the top of his skull into the bottom of the man's chin, snapping the man's open jaw shut.

Tom knew that, at best, he had only stunned his adversary.

He knew, too, that a stunned man could still make effective use of a pistol.

Wasting no time, Tom raised his left leg and kneed the man in the groin.

If once was good, twice was better, so Tom kneed him again, then a third time.

The man was in agony, yes, but all that was needed for him to end the relentless assault was simply to bend his wrist or reposition his arm a few degrees to aim the Glock at some part of Tom.

The man obviously knew this, too, because he began to do both.

His finger was inside the trigger guard, ready to twitch the moment the muzzle was aligned with his attacker.

Tom saw this and did the only thing he could.

He lunged at the man's arm face-first, digging his teeth into the man's forearm just above the wrist.

Dropping to his knees, Tom pulled the man's arm downward, forcing him to bend at the waist.

Screaming but undeterred, the man grabbed the Glock with his left hand, seizing it by the barrel and releasing his right hand.

Holding it like a club, he was raising it in preparation to strike Tom's head when the first shot was fired.

In the confined space of that small room, the retort was like an open-palm slap to Tom's ears.

And it took Tom a second—a desperate second—to realize that the shot had been fired by Hammerton.

Armed with the pistol he had taken from the man he had knifed.

Another shot immediately followed the first—a double tap, both shots hitting the bent-over man above Tom in the top of his head.

Tom would have expected nothing less from a former SAS.

The dead man fell, his lifeless weight crashing down on top of Tom and pinning him with his hands still bound behind his back.

Maybe four or five seconds had passed since Hammerton had first swung into action, Tom right behind him.

During that time the third armed man—the one who had been holding the netbook, the one who had stomp-kicked Hammerton with such power—had dropped the device and begun to guide the limping Slav toward the only door.

The action of a trained bodyguard.

As he did that, he reached for the pistol in his shoulder rig.

The holster was vertical, old school, meaning he had to reach across his broad chest to where the weapon had been positioned under his left armpit for maximum concealment.

Drawing fast from such a rig took two hands—the right hand reached for the weapon while the left assisted by grasping the bottom of the holster and tipping it forward slightly to move the weapon within reach.

But the bodyguard's left hand was still on the Slav's back, pushing his employer forward, which meant he could only reach the firearm's grip with the tips of his right fingers.

Drawing was still possible—it would just take a few seconds of fumbling to get a secure enough hold on the grip to extract the weapon from the molded leather.

And extraction could only be done by pulling straight up.

The bodyguard was in the process of overcoming this problem when Simpson, his hands still bound, crashed into him.

Simpson obviously intended to drive the man into the wall and pin his right arm against his chest with his own body, preventing the man from completing his draw.

A sacrifice play meant to buy Hammerton the time needed to open fire on the last of the Slav's armed men.

But Simpson's all-out tackle did little more than cause the bodyguard to adjust his actions—instead of guiding the Slav through the door, he pushed the limping man through it.

Once his employer was safely out of the kill box the small room had become, the bodyguard turned his attention to Simpson.

A man on whom he had a good forty pounds.

Simpson was still close, crowding the bodyguard, preventing him from completing his draw, but the man was clearly no stranger to close-quarter combat.

Throwing a swift, hooking elbow strike, he broke Simpson's nose.

And like Tom, the bodyguard knew to keep throwing strikes, landing each one on or as close as possible to the same target.

Violence of action and overwhelming force.

Simpson was like a boxer who had been tagged hard—his knees buckled and his eyes glassed over. But before he could drop, the bodyguard grabbed him and spun him around.

Using Simpson as a human shield, the bodyguard completed his draw.

His weapon was no cheap Glock, though.

It was a chrome-plated, .50-caliber Desert Eagle.

Huge by handgun standards—thus the need for the old-school vertical holster.

The bodyguard pressed the weapon's muzzle against Simpson's head and began backing toward the door.

Tom noticed that Simpson looked confused, as if none of what was occurring made any sense to him.

Not scared, not angry, not determined—confused.

Hammerton had already shifted his aim to the man, but Simpson's proximity to his target had prevented Hammerton from firing.

Now the two men were in a standoff.

Once he had made his way to the doorway, the bodyguard made a quick visual sweep of the room before looking back at Hammerton.

Simpson opened his mouth to speak, his eyes turned in a way that made it appear that he was about to address the man behind him.

The man with his left arm around Simpson's neck and the powerful handgun to his head.

But the bodyguard tightened his arm, choking Simpson and keeping him from speaking.

Then the bodyguard smiled.

A smile that was directed at Hammerton.

The smile of a man who enjoyed his work.

Relished in it.

Tom knew what was about to happen.

But there was nothing he could do.

Without hesitation, the Slav's bodyguard squeezed the trigger.

Thirty-Two

In the confined room, the Desert Eagle's retort was unbearable.

Despite being pinned under the dead man, Tom could still feel the concussive wave move through him.

A quick blast of pressurized air traveling at thousands of feet per second.

It hit him like a violent shove.

And once again, Tom could only hear ringing.

He could see this time, though.

But when Simpson dropped into his view, he wished he couldn't.

The top of the man's head and much of the left side of his face were missing.

Sickened, Tom closed his eyes and felt an anger he hadn't experienced in a long time.

A rage that threatened to rise and overtake him whenever he witnessed a pointless loss of life.

But he knew not to grasp on to that rage, or to let it take hold of him.

Giving into anger during battle was a sure way of getting killed.

Calmly but with purpose, Tom scrambled out from beneath the dead man.

Hammerton was beside him, the short blade in his fist ready.

He cut the plasticuffs with one hand while keeping the Glock aimed at the doorway with his other, in case the bodyguard doubled back.

Kneeling beside the man Hammerton had shot, Tom rolled him over and removed the Beretta from his waistband. He then removed the tactical flashlight, which he slipped into his back pocket as he rose to his feet.

The Beretta had been out of Tom's sight for a period of time, so he confirmed that a round was still in the chamber, then dropped, examined, and reinserted the magazine.

He had no time to go looking for the spare mag that had been taken from his pocket.

Eleven rounds—one in the chamber, ten in the mag—would have to do.

As Tom was doing this, Hammerton also recovered his SIG p226, but kept the Glock as a backup, tucking it into his waistband at the small of his back.

Hammerton headed toward the open doorway, Tom following, but the moment they reached it, just as they were about to step over Simpson's body, the end of the dark hallway lit up for a second with a burst of orange light as the Slav's bodyguard, standing at the top of the stairs, fired a single shot.

Even with the distance between them, the shockwave rustled Tom's clothing like a sudden wind.

In the same instant, the thick beam of the door frame exploded, sending splinters into Hammerton's face.

Hammerton screamed and turned away, stunned into brief motionlessness, but Tom yanked him back against the wall.

He saw right away that Hammerton's already-scarred face was bloody.

"Shit," Tom whispered.

Hammerton wiped the blood from his eyes with the back of his hand. "I'm fine. I'm fine."

Tom glanced down, spotting the outlet into which the two flood lamps were plugged.

He saw, too, the night-vision goggles hanging around the neck of the man Hammerton had shot.

Reaching down, he took hold of both electrical cords with one hand and pulled them from their sockets, casting the room into a darkness so complete that Tom couldn't even see his own hands.

Then he knelt and blindly reached around until he'd pulled the goggles over the dead man's bloodied head.

Straightening again against the wall, he listened.

Hearing and touch were the only senses relaying information to his brain right then.

The ringing in his ears was diminishing. He heard footsteps below.

By their broken rhythm, he knew that those steps belonged to the limping Slav.

What Tom could not hear was the bodyguard making his way down the stairs.

This meant that the man was holding his position at the end of the hall, covering the Slav as he made his escape.

But then the Slav's footsteps stopped.

Directly below, from what Tom could tell.

In the room with the vast cache of weapons and demolition.

But had they stopped, or merely passed out of earshot?

Before Tom could decide, Hammerton pointed his SIG around the door frame, bent his wrist so the weapon was aimed down the hallway, and fired.

He got off two rounds before the bodyguard answered back with a single shot that punched several more holes through the door frame.

Scattering yet more wood splinters like shrapnel.

Grabbing Hammerton's collar, Tom pulled him back against the wall again, more roughly this time.

Another's anger could also get a person killed.

He shifted position, pinning Hammerton to the wall. He knew he'd made his point when Hammerton stayed put.

Listening again, Tom wondered where the Slav was.

And why his bodyguard was holding a defensive position at the end of the hallway.

Long moments passed before Tom heard anything.

What came up from below was a single word from the Slav, spoken loud enough for his bodyguard to hear.

"Set."

But it hadn't come from directly below, where the Slav's steps had ended and the weapons were stored.

It had come instead from the machine shop.

The bodyguard opened fire again—two shots—and then immediately displaced from his defensive position, hurrying down the stairs.

He could be heard now moving through the room below them.

More than moving—he was running.

Tom handed Hammerton the night-vision goggles, then moved down the dark hallway in a crouch, Hammerton behind him.

At the least, the device would keep the blood out of Hammerton's eyes.

Hammerton put the goggles on.

Tom readied the tactical flashlight but kept it off as Hammerton moved past him, taking point.

Though the total darkness was disorienting, Tom focused his mind and stayed as close to Hammerton as he could as they made their way down the stairs.

Thirty-Three

On the bottom step, Hammerton paused to make a visual sweep of the room before whispering, "Clear."

He led Tom to the doorway. They paused again as Hammerton surveyed the narrow kitchen area first, then the crowded shop beyond.

Tom had lost track of the sound of the bodyguard's footsteps as they'd made their way across the room, so all he heard now was the sound of the heavy rain drumming on the flat roof above.

He whispered, "Fuse box."

A moment later Hammerton said, "I see it."

Since there was electricity in the room upstairs but none here, it was likely that someone had intentionally tripped the fuses for the ground floor.

Getting to the box and resetting the switches should render the lights operable.

But there was another reason Tom wanted to get to the fuse box besides needing to see.

Carrington had made a point of telling him this building had no active utilities, so turning on the lights would confirm whether that had been a lie.

Tom was not going to take the Slav at his word.

He wanted proof of Carrington's betrayal.

Hammerton stepped away then, and Tom tracked the man by the sounds he made as he moved through the machine shop.

Hammerton took several steps then stopped, likely to take cover behind a piece of machinery.

A few more steps, another pause, then a few more and another pause.

Finally, Tom heard the fuse box's cover swinging open and then the dull taps of breakers being flipped one after the other.

Banks of fluorescent lights suspended from the high ceiling instantly hummed and blinked on.

Tom saw that Hammerton had taken cover behind a steel support beam on which the fuse box was mounted, putting the beam between himself and the door on the other side of the shop.

He had pulled the goggles down around his neck and was carefully leaning out from behind the beam to scan what he could see of the crowded room. Blood streamed from the cuts in the man's already-scarred face.

His Beretta ready, Tom rose and bent at the waist, then moved to the nearest machine for cover.

He'd barely taken a step when another ear-splitting gunshot rang out, this time coming from the direction of the door.

The only exit currently known to them.

Tom had done his best to keep a count of how many rounds the Slav's bodyguard had fired.

A Desert Eagle chambered in .50 caliber held seven rounds in the mag.

That plus one in the chamber, for a total of eight.

The bodyguard had fired six, and though Tom hadn't always been within earshot of the man, he had been for the past few minutes—and hadn't heard a mag change.

He was confident that in this room he would have heard that, especially during those long moments when hearing was pretty much all he had.

Tom got Hammerton's attention, gestured with a bladed hand in the bodyguard's direction, then pointed at the grip of his own firearm before finally holding up his index and middle fingers.

Hammerton nodded that he understood and readied himself, removing the Glock from his waistband with his left hand, holding his SIG with his right.

One for cover fire, one for precision shooting.

He took a deep breath, then moved from his cover behind the beam toward the nearest piece of heavy machinery, firing the Glock without aiming in the direction of the bodyguard's last position.

Tom got down low and also moved closer to the door, counting on the shots fired from the Glock to mask the sounds of his motion.

Hammerton's fire didn't draw any return fire from the bodyguard, but Tom had made it to a position in the loading dock area where he could see the door.

There were three machines large enough to offer cover to the bodyguard, but they were still a good twenty-five feet from Tom.

Controlling his breathing, Tom identified where he would go to next.

A drill press ten feet from the cluster of machines where the bodyguard had to be hiding.

From there he could get on the bodyguard's flank—the man would not be able to hide from Tom without exposing himself to Hammerton, or vice versa.

It didn't take long before Hammerton was in motion again, laying down cover fire with the Glock.

Tom scrambled for the drill press.

This time Hammerton drew the bodyguard's fire—a single shot, and then another.

The eighth shot Tom had been counting on.

But what he hadn't been counting on was Hammerton getting hit.

The man grunted, and though Tom could hear him go down, he could not see him.

There wasn't time to look for him, anyway.

Tom had made it to the drill press. He saw the bodyguard crouching behind a CNC mill just feet from the exit.

Tom also saw that the slide of the Desert Eagle was locked back in the open position, confirming that his count had been accurate—the weapon was empty.

The bodyguard, still crouched, had released the empty mag and was removing one of two backups from his shoulder holster's mag carrier, located under his right arm.

The man was fast, his actions well practiced.

But before he could insert the loaded mag, Tom rose and took several steps forward, his Beretta aimed.

"Don't move," he said.

The bodyguard froze, then turned his head just enough to look at Tom.

His eyes went to the firearm in Tom's hand, and then he did something Tom had not expected and did not understand.

The bodyguard smiled.

"That's a nice Beretta you have there," he said.

His accent was distinctly Russian.

"Place your weapon on the floor," Tom said calmly.

The bodyguard continued to smile.

"Where'd you get that?" he said.

Tom repeated, "Place your weapon on the floor."

"Your new buddy gave you that, didn't he? Simpson, right? That was his name? Simpson?"

"You have one second."

The bodyguard laid the weapon and mag on the concrete, then stood.

"Hands on top of your head, fingers locked," Tom said.

"I have a better idea."

He reached for the cargo pocket of his black pants.

"Don't do it," Tom said.

"Just let me show you what I have. I think you especially will appreciate it."

The man put his hand into his pocket.

"Last warning."

The man didn't stop, giving Tom no choice.

He transferred his finger into the trigger guard and eased the trigger back.

Instead of firing a round, the Beretta simply emitted a dull, metallic click.

Misfire.

The bodyguard continued to smile, his hand reaching deeper into his cargo pocket.

Tom quickly racked the slide, ejecting the faulty round and feeding another into the chamber, then reacquired his target and squeezed the trigger again.

Another dull click.

He repeated the process—rack, reacquire, squeeze—but got the same result.

"Sounds to me like you've got a missing firing pin," the body-guard said. "Hate when that happens."

Simpson has a sidearm for you, Carrington had said. *I'd rather if it comes down to it that your life didn't depend on a relic from seventy years ago.*

Before Tom could even process the betrayal, the bodyguard removed his hand from his pocket.

He was holding an M67 grenade.

190   *Daniel Judson*

"How about a blast from your past?" the bodyguard said.

Without hesitating, he removed the pin and released the lever, then tossed the grenade toward Tom.

The last Tom saw of the bodyguard was out of the corner of his eye.

The man crouched to grab his weapon, then inserted the mag as he bolted through the exit. He pulled the door closed behind him.

There was nothing Tom could do to stop him.

Stunned into motionlessness, he watched the grenade roll across the concrete floor till it came to a stop at the foot of one of the nearby machines.

In that split second, Tom thought of all the things he had done over the past five years—all the decisions he had made, the directions he had headed into, and the directions he hadn't—only to find himself here, face-to-face once again with a live grenade.

It was unfathomable—too much even for his quick mind.

His hesitation ended abruptly as a surge of adrenaline rose through him.

Tom scrambled to put as many of those heavy machines as possible between himself and the grenade.

He passed one machine, then another, then a third, weaving around them all and finally taking cover behind a fourth.

A prewar press brake machine. Identical to the one he operated back home.

Stretched out on his stomach behind the mammoth machine, Tom covered his ears with his arms and his head with his gloved hands.

The blast came less than a second later, the wave of compressed air tearing through the room with the force of a tornado.

It ended as quickly as it hit—a microstorm that scattered countless shards of hot metal—but it took a moment before Tom was able to get up.

And even when he was finally standing, the first few steps he took walking were really just falling turned into forward motion.

Somehow he made his way to where Hammerton had collapsed behind an industrial lathe and knelt quickly by the facedown man.

An initial check showed no indication that the man had taken any shrapnel fragments.

Tom spoke Hammerton's name several times but got no response.

He checked for a pulse and detected one—a strong one.

Rolling the man onto his side, Tom expected blood and torn tissue but saw none.

Examining Hammerton's chest, Tom felt something beneath the man's shirt.

Hammerton was wearing a bullet-resistant vest.

But a .50-caliber AE was a powerful pistol round, and while the vest might stop the round from penetrating, it would not stop the blunt-force trauma of being hit with a 300-grain bullet traveling at fifteen hundred feet per second.

Tom tore Hammerton's shirt open and saw that the .50-caliber slug was in fact embedded in the vest's dense fabric. The angle of the round told him that it hadn't struck Hammerton head-on.

Still, the slug had gone as deeply as it could into the vest without penetrating, and the shock that had been transferred into Hammerton upon impact, even from a glancing hit, would be enough to cause internal injuries.

Hammerton wasn't bleeding—externally, at least—but Tom knew that the man needed medical attention, fast.

Tom said Hammerton's name several more times, wanted to avoid carrying the man if he could because he knew doing so would likely cause even more harm.

But he was still getting no response and was about to pull the man up and hoist him into a fireman's carry when he heard something.

A faint but steady beeping.

One that had just started.

Tom rose and pinpointed the sound's location—a tarp-covered machine just feet away.

Lifting the heavy canvas, Tom saw that beneath it wasn't a machine at all.

It was two twenty-gallon plastic drums strapped together.

Mounted on top of one of the drums was an electronic device encased in clear plastic. And inside the device were four blocks of C-4 and a digital clock counting backward.

The faint beeping was in sync with the seconds ticking away on a clock that had clearly been activated remotely.

2:57, 2:56, 2:55

Tom said, "Shit," and returned to Hammerton, shaking the man's shoulders and calling his name louder and louder.

Hammerton's eyes fluttered beneath his closed lids and his head gradually began to rock from side to side.

Tom had to shout the man's name to bring him all the way to full consciousness.

Hammerton drew a breath and quickly clenched his teeth at the pain simply inhaling had caused.

His eyes were wide, almost wild, blinking.

Baffled, disoriented—but Tom couldn't care about that.

"We need to move, trooper," Tom said. "Now."

As confused as he was, Hammerton must have heard the urgency in Tom's voice because he nodded, braced himself for the inevitable pain as Tom pulled him to a seated position, then got in close beside him and wound the man's left arm around his own neck.

Standing, Tom lifted Hammerton to his feet.

Hammerton gritted his teeth and grunted, but Tom ignored that, too.

He leaned Hammerton against a nearby machine and made sure the man would stay upright before retrieving the two pistols from the floor.

He put the SIG in Hammerton's hand and quick-checked the Glock.

One in the chamber, two in the mag.

Tom stuffed the Glock into his waistband as he got in beside Hammerton again and half-led, half-dragged him toward the door.

As they moved past it, Hammerton saw the truck bomb and said, "Fuck."

He started moving more quickly then, trying to keep pace with Tom.

Together, they were an unwieldy beast, but they reached the door and Tom swung it open, standing to the side of it, just in case.

He heard only the heavy rain.

That was the first glimpse of sky Tom had had since entering the warehouse at four o'clock.

The downpour combined with the low-hanging clouds turned the November twilight as dark as night.

Though they had been in there less than an hour, for Tom it felt as if days had passed since he'd left Stella.

All he wanted was to get back to her.

Seconds were ticking away, yes, but there was no reason now to be careless.

No reason to run blindly into what his gut told him could be an ambush.

Even with the moments they had to spare, they would need to put serious distance between themselves and this building.

The truck bomb combined with the stash of C-4 they had seen would be enough to make an entire city block disappear.

And cause significant damage to the blocks surrounding it.

Tom had no choice but to lean into the open doorway and make a visual check.

The only way to know if the bodyguard was waiting outside was to either spot him or to draw the man's fire yet again.

No easy thing, but those moments they'd had to spare were quickly slipping away, so Tom braced himself, exhaled, and leaned into the open doorway.

He had barely exposed himself when the first gunshot sounded.

Thirty-Four

That first shot was followed by a second, the bullet striking the heavy metal door frame and fragmenting.

Tom felt the skin on his right cheek zip open.

Stumbling backward, he kicked the door closed, turned, and quickly studied the loading dock and cluttered workshop.

There were windows on the opposing wall, six of them in a row, their many panes painted over.

But each window had a grate of iron bars over it.

Tom figured there had to be an exit in the room with the cache of weapons.

That room was located at the front of the building, along Front Street, so it would make sense as a place for a front door.

He hadn't noticed one—it had been pitch-dark the two times he had moved through that room—but if the Slav's bodyguard was intent on keeping Tom and Hammerton inside or killing them as they emerged, that door would certainly be covered as well.

There were any number of positions on Front Street that would give one man a clear view of both doors.

And anyway, the moments they'd had to spare were all used up.

Tom had to find another way out, and he had to find it now.

He scanned the workshop and saw something on the western wall—the wall that ran along the edge of the Quinnipiac River.

It was an elevated office, similar to the one from which Tom's foreman watched him and his coworkers.

The only real differences were that it was smaller and the viewing window had been boarded over with plywood.

Tom grabbed Hammerton and led him toward the office, once again passing the truck bomb as they moved.

Tom glanced at the clock and saw that they had less than a minute.

In his head, he began a countdown.

Despite Hammerton's efforts to be less than dead weight, he stumbled several times before they reached the stairs.

Each time he went down, Tom pulled him back up.

The stairs had only six steps, but they were narrow, so climbing them side by side would be no easy feat.

And Hammerton was reaching the limits of his strength, relying more and more on Tom to not only keep him up, but keep him going.

Still, they made it to the top step fast enough, and to Tom's relief the office door was unlocked.

But it was rotted and loose on its hinges, so its warped bottom edge dragged along the tile floor as Tom pushed the door open with his free hand.

To make things even more slow-going, the doorway was for some reason even narrower than the steps leading to it, so Tom and Hammerton, joined as they were at the hip, had to turn sideways just to move through it.

As Tom overcame these obstacles, he maintained the careful countdown in his head.

Thirty seconds.

Once inside the office, Tom led Hammerton to the window that overlooked the Quinnipiac River.

It was a large window of thick plate glass.

He scanned the office for something he could use to shatter the window, but the small room was utterly bare.

Fifteen seconds.

Though the building was located on the edge of the river, there were rocks visible just above the surface of the water immediately along its side.

He and Hammerton would need to clear a distance of several feet if they had any hope of reaching deep-enough water to break their fall.

Hammerton said, "Back up."

Tom understood what the man meant.

He led Hammerton to the opposing wall—fifteen feet from the window, tops.

Five paces would be all they'd have to build up enough speed.

Directly below the bottom edge of the window was a cast-iron radiator.

Just a foot or so tall, it would serve as the launching point Tom needed.

Ten seconds.

As they readied themselves, Hammerton raised his right hand, aiming his SIG at the window.

Tom did the same with the Glock.

Eight seconds.

"Let's fucking go," Hammerton said.

They ran, Hammerton wedged in beside Tom, Tom's left arm around the man, both of them firing at the window as they rushed toward it.

Each round punched holes in the plate glass, but that was all at first.

Three steps down, two more to go.

Five seconds.

It wasn't until they were taking their last step that a network of cracks crossed the entire sheet of plate glass.

But it remained intact.

Turning at the last second so his right shoulder would hit first, Tom stepped onto the radiator with his right foot and leaped, pulling Hammerton with him.

The momentum and combined weight of the two men sent them through the now-opaque glass and out into the evening air.

Two seconds passed in free fall—seconds during which Tom felt countless more cuts zipping open—and then they hit the rushing water and sank fast into an icy darkness.

Tom opened his eyes, keeping hold of Hammerton as they sank into the river's steady current.

It quickly began carrying them south toward the bridge.

Two seconds.

One.

Tom saw nothing but blackness, felt nothing but the cold water sweeping them and the urge to exhale building in his lungs.

For a long moment it seemed as if this nothingness would never end, and then it came.

The darkness gave way to white light, the water suddenly as bright as swimming pool water in daytime.

Tom could see the stark details of the riverbed below, the rocks and the mud banks.

The bright light was followed immediately by the muffled sound of a tremendous explosion.

Even though he was protected by the several feet of dense water, the blast knocked even more wind out of Tom's already-burning lungs.

The white light lingered, then was gone as suddenly as it had appeared, the river black again, devoid of any detail.

Despite the agony building in his chest, Tom let the current carry them for as long as he could before finally scrambling for the surface, gasping for air as he and Hammerton emerged.

They were lucky; the current was strong and had already carried them thirty feet downriver.

Tom glanced back and saw that the building they had occupied just seconds ago was no longer there.

A fireball still rising above a debris-strewn lot was all that remained.

Tom tried to spot the Slav and his bodyguard, but there was no sign of them.

Of course there shouldn't be; they would have certainly taken cover right before the blast.

But if he couldn't see them, maybe they couldn't see him.

What other choice did he have?

Facing forward, Tom clung on to Hammerton as they continued toward the Grand Avenue Bridge.

Once they had passed under it, Tom grabbed a slick rock and used it as an anchor. He pulled them out of the current and toward the riverbank.

All along Front Street, car alarms were sounding.

Soaked and freezing, Tom and Hammerton made their way out of the water, up the rocky bank, and onto the street.

The rain felt almost warm compared to the water they had just left.

As they crossed the street, Tom asked for the car keys and Hammerton dug them out of his pocket. He still had his SIG in his hand.

Tom had lost the Glock the moment they'd hit the water, but somehow Hammerton had hung on to his weapon.

He helped Hammerton inside the SUV, then covered him with the leather overcoat Simpson had left behind.

Reaching under the backseat, Tom grabbed the lock box and placed it on Hammerton's lap. "Open it." Then he climbed in behind the wheel, started the engine, and shifted into drive. He steered the black SUV away from the curb.

It was only when he looked in the rearview mirror that he noticed the back window was gone—blown out of its frame and into countless pieces by the force of the explosion.

He remembered the neighborhood well enough to find his way out and back to I-91, was doing so when Hammerton reached over the seat with his smartphone.

Tom held the device with one hand, keying in Stella's number with a thumb he could not stop from shivering, though he didn't know how much was because of the cold and how much was from the adrenaline still pumping through his bloodstream.

In the backseat, Hammerton was gasping for air.

"Jesus," the Brit muttered. "Jesus fucking Christ."

Tom glanced at him in the mirror.

"Is this vehicle Carrington's? Can he track it?"

Hammerton was still breathing hard. He shook his head from side to side.

"Are you sure?"

"Yes. I take care of tech stuff."

"You put the tracking device on my pickup?"

Hammerton shook his head again.

"Any idea who did?"

"Simpson, maybe. He was there, in the city."

Tom thought about that, then lowered Hammerton's window and told Hammerton to throw his cell phone out.

He did, then held up Simpson's phone.

"This one, too?"

Potential intel might be stored within its call history or address book. Something—anything—that could help them make sense of what had just occurred.

And Tom was desperate for that.

Desperate to make sense of the long and dangerous road he'd been led on by the one man he thought he could trust.

"No, hang on to it," Tom said. "But disconnect the battery."

Hammerton nodded and did that as well.

He put the phone and the battery into the pocket of the leather coat.

Each breath the man took clearly caused him pain.

Tom saw this and knew what he needed to do next.

There was only one place they could go now.

"Hang in there, man," Tom said.

He looked down at the phone in his shaking hand, entered the last digit of Stella's number, and held his breath as the call connected.

It rang once, then again, and then a third time.

The call was finally answered at the very end of the fourth ring.

Tom was so relieved when he at last heard Stella say his name that he briefly closed his eyes.

"Are you safe?" he said.

"Yes." She paused. "Some men broke into our room."

"I know, I saw."

"You saw?"

"I'll explain when I see you. Where are you now?"

"I'm with Conrad. He's driving me to his place."

"I need you to do something for me, okay?"

"Yes."

"We're done with this hiding out shit. I need you back at your place. I need you surrounded by people. By every state trooper and town cop you know. Throw a party if you have to, I don't care, but be as loud as you can. Do you understand?"

"What's going on?"

"Someone bugged your apartment. I need him to know you're there and that you're surrounded by armed law enforcement. I need him to hear that. I have to be certain he can't come after you again. It's the only way I'll be able to do what I need to do now."

"What is it you need to do?"

"Get answers."

"From Cahill," Stella said.

"Yes. I need the address Conrad gave you."

"Maybe you shouldn't go alone, Tom. He and I can meet you there."

Tom looked at Hammerton in the mirror. "I'm not alone. Please just do what I say, okay?"

Stella recited the address, then told Tom the name of Richard Mercer's daughter.

Sandy Montrose.

"I looked the place up on Google Earth," she said. "It's a decent-size farm about a mile north of Taft. She was an army doctor and is the school physician now. Like father, like daughter. Her husband is a veterinarian. Livestock, horses, big animals. His office and hospital are in the barn out the back."

Tom could think of no better setup for Cahill in his time of need.

His mentor's daughter was someone he had likely known for much of his life and could trust implicitly.

She had medical training, but she also had immediate access to resources as well—through the school or, if needed, through her husband's practice.

And she owned property that was large enough and probably private enough for Cahill to lay low on while he recovered from his wounds.

Property that was less than an hour's drive from New Haven.

The only question that remained now in Tom's mind was what kind of reception he would receive.

Which Charlie Cahill would he find there?

Stella was obviously wondering the same thing.

"What if your friend isn't so glad to see you?" she said.

Tom told her that he didn't have a choice.

Stella was silent.

"Tell Conrad to keep his eyes open," Tom said.

"I will." Stella paused for several seconds—so long, in fact, that Tom feared their connection had been lost.

But finally she broke the silence.

"Tom, I killed three men."

He closed his eyes tight.

Opening them again, he said, "I know."

He wanted to be there with her right now, wanted to go to her and take her far away, begin the long process of forgetting—not that one ever forgets.

But he could not offer her that, not yet.

All he could offer her now was the vague promise that he'd be home as soon as he could.

It was killing him that this was all he could say.

"I'm okay," Stella said. "I'll be okay, really."

It broke Tom's heart even more that she felt compelled to comfort him.

And it was clear to him that she was anything but okay.

He once again felt a rage growing within, a rage toward everyone who was keeping him from being at her side.

For those who'd made it necessary for him to leave her alone in that motel room.

But he needed to think—to outthink—and that required a calm mind.

"Be careful, okay?" Stella said.

"Always."

"I love you, Tom. So much."

"I love you, too, Stella."

He heard her lower the phone, and then the call ended.

Tom looked at Hammerton in the rearview mirror.

The man was struggling for each breath he took, and the blood the river had washed from his scarred face had been replaced with fresh blood.

Tom told him again to hang on.

Then he asked how many rounds remained in his SIG.

Hammerton checked his weapon.

"Two," he said.

Tom nodded and opened the navigation app on his smartphone, then entered the address Stella had given him: 383 Litchfield Road, Watertown.

ETA was forty-five minutes.

Tom knew he would need that time to prepare himself mentally.

To sort through what he didn't know and what he did know.

What made sense and what didn't make sense.

Who was a threat and who wasn't.

Who to trust and, more important, who to punish.

Or, if it came to it, eliminate.

Tom drove on, listening to the rain pounding the roof of the SUV and the hiss of the wide tires slicing the flooded pavement.

Thirty-Five

The farm was located at the crest of a long hill.

Tom turned the SUV from the two-lane road onto the muddied dirt driveway, and as the vehicle's headlights swept the front of the house, he saw an oval-shaped brass plaque indicating that the place had been built circa 1750.

Following the driveway past the main house, Tom steered for the barn located two hundred yards from the road.

He stopped the SUV about fifty feet from the structure, shifted into park, and killed the lights but kept the motor running.

The farmhouse and the barn were both three stories tall, and while the house had seen better days, the barn had undergone extensive renovations.

Modern windows, a new roof, a coat of red paint—all, Tom's experience as a builder told him, completed recently.

There were two entrances to the ground floor—a large garage-style door and a standard-size door to the left of it.

The second story had a row of several windows, the third story just one window and a six-by-six-foot-square hay door.

Behind the barn was a wire fence, and beyond that was a steep decline leading to a bowl-shaped valley below.

The farmhouse was dark, as was the barn. The entire property, though relatively close to the road, struck Tom as secluded—or at least secluded enough.

More than that, this place was one that could be easily defended.

The locations of the farmhouse and the barn turned the part of the driveway he had parked on into nothing less than a kill box.

Once a Seabee, always a Seabee.

Tom took note of the fact that the dirt drive curved off here and wound its way around to the other side of the farmhouse in a horseshoe shape, ultimately leading back to Litchfield Road.

That would be his way out, should he need it.

Opening the driver's door, he got out of the SUV slowly, holding his arms away from his body as an indication to anyone watching that he was no threat.

His clothes were still wet and he was shivering; the vehicle's heater had done little against the damp air rushing in through the missing back window as they'd sped here.

And though the rain had slowed from a heavy downpour to a steady drizzle, it was still a cold and miserable world that he was standing in.

Tom raised his voice and called out, "Hello?"

He heard nothing, saw no one.

Glancing at the house to his left, he scanned it.

All the windows were still dark.

Facing the barn again, he called, "I have a man with me in need of medical attention."

Still nothing.

Tom stepped to the SUV's back door and opened it.

Hammerton was leaning forward and tucking his SIG into his waistband at the small of his back.

Tom waited till the man was ready before helping him out and keeping him upright as they moved a few steps away from the vehicle.

After waiting a moment and getting only more silence, Tom called out again.

"He may have internal injuries. He needs to be looked at. Now."

Still nothing.

He surveyed the property—no vehicles anywhere. But looking down at the driveway, he recognized tire tracks in the soaked ground.

The tires were set wide apart, so maybe they'd been made by a veterinarian's pickup truck.

Or maybe they'd been made by a Jeep Wrangler.

Tom looked at the barn again and called out, "Hello?"

Nothing.

He noticed, though, that surveillance cameras were mounted above both entrances.

Another was mounted outside a window on the barn's second floor and aimed down the long driveway.

Tom looked back at the farmhouse and saw several cameras mounted at strategic locations on that building as well.

As he was looking at these, the camera mounted on the second floor of the barn caught his eye. It was moving.

Facing the barn again, he said, "My name is Tom Sexton. I knew Charlie Cahill. I'm not here to make trouble."

It took another moment, but finally the door to the barn opened and someone stepped through it.

Dressed in a long raincoat and mud boots.

A woman, her hands deep in the pockets of the coat.

Several floodlights mounted along the front of the barn came to life suddenly, temporarily blinding Tom.

Shielding his eyes with his free hand, he blinked, then lowered his hand when he saw that the woman had quickly crossed much of the distance between them.

She was now standing twenty-five feet away.

Though she was merely a motionless silhouette before him, he detected no panic from her.

It was something in the way she stood.

The calmness in her voice when she finally spoke served to confirm his assessment. "What are your friend's injuries?"

Tom had to once again raise his voice to be heard over the rain. "Gunshot," he said.

The woman studied Hammerton.

"He doesn't appear to be bleeding."

"He isn't. Not externally. He was wearing a vest. But the round that struck him was a .50 caliber."

"A vest stopped a fifty-cal rifle round?"

Tom knew that she was testing him.

He also knew that he was more than likely talking to Sandy Montrose.

"Handgun, not rifle," he said.

She was silent for a moment, then turned her head toward the barn and said, "I need this man inside."

The door opened and a solitary figure moved through it, quickly reaching her side.

The figure was expertly shouldering a rifle.

Tom recognized by the weapon's silhouette that it was an AR-15.

The armed man leveled the rifle at Tom and ordered him to drop any weapons.

Tom slowly reached for the SIG at the small of Hammerton's back, removed it, and let the man see it before tossing it into the mud.

After a moment, the armed man moved toward Tom and Hammerton.

Reaching them, he lowered his rifle and proceeded with a quick one-handed pat down.

Hammerton first, then Tom.

The man, Tom noticed, had a second rifle slung over his left shoulder.

Stepping back and raising the AR-15 again, the armed man announced, "They're clear."

Montrose turned to the barn and waved, and all but one of the floodlights went dark.

In the absence of the harsh light, the two people in front of his eyes changed from two-dimensional silhouettes to three-dimensional beings.

Tom could almost see their faces, but it wasn't till another floodlight came on—this one from the farmhouse to the left—that he could clearly see them.

But being able to look them in the eyes was no longer his chief concern, because someone was approaching from the farmhouse.

And when Charlie Cahill emerged from the darkness, Tom recognized not only the man's face but the expression it wore as well.

It was the all-too-familiar mask of a man in grave pain.

All kinds of pain.

Tom had no doubt that it was the same face he himself would be wearing should anyone bring harm to Stella.

More harm, anyway, than she had already endured.

And while he recognized both the man and his agony, it was what Cahill said that made no sense to Tom.

No fucking sense whatsoever.

After looking at Tom for a long moment, Cahill uttered two words.

"Take him," he said.

Though his face was full of emotion, Cahill's voice was void of it.

The armed man moved quickly then, transferring from his AR-15 to the other weapon slung over his left shoulder.

Raising and aiming it, he squeezed the trigger before Tom could even react.

There was, however, no muzzle flash from this rifle.

Nor was there the sonic boom of a projectile traveling at three thousand feet per second escaping a long barrel.

In fact, the weapon made almost no sound at all.

And the only indication that something had actually happened was the sudden pinch Tom felt as the feathered tranquilizer dart punctured his left pectoral muscle.

Within a second, Tom was literally feeling nothing.

Another second later, Tom was down in the mud, a heap of useless limbs, and Hammerton, unable to stand without Tom's support, was down there with him.

The last thing Tom saw before blacking out were hands reaching into his rapidly narrowing vision and struggling to grab Hammerton, who, though injured, was not going to be taken without a fight.

Thirty-Six

He felt as if he were back in the cold, rushing water of the Quinnipiac River.

As if he were being carried, sometimes in total darkness, other times in a chaotic world that was made up of nothing but blurs and shadows.

He saw and heard only fragments, was feeling the same numbness he'd felt that night an army medevac helicopter carried him and Cahill to the aid station. He was feeling, too, that same acute homesickness.

Five years ago, though, he had no home or love to long for.

But things had changed.

Stella was in her apartment, waiting for him. Tom latched on to that fact as if it were a rock he could use to pull himself out of this turbulent water.

But it was more like gripping water itself than stone, and the hope that he could get to her still—break away somehow, find his way back to Canaan—was simply slipping away.

All that was left was the knowledge that Stella was safe, surrounded by men who had cared for her long before he did.

Who had wanted her long before he did.

An odd comfort, yes, but a comfort nonetheless.

But none of those men could protect her from grief if Tom did not return.

Nor could they protect her from worry.

Even as his mind was flooded with opiates and Tom was sinking into darker waters, he understood why men injured in faraway battles cried out for those back home.

Those they cared for and who cared for them.

He'd felt pain before, and loss, but nothing like this.

Nothing like the utter helplessness and deep despair that burned inside him now.

And what drug could dull that?

———

Tom was out of the rain but still in his wet clothes.

He was being helped up a set of narrow stairs, then around a corner and down a short hallway.

There were two men beside him, and as addled as he was, he recognized them.

One was the man who had shot him, the other the man who had ordered it.

Tom stared at the side of Cahill's face as the men shuffled him into a small room and sat him down on the foot of a narrow bed.

Then the men were gone and the woman in the raincoat was leaning down and facing him.

There was no doubt at all now that she was Sandy Montrose.

"We need to get you out of your wet clothes," Montrose said.

Tom nodded and did what he could to help her.

It wasn't easy going—his clothes were soaked with water and river silt and stuck to his skin—but when they were done, Montrose laid him down on clean sheets.

Despite the tranquilizer, he could feel the coldness of the air around him.

A heavy blanket was thrown over his legs, but his torso was left bare.

He tried to focus on the part of himself that was warm, but that didn't stop him from shivering violently.

Montrose checked his eyes with a penlight before listening first to his heart and then his lungs with a stethoscope.

"Breathe in for me," she whispered. "Now let it out."

She repeated this several times before removing the stethoscope from her ears and proceeding to press down on Tom's upper and lower abdomen with the tips of her fingers.

Then she skimmed her hands over his ribs and down his arms.

Pulling the blanket aside, she skimmed over his legs.

When she was done examining him she covered him with the blanket, pulling it up to his shoulders.

"My friend?" Tom muttered.

"My husband's taking X-rays now. We'll take care of whatever he needs, I promise."

She gathered Tom's clothing and started toward the door.

"Phone in my pocket," Tom said.

Complete sentences were beyond him.

Montrose shook her head and said only, "Sorry."

She stepped to the door and opened it.

The dimly lit room was brightened significantly by the light spilling in from the hallway.

Tom was getting the sense that he was a captive.

Scanning the small room, he saw that it had no windows.

And mounted in one corner of the ceiling was a security camera.

It was aimed at the bed.

"I need to call," Tom gasped.

Montrose shook her head again but did not apologize this time.

"He'll want to talk to you when you're awake," she said. "The sooner you give in, the sooner you'll sleep it off."

Then she slipped through the door and closed it.

Tom heard the turning of a deadbolt.

In the renewed darkness, he felt less like a patient being left to recover and more like a man confined to a cell.

It was a reminder that the loss of life was not the only thing for him to be concerned about.

Death was not the only way for him to be separated from Stella.

Struggling to remain conscious, Tom heard voices coming up from below, then footsteps, doors opening and closing.

These could have been concurrent sounds, one immediately following the other, or they could have come long minutes or even hours apart.

In his condition, he had no way of knowing.

Finally, Tom simply could fight it no longer. He felt himself sinking into a deep unconsciousness.

He chose to focus on Stella, safe, as his last coherent thought.

Tom wakes.

He sits up, hears nothing.

He is clothed, has boots on, so he rises and steps to the door.

Testing the knob, he finds it is unlocked.

Opening the door and walking down the stairs he'd been carried up, he explores the farmhouse's ground floor, moving from room to room only to discover that the place is unoccupied.

He is free.

Rushing outside, he finds a vehicle, climbs in, and starts the engine, then speeds away, heading north on Route 63, passing through Litchfield, where he met with Carrington, then continuing till 63 joins with Route 7—the two-lane road that would take him to Stella and the men who surround her.

But just south of Canaan, the engine suddenly cuts out and the vehicle rolls to a stop.

He is out in the middle of nowhere, the road edged on both sides with five-foot-tall weeds.

Determined to run the rest of the way, he exits the vehicle, but the instant he steps out into the night, he sees that he is no longer in Northwestern Connecticut.

He is back in the desert.

Back in the Afghan desert.

Alone in that hellish terrain.

Or, rather, at first he is alone.

Sensing that someone is behind him, he turns and sees a person standing just a few yards away.

It is Carrington, dressed as he was when Tom last saw him at Tallmadge's gravesite.

Neither says anything, but then Tom feels a rush of sudden rage that he cannot control and reaches for a weapon at the four o'clock position on his right side.

Something is there. He draws it.

In his hand is the Beretta Simpson gave him.

The Beretta that Carrington instructed Simpson to provide him.

Before Tom can determine whether or not the weapon works, Carrington says, "Remember what the man said."

Tom stares at his former commanding officer dumbly.

"In the medevac, leaving this godforsaken place," Carrington explains.

He pauses, then repeats what the medic tending to Cahill had shouted to his partner over the rotor noise: "The guy will never be the same."

Tom says nothing.

Finally, he lowers the weapon.

The desert wind picks up and a cloud of sand rises between them.

"Be careful, son," Carrington says.

The man begins to disappear in the confusion.

As he does, he says with a fading voice, "Because we're in more danger than you know, Tom."

Then he is gone and Tom is alone in the desert.

⎯⎯⎯⎯⎯⎯⎯⎯

Waking from the dream, Tom lay still for a moment.

Eventually, his eyes adjusted and he noticed a pile of folded clothes on a chair by the door.

His clothes, washed and dried.

On the floor under the chair were his work boots.

He got up and checked the pockets of his pants, but of course they were all empty.

Inside his boots were electronic boot warmers—no doubt to dry them out.

Tom quickly dressed, pulled on and laced up his boots, then stood and tried the doorknob.

Unlike the door in his dream, this one was locked.

Sitting back down, he wondered what time it was.

However much time had passed, Tom could not escape the dread he felt at the idea of Stella being left to wonder where he was.

She had suffered enough because of him.

It was time to bring an end to all this, once and for all.

Whatever the hell *this* was.

Looking up at the camera, Tom stood and stepped to the door, toe-kicked it once, then a second time, then a third—hard.

He sat down on the edge of the bed again, never taking his eyes off the camera.

For several long moments, the house was as silent as a tomb, but finally from somewhere below Tom heard a door open and close.

This was followed by footsteps.

And then, a moment later, Tom was listening to those footsteps climb the stairs.

Thirty-Seven

The door was unlocked and opened, and the man who had shot Tom with the tranquilizer dart stepped into the room.

Slung over his right shoulder was his AR-15.

"You okay to go for a walk?" the man said.

Tom nodded.

"Sorry about before," the man said. "I'm Kevin, Sandy's husband." He paused and looked Tom over before saying, "Come on, I'll take you to him."

Tom stood.

Exiting that room no bigger than a prison cell was a relief to him, though he found he needed the railing on the stairs to keep his balance.

His head felt heavy, as though it were full of water.

They moved through a narrow pantry and into a country kitchen.

Tom realized that the room he had occupied was some kind of a secret room above the kitchen, accessible only by a set of stairs hidden behind a fake door at the rear of that pantry.

He wondered if the farmhouse had been a place for runaway slaves to hide and rest during their long and dangerous journey on the Underground Railroad.

From the kitchen, he could see into the living room.

He could tell by its layout—large stone hearth dominating a central room—that this house had likely been a Colonial-era tavern when it was first constructed.

The floors were well-worn pine planks held down by wrought iron spikes, the floor and ceiling moldings all dark mahogany.

Built to last centuries—and it had.

Outside, the rain had stopped. By the silvery edge of the clouded eastern horizon, Tom knew dawn was not far off. Kevin was a few feet ahead, walking toward the barn, but halfway between it and the house he stopped and turned to Tom.

Tom's eyes went to his escort's hands, looking for any indication that the man was about to reach for his weapon.

Kevin held his hands out. "It's all right," he said. "I'm going to reach into my jacket pocket now."

He did, slowly, and removed something, holding it up for Tom to see.

It was Tom's smartphone.

"You need to make a call, right? Make it now, but try not to be long."

He tossed the device to Tom.

Tom immediately hit "Redial."

Kevin stayed where he was, watching and listening.

Tom understood that having his call monitored in this way was part of the deal.

Stella answered on the first ring.

"Tom?"

"I'm okay," he said.

"Where are you?"

"At the farm."

"What took so long?"

"I'll tell you later. How are you?"

"I'm okay." She paused. "I was getting worried."

"I know. I'm sorry. It was unavoidable."

He realized only then that he was slurring slightly—the lingering effects, no doubt, of the animal tranquilizer that had taken him down.

That made his head feel so heavy, like he was wearing a crash helmet.

"You sound tired," Stella said.

"I am, a little, yeah. You must be, too. Try to get some sleep."

"When will you be home?"

"I'm not sure."

"Why not?"

"Cahill's here. I'm on my way to talk to him now."

Another pause. "How . . . is he?" she said finally.

Tom knew what she meant.

And he heard the concern in her voice.

"I'm about to find out," he said.

"If you don't call in an hour, we're coming there to get you."

"Don't do that."

"Whatever he has to say to you, he can say it in an hour."

"Stella."

"This isn't negotiable," she said. "Go talk to him, Tom. Then come straight home."

Tom smiled.

How long had it been since Stella texted that same directive to him?

Two days, though it seemed more like months.

Like a long tour of duty.

He was feeling *that* tired, feeling the same profound exhaustion that had numbed him to the bone after his discharge.

That had dogged him as he traveled around, tasting freedom of movement for the first time in eight years and trying to decide whether or not to take Carrington up on his lucrative job offer.

If last Friday seemed like months ago, then those many weeks of drifting five years ago were nothing more than sketchy memories of some other lifetime.

"Okay, you win," Tom said. "I'll call you in an hour."

"Promise?"

"Yes."

"Be careful."

"Always."

They ended the call, and Tom pocketed the smartphone.

Kevin waved for Tom to follow him to the barn.

Reaching it, he opened the door and led Tom inside.

The ground floor of the barn was a vet's office—large animal and equine, Tom guessed by the open layout and size of the equipment and tables.

Along the right wall of the barn, in line with the garage-style door, was a long bay big enough to accommodate livestock trucks.

In it now were three vehicles.

An extended-cab pickup, the SUV Tom and Hammerton had arrived in, and a Jeep Wrangler.

Tom followed Kevin past the vehicles to the far end of the vast barn.

Here was open space.

And no lights were on.

Despite the darkness, Tom saw that the corner at the rear of the barn contained a room with large windows and a stainless-steel door.

The surgery.

It was empty, and its lights were off as well.

"Wait here," Kevin said before backtracking to the front entrance and leaving through it.

Alone, Tom remembered his dream and wondered if he should bolt now. He considered doing so for a few seconds, but didn't.

How far would he actually get?

And if he did somehow make it all the way home, what then?

How far and for how long would he and Stella need to run?

Without even knowing what it was they were running from.

A sound came from the back of the barn. A figure emerged from the door to what looked like a storage room.

It was Cahill. Tom saw that quickly enough.

As Cahill crossed the distance between them, he kept his eyes fixed on Tom.

He still had the hard, lean build of a marine.

And his face still bore the expression of a man in pain.

All kinds of pain.

Tom thought of everything he'd learned about Cahill in the past thirty-six hours.

All the indications that the man was dangerous—to others and maybe even to himself.

Tom thought again of the dream, but this time he was remembering what Carrington had said as the swirling desert sand had risen like a storm between them.

The man will never be the same.

And then the warning he had called out as he was consumed by the chaos.

Be careful, son.

Because we're in more danger than you know.

Thirty-Eight

As Cahill got nearer, Tom spotted a firearm tucked into the waistband of his jeans at the appendix position.

He immediately identified it by its grip as a 1911.

The sidearm of choice of Force Reconnaissance Marines.

Several yards from Tom, safely beyond his reach, Cahill stopped.

He looked Tom up and down.

Tom waited for him to speak.

Or make anything resembling an aggressive move.

"Did you make your phone call?" Cahill said finally.

His voice was even—not hostile, but not friendly, either.

All business.

Tom told him that he had and thanked him for letting him do that.

Cahill nodded, still studying him. "Your friend Hammerton told us what happened," he said.

"Is he going to be okay?"

"Yes. He was lucky. X-rays show no internal injuries. Sandy wants to keep him under observation for a while longer, though."

"Thank her for me. For taking care of him."

"She swore an oath," Cahill said. He studied Tom for another moment. "Before we proceed, I'll need to hear from you exactly what happened in New Haven last night."

Tom understood why.

Cahill wanted to compare his story with Hammerton's.

Tom also understood that while he had been searching for Cahill, Cahill had been waiting for someone to find him.

Find him with orders to kill him.

Hammerton's account proved that Tom was not there for that reason.

More than that, it proved that Tom had refused to kill Cahill, even when the woman Tom loved was being threatened.

Of course, though, Hammerton's account could simply be a story.

And if Tom's version didn't jibe with his, well, then there'd be a problem.

"I'll tell you whatever you need to know," Tom said.

"Then start at the beginning."

"Friday night I was asked to find you."

"By James Carrington. Your former CO."

"No. Carrington arranged a meeting with the people who asked me to find you."

"A man named Sam Raveis."

"Raveis and a woman named Alexa Savelle. He apparently has some personal interest in you. She's NSA."

Cahill said nothing.

"Savelle provided me with files to look through," Tom continued. "She hoped that because you and I had a history that I might see something she had missed. Something that would indicate where you would go for emergency medical assistance. We were getting close to finding you—"

"We?"

"Stella and me. Well, Stella, actually."

"Your girlfriend."

"Yes. We were getting close to finding you when Carrington asked me to meet him again."

"And when was this?"

"Yesterday afternoon."

"And then he sent you to that building in New Haven."

"He provided the address but said the order came from Raveis via Savelle."

"And what were you supposed to do there?"

"I was told that the building was your safe house and that we—Hammerton and Simpson and me—were to look around and gather intel."

"What happened when you got there?"

"We discovered a cache of weapons. A large cache."

"What kind of weapons?"

"Mixed arms. Automatic shotguns, fifty-cal Barretts, grenades, Uzis."

"Do you know which model Uzi?"

"I was told it was the Uzi-PRO."

Cahill thought about that, then said, "Hammerton tells us that men were waiting inside and that you were ambushed."

"Yes."

"How many men?"

"Four."

"And how did they ambush you exactly?"

"Hammerton was the point man. He and I were examining the weapons when Simpson ran upstairs ahead of us. We went up after him and were hit with a stun grenade." Tom paused. "It's pretty obvious now that Simpson was working with the men who were waiting for us."

"We'll come back to that," Cahill said. "The men who ambushed you, they had a leader. Describe him."

Tom sensed that Cahill was eager for this particular information.

"He had a Slavic accent of some kind," Tom said. "I couldn't place it. He was well dressed, though. Well spoken, too. And he walked with a limp."

"Which leg?"

"Right."

"Bad quad, calf, ankle, what?"

"Calf."

Another pause, then: "What did this man want?"

"He wanted me to kill you."

"How was he going to get you to do this?"

"I had hidden Stella in an out-of-the-way motel. I thought she'd be safe there, but the leader had a team in the next room, waiting to take her hostage."

"How did they find her if she was hidden?"

"Someone had attached a tracking device to my pickup while I was in the city meeting with Raveis and Savelle."

"Someone?"

"The leader implicated Carrington."

This was followed by a long silence.

"We'll come back to that, too," Cahill said finally. "How did this man—this Slav—know that you knew where I was?"

"His men had eavesdropped on Stella earlier. They'd heard her tell me over the phone that she'd found you. If I didn't kill you, they'd . . ."

Tom didn't see the need to elaborate.

"She killed the men who came after her," Cahill said.

"Yes."

"And she's okay now."

Tom shrugged.

"Carrington's other man," Cahill said. "Simpson. He gave you a sidearm that was nonfunctional."

"Yes."

"It didn't jam on you."

"No. The firing pin had been removed. And the leader had a bodyguard who confirmed that the weapon had been tampered with. He seemed to enjoy telling me that, actually."

"Describe him."

"Russian accent. Dressed in Blackwater-type tactical gear. Carried a Desert Eagle in a vertical shoulder rig."

"He's the man who shot your friend."

"Yes."

"And who tried to kill you with a grenade."

Tom nodded.

It was obvious that Cahill understood the significance of Tom having come face-to-face again with that particular type of weapon.

He looked Tom up and down once more.

It was obvious, too, that Cahill wanted to ask something.

Maybe he wanted to know what it was like.

Whatever it was that was on his mind, Cahill pushed the thought aside and returned to the cold, hard facts.

He asked if Tom had killed the Russian.

"No. He and his boss got away."

"But not before remotely triggering the timer of an explosive device."

"Correct."

"Did you get a look at it?"

"Yes. Two twenty-gallon containers with a C-4 trigger and digital timer."

"A truck bomb."

"Yeah."

"I understand you two barely made it out."

Tom nodded.

"And you had to all but carry your friend."

Tom said nothing.

After a moment, Cahill said, "What else can you tell me about the leader?"

"He alluded to something Stella had said to me Friday night. While we were in her apartment. Something . . . intimate."

"Was it something she said before or after you went into the city?"

"Before. Right before, actually."

"Someone bugged your place."

"It's the only way."

"The bug is probably still there."

"I hope so."

"Why?"

"Carrington will know that Stella's untouchable right now."

"Untouchable how?"

"She's surrounded by a half-dozen state troopers. In a building we control completely. On a busy-enough street in the town center, a few blocks from the police station."

"Smart," Cahill said. "You know, that might be a good way to plant some misinformation. Should we need to."

"Stella's out of this," Tom said.

Cahill didn't argue with that.

"So our accounts jibe?" Tom said. "Hammerton's and mine? You understand now that I'm not here to kill you."

"I do now, yes."

"Then I'd like to ask you a question."

"Of course."

"What the fuck is going on?"

"That's the million-dollar question, isn't it," Cahill said. "I'm thinking, Tom, that maybe between the two of us, we have a decent shot of figuring that out. But one thing is becoming clear. And I'm afraid it isn't good news for you."

"Carrington," Tom said.

Cahill nodded. "I know what he means to you, the role he played in your life. Sandy's father played a similar role in mine. I'd hate to have to face what you might be facing. But we're talking national security here. High treason." He paused. "And the murder of the woman I loved."

"I'll tell you whatever you need to know," Tom said. "But then I'm gone. I need to be with Stella." He paused. "And this . . . this isn't what I wanted."

Cahill nodded again, as if to say he understood. "I am glad she's okay. Or at least alive and will be okay."

Neither said anything for a moment.

"How was it for you?" Cahill said finally.

"How was what?"

"The first time someone tried to kill me—I mean, when I wasn't wearing a uniform—it was a . . . shock. On the battlefield it's different, you know. It's the enemy who's trying to kill you. And it's your friends you're fighting for, the men you've trained with and lived with. Back here, it's nowhere near as cut-and-dried. Oftentimes it's a friend who tries to end you. And sometimes it's the one person in the world you trust the most. If you're lucky, you survive those. But you never get over them. You're never the same again."

Tom said nothing.

"Come with me, Tom," Cahill said.

"Where to?"

"A place we can talk."

Cahill turned and headed toward the door through which he had appeared.

Tom waited a moment before following.

Unlocking and opening that door, Cahill stepped aside to let Tom in. At the end of the narrow room was another door, this one made of reinforced steel.

As was the frame in which it was set.

Cahill moved to that door and opened it, too.

Tom was now looking down a steep flight of metal stairs.

He knew the entrance to an underground bunker when he saw one.

But he made no move to cross the threshold before him.

"I'm either an insane killer luring you down into his labyrinth," Cahill said, "or we're among the few people either of us can trust right now. Five years ago, you saved my life and I saved yours. That's how I remember it. You led the rescue, and my men would have been massacred had you not done that, me along with them. What I did, when I laid down between that grenade and you, how could I not? For the man who risked everything to save my men?"

This new perspective left Tom feeling stunned, as if he'd been tagged by a punch. All he could really do was wait for Cahill to continue.

"You don't owe me anything, Tom. Do you understand? We were both doing our duty, which was keeping our men alive so they could go home and live their lives and, decades from now, die as old men in their beds. You've more than earned your life with Stella. And it's a life I want to get you back to as soon as possible."

Cahill was face-to-face with him now.

No safe distance between them, no buffer.

It was the closest Tom had been to the man since that cold and violent night in the desert.

"I need to know who ordered the hit," Cahill said. "I need to be certain, though, beyond any doubt, and I can't achieve that certainty without you. So I need your help, for just a little bit longer. I need your help erasing from this fucking world the man who killed a defenseless woman. We suspect he's connected to the same men who tried to kill you and the one thing you hold dear. Men who are at this moment, we believe, preparing to kill a lot more innocent people."

Cahill paused, then said, "Will you do that? Will you help me?"

Tom's answer was to turn and start down the stairs.

The stairwell was dark, but there was a light source below.

Grabbing this railing, too, Tom descended toward that light.

PART FOUR

PART FOUR

Thirty-Nine

A six-foot-long tunnel of galvanized, corrugated steel led into the bunker.

Once inside, Tom determined by its dimensions that the bunker was a repurposed shipping container.

Ceilings nine feet high, length easily eighty feet—so not one container but two that had been welded together end to end and sealed against the elements.

And by the depth of the stairs he'd just come down, Tom estimated that the bunker was a good twenty-five feet underground.

So, there was more to the barn's recent renovations than met the eye.

Tom scanned the bunker, which was more of a state-of-the-art command center than a doomsday prepper's hole-in-the-ground refuge.

There was a workstation with several notebook computers, multiple monitors, and a server, all connected to a bank of a half-dozen backup power supplies.

Next to the workstation was a ham radio setup and four walkie-talkies in a charger.

Beyond the workstation were two purification systems, one for air, the other for water.

Beyond those was a kitchen and dining area, with a table long enough to seat at least eight people.

On that table was a clear plastic bag, the contents of which Tom immediately recognized as the items he had been carrying in his pockets.

His multitool, the single .45 round he had put in his shirt pocket, his driver's license, cash, and keys, plus the paper carry permit Conrad had given him.

What the bag did *not* contain was Simpson's cell.

Cahill handed Tom the bag and led him into the second container. A dozen bunk beds were mounted on its walls.

As they walked deeper into the sleeping area, Tom realized that there was another wing to the bunker—a third shipping container, set perpendicular to the first two to create an *L* shape.

This wing had its own entrance, complete with a heavy-duty door identical to the one up in the barn.

Reaching the doorway, Tom saw that this third container housed the food stores and arsenal, as well as two more bunks and a small medical bay.

So, a panic room inside a panic room.

At the far end of this wing was another table, this one only large enough for four people.

On it were several files, some stacked, others fanned out.

Some of those files were open and the papers they contained spread out as well.

But it was the three people gathered at the table with their backs to Tom that interested him the most.

One of them was Sandy Montrose, who he recognized by her raincoat.

The other two people were busy sorting through files and talking quietly.

It wasn't till they glanced over their shoulders at Tom in mid-sentence that he saw the faces of the last two people he had expected to encounter here.

Sam Raveis and Alexa Savelle.

"There are no recording devices in this room," Cahill explained. "Above us is a foot and a half of concrete, with twelve feet of packed earth on top of that. And the entire shelter is a giant Faraday cage, which of course will shield everything inside from an electromagnetic pulse but also prevents any cell signal from reaching down here. There's no safer place for us to talk. And all of us need to talk freely now. Nothing held back, just the ugly truth."

Cahill gestured toward the table.

"There isn't a lot of time," he said. "We need to get started."

Forty

Alexa Savelle smiled as Tom approached.

The last time he had seen her, she had been leaning against the rear bumper of Hammerton's SUV, her face smudged black by smoke, her eyes glassy with tears, their edges as red as torn flesh.

The last time she'd seen him, he had longer hair and a beard.

Savelle was of course cleaned up now, as was Tom—thanks to Sandy Montrose—but he could tell that she was still shaken.

It was a look in her eyes, one he'd seen before many times in those who'd had a brush with death and survived it only by the grace of another.

He'd seen that look in his own eyes, too.

The stark realization that he owed everything he had, and everything he would have from now on, to someone else.

His life could continue due only to another's bravery.

Tom nodded once, but he couldn't smile.

He was spent, but more than that, he was confused by her presence.

As well Raveis's.

There was no getting his tired mind around that.

As beat and bewildered as he was, Tom didn't fail to notice that Raveis was watching him with a curiosity similar to the one the man had displayed in the town car two nights earlier.

But what had appeared to Tom as slight curiosity then was now nothing short of keen interest.

When Tom reached the makeshift conference table, Raveis said, "It's good to see you, Tom."

Tom didn't reply.

The comments Raveis had made about Stella looking good for her age and the pearls being a nice touch were still fresh in his mind.

And anyway, whatever interest Raveis had in him now, it was no doubt born of the newfound understanding that Tom had more skills than he might have expected from the average Seabee.

So, a man like Tom could be of use to a man like Raveis.

Nothing else could explain the sudden interest.

And nothing could appeal to Tom less.

They gathered around the table—Raveis, Savelle, Tom, and Cahill standing, Sandy Montrose seated in front of the files and documents.

Cahill was facing Tom, and Savelle was to Tom's right, Raveis to his left.

"You don't have clearance for what we are about to share with you, Tom," Cahill said, "but there's no getting around that. We need you to know everything we know so you understand what's at stake."

Tom nodded. "Okay."

"Five years ago, while I was recovering in a VA hospital in New York," Cahill began, "I was approached by a recruiter who offered me a job. The job was subcontract work with the Central Intelligence Agency. The recruiter was a man I'd only met a few times before, back in Afghanistan. He was the CO of the Seabees stationed at Forward Operating Base Nolay."

Cahill paused, but Tom said nothing.

"You had no idea that Carrington was a recruiter for the CIA," Cahill said.

Tom shook his head.

Here was yet another shift in his understanding of things.

He braced himself for more to come.

"No idea at all?" Savelle asked. "Carrington didn't say anything to you? Not yesterday, not five years ago?"

Tom felt all eyes on him. "No. He didn't."

"Carrington's private security firm is a front," Raveis explained. "A fairly lucrative front, but a front nonetheless. He uses it to screen candidates for the Agency's special operations division. Most don't make the cut and end up working in the private sector without even knowing they were being considered. But a select few are recommended for Agency consideration. And an even more select few are accepted and sent off for training."

"You were actually Carrington's first candidate," Savelle said. "He wanted you to be his first recruit. But you passed on his offer so he moved on to others, Cahill being one of them."

"I had reservations," Cahill continued. "And I was in bad shape physically. Carrington convinced me, though, that my skill set, combined with my personal background, meant I had something very specific to offer. Though I was no longer a marine, I could continue to serve my country. As it turned out, by the time I'd healed, I was exactly what was needed for a critical operation. I was in the right place at the right time. This operation was unique, though, in that it required I use my real name. No fake backstory, no false identity. But this would leave my family vulnerable to possible retribution, so a very public battle was orchestrated, one that would make it appear at its conclusion that I'd been disowned and disinherited. This battle would also establish in the press that I had a substantial trust fund. And that I was struggling with significant mental health issues. All these elements were crucial to the success of the operation."

"I understand the need to protect your family," Tom said. "But why was it necessary for it to look like you were struggling with posttraumatic stress?"

"Emotional instability would disqualify him from both government and private sector contract work," Savelle answered. "The lawsuit allowed us to get psychiatric reports into the public record. They were false reports, of course, but no one knew that. This way, anyone looking into Cahill's background would conclude what the Agency needed them to conclude."

"Which was?"

"That he was an imbalanced trust fund kid on some crazy personal crusade," Raveis said. "A Recon Marine once, but in no way the man he used to be."

Tom remembered his dream, but said nothing about it.

"When I informed Carrington that I was in," Cahill said, "he had me transferred to a private hospital. And when I was released, the charade with my family was put into motion. Once enough 'damage' had been done, the lawsuit was settled out of court and I began my training. Six months later, I was given my assignment."

Tom recalled going to the hospital a second time, only to find that Cahill was gone.

He recalled, too, that Cahill had battled his family in the courts, then mysteriously fell off the radar for six months.

Carrington had mentioned that at Tallmadge's crypt but claimed not to know what Cahill had done during those six months he'd been invisible.

Or what Cahill had become. Or for whom he worked.

Of course, Carrington wasn't the only one to have held back information.

Tom looked at Savelle and said, "You knew where Cahill was all the time."

She nodded.

"So why the wild goose chase?"

"We couldn't divulge classified information," Raveis answered. "That alone meant we had to keep you in the dark about a lot of things. But also, we needed you in the dark. We needed it to look like you had found Cahill on your own."

Tom addressed Cahill. "Why?"

"Carrington had to believe that you'd actually found me. We needed it to add up for him."

Raveis said, "Forcing his hand was the only way to expose him."

"As what?"

Without missing a beat, Savelle said, "A traitor."

Tom looked at her. "Traitor how?"

Forty-One

"Imagine six charter buses entering New York City from six different access points," Raveis said. "In each bus are eight six-man squads. Heavily armed men, men with real combat experience. Let's say it's the Saturday of Memorial Day weekend, which also happens to be Fleet Week, so the city is packed with military personnel and tourists. You were a navy man, Tom, you know all about Fleet Week, right? How jammed the city gets. How many of your fellow sailors are strolling about. Now imagine that one of those squads, armed with easily concealed Uzis, deploys to, say, the 6 train. The team separates, each man steps into his own subway car and, at a predetermined moment, each of them begins emptying mag after mag into the people trapped inside. And up on ground level, at the exact same moment, panel vans and box trucks loaded with IEDs take out the bridges and tunnels. Then imagine the remaining dozen or so squads, armed with a variety of automatic weapons, walking down each of the avenues, firing at every person in sight. Men, women, children, law enforcement, sailors all dressed in white. Those who aren't hit in the initial barrage run into stores and restaurants for cover. That's what people do. We saw that on 9/11, remember? We saw it in Paris, too. So now imagine those squads launching grenades through window after window as they move south. Add to all this skilled snipers with fifty-cal

Barretts firing from window or rooftop positions. And add to that men firing M134 Miniguns—at six thousand rounds per minute—from the sunroofs of Range Rovers equipped with armored glass and run-flat tires. Finally, imagine that the charter buses used to transport these men into the city contain explosive devices similar to the one you encountered last night. One bus parks outside the Port Authority, another outside Grand Central, another outside Penn Station, with the remaining three placed at other points of egress where people desperate to flee would flock. And to maximize casualties, as well as the strain on emergency personnel, these buses are all set to detonate just minutes apart."

"The police have been more or less militarized, yes," Savelle said, "but even with Stryker armored personnel carriers, it'd be difficult to navigate the city when the streets are littered with the wounded and the dead, not to mention all the disabled and abandoned vehicles. Cars, cabs, buses. Block after block of them. Just utter mayhem. And of course, personal firearms are as good as nonexistent in New York, so the unarmed citizens, well, they're just target practice."

"The media has done a good job downplaying the danger we all face," Raveis said, "telling us to be on the lookout for lone-wolf attacks, that this is the extent of our enemies' reach into the homeland. But the fact is we have known for years that a major ground offensive is the real threat."

Raveis paused before adding, "We're talking invasion, Tom. And not by an enemy that wants to occupy. By an enemy that simply wants to kill as many of us as they can before blowing themselves to pieces. You fought that enemy in Iraq and Afghanistan, so you know it well. Imagine fighting that *here*. With panicked civilians adding to the confusion. Worse, imagine the carnage men like that could cause. I've seen estimates putting the wounded and the dead in the thousands. One particularly grim assessment puts the casualties at the fifty-thousand mark. That's equal to the number of Americans killed fighting in Vietnam. That's almost the total number of GIs lost in the Battle of the Bulge. But this isn't some war on the other side of the world. And this isn't over the course of months or even years. This is one day in New York City. One fucking bad day."

Tom wanted to ask what this had to do with Carrington and the Chechens, but instead he looked at Cahill and said, "What does all this have to do with your boxing gyms?"

"I set up my charities to gather intel and establish a network of informants. Local street gangs often know more about what's coming through their cities than law enforcement. My objective was to track weapons and explosives funneling in from overseas through key cities. Weapons that were then transported and stockpiled in and around New York City."

"The CIA's charter forbids domestic surveillance," Tom said.

"The Patriot Act is history, but some of the gray areas it created remain. And, of course, being a subcontractor, I'm not technically employed by the CIA."

"Then who does employ you?"

"I do," Raveis said.

Tom looked at him. "And who the fuck are you, exactly?"

"I'm the man your fucking government comes to when it's scared."

"Raveis operates the camp where I received the majority of my training," Cahill said. "And his private security firm allows the Agency to get around certain obstacles."

"Like congressional oversight," Tom said. "All in the name of keeping us safe, of course."

"The world's a dangerous place now," Raveis said.

Tom looked at him. "When hasn't it been a dangerous place?"

"Threats today don't come in the shape of white sails on the horizon. You know this as well as I do."

"So you take it upon yourself to subvert the Constitution. Because you feel threatened."

"I would think a man whose girlfriend came pretty fucking close to having her ass sold into slavery would see things differently."

"I see exactly what you see: an opportunity for you to make even more money for yourself."

"The last I knew, no one was forcing you to be poor."

"We're a nation of laws for a reason—"

Savelle cut in. "Guys, enough, all right? We don't have time for this." She looked at Tom. "For four years, Cahill has been providing valuable intel. Not as a government operative, but as a private citizen. He reported to Raveis, who'd pass on relevant information to his contact at the Agency. Cahill identified several means of entry, for weapons and personnel, as well as transport routes and a number of stockpiles. Each stockpile he found was immediately put under twenty-four-hour surveillance. The Agency shared everything it could with the FBI and ATF, but no one knew how they were getting their intel. Cahill's hiding in plain sight, setting up his charities all over the country, was working. It was brilliant—his cover was holding, nothing connected him to the Agency, everyone was happy. Two months ago, though, we were tipped off that a story was being written about an operation codenamed Voyeur. That was the Agency's cryptonym for Cahill's op. Illegal op, technically. The story was quashed before anything came of it, but it meant someone had talked. Someone on the inside, someone claiming to be a whistle-blower. The journalist had never met his source, though. They had only communicated through codes. That sounds familiar, doesn't it? So even if the journalist had been willing to reveal his source, he couldn't. But there was no way we were going to risk an asset as valuable as Cahill. And a lot of careers were on the line. So he went dark while we scrambled to identify the traitor. The attempt on Cahill's life and the murder of Erica DiSalvo kicked everything into high gear. We needed to act. We needed to find who betrayed Cahill, and fast."

"And at all costs, apparently," Tom said.

"Yes," Savelle said flatly. "At all costs. A lot of lives were at risk, Tom. Tens of thousands. Not to mention the hundreds of thousands that would be killed and wounded if we jumped into yet another war on the other side of the world." She paused before continuing. "And it wasn't just Stella we were putting at risk. You and I were almost burned alive, remember?"

Tom was silent for a moment.

As before, all eyes were on him.

"You believe Carrington ordered Cahill's murder, yet he was the one you asked to help find Cahill. Why?"

"Obviously," Savelle said, "if he was the man who wanted Cahill dead, then he'd certainly be motivated to accomplish the mission we gave him."

"And if he believed we trusted him enough to come to him for help," Raveis added, "then chances were he'd think we weren't on to him. As far as Carrington actually coming here after Cahill once you figured it out—well, obviously Cahill was more than prepared for whatever might show up here."

"But why would Carrington even talk to some reporter in the first place?" Tom said. "And then two months later hire a Chechen hit team to come after Cahill? What would he gain from that?"

"We believe he was building his own secret stockpiles," Savelle said. "Remember *Fast and Furious*? The ATF running guns to Mexico? If our operation was exposed and publicly crashed and burned like that one did, and all the stockpiles currently under surveillance were seized, then Carrington's would be the only ones left, wouldn't they? He'd make a fortune selling to some pretty panicked terrorists who'd had to abandon their weapons."

"Why panicked?"

"Amassing weapons isn't the hard part," Raveis said. "It's gathering the small army necessary for the attack. It's getting them here and keeping them hidden till the time to strike. All three hundred of them. A coordinated attack like that would take months to plan, years even. And if suddenly the weapons they were counting on weren't available, well, it'd be back to square one—unless, of course, another seller with the right weapons was to suddenly step forward."

"But that doesn't explain why Carrington would want Cahill and his girlfriend dead."

"The brutal murder of a journalist and her secret lover by a Chechen hit squad would no doubt get the right people asking questions," Raveis said. "You want to break into the twenty-four-hour news cycle these days, kill a young woman. You want to dominate it for a period of time, kill a pretty blonde."

"All the elements are there," Savelle said. "Cahill is from a prominent family, but so was Erica. The media loves to cover rich people. Also, the rich have political connections. And Erica's husband is a loudmouth with both political *and* underworld connections. Plus, investigative journalists from all over would smell blood and come running, especially since Erica was one of their own. One way or another, the right person would make enough noise."

"We can quietly pressure one journalist into backing off in the name of national security, but we couldn't stop a horde of them caught up in a feeding frenzy." Raveis paused before concluding, "Killing Cahill was obviously another attempt by Carrington to expose and ultimately shut down the operation. There was of course no guarantee his death and the death of his journalist girlfriend would be enough to expose the op, though, so we have to assume Carrington possesses other information. Information that he was going to leak at the right time."

Tom said to Savelle, "But if he wanted me to find and kill Cahill—if that was his objective from the start—then why bring me in at all only to have you and I killed the night we met? I mean, why send men to kill me before I could do what he wanted me to do? And why kill you if you were going to help me help him?"

"He needed Raveis and me to believe he was cooperating," Savelle said. "Just like we needed him to believe we trusted him. Delivering you to us was his way of keeping up appearances. Maybe he was hoping you wouldn't actually answer the coded message. Is that possible? And then once you did, he became concerned that he was somehow on the verge of being exposed and decided he'd better get you out of the game as soon as possible, just to be safe."

"But his own men saved us. They were tailing us on his orders."

"Hammerton confirmed that he and Simpson were on a tail-and-protect detail," Raveis said. "We have no reason to think he's lying. At this point, frankly, we don't know what exactly's in play here. It's possible that the Chechens went too far, as Chechens are wont to do from what I understand. Perhaps Carrington wanted you incapacitated, not dead. Also, Simpson was allied with the men you encountered in New Haven, so it could be they had their own plans for you."

Tom thought about that, then looked at Savelle. "You said Carrington had stockpiles. Plural."

She nodded. "Yes."

"How many?"

"We don't know for sure."

"But the place on Front Street was his."

"We believe so, yes. If it were one we already knew about, one Cahill had discovered, then it would have been under surveillance."

"Carrington told me I was being sent there by you via Raveis."

"He lied, Tom," Savelle said. "Everything he has told you is a lie. He sent you there because he needed to separate you from

Stella so his men could grab her. And he needed a private place for his attack dogs to go to work on you. He needed you desperate enough to do what he wanted. He needed to make you willing to kill the man who had saved your life." She paused. "I'm sorry. I really am. I know what he meant to you."

Tom said nothing.

"I don't think he's the man you knew," Savelle said. "Five years in the real world is a long time."

There was, Tom knew, truth to that statement.

Why else would he have lived the way he did prior to finding Stella?

As far off the grid as possible, minding his own business, reading about those who had founded this country and those who had fought for it.

Uncompromising men, incorruptible, proven.

How many men like that would he encounter in today's world?

Better, then, to rely on himself and only himself.

Looking at his wristwatch, Raveis said, "There's still thirty minutes or so before you have to call your girl back and check in." Addressing the room, he added, "I'm thinking we should be able to lay it all out for Tom in thirty minutes, no?"

Tom stared at him. Why was he surprised that Raveis had listened in on his call to Stella?

He shifted his gaze to Savelle, but she would not meet his eyes.

"I understand you got a good look at the serial number of one of the Uzis you guys found." Raveis's look of keen interest remained. "I'm assuming you memorized it."

Tom nodded again.

"Good," Raveis said. "Why don't we start there?"

Forty-Two

Sandy Montrose opened a file and slid it to the center of the table for all to see.

Tom recognized its contents: copies of police reports.

She wrote down on a notepad the series of letters and numbers that Tom recited. Then she laid the notepad next to the top page of the police report.

Everyone gathered at the table could see that the number on the pad and the serial number of the Uzi listed as having been recovered outside the motel varied only by two digits.

"Both firearms came from the same lot," Savelle announced. "Which means the men who came after Cahill got this weapon from the stockpile on Front Street."

"So who owns the property?" Tom said.

"We're in the process of determining that now," Savelle answered. "So far, it seems to be a string of offshore holding companies and investment banks. Obviously, someone is trying to hide his tracks."

"Make finding that out a priority," Raveis told her.

Savelle nodded.

Tom asked about the lab reports.

"I stabbed the man who shot Erica," Cahill said. "In the right calf. That's how I was able to escape with her. A sample of the blood on my knife matched a profile in the FBI database."

Montrose placed a photograph on the table.

It was a mug shot of the man Tom knew only as the Slav.

"Is this him?" Cahill said. "The leader?"

Tom nodded.

"His name is Umar Kadyrov," Raveis said. "A cousin of the Chechen president Ramzan Kadyrov."

"Over the past twenty years, Chechnya has become a model of human rights abuses and repression," Savelle said. "The president himself condones honor killings. Men murdering their wives for, well, you name it. He has embraced strict Islamic codes and enacted laws that allow for the brutal treatment of anyone accused of a crime, particularly minorities, and often without benefit of a trial. A number of minor crimes are now punishable by death—usually by public stoning or beheading. Torture is the norm, and Kadyrov was one of his government's top torturers."

"Kadyrov is a smart man," Cahill said. "He graduated Oxford, where he learned to alter his accent to mask his country of origin. After torturing and killing for his government—and getting paid shit for it—he moved into the private sector and began providing arms to whoever would pay."

"Despite the leanings of the president he faithfully served," Raveis said, "Kadyrov is a capitalist at heart. He'll arm both sides of a civil war, even if only one side can pay, just to keep the conflict going. He has worked with his own government's enemies, and ours, too."

Tom asked Cahill if there was any proof connecting this man with Carrington.

"You brought it to us, Tom. In the phone Hammerton's partner left behind."

"Simpson."

Cahill nodded. "There were two numbers in its call history."

Montrose handed Cahill a small sheet of paper, which he held up for Tom to see.

"Do you recognize either of them?"

The first listed was the number of Carrington's cell.

The number Tom had been told five years ago would be the only number Carrington would ever use to contact him.

Tom nodded, then said, "I don't recognize the second one, though."

"It appeared to be a dead end for us at first, too," Raveis said. "But then Savelle was able to find it among the numbers listed in an old roving wire-tap warrant for a suspected killer-for-hire turned terrorist named Israilov."

Montrose produced another photograph, this one obviously taken from a streetlamp surveillance camera and zoomed in on a particular person.

Tom glanced at the photo and saw the face of the Russian.

The man armed with the Desert Eagle.

The man who had, among other things, lobbed a grenade at him.

Cahill read Tom's expression.

"This man was Kadyrov's bodyguard, correct?"

Tom nodded.

Cahill listed Israilov's credentials.

Spetsnaz—Russian Special Forces.

Then FSB—Federal Security Service, formerly known as the KGB.

Muscle for hire after that, primarily in Eastern Europe, before working full time for Kadyrov beginning two years ago.

At some point during that time, he had become radicalized.

"What about Simpson?"

"He was Treasury," Savelle answered, "resigning shortly after the Secret Service became part of Homeland Security in 2003. He has worked steadily in the private sector since. His passport shows several trips to Eastern European countries, but each trip syncs up with his employment history. Carrington hired him a little over a month ago and quickly moved him into his own personal security detail."

She paused before continuing, "You have to wonder why Carrington would do that. Assign a man he had just hired to his own protection team."

Cahill said, "Apparently, Hammerton had his doubts about Simpson from day one. Nothing specific, he says, just a gut feeling. And you said it was obvious to you that Simpson was working with Kadyrov. He suddenly took point after you found the cache and led you upstairs. He brought you straight to the room where Kadyrov and his men were waiting."

"It all links up," Savelle said.

"It's still only circumstantial."

"Fortunately, we're not building a legal case here," Raveis said.

"How convenient for you," Tom said. He turned to Savelle and Cahill. "The fact that Israilov's number was in Simpson's phone doesn't necessarily connect Carrington to Israilov. And of course Carrington's number was in Simpson's phone; Simpson worked for Carrington."

Savelle said, "The fact that the phone contains just those two numbers suggests it's a burner phone, Tom. Also, the call history—the calls from it to Carrington and to it from Israilov—only started two days ago. Friday morning, to be specific. Don't you think Carrington would take note if one of his employees suddenly started contacting him from a strange number? Hammerton certainly thinks he would. In fact, according to Hammerton, Carrington provided them both with phones that were designated for business use only, nothing else."

Tom recalled the look of surprise on Simpson's face at the end.

And how the man opened his mouth as if to speak right before being shot.

"So when the first attempt on your life failed," Cahill continued, "Carrington adapted and decided to see if he could use you. He eavesdropped on you, heard you and Stella talk on Saturday, and when he learned she'd discovered where I was, he saw another chance to have me killed."

"How could Carrington have found Stella, though? In the motel, I mean. No one tailed us there, I'm sure of it."

"A tracking device had been planted on Erica's car," Cahill said. "It was well hidden and wasn't discovered by the police till after the preliminary reports you were given had been written. That's how the Chechens knew where to find us. A few hours ago, Sandy's husband went to where Hammerton said your truck was parked. He found an identical tracking device attached to it. And in the exact same, hard-to-find place. Same manufacturer, same model."

Savelle said, "Hammerton tells us that when he and Simpson were sent to tail you in the city, Simpson disappeared for about fifteen minutes, which Hammerton agrees would have been just enough time for Simpson to make it to where you had parked your truck, attach the device, and then catch back up with him." She paused. "How many lies has Carrington told you in the last forty-eight hours? There's a point when even loyalty has to give way to the facts. He betrayed his country, Tom, in the worst way possible. And he betrayed you."

Tom looked at each person in the room.

Cahill first, then Raveis, then Montrose, ending finally with Savelle.

The woman with whom he had almost burned.

"So what now?"

"That doesn't concern you," Cahill said.

His tone was abrupt, almost matter-of-fact.

He was a man ready to take action, at last.

No time to waste.

No need for pleasantries.

Raveis's demeanor was different, however.

"We'll take it from here, Tom," he said.

Friendly and assuring, grateful in a way that was almost fatherly.

There was no doubt in his mind what that meant for Carrington.

What Tom needed to know right then, though, was what it meant for Stella and himself.

He expressed that concern.

"We have no way of knowing if Carrington and Kadyrov believe you and Hammerton were killed in the explosion," Savelle said. "If Carrington is still monitoring the listening device in your apartment, he would have heard Stella on the phone a little while ago, and it would be obvious from her side of the conversation that she was talking to you. Even if that is the case and he knows you're alive, I doubt he'd come after the two of you."

"Why?"

"Because he has bigger problems now," Cahill said.

Tom looked at him.

"Within twenty-four hours, they'll all be dead. Carrington and Kadyrov and Israilov. I can guarantee that much." Cahill paused, then said, "You deserve your life, Tom. You've earned it. I told you I wanted to get you back to it as soon as possible. So return to it, don't look back, and everything will be fine."

Tom knew a veiled threat when he heard one.

Maybe not a threat, exactly.

But a warning to steer clear and forget—and speak of none of this to anyone.

Tom didn't respond to what Cahill had said, nor did he really care how Cahill had said it.

He had, after all, every intention of doing all those things and more.

Savelle instructed Montrose to escort Tom outside so he could make his call.

Tom took one more look at Cahill.

The man's eyes were fixed, narrowed.

Before him stood a man with only one thing on his mind.

Vengeance.

But would any man, knowing what Cahill now knew, appear any different?

Feel any different, think any different?

Before Tom could step away from the table, Raveis extended his hand.

"You did good, son," he said.

Tom didn't see the point in refusing to accept the gesture.

He took Raveis's hand and shook it, then followed Montrose through the mazelike bunker and back to the steep metal stairs that led up.

He suddenly craved the feel and smell of open air.

More than that, he sensed that he was mere moments from heading home.

He told himself that within an hour, barring something he could not foresee, he would be with Stella again.

Forty-Three

Tom stood in the still-muddied driveway, facing east so he could see the dawn breaking as he called Stella.

Standing beside him, Montrose made no attempt to hide that she was listening closely to his side of the conversation.

But it was the possibility that others were listening to Stella as she stood in her apartment that concerned him more.

"How'd it go?" she said.

Tom replied, "It went."

"How are you?"

"I'm okay."

"You sure?"

"Yeah."

"Are you in danger right now?"

"No."

"Are we?"

"They seem to think we're in the clear."

"They?"

"We'll talk when I'm there."

Stella let out a quiet sigh, then asked how much longer before Tom would be leaving.

"A few minutes, I think. I'll text you when I'm on my way."

"Okay."

"Is everyone still there?"

"Yes."

"I need you to do something, but I have to tell you something first."

"What?"

"The bug in the apartment, it seems it was put there some time before Friday night."

Tom heard only silence from Stella's end.

He knew what was more than likely running through her mind.

The frantic calculation of all the things that had been said and done in the apartment since Friday.

It wouldn't take long before that calculation narrowed to what she and Tom had done in the privacy of her dark bedroom that night.

The specific things she had said, for her pleasure as well as his.

Those dark and twisted thoughts she could never explain, and that he would never ask her to.

"You all right?" Tom said.

"Yeah."

"I'm sorry."

"Don't be. What do I care, right? So what is it you need me to do?"

"Ask Conrad and his buddies to locate and disable the listening device. And tell them that with a note; don't say anything. Understand?"

"Yes. Anything else?"

"We're going to need some new phones."

"I'll have someone make a run."

"There's a convenience store just past the McDonald's that's open twenty-four hours. They sell prepaid phones there."

"Sounds good."

"Better get some extras, just in case."

"How many?"

"Make it four."

"Okay."

Tom paused. "I'll be there soon, Stella."

"Good."

"I love you."

"I love you, too, Tom. Very much." She paused. "Come straight home, okay?"

"Yes, ma'am."

They ended the call. Tom looked at his phone before finally pocketing it.

Montrose said, "How is she holding up?"

When Tom didn't respond, Montrose said, "You know, your friend Hammerton will have to keep his movements to a minimum for a few days. It would be good if he had someone to keep an eye on him, just in case. And I'd imagine, for obvious reasons, his apartment in the city is the last place he should be right now."

Without hesitation, Tom said, "He'll come home with me."

Montrose smiled. "Good. Thanks."

Tom looked at the barn.

"Cahill paid for all that? The renovations, the underground shelter?"

Montrose nodded. "He helped us buy this place, too. And helped get Kevin's practice up and running. He has always been extremely generous to me." She paused. "Not a lot of money in being a prep school physician."

"So why do you do it?"

She shrugged. "Tradition, I guess. My father had lived a quiet life. I hated it growing up, but when I got back from Iraq, it was all I wanted. There was . . . I don't know . . . dignity in it. In the things he did behind the scenes. Being a role model to kids like Cahill, changing their lives, setting them on a better course."

"Your father meant a lot to Cahill."

"They were very close. Cahill spent a lot of time with our family. And he joined the marines because of my father. He did a lot of things because of him." She paused. "Men and their father figures, right? It's a bond that lasts, you know."

Tom ignored that.

"You knew the work Cahill was doing?" he said.

"Yes."

"And you knew about his affair with Erica DiSalvo?"

"No. No one did. He kept that a secret."

"Are you sure?"

"Yes."

Tom studied Montrose but said nothing.

It was clear that she was thinking about something.

Something that bothered her deeply.

"He had to bury her body," she said finally. "Can you imagine doing that? Not only watching the person you love die, but having to stick her body in the ground and cover it up, leave her there in the dirt for God knows how long. Like a criminal covering his tracks, but really the act of a patriot, you know? Even in his grief, even at his lowest, he remembered that lives were at stake. If he failed, then others would die, too. I know a part of what's driving him right now is his need to have her family notified. They must be suffering terribly, not knowing if their daughter is alive or dead. That has to be weighing on him, you know. I don't even think he cares what happens after. What happens to him. The legal actions he may face. There's no reasoning with him, no talking him out of it. Trust me, I've tried."

Again, Tom said nothing.

"He hasn't slept since he got here," Montrose continued. "He's hiding it, or trying to, doing what a marine is supposed to do. But he's a wreck inside. He never once regretted doing what needed to be done for his country, over there or here. But I'm not sure he'll ever be right again. Not after this. He blames himself for what happened. He says he shouldn't have loved her, that he put her life at risk. I know he truly believed he could protect her, though."

She paused. "I think he sees this as a suicide mission. I think there's a part of him that welcomes that. And that scares the shit out of me."

Tom wanted to know more, had questions. There were things that didn't completely make sense to him.

But before he could speak, a vehicle turned into the driveway, followed quickly by another.

Two black SUVs, driving aggressively.

Instinctively, Tom stepped between Montrose and the rapidly approaching vehicles.

"It's okay," she said. "It's Raveis's men from the city."

She and Tom moved from the driveway to the wet grass.

The SUVs passed and continued to the barn, where they stopped.

The doors opened and a dozen men in suits climbed out.

The sight of them chased any and all questions from Tom's mind.

It was time to get out of there.

Kevin Montrose emerged from the farmhouse, his AR-15 slung over his shoulder.

Watching the men, he crossed the yard to where Tom and his wife were standing.

"Savelle just called on the landline," he said. "We're leaving right now."

"What's wrong?" Montrose asked.

Kevin addressed Tom as he answered. "Apparently, some of Raveis's men moved against Carrington a few minutes ago. He got the jump on them, killed them all, and has now disappeared."

Montrose looked at Tom, who said nothing.

Tom got the sense that she recognized the significance of this. Of Carrington and Cahill having switched roles.

The irony of the hunted now being the hunter, and vice versa.

Kevin said, "Savelle wanted me to tell you that they doubt they'll need your help flushing out Carrington. But if they do, would you be willing?"

Roughly thirty-six hours ago, Tom had been asked a similar question about Cahill.

Would he help find him and, if necessary, bring him in?

But there was a difference here.

The difference between finding a man in need of aid and finding a man marked for execution.

A man found guilty without the benefit of a trial before a jury of his peers.

Despite Tom's grogginess, he made his decision quickly.

"I have work tomorrow morning," he said.

"So that's a no."

"I can't help. Sorry."

"He was like a father to you, wasn't he?" Montrose said finally. "Your former CO. It's a terrible thing when the person closest to us turns on us," she said. "Uses everything they know about us against us."

Tom thought about that.

The things Kadyrov had known and said—all meant to coerce Tom as quickly as possible.

Force him into embracing cold-blooded murder as if it were self-defense.

The moral thing to do.

The only thing to do.

The only *choice* to make.

"You know, you're welcome to stay," Montrose said. "Stella, too. Till all this blows over. You'll be safe here. And this way you'll be in the loop. When Carrington is killed, you'll know it right away. Same with Kadyrov. That might be better than holing up in your place, waiting for the worst."

Tom shook his head. "No. But thanks."

"I guess I'd rather be in my own home, too," she said. "At some point, we have to stand our ground, right? If you change your mind, though, or if something does happen, we're here, okay? We'll help. And meanwhile, Kevin will drive you and your friend back to your truck."

Tom thanked her.

As he stepped away, Montrose reached into the pocket of her raincoat, removed an envelope, and offered it to him.

"I almost forgot," she said. "I was told to give this to you."

He could tell by the shape and thickness of the envelope that it contained cash.

A stack of it.

"Who told you to give that to me?"

"Raveis."

Tom said, "Keep it."

Then he turned and took one last look at the men in suits.

Two stood on either side of the door, guarding it, while the rest entered the barn.

He thought of Carrington getting the better of men like them.

Fighting his way through an ambush before running for deep cover, which was likely what the man had done.

But could he stay hidden forever?

Could anyone, really, in today's world?

Tom knew the answer to that.

Knew it was only a matter of time before Carrington was hunted down.

The combined resources of Raveis and Savelle and Cahill were just too formidable.

Tom didn't care, though—couldn't care.

Like Cahill, there was only one thing on his mind now.

One direction in which he wanted to head.

Forty-Four

Tom followed Kevin to the farmhouse.

Inside the kitchen door, Kevin paused and reached into his shirt pocket.

Removing a slip of paper, he showed it to Tom.

On it was a phone number.

Tom recognized the handwriting as Savelle's, but the number was different from the one she had shown him two nights before in the sedan.

"If you have any trouble, call this number," Kevin said. "A suspicious car you don't like the sight of, a medical emergency or quick exfil, even trouble with the law, anything from a traffic ticket to a weapons charge. You name it and they will take care of it, and fast."

Tom took the card and placed it in his shirt pocket, along with his single .45 round.

"So let's get you guys on the road," Kevin said.

Hammerton was in a small room off the tavern-style living room.

Cleaned up like Tom, his cuts tended to, he was stretched out on a cot placed against the wall, one arm at his side, the other draped over his eyes.

He looked anything but comfortable.

Tom approached and asked how he was doing.

"I'm good," Hammerton said.

It was an obvious lie, spoken more for Hammerton's own benefit than Tom's.

Tom helped him up to his feet and wedged in beside him, then wound Hammerton's right arm around his neck.

Together they made it outside to an extended-cab pickup parked behind the farmhouse.

Hammerton sat in the back, Tom in the passenger seat, Kevin behind the wheel.

From his jacket, Kevin removed Hammerton's SIG p226, its slide locked back and breech open.

He handed the empty pistol back to Hammerton, along with its magazine.

"I don't have any spare SIG mags," Kevin said. "But I loaded yours for you."

Hammerton took the pistol, inserted the mag into the grip, and released the slide.

"Thanks," he said.

Another pair of black SUVs was just arriving as Kevin steered the truck around the horseshoe-shaped driveway and down to the main road.

The sudden activity overtaking the small farm reminded Tom of the forward operating base where he and Cahill had met.

Rushing vehicles, armed men moving about with purpose, an atmosphere of imminent danger—this had been their daily life back then.

Tom had left that world behind, though the war he'd been a small part of was still ongoing.

He would be glad to leave this world behind as well, its own secret war just gearing up.

He'd chosen a different life for himself and was finally free now to return to it.

Return to it and never look back.

He embraced that phrase like a new mantra, replacing the one he'd been taught by Carrington more than a decade ago.

The one he'd hung on to for all that time.

The only way out is through.

Once Kevin Montrose's pickup was northbound on Route 63, Tom sent Stella a text that contained just two words.

Coming home.

Once they reached the commuter lot off Route 8, Tom retrieved a flashlight from the toolbox mounted to the truck's bed and searched every inch of his vehicle, top to bottom, engine compartment to rear bumper.

Only when he was certain that there was no tracking device anywhere did he help Hammerton into the passenger seat.

Every movement caused the man pain, but he bore it well, like a former SAS trooper would.

Hammerton settled into the seat, the SIG resting in his lap, his right hand loose around the grip. Tom retrieved the empty Colt 1911 from his toolbox mounted to the truck bed.

Getting in behind the wheel, Tom handed the pistol to Hammerton and told him that the magazines were in the center console.

As Tom drove, Hammerton inserted a mag into the Colt, then racked the slide, chambering the round.

Tom removed the cartridge from his shirt pocket and gave it to Hammerton, who dropped the mag from the Colt and topped it off with that round.

Reinserting the fully loaded mag, he passed the locked and cocked Colt to Tom, who placed it between the driver's seat and center console.

Neither said anything for much of the ride.

At first, Tom checked the rearview mirror frequently to make certain they weren't being followed.

Hammerton did the same with the side view mirror beyond the passenger window.

As the miles ticked by, neither man saw anything he didn't like.

By the time they had passed through Litchfield, it became clear that they weren't being tailed or driving into an ambush.

It seemed more and more likely they just might make it home without a fight.

Eventually both men, exhausted and injured, became lost in thought, Tom finding himself driving for long stretches at times as if on automatic pilot.

Barely seeing the road ahead, his numbed mind wandering.

Still, he had the presence of mind to recognize, when he reached it, the exact strip of grass-lined road he had dreamed about a few hours before.

The spot where the vehicle he had stolen simply died and, stepping out, he had found himself back in the desert.

And face-to-face with Carrington.

We're in more danger than you know, the man had said.

It seemed to Tom that even in his dreams, his former commanding officer only spoke lies.

It was just after seven when Tom pulled into his spot in the lot behind Stella's building.

Looking up at the bedroom window, he saw that Stella was standing in it.

Just as she had been when he'd left for New York City two nights before.

They stared at each other for a moment before Stella stepped quickly away. Tom opened the driver's door and climbed out.

Two state troopers dressed in street clothes appeared and escorted Tom as he helped Hammerton around to the sidewalk.

Canaan Village was empty, as it should be so early on a Sunday morning.

Empty save for the five state trooper cruisers parked like a blockade along the curb outside Stella's building.

Tom got his friend as far as the front entrance.

Once inside the stairwell, the door closed and locked behind them, the two troopers took over and together got Hammerton up the narrow stairs.

It was only after the three of them were inside the apartment and leading Hammerton to the couch that Stella appeared in the open doorway above, Conrad standing behind her.

She said nothing as Tom began to climb the steep steps.

He moved steadily upward, never taking his eyes off her.

At the top, Tom closed the remaining distance between them and wrapped his arms around Stella, pulling her close.

Conrad quietly retreated into the kitchen as Stella wound her arms up and around Tom's back, clinging to him fiercely.

They stayed that way for a while.

Forty-Five

Tom struggled all that day with a troubled sleep.

This was not the restorative sleep he had counted on.

The sleep that would prepare him for work tomorrow morning, the sleep during which his cuts and burns and bruises would begin to heal.

This was the restlessness of a man wrestling with doubts he was as yet unable to fully understand.

Lying still, Stella motionless beside him, Tom's tired mind was plagued by images he could not shake.

Images of what Stella had endured—what he had viewed, helpless, via the webcam.

More than any other image, he saw Stella in a prone shooting position on that motel bathroom floor, firing her .357 at her attackers.

Men who had come to take her.

Men who would not hesitate to torment her, if ordered.

But it wasn't just images that replayed for Tom.

He heard the words Kadyrov had spoken, too.

The threats the man had made in an effort to coerce Tom.

As well as the private details Kadyrov had shared.

Details that only someone who had been eavesdropping on Tom and Stella on Friday night could know.

You two like it rough, no?

She says things to you about all the other men in town.

Tom's tumbling mind eventually shifted to events that had not occurred.

He saw self-inflicted projections of the terror Stella would have faced had she not been armed.

Had her father not passed on to her certain skills—skills that Tom had no idea she possessed but was immensely grateful that she did.

Gradually, though, Tom began to realize that it was more than that, more than Stella's retreating to the bathroom and running the shower as a diversion and positioning herself on the floor that had saved her.

More than her marksmanship and ability to stay calm and think.

Because her skills would not have mattered had the men sent by Carrington been smarter.

Had they known that she was armed and acted accordingly, had they adjusted their approach to the closed bathroom door, as Tom would have done.

A frightening thing, then, Tom thought, for Stella's life to have hinged on Carrington not passing along that one simple but crucial detail.

On Carrington failing to warn the men he had sent to abduct Stella of the powerful firearm in her possession . . .

The gray November sky beyond their bedroom window was beginning to darken when Tom finally gave up on sleep.

Sitting up, he moved to the edge of the mattress, doing so carefully so as not to disturb Stella.

He felt as if his unconscious mind had been building a case.

Had been working to filter through the noise of the past two days and eventually lock on to something that Tom could not ignore.

A singular fact that stood out.

A contradiction that had to be reconciled.

In the name of justice.

He worked backward, starting with the conversation he had with Sandy Montrose prior to leaving her farm.

You knew the work Cahill was doing? Tom had asked.

Yes.

And you knew about his affair with Erica DiSalvo?

No. No one did. He kept that a secret.

Something else she had said emerged.

I know he truly believed he could protect her.

And then another comment.

It's a terrible thing when the person closest to us turns on us. Uses everything they know about us against us.

From there Tom moved farther back, to when he was standing in the underground bunker with Savelle and Raveis and Cahill.

A tracking device had been placed on Erica's car, Cahill had said. *That's how the Chechens knew where to find us.*

Then Cahill had concluded, *Same make, same model.*

And finally, Raveis had said, *It's clear what this evidence tells us.*

It's still only circumstantial, Tom had protested.

Fortunately, we aren't building a legal case here.

Tom dwelled on that for a while before recalling the things that had been said to him by Kadyrov, captor to captive.

I'm told the freedom to choose is important to you, and that giving you a choice in this matter might make things go more quickly.

That's all that's being asked of you. To kill for your country one more time.

You can save her. You can choose to save her. Simply kill a traitor.

You needn't bother yourself with the why, Tomas. It's best for men like us to leave the big picture to those who are paid to think on that scale . . .

Finally, Tom remembered meeting with Carrington at Tallmadge's tomb in Litchfield.

Keep your eyes open, okay? Carrington had said. *Trust your gut. If you see something you don't like, just get the hell out of there. You owe Cahill, yes, but he may not be the man you remember.*

And then, moments later:

Simpson has a sidearm for you.

I'd rather if it comes down to it that your life didn't depend on a relic from seventy years ago.

Simpson had handed him the Beretta and spare magazine.

After Carrington was long gone.

———

It didn't take long before Tom was on his feet and pulling on his jeans.

From the darkness, Stella whispered, "Everything okay?"

Tom zipped up and sat on the edge of the bed.

"We're okay," he said. "But we need to leave."

"Why?"

Several strands of Stella's curls obscured her eyes.

Tom gently brushed them away as he thought of his drug-induced dream about Carrington.

The two of them back in the desert, Carrington disappearing into the rising sandstorm, speaking as he did.

Tom had no intention of keeping the truth from Stella.

She deserved to know everything he knew.

"Because I think we're in more danger than I realized," he said.

Stella nodded and asked Tom what he needed her to do.

He told her to get dressed, and that he was going to talk to Hammerton for a few minutes, after which they would be heading out.

"Where to?"

"I'm not sure yet. I'd like you to call Conrad, okay?"

"Why?"

"So he can take you somewhere safe. Somewhere I don't even know about."

"Why somewhere you don't know about?"

"Just in case."

"In case of what?"

"In case this goes wrong again."

Stella shook her head and said flatly, "No, Tom. I'm coming with you."

"It will be easier for me to do what I have to do if I know you're safe."

"Will I really be safe anywhere? And anyway, that's not the point. I can't sit in some motel again, staring at a can of coins balanced on a doorknob. And I don't want to be surrounded by a bunch of men, waiting for a cell phone to ring or not ring. I need to be beside you, okay? I'd rather die with you than live without you. So I'm either riding along with you or following you in my own car. That much is your choice. But the rest isn't negotiable. Okay?"

Tom didn't have it in him to fight her.

And anyway, he knew she was right.

He said, "You'll do what I say, when I say it."

"I won't let you down, Tom. I promise."

They looked at each other for a moment.

Tom remembered what Sandy Montrose had said about Cahill's guilt over Erica DiSalvo's death.

I know he truly believed he could protect her.

Tom would have no choice, then, but to succeed where Cahill had failed.

It was as simple as that.

"Pack only what you need," Tom said. "I'll be in the living room."

Tom stood and finished dressing—T-shirt, black sweater, work boots.

On his nightstand were the cocked and locked 1911, the two spare mags, his multitool and keys, driver's license and pistol permit, as well as a new prepaid smartphone and emergency cash.

One thousand dollars.

Not a lot to run on.

Nor the biggest operational budget, especially when compared to what those he might have to stand against had at their disposal.

But it was something, and every edge counted now.

Tom picked up the 1911 and confirmed that the thumb safety was engaged before tucking the firearm into his waistband at the small of his back.

Distributing the other items among various pockets, he waited till Stella was dressed—jeans over boy shorts, black T-shirt over her pearls, cardigan over that.

Another phone, identical to Tom's, was on Stella's nightstand alongside her .357 Smith and Wesson.

Stella was reaching for them both as Tom left the bedroom.

Hammerton was asleep on the living room couch.

Despite the fact that the room was lit only by the pale glow of the streetlights outside the windows, Tom could see his SIG p226 resting on the coffee table.

Within Hammerton's easy reach.

Tom quietly walked to one of the two front windows that overlooked Main Street.

He scanned the sidewalks and street thoroughly, saw nothing he didn't like, nothing he hadn't seen every evening during his six months there.

A peaceful and isolated small town, more or less unchanged for decades.

The kind of place in which a man like him could come safely to a stop for a time.

But that time may have run its course.

Tom was aware that there was a very good chance they would not be returning anytime soon—if at all.

Stepping away from the window, he entered the small kitchen.

On the table was a glass of water containing the listening device that Conrad and his buddies had found during their basement-to-attic search of Stella's building.

Smaller than a housefly, it had been dropped in the water immediately upon discovery to render it inert.

Also on the table was Tom's Kindle.

He stared at both items for a moment before finally returning to the living room.

The sound of his approach woke Hammerton, who immediately reached out for his weapon.

"It's okay," Tom said. "It's me."

Hammerton's arm remained extended, his hand lingering on the pistol's grip. "What's up?"

"We need to talk."

"What about?"

"Carrington."

Hammerton paused before withdrawing his hand.

"Something on your mind, Tom?"

"Yeah."

Hammerton nodded. "All right, mate," he said. "Pull up a chair. Let's talk."

Forty-Six

Tom sat leaning forward, the narrow coffee table between himself and Hammerton.

Sitting up on the couch, Hammerton breathed out sharply.

"You okay?" Tom said.

Hammerton nodded.

It was obviously yet another attempt to deny his condition—for his benefit as well as Tom's.

Before Tom could say anything more, Hammerton said, "So what's got you up?"

"Carrington's on the run, which means he either deactivated or disposed of his cell phone. I have no way of reaching him, but I'm hoping you do."

"Why?"

"I want to talk to him."

Hammerton thought about that, then said, "What are you thinking?"

"What if Carrington wasn't behind this after all?"

"How could he not be?"

"Exactly."

"I'm not following."

"It all adds up, right? Carrington sent us to where Kadyrov and his men were waiting to ambush us while another team of men took the room next to Stella's, ready to ambush her. Men who were listening to her, just in case she put together all the clues that had been laid out for me and figured out where Cahill was hiding."

"What do you mean by laid out for you?"

"Kadyrov said it himself, remember? Not only did those files contain everything I would need to find Cahill, they contained everything that would make me *want* to find him. Feel obligated to find him."

Hammerton nodded, then said, "I remember that, yeah."

"And how did Carrington know where Stella was? Because a tracking device on my pickup led him there—a device Simpson likely planted while I was meeting with Raveis and Savelle. One virtually identical to the tracking device the police found on Cahill's girlfriend's car. Obviously, Simpson was working with Kadyrov, right? Simpson took point and led us right to where he was waiting. And Israilov killed Simpson before he could blow his cover. Also, Simpson's cell phone very nicely connects Carrington with Kadyrov, and Carrington ordered Simpson to provide me with a sidearm—one that, it turns out, had its firing pin removed. To top all this off, you and I found a cache of weapons, including a crate of Uzis from the same lot as the Uzi used by the Chechen hit team sent to kill Cahill. Open-and-shut case, right?"

"Right."

"And Carrington knows me, knows what matters to me. So obviously he had to have been the one who instructed Kadyrov on how to manipulate me. Everything Kadyrov said had to have come straight from Carrington's mouth, right? From the one man who knew me better than anyone else, who knew things about me even Stella didn't know."

"But if it wasn't from Carrington, who did it come from?"

"You've been working for Carrington from the start, right?"

Hammerton nodded.

Tom leaned closer.

"I know that Carrington recruits for the CIA," he said. "Identifies and screens potential candidates. I take it you helped him with that."

Hammerton hesitated, then nodded again.

"How was that done? What were the protocols?"

"We'd monitor computer and cell phone usage, credit card charges, family history, affiliations, travel history, sex life, you name it. Full and complete surveillance, twenty-four-seven."

"Illegal surveillance."

"Yes."

"Did that include hacking e-mail accounts?"

"Yes."

"What about a potential candidate's reading habits? Wouldn't that tell you a lot about him? What was important to him?"

"Of course."

"So anyone who knew what I had read over the past five years would have a tremendous insight, right? They'd distill and compile and from there know what makes me tick, what buttons to push, right?"

Hammerton said, "All that stuff about it being your choice. And the appeals to your patriotism."

"Everything Kadyrov said led me to believe it was coming from Carrington. He even implied Carrington apologized for what he was about to do. But it could have just as easily come from anyone who had access to my reading list. Who either hacked my Kindle or hacked my e-mail account, which contained the receipts for every book I had purchased."

Hammerton looked at Tom. "Okay, but who?"

"That's the question, isn't it?"

The bedroom door opened and Stella stepped into the living room, carrying an oversize purse.

She placed it on a chair, then stood behind Tom.

He said to Hammerton, "If one of the protocols for choosing candidates was illegal surveillance, does that mean you and Carrington bugged private residences?"

"Yes."

"Did you have anything as advanced as what's at the bottom of that glass of water in my kitchen?"

Hammerton shook his head. "I've never seen anything like that before. Anything that small. Usually by the time a piece of tech reaches the private sector, we've heard about it. Speculation, rumors, often for years. But I've not heard one thing about something like that. That's top secret, no doubt about it. But that doesn't rule out the possibility that Carrington got his hands on it somehow."

"That's the thing, though," Tom said. "Kadyrov alluded to some things only someone who had been listening to Stella and me on Friday could have known. Things that were said *before* I went into the city. Carrington was eavesdropping on me from the time I met him in the city Friday night to when I met with him again on Saturday afternoon in Litchfield. He admitted to that much."

"The flip phone with the hot mic," Hammerton said.

"Right. During that time, he would have heard Stella offering me her .357 and me refusing it. That happened Saturday morning. A few hours later, a friend of hers showed up with her father's old 1911. Carrington heard that, knew Stella had given the 1911 to me, which is why he wanted me to take the Beretta instead. And yes, it was on Carrington's orders, but it was Simpson who handed me the Beretta. He had his hands on the weapon last. And you and I both know it would take two, three minutes tops to remove the firing pin from a Beretta with just basic tools. Do you think Simpson would have had the time to do that between when Carrington told him to bring along a spare sidearm and when he had handed it to me?"

"Yeah, he would have. Actually, he would have had several chances to do that."

"And the three men who came after Stella in the motel, they weren't acting like men who knew their target was armed. You were right next to me; you saw the video feed. They entered like their target was soft. They walked right up to the bathroom door and stood in front of it, didn't fan out, didn't use the door frames as cover. Remember, Carrington *knew* Stella was armed because he was listening when she offered me her .357 and I refused it. So if those men were working for him, if he'd been behind this from the start and thinking moves ahead of all of us, wouldn't he have tipped them off that she had a weapon? And if they had been tipped off, wouldn't they have approached her more cautiously?"

Hammerton nodded and said, "You would think so, yeah."

"Whoever was listening to Stella and me on Friday night, though, wouldn't have had that information. That tells me that it couldn't have been Carrington who bugged us Friday. It had to be someone else. Someone who had been listening Friday night here but not Saturday morning in the motel. Someone who told Kadyrov what to say."

"Who wanted to convince you that Carrington was behind this."

"Yeah. And if Simpson was working for someone else—if he planted the tracking device on my truck for them while I was in the city Friday night—then there is no way Carrington could have known what motel Stella was in. And if he didn't know, then he couldn't have sent those men there to abduct her."

Hammerton was silent for a moment.

"But why would someone want that?" he said finally. "Want you to believe it was Carrington who wanted you to kill Cahill?"

"If they got me to do what they wanted—and I somehow came out of it alive—then I'd spend the rest of my life hunting

Carrington down. And if I found him and killed him, that would be that, wouldn't it? Cahill would be dead, Carrington would be dead, and I'd spend the rest of my life in hiding, which was more or less how I lived before I met Stella. I'd just disappear again, right? Only this time I'd go off the grid completely."

Hammerton thought about that, then said, "So Carrington had no idea what was waiting for us when he sent us to Front Street."

"He was just following orders. Savelle's orders via Raveis, to be precise."

"So either Savelle or Raveis set us up. Sent us to that building so Kadyrov and his goons could go to work on you. But which one, Tom? I mean, for that matter, they could be working together, right?"

"Add up all the hurt," Tom said. "Cahill was attacked and almost killed. You were attacked and almost killed. Savelle and I were almost burned alive. And this morning, Carrington was attacked. There's only one person in this whole mess without a mark on him. And who has managed to keep himself from being directly linked to any of the murders or attempted murders."

"Raveis," Hammerton said.

Tom nodded. "Carrington gave Savelle my cell number so she could contact me. I'm willing to bet that's how Raveis determined my location, either through Savelle or someone else. He has the connections—CIA, FBI, you name it—so she's not his only asset. And Savelle first started calling me on Friday morning, which would have given Raveis enough time to send a team up here to plant the bug. I was at work and Stella was out all day. Plus we have no security system, so slipping in and out wouldn't take much at all."

"But if Raveis was behind the hit on Cahill—if he hired the Chechens to kill Cahill and his girlfriend—then why would he recruit you to track Cahill down only to send another hit team after you and Savelle a half hour later? That doesn't make sense."

"Everybody works for someone," Tom said.

"Meaning Raveis needed someone to think he was seriously trying to find Cahill."

"He's desperate to hide his crimes. Maybe everything he said to me about Carrington was really about himself. Maybe he's playing all of us against one another. I don't know, but when that second hit team failed, thanks to you, he adapted, saw his chance to use me after all."

Hammerton said nothing.

"You know the first law of combat," Tom said. "No plan ever survives first contact."

"But why would he want to kill Savelle, too? I mean, she's his asset. And a valuable one."

Tom shrugged. "Collateral damage. Don't imagine he'd care much about that. Or maybe Savelle suspected he was up to something. He could have known that and panicked."

"First of all, Tom, men like Raveis don't panic. And they don't hire blunt instruments like Chechen gangs to go after loose threads. Second, you said he was desperate to hide his crimes. What crimes?"

"Treason, for starters," Tom said. "The weapons cache we found. The means to purchase a building and hide the paper trail through a series of dummy companies. Not to mention the connections necessary to get his hands on a top-secret listening device. And who better to outsmart Cahill—find his secret girlfriend, someone Cahill's closest friend didn't even know about, and use her to ambush him—than the man who trained him? It's all Raveis. It has to be. Simpson, Kadyrov, both Chechen hit teams—they were all working for Raveis."

Hammerton thought about all that, said finally, "This is a big can of worms we're thinking of opening. Raveis's organization, it's . . . monstrous. The guy isn't even a person, technically. He's a multimillion-dollar corporation with his own private army. You've seen his personal protection detail. That's just a fraction of the men he employs. And he has created dozens of Cahills. Hundreds maybe. Which is why I don't see him hiring a bunch of thugs he couldn't count on or control. But with all his resources, all his money and manpower, we can forget about fighting him. I'm not even sure we could hide from him for long."

"Maybe we won't have to do either."

"What do you have in mind?"

"Cahill needs to know he's hunting the wrong man. I can't reach him, but I'm betting Savelle can."

"And he'll just believe you?"

"He can't ignore the facts."

"You *want* to believe, Tom. He doesn't. He won't. I saw the look in his eyes. He's out for blood, and right now he smells it. You'll need proof. Something more than all this, anyway."

"Then we'll get proof."

"How?"

"We need to talk to Carrington."

"What good would that do?"

"You had your doubts about Simpson all along, right? And Savelle said it didn't make sense for Carrington to hire someone like Simpson and move him into his private detail right away. Any idea why Carrington would do that?"

"All he ever said to me was that he was doing someone a favor."

"I'd be interested to know who that someone was, wouldn't you? Because I'm thinking it was Raveis. That's the only way all this was going to work. Raveis needed Simpson close to Carrington, and who's closer than a bodyguard? Simpson had to be there to put the device on my truck and, the next day, hand me a disabled pistol. He had to be there to get us up those stairs and off our guard. If we can prove this—prove to Cahill that it is Raveis and not Carrington who is behind all this, and if we can get Cahill on our side—then maybe we have a chance."

"A chance at what? Killing Raveis?"

"Getting our lives back."

"And if Cahill won't listen to reason? If it comes down to you having to put yourself between him and Carrington? Could you do that? Could you make that choice?"

Tom was silent for a long time.

Finally, he said, "Does Carrington have another contact number? An emergency burner phone, something?"

"He does. But if he believes we're dead, he'll think it's a trap and won't respond."

"I might have a way around that."

"How?"

"I'll tell you on the way. Are you able to move?"

Hammerton nodded. "Yeah."

Another lie, but neither man cared about that just then.

Forty-Seven

They left the apartment lights on and moved to the empty retail space below to use it as a staging area.

The dark storefront crowded with stacks of furniture would also provide them with cover, should the building be under active surveillance.

Or should someone suddenly storm it.

They'd come too far and sacrificed too much to act foolishly now.

In the small back room, out of sight, Hammerton keyed the number of Carrington's emergency burner phone into one of Tom's four "clean" phones.

Once the last digit had been input, Hammerton looked at Tom and said, "So what do I text?"

Tom recited four numbers.

Hammerton entered them, asking what those numbers were as he did.

"The year Benjamin Tallmadge died," Tom said.

Hammerton pressed "Send," then looked at Tom. "And who the fuck is Benjamin Tallmadge?"

Tom smiled but said nothing.

"How long do you think we'll have to wait?" Stella said.

Before Tom could do more than shrug, the phone in Hammerton's hand rang.

He handed it to Tom.

"I'm guessing this is for you," he said.

Tom quickly pressed the "Speaker" button.

From the other end, a familiar voice came through. "You're alive."

Tom said, "It's good to hear your voice, sir."

Carrington being Carrington, there were safeguards to address first.

"Where were you when I first saw you?" he said.

"Naval Construction Battalion Center, Gulfport, Mississippi."

"Be more specific."

"On the shooting range during expeditionary combat skills training."

"What weapon were you qualifying on?"

"The M16A3."

There was a pause.

"Five years ago in New York, when you turned down my job offer, what hotel were you staying at?"

"The Chandler."

Another pause.

"It's good to hear your voice, too, son," Carrington said.

"We need to meet."

"We?"

"Hammerton's with me. We need to talk."

Yet another pause, longer than the others.

"Destroy this phone the moment this call ends," Carrington said finally. "Understand?"

"I do, yes."

"I'll be destroying this phone, too, which means this will be our only chance to meet."

"Just tell me where. We'll be there."

"Let's take a play out of Tallmadge's book," Carrington said. "Seven eleven, White Plains," he said. "Got it?"

But before Tom could even think to say that he didn't understand, the line went dead.

Stella was obviously confused. "He wants to meet at a 7-Eleven in White Plains?"

"Not the most secure place," Hammerton added.

Tom stepped away, removing the battery from the phone.

He dropped the device to the tile floor and crushed it beneath the heel of his work boot, then tossed the battery onto a nearby desk.

"Tallmadge was Washington's spymaster during the Revolution," Tom explained. "He had a codebook with all the designations to be used in all secret correspondence. Washington's designation was seven eleven."

"So a code," Stella said. "But what does it mean?"

Tom asked her for another smartphone.

She handed it to him, and he opened an Internet browser and began to key in words.

"What are you looking for?" she said.

Tom finished his phrase—*George Washington White Plains*—and hit "Search."

"Revolutionary War landmarks," Tom answered.

He held the phone so all of them could see the display.

The first hit that came up was a photograph of a stone monument, complete with an engraved brass plaque and topped with a small cast-iron cannon.

The caption below that photo read: THE MONUMENT OF THE BATTLE OF WHITE PLAINS.

Tom scrolled down and saw a second photo, this one of a modest-size red cottage, its shutters closed.

The caption below that identified the building as the Jacob Purdy House, a private residence used as Washington's headquarters during the Battle of White Plains in October 1776.

"So which place?" Stella said.

From one of the other burner phones, Hammerton navigated to a satellite map of the Purdy House.

Tom and Stella studied it with him.

The house, on what appeared to be a residential block just east of the Bronx River Parkway, was set within a cluster of trees.

Hammerton then searched for the monument site, which turned out to be just six blocks to the south and three blocks to the west, located on the other side of the parkway.

Tom noted that the White Plains train station was a short walk from the monument site.

"The house would offer Carrington more cover," Hammerton said. "Residential street, the cluster of trees. The monument is in a park, which would put him out in the open."

"But it would put us in the open, too, right?" Stella observed.

From his reading, Tom knew that Washington had retreated to White Plains after a series of defeats that led to the loss of Manhattan.

Unable to maintain the high ground in White Plains, Washington lost there as well and was driven even farther north.

Another defeat in that long list of defeats, but which ended up perfectly positioning Washington for his resounding victory at Trenton.

Tom remembered what Carrington had said about Washington as they stood at Tallmadge's tomb.

The man lost more battles than he won.

This was enough to lead Tom to his decision.

And also cause him to begin seeing his former CO in a new light.

Was Carrington really thinking moves ahead?

And that many moves ahead?

Casually planting clues in Tom's mind, should Carrington, like Washington, need to retreat from defeat?

Had Carrington seen this coming—whatever *this* was?

"It's the monument," Tom announced.

"What makes you so sure?" Hammerton said.

"Of the two places, the park is more secluded. He'd want that. And Stella's right, we'd be out in the open as we approach the monument. All of us would be—Carrington, too—and that levels the playing field."

"So we're going there now?" Stella said. "To New York?"

"Yes."

She paused before saying, "Our carry permits aren't valid there, Tom. If we're caught, the penalties are pretty harsh. Fines, mandatory jail."

"I have a New York State permit," Hammerton said. "If we get pulled over, just pass your firearms to me."

Tom appreciated the offer but knew it wouldn't be enough.

It wasn't just the idea of a potential traffic stop that concerned him.

He knew there was no way he could convince Stella to stay behind.

He remembered then the slip of paper Kevin Montrose had given him.

Removing it from his shirt pocket, he handed it to Stella and said, "Keep this."

"What is it?"

"Help, if we need it."

"What kind of help?"

"Any kind. Every kind."

She looked at the paper before pocketing it.

Tom told them that they would be leaving as soon as they were ready.

He had to take care of something first.

And Stella would have to do something for Hammerton.

Forty-Eight

Hammerton sat on the edge of an old desk as Stella wound silver duct tape around his bare torso to ease the pain caused by even the slightest movement.

Despite Hammerton's refusal to admit the reality of his condition, Tom knew that for even the toughest and most determined person, the body had its limits.

The potential for Hammerton's condition to turn from bad to worse was enough for Tom to start thinking moves ahead as well.

He recognized that this was another reason for Stella to come along.

Should he need to leave Hammerton behind at any point, Hammerton would have her to rely on.

And Stella would have Hammerton.

In the darkest corner of the retail space, Tom put on a pair of work gloves and field-stripped the 1911 to confirm that it was in working order.

Every piece was close to pristine, every mechanism operating as it should, including the firing pin.

Wiping the individual parts down, he reassembled the pistol, then inserted the original magazine and repeatedly racked the slide, ejecting the live rounds into a small cardboard box till the magazine was empty and the slide locked back in the open position.

The springs in old Colt mags could be finicky, he knew, and better that they failed to feed now than in a firefight.

But the mag had performed perfectly, so Tom inserted one of the McCormick mags into the 1911 and depressed the catch lever, sending the slide forward with a sharp snap and chambering a round.

Ejecting that mag, he topped it out with a round from the cardboard box, reinserted the fully loaded mag into the grip, and set the thumb safety before laying the pistol down on the table, the muzzle pointed in a safe direction.

Reloading the original Colt mag with the ejected rounds, he placed it in his left hip pocket along with the second McCormick mag.

Seven rounds in the Colt mag, eight in each of the McCormicks, and one in the chamber.

Twenty-four total.

Stella had six in her .357, Hammerton just ten in his SIG.

Hardly a well-equipped force.

But it would have to do.

Tom was aware that New York State law not only banned the possession of magazines with a capacity greater than ten, it also required that ten-round magazines only be loaded with seven rounds.

His eight-round McCormicks and Hammerton's ten-rounder put them both in violation of state law.

But like those who were likely to oppose them tonight, Tom didn't care about that.

He couldn't care about that.

He had no intention whatsoever of losing those he cared about.

And he had every intention of getting them—and himself—out of New York alive.

For the first time in Tom's life, he was about to intentionally step outside the law.

His only consolation was Carrington's favorite John Locke quote.

The first law of nature is self-defense.

It would be his mantra for the night.

The retail shop below Stella's apartment had a rear door, and they exited through that.

Tom's pickup had been out of his sight since morning, so he got out his flashlight and made another bumper-to-bumper sweep of the vehicle to make sure no tracking device had been planted.

After that, he steered out of the parking lot and onto Main Street, Hammerton by the passenger door and Stella between them.

There was comfort in having her so near.

But there was also concern.

This was his razor's edge to walk.

It would be a two-hour-plus ride to White Plains, south at first on a two-lane country road that wound through farmlands and historic villages and small towns, then on a state highway past failed industrial cities, and from there an interstate freeway west, which would carry them across the state line and into New York.

And, for two of them, into lawlessness.

It was during the final leg of their journey, south on I-684, that Tom realized the true nature of their situation.

The problem with being outside the law was that you could no longer count on it for protection.

The list of those against them had just multiplied exponentially.

In every way imaginable, they were on their own now.

Forty-Nine

White Plains was a quiet city.

There was barely any street traffic as they crossed through the business district, and no vehicles parked at the curb for blocks at a time.

In fact, the only businesses open were a handful of restaurants that appeared all but unoccupied.

Tom understood the reasoning behind choosing such a sleepy place as a fallback position, if that was in fact what Carrington had done.

Tom had recognized similar advantages when he first arrived in Canaan.

The monument was located off Battle Avenue, between the Bronx River and Chatterton Parkways.

A small, tree-lined park on a slight incline with a narrow paved path led to the less-than-impressive memorial.

And if the city of White Plains was quiet, the park was desolate.

Tom parked in a deserted municipal lot.

Together, he and Stella and Hammerton exited the truck and approached.

The tape around Hammerton's ribs helped him stay upright and move, but even with his well-practiced SAS stoicism, the exertion showed.

Both Tom and Stella saw it.

As Tom led, she remained close to Hammerton.

They paused when they reached a grove of trees at the park's northern edge.

These trees were half-bare, so the cover they offered was minimal at best.

The lawn in front of them was blanketed with yellow and orange fallen leaves that appeared untrampled.

Perhaps even when the city was busy, this landmark remained unfrequented.

The only sounds that could be heard were the vehicles passing on the Bronx River Parkway.

A hiss that, while steady, rose and fell in volume as vehicles from two directions approached, passed, and then sped away.

Looking behind them, Tom saw a number of streets, some of which were one-way.

These streets were not set up on a grid pattern like Manhattan's Midtown but rather at angles that created a confusing geometry more like Washington, DC.

One glance showed at least a dozen means of approach and egress.

Carrington couldn't have picked a more suitable location for the meeting.

The only thing missing, really, was high ground from which Carrington could observe them.

But a position behind any of the trees surrounding the park would provide close to the same advantage.

Tom looked forward again, scanning the area.

"I don't see anyone," Stella whispered.

"We wouldn't," Hammerton said.

Tom told them to wait there and stepped onto the lawn.

He took a few steps—noisy, due to the brittle leaves—and stopped.

Scanning again, he saw nothing—no hint of movement, no figure in any of the shadows of the trees.

He continued walking, the leaves announcing every step he took.

Even the paved path, which he eventually reached, was covered.

He approached the monument, stopped a few feet from it, casually looking around again before closing the remaining distance.

And that was when he heard the sound of a cell phone ringing.

Both muffled and echoing.

It took a few seconds for Tom to determine that the ringing was coming from the mouth of the cannon.

Leaning close to it, he reached inside and felt a vibrating phone.

When he answered, Carrington said, "Is that Stella with Hammerton?"

"Yes."

"She's a beautiful woman, Tom."

Tom ignored that. "Cahill thinks you ordered the hit on him."

"I figured that out, yeah."

"The way Hammerton and I see it, Raveis was the one behind it. But I need to prove that to Cahill."

Tom heard only silence from the other end.

Several seconds of it.

"You still there?" he said finally.

"I am."

"The only real evidence against you is Simpson's cell phone," Tom said. "A burner phone with only two numbers in it. One of them was yours, and the other was linked to a Russian named

Israilov, who is the bodyguard to a weapons dealer named Kadyrov—"

"Tom," Carrington said.

"Simpson was working for Kadyrov, and Kadyrov is somehow linked to Raveis. He has to be—"

"Tom, Israilov is dead. Shot in the head a few hours ago in the city."

"Cahill?"

"Yes. My sources say there's surveillance footage from a street camera. It shows the whole thing." Carrington paused. "Cahill crossed a line, Tom. He murdered a man in broad daylight."

Tom was silent for a moment.

He thought about Cahill's promise in the bunker.

In twenty-four hours, they'll all be dead.

Finally, Tom asked about Kadyrov.

"It seems he got away. The man's not without friends. Or resources of his own. Cahill has a war on his hands now. It's bad, and it's only going to get worse." Carrington paused. "I'm going to give you an address. It's not far from here. The three of you will meet me there, and we'll talk about this in person."

Tom hesitated, remembering the last time Carrington had sent him to an address.

Sent him and Hammerton then, but was also sending Stella now.

Carrington obviously understood Tom's hesitation, because he said, "It's a house in a residential neighborhood. I rent the basement apartment. No lease, all cash. It's safe. Trust me. Okay?"

Tom glanced back at Stella and Hammerton standing among the trees.

They were watching him intently but were too far away to hear what was said.

But not so far away that they couldn't see the look of concern on his face.

Turning back and facing the monument, Tom said, "What's the address?"

Fifty

Robertson Avenue was just as Carrington had described it.

A residential street in the heart of White Plains, a mix of pre-war and postwar homes, the majority of which were three stories tall.

Yards nonexistent, the houses crowded together.

Nothing, then, like Front Street.

The opposite, in fact, of the relative privacy offered by a semi-industrial area located on the far edge of a large city.

Violence here would not go unheard.

And response time, once the authorities had been called by countless neighbors, would certainly be swift.

The address Carrington had given Tom was the last house on the right before Robertson crossed with Harding Avenue.

Just past that house was a sloping driveway leading down at a steep grade to an exposed basement at the building's rear.

Tom parked his pickup at the curb, killed the lights and the motor, and saw that Carrington was standing at the top of the driveway.

The man scanned the street quickly, then turned and started down the slope, waving for Tom and the others to follow.

There was something in the way Carrington moved that struck Tom as odd.

He had wavered slightly as he turned, lumbered just a little as he walked.

Tom had no time to study him. The driveway was so steep that it only took a few clumsy strides for him to completely disappear from Tom's line of sight.

Tom's first thought was that Carrington's basement apartment must be a stripped-down version of Cahill's underground bunker.

A place to stash gear and supplies and, should it come to that, to lay low for as long as necessary.

It was a single large room in a roughly finished basement, containing a bed, a desk with computer and printer, a table with a television, and a small kitchenette.

Exposed sheetrock, cement floor with a ratty throw rug, stale air.

Canned goods, bottled water, a small safe—likely for firearms and emergency cash.

Nowhere near as fortified or elaborate as Cahill's safe house, but ideally located just thirty miles north of Manhattan—accessible by train and several different highways and parkways.

If Carrington had taken the steps necessary to keep this place a secret, then it would do its job despite being so decidedly low-tech.

Carrington was on the verge of doing what Tom had done five years before. Roam from place to place, leaving as small a footprint as possible—even none at all when he could.

But Tom had drifted to wash away the effects of war, and had done so causally.

Carrington would have to drift to avoid being pulled into war, and would have no choice but to do so expertly.

Stella led Hammerton to the table and helped him down as easily as she could onto one of the two chairs. All this moving around was clearly taking its toll on the man.

Tom stepped farther into the room. Carrington stood at the computer, his back to his visitors. The printer kicked on.

Next to it was a bottle of Oban scotch and a glass.

The bottle was more than half-empty, and the glass contained an inch of amber-colored liquid.

Tom recalled when he had arrived at the Gentleman Farmer in New York.

Seeing Carrington seated at a table, a drink before him.

And Carrington quickly downing his glass of liquor as he rose to greet Tom.

What was it Raveis had said in the limo?

He drinks too much now and then, but not so much that it interferes with business.

At least it hasn't yet.

Carrington reached for the paper being ejected from the high-speed printer, and Tom finally recognized what it was about the man's movements that had struck him as odd.

Carrington was drunk.

Taking the printout from the printer tray, he turned and faced Tom.

His breath reeked of booze.

In all the years he had known Carrington, Tom had never seen him inebriated.

"You okay?" Tom said.

Carrington nodded and offered the page to Tom.

Looking at it, Tom saw what appeared to be a screen capture of a smartphone's display.

As Tom studied the photo, Carrington said, "I took this before I destroyed my phone. Like you, I don't answer calls from numbers I don't recognize. There are two calls in my call history from a number I'm now guessing is the number of Simpson's burner phone. As you can see, both calls are labeled as missed calls, meaning I didn't answer them."

"He called your phone from his burner so there would be a record of him contacting you," Tom said. "To frame you."

"It's starting to look that way, yes. As you can see by the time stamp and date, the calls came the morning after you and Savelle were attacked. A few hours before you and I met at Tallmadge's grave."

Tom wondered if Simpson had made the calls while he was removing the firing pin from the Beretta.

Which of course raised a question.

"When did you tell him to bring a sidearm for me?" Tom said.

"That morning."

"Before the calls to your phone started."

"Yes. Why?"

Hammerton answered, "Because the Beretta had been tampered with, Jim. It was inactive."

Carrington looked at Tom.

"Simpson put a tracking device on my pickup while I was meeting with Raveis and Savelle," Tom said. "The same make as one found on the car belonging to Cahill's dead girlfriend. We need to connect Simpson to Raveis if I'm going to convince Cahill. Hammerton says you hired Simpson as a favor to someone. Was it Raveis?"

Carrington looked at Hammerton.

It didn't take long before his eyes shifted to Stella.

Tom said, "Was it Raveis who asked you to hire Simpson? As a favor? And asked you to put him on your private detail?"

Carrington looked back at Tom.

The man's processes were slowed significantly.

"Yes," he said finally. He paused, then added, "Well, sort of."

"What do you mean?"

"Raveis doesn't give orders. Not directly. The request came to me via Savelle. Just like when I sent you to that building in New Haven."

"What was the reason Savelle gave for asking you to put Simpson on your private detail?"

"I didn't ask for one. You don't question it when one of Raveis's people asks for a favor. But I'm guessing Simpson was related to someone important to Raveis. And that he left the Treasury for reasons that would keep him from landing work without Raveis's help." Carrington glanced at Hammerton, then said to Tom, "Hammerton never liked the guy. Said he was too gun-happy. Too . . . reckless. I could see that kind of thing not going over well with Treasury."

"And you never talked to Raveis about that? Complained about the guy, asked if you could take him off your detail?"

"I don't think you understand, Tom. I don't interact with Raveis. I don't have direct contact with him. He's high up in the food chain. At the end of the day, I'm just a recruiter." Carrington paused, then said, "I'm sorry for the runaround these past few days. For withholding certain things from you. I swore an oath when I signed on with the Agency. I couldn't tell you about me or Cahill. I tried to tell you as much as I could without actually coming out and saying it. But I never lied to you for the sake of manipulating you. And I wouldn't have sent you to Front Street if I even suspected a trap."

Tom glanced at Stella and Hammerton.

Carrington followed his line of sight and took his first good look at Hammerton.

He said to Tom, "What's happened to him?"

"He took a fifty-cal to the torso. Luckily, it was a glancing blow and he was wearing a vest." Tom paused. "It's been a shitty few days for all of us."

"I'm sorry I got you involved in this, Tom."

"Then help me get out of it. Help me get out of it with a clear conscience."

"How?"

"Give me something I can use to prove to Cahill it was Raveis behind the attack on him, not you. After that, we're all on our own, right? I have to do this much, though. For you and for Cahill."

"Raveis is too smart, Tom. He knows how to move the pieces without leaving any prints—always does."

"Savelle said that the building on Front Street had been purchased through a series of holding companies and dummy businesses. If we can tie that building somehow to Raveis—tie it and the weapons it contained, one of which was found outside the motel where Cahill was attacked—then Cahill has to at least begin to suspect him."

"It's not going to work, Tom. If Raveis wants to hide his hand, it stays hidden. That's his genius. That's his bread and butter."

"Back up a minute," Stella said.

Tom and Carrington looked at her.

"You said the building where you were almost killed had been purchased through a series of holding companies."

Tom nodded. "That's what Savelle said, yeah."

"But that's not really how that works."

"What do you mean?"

"I was in real estate, remember? People—famous people, rich people, investors—often don't want their names to be linked to the properties they own, for privacy or inheritance reasons. You don't need to use holding companies or dummy businesses to hide ownership. Actually, that would do the opposite of what you'd be trying to achieve."

"How so?"

"It would catch the eye of the IRS or FBI—or these days, the Department of Homeland Security. Especially if the property is an abandoned workshop or warehouse. Either way, a property changing hands several times over a short period would send up red flags."

"So how can someone buy property anonymously?" Tom said.

"It's easy—that is, if you aren't looking to get a mortgage. Create a land trust and appoint a trustee with yourself as beneficiary. The only name connected to the property would be the trustee, who is forbidden to reveal the name of the beneficiary. Or you could create an LLC and appoint an attorney as its sole member. Like I said, it's actually very easy, and common. But if you don't have the cash and need to get a mortgage, there's going to be a paper trail leading back to the holder of the mortgage."

Hammerton observed that he didn't imagine Raveis having a problem coming up with the cash necessary to buy a derelict workshop.

"And isn't he a walking, talking corporation, anyway?" Tom said. "I would bet nothing he owns is actually in his name."

"We can find out one way or another right now," Stella said.

"What do you mean?"

"It's all online. Current owner, complete deed history, tax information—everything. I can find out who holds the deed from this computer right here. All I have to do is log in to the MLS. It should only take a few minutes."

Tom looked at Carrington.

The man nodded and swiveled his chair so it was facing Stella.

"Let the lady do her thing," he said.

Fifty-One

Tom joined Hammerton while Stella ran the online search, Carrington beside her.

"How are you holding up?" Tom said.

Hammerton shrugged the question off and said in a hushed voice, "I've never seen Carrington this bad before."

"I'm not worried about him right now. I'm worried about you."

"No need to be."

"Look, I know you're a badass, but you don't have much left. I can see it."

"It's a mistake to count me out."

"I'm not. I'm counting on you. No matter what happens, no matter what I do, your job is to keep Stella safe. Do you understand?"

Hammerton nodded. "What are you thinking, Tom?"

"To get the word to Cahill, I'm going to have to meet with Savelle. Carrington told me that she lives in the city, so if that's where she wants to meet me, I'll have to go in alone. I can't let Stella take any more risks."

"Tell me what you want me to do."

"You'll see it when I make my move. Once I'm gone, take Stella to any Midtown hotel. I don't want to know which one. If you don't hear from me by dawn, get out of the city."

"And then?"

Tom pulled his $1,000 from his pocket and offered it to Hammerton.

"It's all I have," he said.

"Keep it, mate. I've got money." Hammerton paused, then said, "I'll take care of her. You have my word."

"Thanks."

Hammerton smiled. "No problem, Seabee."

Neither said anything for a moment.

The silence was finally broken by Stella.

"I've got it."

Tom approached her as she read from the computer display.

"The deed is listed as being held by Jenna Walewski as trustee of an 'S.A.R. Trust.'"

"You're kidding me," Carrington said.

Tom looked at him. "What do you mean?"

"Those are Raveis's initials. Samuel Arthur Raveis."

"Why the hell would Raveis try to hide ownership of a property with a land trust that bears his initials? That makes no sense."

Carrington shrugged. "Got me."

Tom asked Carrington if he knew anyone named Jenna Walewski, and Carrington replied that he did not.

"The property was purchased six months ago," Stella said, still reading from the screen. "There's no lender listed, so it was a cash deal. And the prior owner was Maritime Tool Works Inc. They owned it for close to twenty years. Apparently the building sat on the market for five years before S.A.R. Trust came along and bought it."

"So no series of holding companies passing it around," Tom said.

"No."

Tom addressed the room. "Then why would Savelle say that?"

Carrington said, "If she knew the trust could identify him, she might have said that to dissuade you from bothering to look up the deed. She's smart, Tom, and she does her homework. She'd know that Stella here had been in real estate and could easily do what she just did."

"I don't buy it," Tom said. "I don't buy that Raveis would do that. Is he arrogant enough to actually put his initials on the deed to a building that contained an arsenal of military-grade weaponry and munitions?"

"Sam Raveis's arrogance knows no bounds," Carrington said.

"But a man doesn't get and hold on to the power Raveis has by doing stupid things like that," Hammerton countered.

"The man has a God complex, thinks he's indestructible and untouchable." Carrington paused, shrugged, then said, "He isn't wrong."

Stella turned from the computer screen and faced the three men.

"Then maybe we can connect Raveis to this S.A.R. Trust through Walewski," she said. "Maybe Walewski is the trustee to other properties Raveis owns, or would be likely to own. Or maybe she's an attorney he has worked with before. If we can tie her in some way to Raveis it would at least make it plausible that he's the actual owner, right? And that would give Tom something to show Cahill." She looked at Tom. "I could call Joe and ask him to run a background check. It might take him a while, though. He's off duty right now."

Tom turned to his former CO and said, "You run background checks all the time, don't you? And I'm not talking standard checks—I mean illegal surveillance. That was part of your recruiting process, right?"

Carrington was obviously reluctant to admit to Tom that he frequently invaded the privacy of former military members.

Men and women who had served their country and were simply looking for work.

Finally, though, Carrington nodded.

"Then find everything you can on Jenna Walewski," Tom instructed.

Stella stood and held the seat as Carrington sat down.

Tom glanced at Hammerton.

Though not inebriated like Carrington, Hammerton was none-theless wavering as well.

Doing his best to hang on, but his best was all used up.

"And please hurry," Tom said to Carrington. "There isn't a lot of time."

Stella placed a cold compress on Hammerton's forehead.

"He's running a fever," she said.

"Bad?" Tom asked.

"Bad enough."

Tom said that he needed to contact Savelle to set up a meeting as soon as possible.

It was the only way of getting to Cahill.

Stella, of course, reminded Tom that she would be coming with him.

Tom didn't put up a fight.

But he also couldn't meet her eyes.

And Hammerton did his part, as promised, said, "I'm coming, too."

Stepping away, Tom powered up one of the three remaining disposable prepaid phones and entered the number Kevin Montrose had given him.

Then he sent off a three-word text:

Need to meet.

There was nothing for them to do but wait for a reply.

As they did, Hammerton said, "Listen, there's something I didn't tell you, Tom. I didn't really think anything of it at first. He was like that, you know. Compulsive, eager. But I'm thinking that it's significant now."

"What is?"

"That night you and Savelle almost burned in that car, when Simpson and I arrived on the scene, he took point."

"What do you mean?"

"He saw the sedan upside down and on fire—Savelle's sedan, and the Chechens waiting all around it—and he just rushed right toward it. But that was him, you know—gun-happy, itching for action—so like I said, I didn't think anything of it."

"But now?"

Hammerton thought for a moment before saying, "What if it were something else?"

"Like what?"

"What if Simpson wasn't rushing to carry out Carrington's orders to protect you? What if he was rushing to save Savelle? What if it was Savelle who told Simpson to pull the firing pin from the Beretta? And had Simpson call Carrington's phone from his burner so there'd be a record of it—one that Savelle herself would 'find' since she seems to be Raveis's main source of intel? I mean, when they interviewed me back in the farmhouse, she was the one with all the info. Was it that way with you? Did she seem to have all the answers when they were talking to you?"

Tom recalled his conversation in the bunker.

Nearly every piece of information provided to him had come from Savelle.

Maybe even every piece.

And never for one moment did Cahill and Raveis seem to doubt or question her.

In fact, they invariably deferred to her.

"What if Savelle ordered Kadyrov and his men to be waiting for us?" Hammerton said. "Told Kadyrov what to say to you because she was the one who bugged your apartment on Friday? What if she's the hidden hand behind all this, Tom? Playing Raveis and Cahill and you against one another."

"That would explain Raveis's initials being used as the name of the land trust," Stella said. "Wouldn't you do that if you wanted to cover your tracks? Implicate someone everyone disliked and distrusted? Do whatever it took to assign your motive to that person?"

Hammerton said, "For that matter, maybe framing Raveis was her original plan."

"What do you mean?"

"Make it look like Raveis was the one who had Cahill killed. But when Cahill survived the ambush and Raveis had you brought in, she had to come up with a new plan on the fly, decided instead to get you to kill Cahill for her, and in a way that would leave you convinced that Carrington was behind all of it."

"And if for some reason you dug deep," Stella said, "the name of the trust would point you to Raveis."

"She's scrambling," Tom said. "Desperate to achieve her goal."

Hammerton nodded. "Yeah. More like fixated on it, if you ask me. Locked into it, can't see any other way out."

"But Savelle would have to know anyone would see Raveis's initials on a trust and not buy it. Hammerton's right. A man like Raveis doesn't get where he is by being stupid."

"Maybe all Savelle wanted was to create an abundance of confusion," Stella said. "And maybe she was counting on you being so blinded by rage that you wouldn't care. Like Cahill is."

"That would explain Kadyrov taking his time to paint an ugly portrait for you of everything he was planning for Stella," Hammerton said. "And anyway, whether you bought it or not, Tom—whether you saw Raveis's initials and jumped to the conclusion she wanted you to jump to, or doubted it and stopped to think it through—the confusion would make a pretty good smoke screen, providing just enough cover for her to get away."

"But the Chechens ambushed me *and* Savelle," Tom said. "They tried to kill us. If she had hired them to kill Cahill and his girlfriend—if they worked for her—why would they come after her the very next night?"

Hammerton shrugged, as if the answer were simple.

"To avenge their fallen brothers," he said. "If any of my SAS mates got killed, I'd seriously consider going after the person responsible. And chances are Savelle didn't bother to warn them that Cahill was a Recon Marine turned special operator. She might have even outright lied to them about him."

"It would be easy enough to confirm if they were in fact gang brothers," Stella said. "The Chechens who attacked Cahill at the motel bore gang tattoos. I'm willing to bet that the ones who attacked you and Savelle had identical tattoos."

Tom said nothing.

In his mind, he pictured Savelle and Cahill standing next to each other in the bunker.

He saw, too, the smile on Savelle's face when he joined them in the bunker's makeshift conference room.

And the look of gratitude she had displayed as she leaned, her face stained with smoke, against the bumper of Hammerton's SUV.

Tom was thinking of all these moments when the phone in his hand rang.

All eyes went to it.

Tom saw a reply text on the display.

It contained a New York City address, just as Carrington had said it would.

The only instructions the text included were precisely where Tom should wait at that location and that he would need to be there by ten.

Just a little under three hours away.

Which was exactly how long it would have taken Tom to make the drive from Canaan to New York City.

Tom memorized the address, then deleted the text.

There was, now more than ever, no way in hell that he would allow Stella to come with him.

Nor was there any way in hell that he was going to let Stella know where he was headed.

"It's her?" Stella said.

Tom nodded.

The fact that Savelle hadn't needed confirmation of the sender's identity told Tom that she had only given him that number.

It also told him that Savelle, as Hammerton had suggested, was capable of thinking moves ahead.

More than capable, in fact.

An expert at it.

But all this simply brought them right back to the same predicament as before.

They needed definitive proof.

Something to show Cahill that would cause him to end his war, or at least call a cease-fire.

From behind Tom, Carrington spoke.

"Jesus Christ," he muttered. "Jesus Christ."

All eyes now turned to him.

"What?" Tom said.

"There are several Jenna Walewskis, believe it or not, but one stands out. KIA in Iraq seven years ago. A Humvee driver. Her vehicle was taken out by an IED. Riding with Walewski was her platoon leader. A lieutenant fresh out of West Point. Anyone care to guess her name?"

No one needed to.

"Alexa Savelle." Carrington spoke as he skimmed a newspaper article. "Wounded, fought off an ambush, saved a whole bunch of lives. Bronze Star, honorably discharged." He paused before concluding, "Returns home a war hero."

"A war hero who fucking steals a dead soldier's identity," Hammerton said. "One of her own, too."

"And uses it to appoint a ghost as trustee," Stella added. "This explains why she didn't want you looking up the deed, Tom. That bullshit comment of hers about holding companies . . . she knew that a couple of computer key strokes by the right person and up comes Walewski's name. A few more keystrokes and, boom, there's a direct link between the two of them. And from there everything would start to fall apart fast."

Tom turned back to Carrington. "Do me a favor, pull up the train schedule."

"You're not still thinking about meeting with her?" Stella said.

"We need Cahill to know. Not only that Carrington had nothing to do with this, but that a person he trusts—one of the two people with access to him—is the one who betrayed him. The only way I can get to Cahill is through Savelle. And Savelle won't talk over the phone, so I need to meet her face-to-face."

"She also tried to have you killed, Tom. What's to stop her from trying again?"

"She has no idea what I know."

"You can't be sure of that. You can't be sure of anything right now."

"It has to be this way, Stella. I just need to get to Cahill tonight. I need to tip him off. And then all this will be over for us."

"Can't you talk to Raveis? You said two people had access to Cahill. He's the other one, right? I'm sure he'd be interested to know that Savelle tried to set him up. Better Raveis take care of this, Tom, than you go running off on another mission to rescue Cahill."

Tom shook his head. "I still don't trust Raveis. It has to be this way. I have to do this. And anyway, we're running out of time."

"What do you mean?"

Tom ignored her question and stepped to Carrington's side just as Carrington was bringing up the Metro-North schedule.

Scanning the departures, Tom determined that the next train to the city would be leaving White Plains in thirteen minutes.

Carrington asked why Tom was going by train and not driving.

He spoke quietly, as if he knew Tom was up to something.

But Tom ignored that question as well, saying instead, "Savelle gave me three hours to meet her, so she still thinks I'm up in Canaan, which means she isn't tracking me. But you should still get out of here, I think. Just in case."

"I'll come with you. You're going to need all the hands you can get."

Tom shook his head. "You're not exactly combat-ready right now, sir."

"I can sober up fast."

"Not fast enough. And someone who knows the truth needs to stay behind. Keep your phone on, but keep moving. Understand?"

"I can do better than that," Carrington said.

He rose and stepped to his safe, opened it, and reached inside to retrieve something.

Returning to Tom, Carrington offered him a smartphone.

"It's equipped with a hot mic, so like before I'll hear everything and the device will record it. If you can't get Savelle to bring you to Cahill, then maybe you can get her to confess, say something, anything that we can use. And it'll let me track you, tell me exactly where you are at any given time, which I think isn't such a bad idea tonight."

Tom looked at the device but made no move to accept it.

As if he understood what Tom was thinking right then—and what Tom was planning to do—Carrington stepped close and said quietly, "I'll be discreet, Tom. I promise."

Tom took that to mean Carrington would not share his location with anyone.

More specifically, he would not share it with Stella, should she try to get it out of him.

As he had done outside the Gentleman Farmer, Carrington placed the phone into Tom's palm.

Stella and Tom were getting Hammerton to the door when Carrington stopped them.

"Kadyrov no doubt has men hunting Cahill. And Raveis's men are still looking for me. Watch your backs," he said. "All of you."

Hammerton stumbled several times up the steep driveway. The man was in agony.

Stella looked at Tom in a way that told him she understood what he had meant when he said they were running out of time.

They were rapidly approaching the tipping point when Hammerton would go from being a significant asset to a burden that could not be managed.

All Tom could do was hope that Hammerton could hang on just a little longer.

———

The White Plains train station was a ten-minute drive from Carrington's apartment.

Tom was parking his pickup in the vacant lot when the train came into sight.

Stella helped Hammerton out. Tom placed the ignition key under the driver's side rear tire, pushing it as far as it would go so that it would not be easily seen.

There for whoever, for whatever reason, got back to his pickup first.

Together, he and Stella scrambled to get Hammerton up the platform stairs. They all but dragged him through the train's doors just as they closed.

Tom was fairly certain that a Sunday-night, city-bound train would not be crowded, but he was pleased to find that the first car they entered was completely empty.

He made a point of choosing seats that were near the front of the car, close to an exit.

Hammerton sat by the window, then leaned his head against the tinted glass.

Stella was in the middle seat, Tom on the aisle.

They sat in silence as the train began to move, each person lost in thought.

Each person dealing with what lay ahead of them—the knowns and unknowns.

Every few minutes, Tom would look at Hammerton and see that the man had slumped just a little deeper into his seat.

His scarred face—scars that had healed long ago, and those that had only begun to—was pale and waxy.

This only deepened Tom's resolve, removing any doubt from his mind that what he was about to do was the right thing to do.

The only thing to do.

Savelle's promise of any and all kinds of help was null and void.

There was no magic phone number that Tom could call should they run afoul of the law.

Or worse, should they need medical help or a quick extraction from a hostile situation.

No, he had to go on alone from here—and in a way that Stella could not follow.

Fifty-Two

With each town the train passed through as it headed south, Tom's dread increased.

He didn't want this, had never wanted this.

He had said no to Carrington's job offer five years ago, the two of them standing in Tom's room in the Hotel Chandler, and had made that difficult decision to guarantee that he would never have to face this.

A world occupied by those who embraced violence.

Each place he had paused after leaving the city—each job he had taken before eventually moving on to the next place and the next job—had brought him closer, step by step, to the day—the hour, the minute—when he had happened to stop for an early lunch at a railroad-car diner in a quiet town and spot a woman he knew he would never forget.

A woman deeply anchored in her community, whose life, as broken as it was, still had gravity sufficient to pull Tom toward it.

You don't happen to know of any apartments for rent around here, do you?

And he remembered her reply.

I could probably help you find something. Month-to-month or a lease?

He recalled, too, their first date.

And their first night together not long after that.

Stella tenderly touching his scarred torso with the tips of her fingers, afraid to ask how he had gotten those wounds but clearly curious.

Tom had quickly brushed away the entire issue with his clumsy joke.

You should see the other guy.

Tom had always believed that his journey, his wandering, had ended that night. He saw now that these six months of domestic life—his first and only attempt at it—had simply been a long pause between steps.

Month by month, day by day, events far beyond his control were directing him—hurtling him—closer and closer to this very moment.

When he would need to leave Stella.

And face the possibility of having to run once more.

And run, maybe, for her sake, without her.

As determined as Tom was to see her again, no matter what it took, he was keenly aware of the number of terrible things that could prevent that.

As much as he would have regretted not coming to a rest for Stella, it was nothing compared to the emotions he was feeling now.

The regret and dread, growing stronger with each town that flew past his window in a blur.

With every mile closer to New York City—and Cahill's war—that they got.

The train crossed over the Harlem River and into Manhattan.

They were just moments away from the 125th Street station, so Tom leaned close to Stella and whispered, "I love you."

Pulled from her thoughts, Stella looked at him. "I love you, too."

Tom reached into his pocket and removed his cash.

"I want you to hold this for me."

"Why?"

"I don't want to be weighed down."

"A thousand dollars weighs you down?" Stella teased.

He forced a smile. "Just take it, please."

Stella did, pocketing it.

"I can't lose you, okay?" Tom said.

"You won't."

"I wouldn't have made it this far without you. You know that, right?"

"I'm not so sure that's a good thing." She paused, then kissed him. "We'll see this all the way through, okay?"

The train began to decelerate as it approached the Harlem platform.

After this stop, there wouldn't be another till Grand Central in Midtown, fifteen minutes from now and eighty-some-odd blocks south.

Tom looked again at Hammerton.

The man met Tom's stare.

You'll see it when I make my move, Tom had told him in Carrington's apartment an hour before. *Once I'm gone, take Stella to any Midtown hotel. I don't want to know which one. If you don't hear from me by dawn, get out of the city.*

Hammerton smiled, or tried to, and nodded once.

A gesture that said, among other things, *Good luck.*

Tom did the same, then waited as the train came to a stop at the elevated platform.

Its door opened and Tom said to Stella, "Promise you'll forgive me."

Though Stella smiled, she was obviously confused by what he had said.

"What are you talking about, Tom?"

"You two take care of each other. And I'll see you soon, okay?"

Stella's smile quickly faded and her eyes shifted to the still-open doors.

The look of confusion was replaced by concern.

And that was replaced by a flash of anger.

This was the last Tom saw of Stella, because he was up on his feet and moving down the aisle, racing to beat the doors before they closed.

He heard Stella calling his name, but he didn't stop.

Reaching the doors just as the hydraulics engaged, he slipped through and out onto the platform.

The doors closed with a hiss, and Tom couldn't bear to see the look of hurt and anger he was certain to see on Stella's face as the train carried her away, so he bolted for the stairs leading down to the street without looking back.

He was halfway down by the time the train cleared the long platform above.

It was out of his sight completely by the time he reached the street.

Harlem was eerily silent. Tom made his way toward the entrance to the subway at the corner of 125th and Lexington Avenue.

To get there he had to pass an MTA police cruiser parked at the curb.

The two uniformed officers inside studied him as he walked past, his jacket hiding the 1911 tucked into his waistband at his right kidney.

His dread and regret were replaced now by a deep, icy fear.

All he could think of was everything he had to lose.

The woman he loved deeply, and the freedom of movement he cherished.

Not to mention his very existence.

Any and all of those precious things could be gone in the blink of an eye—or the pull of a trigger.

Tom had killed before, but the taking of those lives had been sanctioned by both war and John Locke's first law of nature.

A world of black and white back then, no reason to doubt or hesitate, nothing more to do than act in accordance with one's duty.

But there was less clarity here in the civilian world.

A world that was, at times, surprisingly uncivil.

An act of self-defense here could easily become something Tom would have to pay for with the loss of his freedom and separation from Stella.

John Locke's philosophy—all philosophy—was of little comfort now.

Despite his fears, Tom pressed on toward the subway entrance.

He repeated the words taught to him by Carrington so many years before:

The only way out is through.

The only way out is through.

The only way out is through.

Reaching the subway entrance, Tom heard the echoing clamor of an incoming train from below.

He ran down the steps to meet it.

PART FIVE

Fifty-Three

Tom entered Madison Square Park through its southeast corner, then walked north along the eastern edge.

Alexa Savelle had instructed him to meet her by the benches in the northwest corner.

Following the perimeter, he saw that the small park was empty.

Madison Avenue and Twenty-Sixth Street, the eastern and northern boundaries of the park, were also quiet.

Fifth Avenue and Twenty-Third Street, the park's western and southern boundaries, were busier, but only slightly.

The northwest corner was the closest thing to a secluded area the park offered. There were trees whose branches made a thick canopy that all but blocked the overhead streetlights, creating pockets of shadows.

Savelle, Tom was certain, would prefer whatever darkened place she could get.

Twenty-Sixth was a one-way street that ran from Fifth to Madison.

In the time it took Tom to make his way around the park, no vehicle had traversed Twenty-Sixth, while dozens had come down Fifth Avenue.

This would make Twenty-Sixth a perfect place for Savelle to park unseen, and from which to egress, quickly, if necessary, without contending with traffic.

Or witnesses.

She had chosen her location well.

Tom had been instructed to arrive by ten, but it was not yet nine.

If Savelle believed he was coming in from Canaan, there would be no reason for her to be here this early.

This extra time would allow him to do some recon of the area.

But first he removed one of the spare mags from his pocket—the eight-round McCormick—and dropped down to one knee, slipping the mag into his right sock and wedging it between his Achilles tendon and boot.

It was uncomfortable, but he would bear it.

Taking Carrington's smartphone from his jacket pocket, Tom quickly loosened the laces of his boot, placed the phone display-up beneath them, then drew the laces tight again, securing the phone in its hiding place.

Standing, he shook his right foot to confirm that the items would not fall out as he moved.

There was a little play with the mag, which also dug into his ankle slightly, but the phone was there to stay.

Tom rose and was about to begin his recon of the area when a black sedan turned onto Twenty-Sixth from Fifth Avenue, traveled midway down the block, and parked at the curb.

It was the only vehicle on the street, and a short walk from the park's northwest corner.

Tom made no move to approach it, was standing where he had been instructed to stand.

The presence of a black town car in the Flatiron District, he supposed, was not an uncommon thing, even on a Sunday night.

But who else could it be?

Arriving early, the way a trained soldier would.

It wasn't long before the rear passenger door of the sedan opened and a figure emerged.

Tom recognized Savelle immediately.

She started walking west on the sidewalk, her eyes fixed on him.

Tom saw the same smile she'd used to greet him in Cahill's bunker.

Nothing but warmth and fondness for the man who had struggled to free her from a burning vehicle.

The man who had saved her life.

Facing her, he watched as she entered the park and approached him.

"You got here early," she said.

"You, too."

"I was in the area already." She studied his face. "You look tired, Tom."

"I am."

"How's Stella?"

"She's fine."

Savelle nodded. "Good. I'm hoping she won't face any legal troubles for what she did at that motel. Firing through a closed door. Clearly in self-defense, but you never know when a prosecutor's going to try to make an example or gain political points."

Tom said nothing.

He'd faced enemies before, but this was different.

This was a new kind of enemy.

An enemy disguised as a friend.

They looked at each other for a moment, Savelle still smiling.

She was relaxed but poised, both gracious and grateful.

What was it she had said when they'd first met?

People who have almost died together in combat share a bond that can never be broken.

It was difficult for him to look at the woman standing before him and reconcile her current demeanor with what he now knew about her.

With all that she had done and all that she would no doubt do.

Tom realized that he had crossed a boundary, had entered into that dark world, the one he had desired to avoid—one for which he was ill-suited.

He had no choice, though, but to adapt, and adapt fast.

"I need to talk to Cahill," Tom said. "Face-to-face."

"Why?"

There was only one thing he had to offer.

"I can give him Carrington," he said.

"You know where Carrington is?"

"He's waiting for me somewhere, yes. It wouldn't be difficult at all for Cahill to show up there instead of me."

Savelle studied him for a moment, then said, "I think your first instinct was right, Tom. You're better off staying out of this."

He shook his head decisively. "No, I need this to end. Carrington already tried to kill me once. And he sent men after Stella. Not even men—animals. I'm finding it hard to sleep knowing he's still out there. Smart people tie up loose ends, and if Carrington is anything, it's smart."

"And that's the only reason you're doing this? For a little peace of mind?"

"What other reason is there?"

"I just don't like to see you selling yourself short. I have no doubt Cahill would be happy to pay for this information. I know you turned down Raveis's compensation. This might be a chance for you to change your life—and Stella's. And change them in a big way."

So is that it? Tom wondered. *Money? Her reason for doing what she did?*

"I just want this to end," he told her. "So will you help me? Will you get me a meeting with Cahill? Or do I need to go to Raveis directly?"

Savelle stared at him for a moment, then glanced at her watch.

Looking at Tom again, she said, "I can try. I mean, I owe you, right? I owe you everything and anything you'd want."

Tom didn't respond.

"I'm curious about something, though, Tom. How do you know where Carrington is? Last reports indicate he killed three of Raveis's men before going black. Do you and he have another one of those codes of yours worked out?"

"Something like that."

She stared at him for a moment longer.

Tom simply stared back.

Finally, Savelle removed a smartphone from her jacket pocket and stepped away to key in a number.

"I'm with Tom right now," she said. "He needs to talk. It's important." She paused to listen, then said, "We'll meet you there. Give us an hour."

Ending the call, she pocketed the phone.

"It's all set," she said. "I'll take you to him."

The ease of this caused Tom's gut to tighten.

How could it not?

"Maybe I should go alone," he said.

"He's expecting me there, too."

"Call him back; tell him it will be just me."

"Strength in numbers. And anyway, Cahill is a little keyed up these days. You wanting to meet him alone might strike him as suspicious. In his current frame of mind, well, things could easily get out of hand. We don't want that, do we?"

This was Savelle's world.

He had no choice but to follow her lead.

They exited the park and headed toward the sedan waiting at the curb.

As they approached, the driver's door opened and a man climbed out from behind the wheel.

A hulking man in an ill-fitting suit.

He stepped around to the rear passenger door, opening it as he alternately looked at Tom and scanned the street.

"One of Raveis's men?" Tom said.

"Yes. He insisted."

Tom studied the driver.

A hard, scowling face; dark, coarse stubble; focused eyes.

As intense as the men who had occupied Raveis's SUV Friday night, who had accompanied Tom as he was transported to that parking garage on the Upper East Side.

But something was different.

There was something *unpolished* about this man.

Something *unprofessional*.

Or maybe it was just that he was a different kind of professional.

Before Tom climbed into the sedan, he nodded his thanks to the hulking man holding the door.

The man nodded back but said nothing.

Tom had little doubt that if he had spoken, the man would have done so with some kind of Slavic accent.

Tom slid across the leather backseat, then Savelle got in and sat beside him.

The door closed and the bodyguard stepped around the rear of the vehicle.

In the moment it took him to do so, Tom glanced down at Savelle's hands to look for her West Point ring.

He saw it.

And saw, too, that her hands were trembling.

Like Tom's, they bore multiple recent scrapes and burns.

But Tom didn't look there for long.

The driver was behind the wheel, his gaze fixed on Tom in the rearview mirror.

Tom recognized the look as an attempt at intimidation.

But he didn't care.

All he saw as he stared back at the narrowed eyes framed in the mirror was an obstacle he would tear his way through when the time came.

Without hesitation or mercy.

"Take us to the garage," Savelle said.

The driver shifted into gear, then broke off his stare as he steered the sedan away from the curb.

Tom recalled the last time he and Savelle had been seated together in the back of a sedan.

The ride they had shared, nearly the last of their respective lives.

With Carrington listening in then, too.

The sedan made its way east.

Several blocks later, it drove on to the FDR and headed north.

At that point, Tom knew their destination was again the Upper East Side parking garage where he had first met Raveis and Savelle.

Fifty-Four

The sedan entered the eight-story garage, but instead of following the gentle curve of the ramp that led to the floors above, it made a sudden, sharp turn onto a steep downward ramp.

Winding around to another ramp, the vehicle descended into an underground parking area.

This floor was empty.

Winding around one more time, the vehicle reached a third ramp, the access to which was blocked by a heavy chain draped between two cement columns.

Here the driver stopped, shifted into park, and switched off the motor.

Tom studied the area but saw no other vehicles.

He looked at Savelle.

"Back where we started, right?" she said. "Well, more or less."

Tom said nothing.

Savelle smiled. "He's going to meet us on the floor below. We'll take the elevator down."

Stepping out of the sedan, Tom could hear the faint, echoing sounds of the city above.

As the driver escorted him and Savelle to the elevator at the far end of the floor, the city sounds grew even fainter.

They rode the elevator to the final floor, deep in the building's substructure.

Tom noticed that a convex, disk-shaped mirror was mounted where one of the back corners met the ceiling.

The mirror would allow anyone about to enter the elevator to confirm that no one was lurking in the corners to either side of the door.

A security measure for those who made use of the parking garage late at night.

When the elevator reached the bottom and the doors opened, Tom immediately noticed the lack of any city sounds at all.

Nothing but total silence.

Emerging from the elevator, he saw that the area immediately beyond the doors was the only section lit.

Within that limited patch of illumination, no vehicles were visible, and beyond its edges were shadows so dark that Tom couldn't even see the corners of the structure a hundred feet away.

Or know what those corners contained.

What he did know was that Savelle had taken him to a location that was as private and secure as one could hope to find in the crowded city.

Tom glanced at the hulking driver, who had taken a position at his right side, then looked at Savelle.

She was facing him.

"The building belongs to Raveis," she said. "The security cameras at the entrance went offline prior to our arrival. And as you can see, there are no cameras on this level."

Tom took a quick look around to confirm this.

As he searched, he took note of the only other exit.

A fire exit comprised of a pair of double doors, directly across from the elevator.

Mounted on the wall next to that door was an emergency phone.

Tom looked to his left and saw that beyond a pair of concrete columns—a good two hundred feet away—was the ramp that had been blocked off above.

The other way out, and a long way off.

Savelle observed Tom making his visual scan and said, "Meeting here is standard protocol. Cell signals can't reach this far underground, so no one can listen in. And Raveis recently had this entire level shielded to prevent radio waves from penetrating, so even if someone managed to plant a bug or came down here wearing a wire, they'd only hear static. It's safe here, Tom. Even the attendants upstairs are Raveis's men, so they know to not come down here no matter what."

Tom understood that his having been brought to this place to meet with Cahill made perfect sense.

But he wasn't buying it.

While this place clearly provided the privacy and level of security that Cahill would no doubt require, a number of other reasons for choosing this locale came to Tom's mind.

None of them were good.

In fact, each one of them caused his gut to tighten sharply.

He didn't see the point in masking his doubts.

"You told Cahill it would take us an hour to get here," Tom said. "But it only took half that."

"I wanted to leave extra time in case there was traffic on the FDR."

"It's Sunday night. Traffic would be southbound."

"Better safe than sorry, right? Anyway, like I said, Cahill is a bit keyed up. I can't be certain what he might do if we weren't here when he arrived."

Tom could have let that go but decided not to.

The time for games had passed.

The time for all hands to be laid on the table was here.

"That's the thing," Tom said. "It's hard for me to imagine Cahill being keyed up. He was a Recon Marine, elite of the elite. And don't forget, I fought beside the guy. I've never seen anyone as composed under fire as he was."

"I don't think he's the man he used to be."

"Yeah, that seems to be the consensus."

"Grave injuries can change a person," she said. "So can watching the one you love bleed out and die."

"You know that firsthand, I take it?"

Savelle continued to stare at him.

Tom thought of the smartphone secured beneath the laces of his boot.

The lack of a cell signal meant Carrington could no longer listen, but the device was still recording what was being said.

No battle plan survives first contact.

And the only way out is through.

All Tom could hope for now was to get what he could and escape with the smartphone.

And his life.

Fifty-Five

"I'm too tired to play pretend with you right now, Savelle," Tom said. "Cahill isn't meeting us here, is he?"

"No, he is, Tom. Just not right away." She studied him, then said, "How much do you know? I mean, if we're not pretending anymore."

"I know that you sent the Chechens to kill Cahill. And I'm guessing their gang brothers came after you for revenge. I'm guessing, too, your men were rivals to the men loyal to Kadyrov. I also know that you had Carrington send Hammerton and me to the property on Front Street, a property you had purchased anonymously using the stolen identity of a soldier who died under your command."

"She wasn't just a soldier," Savelle said. "Not to me."

Tom thought about that, then nodded. "I'm sorry. For your loss."

"It was a long time ago."

While that may have been factual, Tom knew it wasn't the whole truth.

He recognized hollow words when he heard them.

For Savelle, it still felt as though it had happened yesterday.

And likely would for the rest of her life.

"So Stella figured that part out, did she?" Savelle said. "She looked up the property?"

"That doesn't matter."

"It matters who else knows, Tom. Your girlfriend? Your new best friend? Carrington? You don't think I actually believed you'd turn over your former CO? I need to know what you know. And who else knows it."

"Raveis knows by now," Tom said. "I told Carrington to fill him in."

"I doubt that. Raveis is the last person you'd trust. And for good reason. Also, you wouldn't be here if Raveis knew. You wouldn't be here trying to save Cahill one more time. No worries, though. I'll be long gone before Raveis figures out what really happened."

"Living off the grid isn't as easy as it seems."

"Maybe not on a Seabee's savings. But for someone with the right resources—someone who knows how the intelligence community works and has the necessary cash—trust me, it can be done."

"The weapons cache was destroyed. You and Kadyrov have nothing left to sell."

"*That* cache was destroyed. There are others. But we need Cahill dead, and we need him dead in a way that will lead to a Senate investigation. Like I said, Tom, kill a pretty journalist, throw in an extramarital affair, and you own the news cycle for days. But all we need is one journalist to put the pieces together. Once Cahill's op is exposed, Senate hearings will feed the public outrage over the government knowing about massive weapons caches in our major cities—knowing about them and doing nothing. No one will care that the caches were under twenty-four-hour surveillance by multiple agencies. All people will need to hear is 'guns' and 'Islamic terrorists' and 'government cover-up' and 'rogue CIA op.' And then all hell will break loose."

"You were the source," Tom said. "Not Carrington. You tipped off that journalist, the one Raveis bought off."

"And by doing that, Raveis forced me to adapt."

"But how did you know Erica DiSalvo and Cahill were together? It was a secret. Not even Cahill's oldest friend knew."

"Because I know every trick Cahill knows. I learned them from the same man he did. But more important, I *knew* Cahill. He's a man, like every other man, with his own set of weaknesses. One look at their photo in the paper and I knew. I knew because I wrote the file on him. Just like I wrote the file on you. I know you and your weaknesses, too, Tom. Which is why I know you will kill Cahill for us the moment he steps off that elevator." Savelle paused. "Like I said, here we are, right back where we started."

"Except that you have no leverage this time," Tom said.

"I know you think that, but you're wrong. Dead wrong."

Tom said nothing.

Savelle took a breath, then let it out.

"Let me guess, Tom. Your new friend isn't feeling well," she said. "Hammerton. He's running a fever, right? That's his immune system treating the implant as a foreign body."

"What implant?"

"The implant I injected under his skin while he was sedated. At the farm. And by implant, I of course mean tracking device. The immune system's reaction is a side effect, one we haven't found a way around yet, but the device is still only in the prototype stage. The real issue is the power source. A transmitter powerful enough to be read by a satellite has to have a power source. Microscopic batteries don't last very long yet. It's a good thing for us you acted when you did. Good thing for us, too, that you were kind enough to take your injured friend home with you. But what soldier leaves another behind, right? Not you. That was one thing I knew I could count on from you."

"You're bluffing," Tom said.

"According to the latest update, they're in a hotel in Midtown. The Hotel Chandler, to be precise. Does that sound about right? By the time our people got to Carrington's safe house in White Plains, he was long gone. But we'll find him soon enough. Find him and kill him, too. Just like we will kill your Stella and Hammerton. Kill them in terrible ways—unless, of course, you do what we want you to do. That's all you need to do to ensure a quick and painless death for them. And for yourself."

"You have men, Savelle. Have them kill Cahill. Or just kill him yourself. You don't need me."

"No, Tom, it has to be you. It has to be the man whose life Cahill saved. The unstable drifter stuck in a dead-end job. The homeless PTSD case Carrington foolishly recruited for a highly sensitive search-and-rescue mission."

"And how is that going to achieve your objective of getting an investigation launched?"

"Turn on a TV, Tom. The feeding frenzy has already begun. Remember, Erica DiSalvo is missing. Cahill buried her body somewhere, so no one knows for sure yet if she's dead or not. But maybe missing is even better than dead. Missing keeps the hope alive, you know. Missing keeps people tuned in to the news for the latest update. Missing gets anguished family members on TV, and that always stirs things up. The pieces will begin to fall into place when Cahill is ambushed and killed by the basket case Carrington sent to find him. And when classified files are found on Carrington's computer—files detailing Operation Voyeur, files implicating DC insider Sam Raveis—well, all hell will break loose then."

Tom quickly realized something.

"You're up against a timetable, aren't you?" he said. "You need those other caches confiscated now. Why?"

"Raveis's theory about the attack coming during Fleet Week is wrong. The time to strike—for the greatest psychological and emotional impact, not to mention the highest casualty rate—is Christmas. As in weeks from now. Imagine Manhattan streets crowded with families from around the world, all of them here to see the window displays and shop. Hotels full, theaters full, restaurants full. An environment rich with soft targets. The loss of life would be staggering, the scars left on the American psyche devastating. The world would never be the same again."

Tom had heard enough, reached fast for the 1911 hidden under his jacket, but before he could do more than palm the grip, he felt the cold steel of a pistol's muzzle pressing against his right temple.

Savelle's driver had moved, and moved fast.

A Glock was in his right hand, his left grasping Tom's right wrist.

Savelle removed a pair of leather driving gloves from her jacket pocket and pulled them on.

Moving close to Tom, she reached around his torso and pulled the pistol from his waistband.

Stepping back, she examined the weapon.

"You aren't messing around, are you, Tom," she said. "I love an old government-issue Colt. By the shape of the hammer spur and the markings, this is old military surplus. I'm guessing this makes it untraceable, right?"

Tom ignored that. "Storming a motel in the middle of nowhere is one thing, Savelle. You're not going to have men storm a crowded New York City hotel. You may know where Stella and Hammerton are, but you can't get to them. Not without a shitload of shots being fired, and I don't think you're crazy enough to want that kind of attention."

Savelle removed the mag from the Colt, then expertly racked the slide, her waiting palm cupped over the ejector port to catch the ejected round.

Pocketing the mag and the round, she said, "I'm a little surprised at that, you being a Seabee and all. I would think you'd know better than anyone that there are more ways than one to breach a perimeter."

Holding on to the empty Colt with her left hand, Savelle searched Tom with her right.

"I'm fortunate to be associated with a man who is capable of anything. You've dealt with him already, so you know what I'm talking about."

She found the mag in his jeans pocket and the cell phone in his jacket, taking them both.

The mag she also pocketed, but the cell she dropped to the cement floor and crushed with the heel of her shoe.

Then she patted down Tom's torso and crotch.

"No wire," she said. "Not that it would have done you any good down here, but I'm surprised."

She finished by moving her hands down Tom's legs, never going below his ankles.

Finally, she rose and stepped back.

"I'll need you to lose the gloves, Tom."

Tom didn't move.

Savelle's driver shifted the muzzle from Tom's temple to his ear, left it there for a moment, then moved it back to Tom's temple.

He pressed the cold steel even more firmly against Tom's skin.

Tom removed his work gloves and dropped them to the pavement.

"This is the big leagues," Savelle said. "You understand that, right? This is the world stage we're on. It doesn't get more important than this. Kadyrov will have no problem setting an entire city block on fire if that's what it takes to get to the people he needs to get to. The people who matter the most to you. People you would do anything to keep from burning to death in some tragic hotel fire. Do you really want that, Tom? Stella dying like that? In prolonged agony? The way you and I almost died? Remember the heat? The smoke burning our lungs? The panic? Is Cahill really worth that? Is his life worth letting others die so horribly?"

"If that's what it takes to keep you from arming our enemies."

"Now who's bluffing, Tom?"

It took all Tom had to keep his rising anger from showing.

Anger toward Savelle for what she had done, yes, but also because she was right.

Tom had no intention of letting Stella or Hammerton—or anyone—burn.

Nor was he going to give Savelle what she wanted.

All he needed to do was wait for his chance to move.

Or better yet, create his chance.

"How much is Kadyrov paying you?" Tom said. "How much did it take for you to betray your country?"

"More than I can ever spend. But I would have done it for less."

"Why, Savelle? You're a fucking West Point grad. Bronze Star, Purple Heart, the whole thing. Why do this?"

"Because scars on a man aren't the same thing as scars on a woman. Do you want to compare torsos? Right now? Do you? Want to see the scar that was left after they took out my uterus because it was full of metal fragments? Want to see what's left of my genitals? My breasts? Want to see what reconstructive surgery at the hands of VA surgeons gets you? Because it isn't much."

Tom said nothing.

All he could think of was what Carrington had said about Benedict Arnold.

A hero of the American Revolution before he turned traitor.

Not for ideological reasons, but simply because of insults and injuries he'd been forced to bear.

"I know you know what it's like to be torn up, Tom. You wandered around for five years, no girlfriend, not even a one-night stand as far as we can tell. Nothing—till you met your precious Stella, that is. Beautiful face, flawless body, which she's more than willing to flaunt, to send you naked pics of while you're at work. Was it a relief, Tom, to finally be touched after five years? To lie naked with someone when you finally got up the nerve? I'll never know that. Not now, not five years from now, not five years after that. No one will want me. Not the way *she* did. No one will want to look at me or touch me or want me to touch them. I would have rather been killed over there than to come back like this. Come back to hear all the promises. That they were going to do right by me, that all the doctors and nurses were going to put me back together again, that this country takes care of its soldiers, that there was nothing for me to worry about. All of it was lies."

Savelle stopped short.

A thick vein throbbed in her forehead.

Tom was staring at it when he heard a voice emerge from the surrounding darkness.

A voice he immediately recognized, and would never forget.

Kadyrov's voice.

Fifty-Six

"*Enough,*" the man barked.

Tom and Savelle looked toward the voice.

But Savelle's driver kept his eyes on Tom and the muzzle of his Glock pressed against Tom's temple.

Tom watched as Kadyrov emerged from the farthest and darkest corner.

Still limping, and flanked by four bodyguards.

Men identical in almost every way to the man to Tom's right.

"We're wasting time," Kadyrov said. "He will not cooperate. Kill him now and be done with it before Cahill gets here."

"That's not the plan," Savelle protested.

"It is now," Kadyrov said.

"I can fix this. Let me fix this."

Tom could see that Savelle was unraveling.

"You've had your shot, Alexa," Kadyrov said. "But right now I need you to follow my orders."

"Just let me fix this."

Kadyrov came to a stop a good twenty feet from Tom, his bodyguards behind him like a wake.

"No. Kill this man with his own weapon. Now. I will see that the others are taken care of later."

Savelle hesitated, but only briefly.

Retrieving one of the mags from her pocket, she slapped it into the Colt's grip and racked the slide, chambering a round.

She looked at Tom but didn't raise the pistol.

Kadyrov asked if there was a problem.

Tom glanced at the driver's hand grasping his right wrist.

Savelle began to raise the pistol and Tom was about to make his move when a noise came from above.

It was the echoing clang of elevator doors opening.

Savelle stopped.

Everyone froze.

Kadyrov said, "I thought you had men posted upstairs."

"I do. I replaced Raveis's men with two of ours. They were supposed to call when Cahill arrived."

Savelle looked fast at the emergency phone mounted by the fire exit.

Tom fixed his peripheral vision on the man beside him, waiting for the first indication that his attention was wavering.

Then there was more clanging as the elevator doors closed.

This was followed by the rapid whir of an electric motor as the elevator began to descend.

Savelle's driver spoke to her in broken English.

"I kill him?"

"It's too late," Kadyrov snapped.

Shots fired now would alert Cahill to the trap awaiting him.

Kadyrov ordered Savelle and her driver to get out of the way.

The driver did as commanded, releasing Tom's wrist and backing up, his Glock still aimed at Tom's head.

Savelle, though, hesitated.

Her eyes flashed with defiance.

And determination.

Releasing the mag from the Colt, she gripped the weapon by the barrel with her left hand and handed it grip-first to Tom.

There was one round in the chamber.

Tom noted that the safety was set.

"Kill Cahill," Savelle said, "and Stella won't burn. You'll die quickly, and when her time comes, she'll die quickly, too. I promise, Tom. Okay? Just do this. Forget everything else. The best either of you can hope for now is not to suffer. So just do it, okay? One shot, right in the head. Don't do it, and the men standing by outside Stella's hotel act. Do you understand? I make just one phone call and Stella burns. Tonight."

Savelle took two steps back and stopped.

Cahill would initially see what he expected to see when the doors opened.

Tom and Savelle, waiting for him in Raveis's secured area.

Savelle's driver, to the right of the elevator and just out of the sight of its occupant, stood ready to execute Tom, his Glock now in a two-handed grip.

In anticipation, Kadyrov's bodyguards broke from their formation. Two of them took position in front of him, the other two stood close beside him.

The two in front had their hands on their holstered weapons, ready to draw.

The two beside stood ready to grab Kadyrov and shield him as they rushed him away.

Tom faced the elevator, the 1911 in his grip.

His hand was hanging at his side, the safety still engaged.

"Just kill him, Tom," Savelle urged. "For Stella's sake. Kill him and this will all be over."

There was panic in Savelle's voice.

A woman on the verge of losing everything for which she had worked.

Everything for which she had already killed and would continue to kill, if necessary.

The whirring of the electric motor ceased as the elevator reached the bottom of the shaft.

Less than a second later, the doors began to part.

Tom still didn't raise his weapon.

As the doors opened fully, he stood facing the last thing he was expecting.

An empty elevator car.

Savelle, facing it, too, froze in confusion.

Tom's eyes went to the disk-shaped, convex security mirror mounted high in the right-hand corner of the ceiling.

He saw movement in that mirror.

The reflection of the fire exit behind Tom opening.

And a figure stepping through it.

Fast, efficient, silent.

Despite the distorting aspects of the mirror, and the distance between it and the fire exit, Tom recognized the figure right away.

It was Cahill.

And he was armed.

The sound of the swinging door was the only indication of his sudden presence.

It was enough, though, to catch the attention of Savelle's driver.

And Tom finally saw the break in concentration for which he'd been waiting.

The moment when he would make his move.

The only move left for him to make.

Tom clicked the thumb safety off and instantly dropped into a deep crouch, raising the 1911 as he did.

At such close range, there was no need to pause to take careful aim.

He simply extended his arm till his weapon was in line with the hulking driver's head, then eased the trigger back and fired his one shot.

Fifty-Seven

The retort of the plus-P round—of the bullet leaving the muzzle of the 1911 at close to two thousand feet per second—was as loud as a thunderclap in the enclosed garage.

The compression wave emanating from the weapon in Tom's hand blew his jacket open like a sudden gust of hot wind.

Before his body even hit the pavement, Savelle's driver was dead from a round that struck the bridge of his nose and penetrated his skull.

But Tom knew this was only the start of the work ahead.

He dropped flat onto his back, Kadyrov's men sighted squarely between his feet as he reached down for the magazine hidden in his right boot.

The two men taking point had already drawn their weapons, while the other two had grabbed Kadyrov and were ushering him back toward the shadowed corner from which he had emerged.

Where, no doubt, some unseen means of escape waited.

The first of Kadyrov's bodyguards was taking aim at Tom—a relatively small target, now that he was lying on his back.

The second was zeroing in on Cahill, who was approaching both men steadily, a compact pistol held in both hands.

Tom had little time, was pulling the mag from his boot when the first bodyguard found his target.

But Tom still had to bring the mag to his weapon, insert it, and release the locked-back slide before he could even think about taking aim.

There was, he knew, no way he could accomplish all that in time, felt his heart pounding and adrenaline spilling down his limbs and was looking down the barrel of the man's weapon when a shot was fired, quickly followed by another.

The bodyguard suddenly dropped.

Tom quickly surmised that Cahill had chosen the man who had drawn a bead on Tom as his first target, taking him out with a double tap.

Tom didn't flinch, knew that the second bodyguard would have a line on Cahill by now, so he scrambled to complete the loading of the Colt, then took aim at the second bodyguard and fired. He felt the heavy recoil of the .45 and waited for the full second it took for the muzzle to lower into place again before firing once more.

Both shots struck the man in the chest.

He, too, fell fast.

Cahill instantly turned his attention past Tom, his pistol aimed in the direction of the elevator.

Tom understood that Cahill was targeting Savelle.

Still on his back, Tom rolled onto his left side and aimed toward the elevator as well but was too late.

The doors were closing automatically.

And Savelle had already moved through them and taken cover by the control panel.

Before Tom knew it, Cahill was crouched at his side, putting himself between Tom and the dark corner into which Kadyrov and his two remaining bodyguards had disappeared.

Facing in that direction, his compact 1911 raised and ready, he asked Tom if he was okay.

Tom replied that he was.

"Good," Cahill said. "Now get up and follow me."

Scrambling to his feet, Tom did a quick search of the spot where Savelle had been standing before the firefight had begun.

He saw what he was hoping to see.

She had dropped the mag she'd been holding to the pavement.

Tom hurried to it and grabbed it, checking the bottom and seeing the Colt logo stamped into its metal floor plate.

This was the original mag, the seven-rounder, which meant the 1911 was currently loaded with one of the two eight-round McCormicks.

A single shot had been fired from the Colt mag, so it now contained six.

Two had been fired from the McCormick, leaving only six in that one as well.

Twelve rounds total, then.

Tom slipped the spare mag into his back pocket as he followed Cahill to the fire exit.

Moving in a two-man-team formation, they cleared the stairwell as they made their way to the next floor.

Tom assumed there was another fire exit in the dark corner below, and that Kadyrov and his men had made their way to it and were ascending as well.

The heavy chain at the top of the ramp would prevent any vehicle from either entering or exiting that lower level.

But all Tom cared about was Savelle in the elevator, rising closer to where her cell would get a signal.

Allowing her to make the call she had threatened to make.

Reaching the doorway—double doors, identical to the ones below—Cahill paused on one side, Tom on the other.

After a brief pause, Cahill leaned forward and quickly peered through the small window inset in the doors.

He announced, "Clear," and leaned back, grabbing the door handle and pulling his door open.

Tom was the first through, crouching low. Cahill was right behind him and upright. Each man scanned the area ahead of him, weapons raised and ready.

They moved in that way through the garage, heading for the other fire exit, checking corners, keeping their formation tight, pausing only to quickly clear potential ambush points.

They had to reach the concrete columns at the center of the structure and round them before either could even see the other fire exit.

It was as they were making their way around the massive columns that Tom recognized the hornet's nest they had walked into.

No sign of Kadyrov or his two bodyguards.

But there were three other men.

Two armed with handguns, one with a semiautomatic rifle, standing shoulder to shoulder.

While Tom and Cahill were surprised by the sudden appearance of the men, Tom got the sense that they were just as surprised to see him and Cahill.

And by their lack of formation—running abreast instead of moving in a tight single file—Tom knew they were untrained street thugs.

The panic in their faces told him that they were in over their heads.

There was no time for Tom to retreat or take cover, so he dropped down to one knee and took aim at the center man.

At the same instant, Cahill swung around Tom, away from the column and out into the open, drawing the attention of the man armed with the rifle, firing as he moved.

An application of overwhelming force.

Cahill's two fast head shots took the rifleman down.

Tom knew not to bother with body shots—thugs or not, there was the chance that these men were wearing protective vests—so he raised the 1911 till the front sight all but obscured the center man's face.

His first shot was dead on, his follow-up merely a safeguard.

That man went down as well.

Cahill continued moving in his wide arc, the one remaining man mistaking him for the greater threat and firing wildly at him.

This allowed Tom time to shift his aim a few inches to the left and fire another controlled pair, killing that man on the spot.

Four shots fired, two remaining.

One in the chamber, one in the mag.

Tom released the near-empty mag and replaced it with the original Colt mag.

Counting the round in the chamber, he now had seven rounds ready and a single round left in the McCormick mag, which he had shoved into his back pocket.

Without ear protection, Tom's ears were ringing badly, but he could still make out Cahill's commands.

"Take right!"

Splitting up now, keeping a good twenty feet between them, Tom and Cahill moved forward once more.

Tom took the right, Cahill the left.

The distance between them would prevent another head-on collision with any other men they might encounter and would also set them up for a possible pincer movement once they caught up with Kadyrov.

Finally rounding the center column, they spotted the fire exit.

Reaching it, Tom held back slightly as Cahill approached the doors, quick-checked the window, then pulled one door open.

Tom entered the stairwell, Cahill right behind him.

Tom covered the stairs leading down, Cahill the stairs leading up.

Each man as much listening as looking.

It was just a few quick seconds after that that they heard the sound of a door closing above.

Taking off, they moved up the stairs as fast as caution would allow, then reached the doors to the next floor, pausing again on both sides.

As before, Cahill took a breath, then leaned forward and checked the window.

He peered through, then pulled his head back reflexively, doing so just as Tom heard gunshots.

He had barely gotten his head out of the way before the window's glass shattered.

Cahill crouched and took cover against the cement wall, and Tom saw blood on his face.

But before Tom could say anything, Cahill wiped away the blood with the back of his hand and shook his head, as if to say, "It's nothing. I'm okay."

Rising, Cahill shoved his compact .45 through the broken window and fired one shot after another, laying down suppressing fire. Tom pulled the other door open and, crouching low, moved through.

This parking area was full, and Tom found cover by the nose of the nearest vehicle.

Scanning over the hood and through the vehicle's windows, he saw no shooter, only other cars.

Each one offered some degree of cover.

Tom knew what Cahill would do next, so he waited, ready.

Pulling the door open, Cahill appeared in it for a second, then darted out of sight again.

Shots were fired, rounds hitting the closing door.

Rising, Tom spotted the shooter.

One of Kadyrov's two bodyguards, covering Kadyrov's retreat, firing from behind a sedan parked directly across from the exit.

Extending his 1911, Tom fired twice.

The first shot only grazed the man's head, but the second went through his eye.

Cahill cleared the door and was on his way to join Tom by the nose of the nearest vehicle when something seemed to catch his eye, causing him to deviate from his path and take off running.

Tom followed Cahill's line of vision and saw a sedan backing out of a parking spot.

In it were Kadyrov and his last remaining bodyguard.

As he ran, Cahill did a mag switch, dropping the empty one to the pavement.

His compact now fully loaded, he ran at an all-out sprint, closing in on the sedan as its driver paused to shift from reverse to drive.

Tom took off, too, was maybe twenty feet behind Cahill, who was still fifty feet from the sedan.

The front wheels squealed as the driver hit the gas. The sedan lurched forward, gunning for the ramp that led up to the exit.

Cahill stopped running, assumed a shooter's stance, and began to unload on the sedan's rear window.

The bullet-resistant glass cracked but did not shatter.

The sedan continued forward, and Cahill continued to fire.

One round, another, and another.

Each bullet landing in a tight group in the center of the window.

The glass, though now opaque, remained intact.

Cahill was still firing when Tom reached his side.

The sedan was closing on the ramp, which exited to the city street.

Taking careful aim at the impact point left by Cahill's shots, Tom fired.

He hit dead center, but the glass remained.

Five rounds left.

He fired again, hit his mark. Nothing. He fired a third time.

This time the distressed glass finally shattered, its shards dropping like rain and leaving a clear view of the heads of both the driver and occupant.

Tom knew which target to take and which target to leave for Cahill.

He knew, too, that he was down to three rounds.

He fired at the driver, missed him, but struck the windshield, shattering it.

His second shot found its target.

Much of the man's head was gone.

And the slide of Tom's 1911 locked open on the empty mag.

Cahill got a shot off as well—the shorter barrel of the compact .45 required more care when aiming at a distant target—but he did so just as the speeding vehicle veered.

As it crashed into a cement wall, the sedan came to an instant stop.

Cahill ran, Tom following, dropping the empty mag from the Colt and grabbing the one from his back pocket.

The only mag he had left—containing a single cartridge.

He released the slide, chambering that last round.

Cahill reached the sedan and moved along its right side, stopping at the rear passenger door, his weapon aimed at the window.

He pulled open the door with his left hand, then just stood there, the firearm in his right aimed at the occupant inside the vehicle.

As Tom reached Cahill's side, he got a look at Kadyrov.

The man's left ear had been torn off by Cahill's shot.

The Slav was covered in his own blood.

Visibly stunned by the sight of it, as well as the force of the crash, Kadyrov looked at Cahill.

Looked, but said nothing.

Cahill kept his weapon aimed at Kadyrov's head, his index finger on the trigger, his face blank.

"There are other caches," Tom said. "He knows where they are."

This obviously didn't matter to Cahill.

He simply shook his head, continuing to stare at Kadyrov.

Tom understood the significance of this.

Of Cahill standing outside a vehicle in which Kadyrov sat.

Helpless, trapped.

Just a few nights ago, Erica DiSalvo had been seated in Cahill's Jeep while Kadyrov stood outside the vehicle.

It was clear what Cahill was thinking right now.

The only thing on his mind.

Tom knew it would have been the only thing on his, too.

Cahill lowered his aim from Kadyrov's head and fired into his chest.

The wound was not immediately fatal, as was sometimes the case with chest wounds. Nor was it intended to be so.

Cahill watched as Kadyrov bore the initial agony of flesh and bone being torn and shattered.

Then, still conscious, the Slav began to gasp as his punctured lung struggled to inflate.

A lung quickly filling with blood.

Each autonomic function causing more and more tissue to tear against the jagged edges of a mushroomed hollow-point bullet.

Cahill allowed this struggle to go on for a time. Five seconds, then ten, never taking his eyes off Kadyrov's face.

Finally, though, he raised his pistol once more and aimed it at Kadyrov's temple.

Their eyes met, and there was a moment of cognition.

Cahill paused for a second more, then squeezed the trigger.

His expression did not change.

Not during the execution, nor after it.

The echo of his single shot was still ringing when Tom heard the high-pitched shriek of screeching tires.

It was the sedan in which he had arrived, rushing up from the floor below.

Cresting the ramp, it turned sharply, was coming up behind them fast, its engine gunning.

Savelle was visible behind the wheel.

Cahill was still staring at Kadyrov, seemingly unaware of the vehicle bearing down on them.

Tom grabbed him and pulled him out of the way just in time.

The sedan sped past them, heading for the ramp.

It was now Tom who took off in blind pursuit, sprinting after the vehicle.

He heard Cahill call his name but ignored it, just kept running.

While making the turn onto the ramp, the vehicle slid sideways, colliding with the wall and slowing, though only briefly.

Savelle gunned the engine again and the sedan sped upward.

Tom reached the bottom of the ramp several seconds later and looked up to see the sedan skidding to stop to avoid colliding with an SUV parked near the top of the ramp.

Three of its four doors were open, and Tom knew it belonged to the dead men on the floor below.

Men who had clearly arrived in haste.

Savelle steered around the vehicle, scraping its bumper, then exited the garage.

Tom ran after it with everything he had.

He reached the SUV and was climbing in behind the wheel when he spotted two men facedown on the pavement.

Two men wearing attendant's uniforms.

The men who had replaced Raveis's men, who Savelle had tasked with warning her of Cahill's arrival.

Caught off guard by the former Recon Marine, they were now among the dead.

The many dead.

But Tom couldn't care about that.

About the bodies here and the fallout that was sure to come.

How could he possibly get away with what he'd done?

With his part in all this?

His fingerprints and DNA were now all over the Colt.

And while Raveis had control over the security system inside the garage, the city was a net of public and private surveillance cameras.

Street cameras, shop cameras. Every inch of Tom's movement from the moment he exited this structure would be recorded.

It wasn't a matter, though, of getting away.

It was a matter of stopping Savelle, no matter what it took.

Tom caught a break—the keys were in the SUV's ignition. Starting the engine, he shifted into gear and gripped the wheel with both hands as he pressed the accelerator to the floor.

The motion of the vehicle lunging forward swung the doors back.

They slammed shut as Tom exited the parking garage and turned onto Seventy-Second Street, racing after Savelle.

Fifty-Eight

The southbound traffic on the FDR was heavy but moving.

Savelle's sedan was three car lengths ahead, weaving in and out of lanes as she passed slower vehicles.

Her sedan was more maneuverable than the SUV, but Tom had horsepower on his side.

And weight.

His vehicle itself was a weapon.

If need be, he'd drive Savelle—and himself—into a wall.

But the speeds he was traveling required two hands on the wheel, so Tom opened the console between the two front seats and placed the Colt 1911 inside.

It was then that he saw a cell phone.

Grabbing it, he closed the console lid and, holding the phone with one hand, entered Stella's current number with his thumb.

There was no time to talk to her, so he typed out a single word, one that he could write quickly and that Hammerton, if not Stella, would understand.

Displace.

Hitting "Send," he looked up in time to see that he was about to ram a slow-moving vehicle in front of him.

Cutting the wheel sharply to the right, he swerved to avoid it, barely missing sideswiping the vehicle in the next lane.

Recovering, he spotted the sedan, now even farther ahead.

Still, he held on to the phone, driving one-handed as he waited for a reply.

Finally, a message came through.

One word, but it was enough.

Affirm.

Tossing the phone onto the seat, Tom gripped the wheel with his right hand and flattened the accelerator.

The sedan continued to change lanes, maintaining its lead.

It was all Tom could do to keep from losing even more ground.

They passed several exits before traffic thinned slightly and the sedan entered a relatively empty patch of highway.

Savelle gunned it, pulling ahead even more.

When Tom reached the empty stretch, he gunned it as well. The gap between the two vehicles instantly began to close.

Tom could feel that the SUV was on the verge of flying out of control, but he kept the accelerator to the floor.

He was less than a car length behind the sedan when it entered yet another cluster of heavy traffic and began cutting in and out of lanes.

Tom was forced to slow, and immediately the gap began to widen again.

Two car lengths, three, then four.

Tom knew he had to be more aggressive and started pushing the SUV even more, clipping first one car, then another as he maneuvered up the pack.

Glimpsing ahead, he saw another open patch, waited for it as they rushed to reach it.

The sedan cleared the pack first and shot forward.

As much as Tom couldn't stand holding back, he knew he had to wait or risk colliding with other cars, putting innocent people at risk.

Fortunately for him, the driver of the vehicle in front of him sensed trouble and veered onto the narrow shoulder.

Tom barreled through the now-open lane, once again closing on the sedan fast.

It swerved from the right lane into the far left, and Tom followed it.

The front bumper of the SUV was yards from the rear of the sedan.

Then feet.

Then inches.

Tom didn't have to ram it, just tap it right, to cause the sedan to fishtail into a spin.

But before he could close the remaining inches, the sedan cut to the right suddenly, crossing lanes as it headed toward an exit ramp at the last possible second.

Tom did the same, but the SUV was too cumbersome and threatened to roll.

He maintained his reckless course, though, holding steady, the SUV turning into a sideways slide.

He watched through the windshield as Savelle's sedan made the exit ramp, only to slam sideways into the concrete barrier.

But this barely interrupted the vehicle's forward momentum.

His SUV was in a clockwise spin, so that was all he could see of the exit and the sedan before he was facing north—and an oncoming wall of speeding headlights.

The spin continued. He briefly faced the East River at the edge of the highway.

And then the SUV completed its roughly 360-degree ride and collided sideways with the water-filled plastic safety barrels just past the exit.

The barrels exploded upon impact as designed, sending columns of water up into the air.

Tom made a quick check of the rearview mirror, saw the oncoming traffic but didn't care, shifted into reverse anyway, and backed up till he could make the turn onto the exit.

He was halfway down the ramp when Savelle's sedan reached the bottom.

The intersection was blocked by stalled traffic, causing the sedan to stop.

Savelle couldn't turn right or left or even go straight.

Tom saw his chance to overtake her once and for all.

End this in whatever way he had to.

He grabbed the seat belt with one hand, pulled it across his chest and latched it, then punched the accelerator, the engine roaring as he set the SUV on a collision course.

Traffic in the intersection began to move slightly, opening a hole for Savelle.

She steered the sedan into it, forcing the vehicles to her right to stop.

A second lane of cars beyond the first also began to move, but even more slowly.

Savelle was creeping into that lane as well, cutting those vehicles off, wedging her way through.

She would be on her way again once she cleared this obstacle, was moving around a driver who had no intention of letting her cut him off when she ran out of time.

Tom saw that the speedometer was reaching sixty when the SUV collided with the sedan, instantly crumpling the tail end as it drove the lighter vehicle through the intersection and onto the wide cross street.

Savelle attempted to steer out of the crash, but her efforts only served to send the sedan into a sideways slide.

The SUV was well out of Tom's control now, and it rammed the sedan's passenger side, tipping the vehicle into a violent roll.

Its forward momentum continuing, the SUV itself veered sharply to the right, turned sideways, and was about to begin its own roll when it crossed onto the sidewalk and collided with a lamppost.

Tom felt the impact, heard glass shattering, metal twisting, and automotive plastic splitting.

Then he felt and heard nothing, saw only blackness.

When he regained some of his senses, the first thing he noticed was blood on the left side of his jacket.

It was shortly after that that he became aware of the deafening ringing in his ears.

This was all he was aware of for a time.

Orienting himself, he looked out his window and saw the battered sedan resting on its roof.

He realized that he must not have been unconscious for too long because the sedan's tires were still spinning, a haze of dust only beginning to rise.

There was no knowing how badly he was injured, but there was also no knowing how long he would hold on to consciousness, so he decided to move while he could.

Opening the center console, he grabbed his 1911 with his right hand and the door handle with his left.

But the driver's side had struck the lamppost, and the vehicle had folded around it, bent at close to a fifteen-degree angle.

The brunt of the collision had been taken by the rear door, but the damage was enough that the driver's door wouldn't open. Tom would have to exit through the window, which he only now realized had no glass, or cross to the passenger side.

As he pulled himself across the seat, bits of glass covering him poured off his clothing.

He felt pain, but wasn't sure from where, so he ignored it.

He could move, and that was all that mattered now.

Making it out through the passenger door, he walked around the back of the SUV and started toward the overturned sedan.

He could still hear only a deep, metallic ringing, and his view of the world tilted sharply to the left as he walked, then corrected itself, only to tilt to the left again.

He stumbled forward like this, the weapon in a hand that was numb.

Reaching the sedan's passenger side, Tom clicked off the safety and knelt down.

His balance shifted—it was almost as if his head was suddenly filled with gallons of water—and he nearly fell but caught himself with his left hand.

When he was ready, or ready enough, Tom bent forward till he was able to look into the vehicle's compartment.

Savelle was suspended upside down in the driver's seat, but it wasn't the safety belt that was holding her there.

The steering column had bent upward, the broken wheel piercing her midsection.

Her silk blouse was soaked with blood.

Blood also dripped from a deep gash in her head.

But Savelle was still conscious, and though she couldn't move her head, her eyes found Tom.

She whispered something, but he couldn't hear it.

By the way her jaw barely moved, he knew it was broken.

Savelle whispered again, and this time Tom heard it over the ringing.

"Kill me," she said.

Her eyes went to the pistol in his hand.

"Did you make the call?" Tom said.

She didn't respond.

"Did you make the call?"

"Please just kill me."

Tom thumbed the safety upward and tucked the pistol into his waistband at the small of his back.

"I'll get you out of there. Hang on."

Savelle flashed with anger. "*No!*"

Her voice was a scream, not a whisper.

Tom tried to calm her. "You're going to be okay," he insisted. "I'll get you to the hospital."

Her anger was gone as fast as it came. Tears filled her eyes.

"No." Her voice was barely a hush. "No more hospitals. No more doctors. Just kill me. Now. Please."

"Just hang on, Savelle."

She stared at him.

Her eyes were pleading.

Tom couldn't look away.

"Please, Tom," she whispered. "Please."

Her eyelids fluttered, then closed.

It took only a few seconds for her face to completely drain of all indications of life. All Tom could do was watch her die.

To his surprise, he felt a wave of grief.

After a moment, he sat down on the cold pavement.

Numbness washed over him.

He let it, felt no desire to move, felt nothing, thought nothing.

It was, however, a false peace.

His still-addled mind went to Stella, that he had to get her, had to get Hammerton, too. Despite his warning, they were likely still in danger.

Pushing himself up to his feet, he looked for the nearest street sign to tell him where he was.

And how far he had to go.

He was able to work out that if the highway behind him ran down the east side of Manhattan, then what was in front of him had to be west.

He started walking in that direction but only made it a few steps past the sedan before his legs gave out and he tumbled to the pavement.

As he lay there, the ringing in his ears was joined by the sound of sirens wailing in the distance.

He needed to get up again, so he placed both hands on the pavement and pushed till he was on his hands and knees.

From there he got up onto one foot, had to pause there, noticed as he did that the smartphone he had secured beneath the laces of his work boot had been smashed in the crash.

Its display screen was shattered, but it was not dead.

Still active, still recording.

Rising to his feet once more, Tom lumbered in the direction he believed—hoped—was west.

He really couldn't be sure now.

The dual notes singing in his ears were growing louder.

The cacophony became a frantic shriek that somehow served to drive him forward.

He was, at best, stumbling, but soon enough he found a rhythm that wasn't too awkward.

And not long after that he was running.

Or close enough to it.

He had barely covered a quarter of the block, though, when a vehicle pulled up beside him.

It was a ten-year-old black Mustang, matching his slow pace.

The passenger door swung open, the man behind the wheel calling to Tom by name, waving for him to get in.

It took a moment before Tom even realized that it was Cahill.

He was shouting now, leaning across the passenger seat, still waving.

Tom as much read the man's lips as heard his words.

Stella's safe, he said. *Hammerton, too. Carrington is getting them out of the city now.*

Tom understood the words, even nodded to indicate that he did, but for some reason he continued his slow running.

Eventually, though, after a half-dozen steps, he came to a stop.

And so did the Mustang.

For a second, Tom didn't know what to do.

He stared dumbly at Cahill, who was looking at his left arm.

"Tom, your arm is broken."

Tom continued to stare at him.

Cahill said, "Can you hear me, Tom? Your arm is broken."

Looking down, Tom saw a sharp jigsaw bend just below his elbow joint.

"C'mon, Tom. Get in the car."

Cahill glanced quickly in the rearview mirror.

Tom turned his head and saw what had caught Cahill's eye. Flashing lights were approaching the crash scene. The police were almost there.

"C'mon, Tom," Cahill said. "We have to get to the extraction point. Now."

It took another second, but finally Tom climbed into the passenger seat and pulled the door closed.

He felt gravity tug at his core as the Mustang took off down the street.

The speed further overwhelmed his limited senses, but he was determined to hang on to consciousness, or what passed for it.

Cahill raced westward, heading across town, weaving around vehicles to catch green lights and pausing at red lights only to jump them when he could.

It wasn't long before they reached their destination.

The commercial heliport at West Thirtieth Street, on the edge of the Hudson River.

Cahill led Tom toward a waiting black EC-135, its rotors spinning.

Once on board, Cahill pulled the door closed and took the seat directly across from Tom.

They were facing each other as the copter lifted off, carrying them up and out over the river.

The cabin of the 135, unlike the interior of the Huey that had transported them across the nighttime desert five years ago, was sealed tight and surprisingly quiet.

A luxury transport, designed for maximum comfort.

For men of means with no time to waste and high-stakes deals to make.

But Tom and Cahill simply sat in that silence and looked at each other.

Tom was of course grateful that for this ride—his second such journey with Cahill—neither man was stretched out on a gurney, broken and bleeding and fighting to stay alive.

And it was obvious to him that Cahill was thinking the same thing.

After heading south at first, along the edge of the Hudson, the copter banked sharply to the left and crossed eastward over Lower Manhattan, heading for Long Island.

Reaching down, Tom removed the phone from beneath the laces of his boot and tossed it to Cahill.

Fifty-Nine

Tom awoke with Stella beside him.

The bed was large and soft, the linens crisp.

But it was a strange bed, as was the room it occupied.

Whitewashed walls, bright pine floor, and a row of windows with a view of tranquil waters.

It took Tom a moment to orient himself.

The helicopter ride with Cahill had taken close to a half hour.

Though Tom didn't know the exact cruising speed of an EC-135, he estimated that it had carried them anywhere between seventy-five to one hundred miles, most of it due east.

And though they had landed in the darkness in an open field, Tom had managed to determine that the field was part of the grounds of a large hilltop estate—manor house, stables, five-door garage—and that the estate was located on some island nestled within what appeared to be a bay.

Tom remembered little after that—men had helped him from the helicopter and into a house. Another man that Tom assumed was a doctor told him to brace himself as he prepared to set Tom's broken bone; Raveis and an older man with deep-set eyes and buzz-cut hair watched from a corner; Cahill and a man with long-ish gray hair looking at each other for a moment before embracing, both men smiling.

After that, Tom had been brought to a large study with floor-to-ceiling bookcases and a set of French doors overlooking a lawn that ran at a gentle slope toward tall reeds, beyond which was the same tranquil water.

He lost track of how long he'd been left to wait in that room, fighting his growing fatigue. Eventually, he heard doors opening and closing somewhere inside the house, followed by the sound of footsteps.

Two sets of footsteps, one heavy, the other not.

The study door opened and Tom saw Cahill.

Standing beside him was Stella.

Cahill closed the doors as Stella walked into Tom's arms.

Next to her now in this strange bed, Tom looked at his left forearm, encased in a cast.

He realized that he was feeling no pain.

More than that, his entire body was alive with a buzzing numbness.

It was more than pleasant.

No doubt the man who had set his arm also shot him up with a dose of painkillers.

Tom might have preferred the pain over the slowing effect the drug was having on his thoughts and movements.

He sensed that he needed his wits about him, now more than ever.

A quick check of the nightstand for their belongings—phones, ID, cash, Stella's .357, Tom's 1911—came up short.

Then he realized he didn't know the time, and there was no clock in the sparsely furnished room.

What Tom did know was that this was Monday morning, so no matter what time it was, he was missing his shift.

And so was Stella, who had already missed her Saturday and Sunday double shifts.

Living paycheck to paycheck meant they would be short at the end of the month.

And working for the kind of man Tom worked for meant there was a very good chance he was out of a job.

Later that morning an attractive woman in her fifties, dressed in jeans, a white fisherman's sweater, and deck shoes brought Tom and Stella breakfast on a silver tray.

She also brought them clothing.

Slacks, tank top, cardigan, and sneakers for Stella.

Heavy work jeans, T-shirt, hooded sweatshirt, and hiking boots for Tom.

All brand new, store tags still attached.

The woman said her name was Eileen and asked if they needed anything else just then. She was smiling, gracious.

Her demeanor struck Tom as that of a hostess tending to welcome guests, not a jailer minding her charges.

Tom asked where Cahill was.

"He flew back out this morning," Eileen said. "I'm surprised the two of you slept through the noise. The house always shakes whenever that thing takes off."

She asked again if she could get them anything else.

Stella examined the tray and said they were good.

Eileen said to Tom, "They'll talk to you when they're ready. There's nothing to worry about. You're both safe here. Just rest up. I'm just downstairs if you need anything."

She left then, closing the bedroom door behind her.

Tom listened, but heard no indications of a lock being turned.

Stella picked up a piece of buttered toast and tore it in half, handing one of the pieces to him.

He took it.

As they sat in the large bed and ate, neither spoke for a while.

Eventually, Stella said, "Isn't Cahill's mother named Eileen? I think I read that in his file."

———

Eileen collected their tray after lunch.

"You're welcome to walk the grounds if you feel up to it," she said.

Though it was a blustery November day, the sky crowded with clouds the color of brushed steel, Tom and Stella headed down the sloping lawn to the water's edge.

It was here that Tom began his recon.

He waited till there was a break in the clouds and used the angle of his own shadow to determine that this part of the property was facing east.

The nearest land was well off in the distance.

Turning right, he and Stella strolled to the southern side.

Here, the nearest land was only a few hundred yards away.

"How long will they keep you waiting?" Stella asked.

Tom said that he didn't know.

Scanning the southern bank of the grounds, he spotted a boat launch and small wooden dock.

Moored to the dock was a rowboat.

Rocking quietly with the gentle tide.

———

As the sun was close to setting, Eileen knocked on their door.

"They're ready for you."

She led Tom back to the study where he had waited for Stella. Three men were there.

Raveis, of course, as well as the man with longish gray hair who had embraced Cahill, and the older man Raveis had been talking with as Tom's arm was set.

Tom estimated that the man with the longish hair was in his fifties, the other man in his sixties.

And by the way Raveis and the gray-haired man stood facing the older one, it was clear to Tom who was in charge.

Everyone had a boss, even men like Raveis.

The older man looked at Tom as he walked into the room.

Raveis and the gray-haired man turned and stepped quickly toward Tom, leaving the older man to stand back and observe.

Approaching Tom, Raveis said, "It's good to see you, Tom."

Tom said nothing.

He locked eyes with the older man, studying him as he studied Tom.

Barrel-chested, bull-shouldered, six feet, salt-and-pepper hair buzzed close to his scalp, like Tom's was now.

Powerful and commanding, despite his age.

Tom knew former military when he saw it.

He also knew power—real power—when he saw it.

"These men are associates of mine," Raveis said.

Tom didn't care who they were. There was one thing he wanted to know first.

"Where are we?" he said.

"It's called Shelter Island. It's between the two forks of Long Island—"

"This place belongs to Cahill's family," Tom said. "Right?"

Raveis smiled in a way that indicated Tom had caught him off guard. "What makes you think that, Tom?"

"The woman taking care of us is Cahill's mother." Tom nodded toward the gray-haired man. "And he and Cahill looked a lot like a father and son who hadn't seen each other in a long time."

The gray-haired man stepped forward, extending his hand.

"I'm Robert Cahill," he said. "It's very good to meet you, Tom. I've been wanting to for a long time."

Tom shook his hand. "I appreciate you taking Stella and me in."

"Of course."

Tom looked at Raveis. "I have questions."

"Go ahead."

"Where's Hammerton?"

"In the hospital."

"Which one?"

"New York-Presbyterian, in the city."

"Savelle put an implant in him."

Raveis nodded. "It has been removed. His fever is already down. He's fine, Tom. A single phone call was made, and within hours, two of his SAS brothers arrived, one to guard his door, the other to sit at his bedside. They won't leave till he does. He'll be well taken care of, I can assure you of that."

"And Carrington?"

"He's fine, too." Raveis smiled. "A little hungover, but fine."

"I'd like to talk to him."

"Not yet, Tom."

"Why not?"

"We'll get to that in a minute."

Tom thought about that, looked at each man, then said, "How did Cahill know the meeting in your garage was a trap?"

"Carrington tipped us off."

"He contacted Cahill?"

"No, he surrendered to me. Came in with his hands up. A ballsy move, considering we'd put a kill order out on him."

Tom took note of the use of the plural pronoun.

He glanced at the older man.

Still standing back, still observing.

Tom said to Raveis, "Carrington was innocent, but because of you he was forced to kill three of your men in self-defense."

"This is a dangerous business. Dangerous, but vital to national security. Those men knew the risks yet still showed up for work every day." Raveis paused. "But we've gained more than we lost. A lot more. And that's what matters."

"And what was it exactly that you gained?"

"I know what you think of me, Tom. And believe me, you aren't that far from wrong. I'm a capitalist to the core, but like you, I'm also a patriot. Like you, I fought for my country and nearly died for it. I still fight for it every day. Which is why I consider what you achieved here to be a significant gain."

Tom said nothing.

Raveis took a step closer. "Three more weapons caches have already been found. Each one of them purchased through land trusts listing Jenna Walewski as trustee. Each one of them just outside New York City. One was triple the size of the cache you and Hammerton found. Joint ATF and FBI task forces have already set up twenty-four-hour surveillance on all of them. No one enters those buildings—no one leaves them with so much as a box of ammo—without us knowing about it."

Tom looked at Robert Cahill, then at the older man.

"You saved a lot of lives, Tom," Raveis said. "And not just the would-be victims of an attack on New York City. We're talking about the tens of thousands of lives that would have been lost in another full-scale war in the Middle East. How could our leaders not avenge such an attack? The danger of fighting an enemy you demonize is that you will always underestimate them. Our current enemies are convinced that America would cower after such an attack. That our government would retreat from their part of the world—every other part of the world—never to come back again. It's a mistake they make over and over. A mistake every single one of our enemies has made throughout history. Al Qaeda, the Nazis and Japanese, the British in 1812, you name it. And it's a mistake the entire world always ends up paying for, one way or the other."

The older man spoke. "That's enough, Sam," he said softly.

The three men turned to look at him.

"We brought Tomas here so he could hear good news. We've kept him waiting long enough."

Raveis nodded and faced Tom. "Half an hour ago, the mortgage on Stella's property in Canaan was paid off. That's one of the reasons why it took us so long to meet with you today. We wanted the matter to be settled before we told you. In his debriefing, Carrington pointed out that things would have no doubt ended differently if it weren't for Stella. Relieving her of the last of her debts is the least her government could do."

Tom said nothing.

"Also, a two-year lease for the retail space below her apartment has been drawn. To our accountant's dismay, we calculated that ten thousand dollars a month would be a fair price. The two years paid up front, in full. In fact, that amount has already been wire-transferred into her bank account."

Tom wouldn't have been able to say anything even if he could think of something to say.

But the older man wasn't yet done.

"Finally, a phone call was made to the Litchfield County prosecutor. He has assured us that Stella will face no charges for what was a clear case of self-defense."

Tom closed his eyes, then opened them again and said, "Thank you."

The older man nodded. "Please come here, Tomas."

He pronounced Tom's name correctly.

Tom looked at Raveis and Robert Cahill before stepping toward the man.

They stood facing each other.

"Do you know who I am, Tomas?"

"No."

The man smiled and nodded. Despite his hard features, there was genuine warmth in his expression.

"Good," he said. "Let's keep it that way for now, okay? But you'll need to call me something, so why don't you call me what most people call me?"

"What's that?"

"Colonel."

Tom nodded. "Yes, sir."

"There's another reason why we waited till now to meet with you. Would you like to know what that reason is?"

"Yes."

"We wanted to be certain that relevant members of New York law enforcement had been informed of your status. And we also wanted to ensure that certain pieces of evidence had been claimed and destroyed or went missing."

Tom understood what part of that meant.

He would never see again the Colt 1911 that Stella had given him.

The weapon he had used to shoot four men in New York City.

On which was his DNA.

And while Tom had a pretty good idea what was meant by evidence going missing, his real concern was the first half of the Colonel's statement.

"What do you mean by my status?" Tom said.

"Employment status. Every action taken by you over these past seventy-two hours was done in the service of your country. Your orders, in fact, had come down to you from the highest levels of our government. Of course, those involved in classified operations are afforded certain immunities. Even those involved in domestic ops—ops that aren't technically legal but are recognized as necessary for national security—are afforded certain . . . courtesies. Quietly, of course. And always behind closed doors. Do you understand what I'm telling you, Tomas?"

Tom said, "That I'm in your debt."

The Colonel smiled. "I can assure you, son, it is quite the opposite."

Tom glanced again at Raveis and Robert Cahill.

Facing the Colonel once more, he said, "Then maybe Stella and I can get our personal belongings back."

The Colonel nodded. "Yes, of course. Right away." He looked at Raveis.

A look that carried the weight of an order.

Raveis left the room.

"Are Stella and I free to leave?" Tom said.

"I'm curious. Where would you go?"

"Does it matter?"

"You've made important friends here, son. But you've also made powerful enemies. Kadyrov was not a one-man show. He was in business with others, worse men than he, believe it or not, and they are about to lose a lot of money. There will be significant fallout from that. I'm afraid you and Stella returning to your life in Canaan won't be possible right now. Let's call it an abundance of caution. Frankly, you may never be able to go back."

The Colonel paused, then said, "Sam is correct. You've not only saved countless lives, but you've spared the world from yet another gruesome and costly war that can't be won—by either side. But this doesn't mean our work is done. Not by a long shot. They will keep trying and we will keep doing what it takes to stop them. Cahill is back out there, doing what he can. Fortunately his cover is still intact, so his family remains safe. We were hoping, Tomas, that you would reconsider a career with us. I realize that this is what you turned down five years ago when Carrington first tried to recruit you. But you're a damn good man, and I'd like you on my team."

"You didn't really answer my question," Tom said. "Are Stella and I free to go?"

"Yes."

"How soon can we leave?"

"The ferry doesn't start running again till five-thirty."

"How far is the landing from here?"

"My driver is at your disposal. He will take you anywhere you want to go."

"We can find our own way."

"No doubt." The Colonel paused. "The landing is about half a mile west of here. At least let my man drive you to the train station on the mainland."

Tom said nothing.

"I answered your question, Tomas, so how about answering mine? Are you interested in a career with us?"

"No," Tom said. "But if there is anything I can do for you, I will do it. On one condition, though."

"Go ahead."

"The only person I want to contact me is James Carrington. I won't deal with anyone else. My phone rings and it's not him, I don't answer. There's a knock on my door and it's someone else, I walk out the back. And I keep on walking. We clear?"

"Very clear," the Colonel said. "May I ask why?"

"Because he risked his life to save mine. It's as simple as that."

"And what if something were to happen to him?"

"You'll have to make sure nothing does."

The Colonel thought about that, nodded once, and said, "You look out for the people who mean something to you. We have this in common."

He reached into his jacket, removed a card, and handed it to Tom.

"We don't give these out often," the Colonel said.

Tom expected a business card, something made of paper or card stock, but right away he knew he was holding something different.

This card, slightly thicker than a credit card, was made of copper.

One of the metals Tom had worked with often during the past six months.

Tom's full name was stamped on the card, identifying him as the bearer of the card, and the name of the attorney general of the United States was stamped below it, along with a phone number.

The card also bore the official seal of the office of the attorney general.

"That phone is monitored twenty-four-seven," the Colonel said. "Show this card if you find yourself in trouble with the law. Any trouble. If it doesn't get you immediately cut loose and you end up at the station house, request that the shift supervisor or precinct captain call that number. If you are refused, ask for your one call and dial the number yourself. Of course, this doesn't mean you shouldn't avoid trouble, Tomas. But something tells me I don't need to remind you of that."

Tom held the card, looking at it.

He was now in possession of a courtesy card from the highest-ranking law enforcement officer in the nation.

The one person who could, with a single phone call, make virtually any problem go away.

And the Colonel seemingly had this person in his pocket.

Raveis returned then, holding a gallon-size Ziploc bag.

He crossed the study and placed the bag on a table near Tom.

Inside were Stella's smartphone, wallet, and keys and Tom's driver's license, carry permit, and cash.

The bag also contained Stella's .357 Magnum, its cylinder open, the weapon unloaded.

Its six hollow-point rounds were in their own smaller bag.

All that they had in the world, but exactly what they'd need for now.

Tom barely glanced at the items, though.

He didn't want to take his eyes off the Colonel for too long.

He was standing his ground with a man in possession of unfathomable power and influence.

And one didn't look away when face-to-face with someone like that.

After a moment, the Colonel stepped closer to Tom and extended his hand.

Tom took it, felt a powerful grip. He easily matched it with his own.

"Rest up," the Colonel said. "Let those wounds of yours heal. Because when we do need you, we will need you at your very best."

The Colonel released his hand. "Good luck, son," the man said. "We'll be in touch."

Sixty

They slipped away not long after midnight.

Making their way through the darkness to the rowboat Tom had seen earlier, they quietly climbed in, untied the mooring line, and pushed off.

Despite his broken forearm, Tom took the oars.

The pleasant numbness he'd woken to eighteen hours ago had long since worn off, but he didn't care.

Only getting Stella far away from there mattered.

Far away from this world of power and violence.

And the men, both good and bad, who occupied it.

Stella's smartphone had been out of sight—and in Raveis's possession—for too long, but Tom had no choice except to use it once.

Prior to their leaving, he had called for a cab to meet them at the ferry landing, then left the phone behind in their room.

To anyone tracking the phone, it would appear that Tom and Stella were still in their room.

And he suspected that anyone listening wouldn't let them get out the door.

But they made it out of the house and down to the dock without interference, which meant no one had eavesdropped.

Tom knew such a courtesy wasn't likely to last forever.

While rowing the half mile to the landing, Tom wasn't sure what he and Stella would do if the cab didn't show.

They had no outerwear, only the clothes Cahill's mother had given them, and the November night was windy and cold.

They were both already shivering.

But as the landing came finally into view, Stella spotted the cab.

Steering to the shoreline, Tom hopped out and grabbed the bow with his good hand, hauling the boat onto the bank.

He and Stella hurried to the waiting vehicle and got in.

The nearest train station, the cabbie told them, was in East Hampton.

The last train to New York was at 1:22 a.m.

Tom and Stella made it with time to spare.

But the small station house was closed, so they huddled together and waited on the open platform.

The train was ten minutes late, and Tom and Stella were the only two to board.

They sat in an empty car, saying nothing, Stella leaning into Tom, his arm around her shoulder.

At one point she fell asleep and Tom just looked out the window.

—————

They reached Penn Station at just after 4:00 a.m., then made their way on foot to Grand Central.

Two refugees crossing streets that were all but empty. The train from Grand Central to White Plains didn't depart for another hour, but there was food and water to buy.

And books, too.

Paperbacks this time, and magazines.

Tom knew that with wandering came plenty of time to read.

―――――

It was first light when the Metro-North train pulled into the White Plains station.

Tom's truck was still in the lot.

Seeing it, he felt relief.

Its not being there would have been the last possible glitch in his escape plan.

Retrieving the key from its hiding place behind the driver's side rear wheel, Tom unlocked the passenger door and helped Stella in.

He did a quick recon of the area as he walked around to the driver's door, but he saw nothing he didn't like.

Climbing in behind the wheel, he started the motor and steered out of the lot, following the signs to the interstate and checking his rearview mirror often.

No one was behind them.

His instinct was to head north.

He had done that when he'd first left the city, five years before.

Passing on Carrington's job offer as they stood in Tom's hotel room and slipping out in the middle of the night then, too, because he simply couldn't wait any longer.

He was craving motion and the feeling of freedom that came with it.

Got in his pickup and just drove.

Now, he was making that same journey again.

Only not alone this time.

It was when they were on the New York State Thruway, heading north at last, his truck the only vehicle in sight, that Tom asked Stella where she wanted to go.

She thought about it for a moment, then said, "Show me the places you've been."

Tom asked if there was any place in particular she wanted to see first.

She thought about that, too. "Actually, there is."

"Name it."

Stella looked at him.

"Take me to where you were born," she said. "I want to see where you come from. I want to know everything about you. And I want you to know everything about me."

Tom smiled and nodded.

"Okay," he said. "You got it, Stella."

She was smiling, too.

Touching his face, she looked out the windshield at the road ahead.

"I mean, hey, we've got nothing but time now, right?" she said.

Epilogue

Cahill took a room in a motel a mile from the cemetery.

He had arrived after dark and secured the door and windows, then sat on the edge of the bed with the lights off.

He'd been on the road for three days, taking a circuitous route to his destination—an affluent suburb north of Chicago.

This was as much to conceal his movements as to allow Erica's family the time necessary to claim their daughter's body, arrange to transport it back home, and schedule the burial.

It would be dangerous at this point for him to stay in one place for too long.

Tired upon his arrival, his physical wounds only just beginning to heal, Cahill sat still for a long time before finally removing his compact 1911 from his boot, placing it within easy reach on the nightstand, and lying down.

Sleep had become tricky; he dreamed of her alive and happy, only to see her dead again.

The lifeless corpse he'd covered with dirt and left behind.

He woke several times that night, was able to get back to sleep sometimes, though other times he needed to get up and splash his face with water.

Naked, he looked at his scarred torso in the bathroom mirror, to remind himself that he was a survivor and would, too, survive this.

The next morning, shaved and showered and dressed, Cahill walked to the cemetery.

It was a cold November morning, the winds gusting, the sky crowded with clouds the color of battleships.

By the time Cahill arrived, the narrow roads that wound through the cemetery were lined with dozens of cars.

Maybe even a hundred.

It pleased him that there were so many here to see her off.

He had no intention of joining the mourners. The nature of their relationship—an extramarital affair—meant that her family had known nothing about him prior to her murder.

They still knew very little.

He was her secret, then and now.

He would always regret that he had failed to keep her as his.

Walking the perimeter of the grounds, Cahill positioned himself so he could view the burial rites while remaining unnoticed.

Her parents and sister were easy to spot; they were the closest to the casket, at the very edge of the grave, the crowd fanned out behind them.

A man he assumed was Erica's husband stood behind them, though Cahill didn't look at him for long.

The distance and wind prevented Cahill from hearing the Catholic priest's words.

So he once again whispered his own prayers for Erica's soul.

When the priest was done, the casket was lowered into the ground.

Erica's family was tossing spades filled with dirt into the grave when Cahill turned away and began the walk back to his motel.

He waited there till dark, a wounded man alone with his many pains, then left to catch the seven o'clock bus out of town.

Acknowledgments

Much appreciation for the hard work (and patience) of the following kind souls, in order of appearance:

Scott Miller, Alison Dasho, Alan Turkus, Jacque Ben-Zekry, Bryn Savage, Gracie Doyle, and Caitlin Alexander.